THE
RED
CASTLE

THE
RED
CASTLE

NOAH VERHOEFF

atmosphere press

PRELUDE

We are not judged by the outcome of our deeds, nor the deeds themselves, but by the intent that drives them. This phrase echoed in the boy king's mind as he sat patiently in wait for Walter and his travelling band of Thespians to finish setting up. It reminded him of his father, a warrior king whose shadow would cast itself across the next dozen generations. After a few moments, the curtains unveiled.

"Lords, ladies, gather round. My travelling band of troubadours are proud to present to you all the troublesome tale of King Arthur on this fine occasion," announced a minstrel. Just before he began to play, the boy king interrupted him.

"Come now, Walter. I've heard you and your band quite a few times now – at least a dozen, and each time, you plague us with the same dreadful tales. King Arthur this, Holy Grail that. Can't you entertain us with something more... interesting?"

"Interesting, King Henry?"

"Yes, interesting. A tale of real men in real wars, not this precomposed rubbish from centuries ago. That stuff's ancient. I crave real adventure: real knights, in real armour, fighting real monstrous beasts."

"Well, sir, we have only rehearsed tales from *Le Morte d'Arthur*..."

"Walter, to be frank, anything would be better than another tale from *Le Morte d'Arthur*. Anything! Make something up if you have to."

"Hmm... Very well. I suppose I shall entertain you with a melancholy tale I heard once in my youth. This tale recounts a young man, not much older than you, my King, who yearned for adventure. He lived all the way over in Göttingen. You are aware of this region my Lord, are you not?"

"I have a rough idea."

"Very good. Then, with all the powers vested in me, by the mighty God, I recollect a tale so epic and tragic, that even the fools will cry and the ladies will get up and swing around sticks like swords as children do. Lord, give me the inspiration, skill, and knowledge to present this tumultuous tale to these merry folks of the English court with accuracy and drama. Let me recount the perils endured on the road, the battles fought, the wars waged, the love that could have blossomed if only death hadn't knocked on their door. I warn you all - there be no fairies or giants in this tale; only beings that still existed a mere fifty years ago, like wild wolves and wretched witches. Without further ado, ladies and gentlemen, come one and all, and listen to the tale of the bold, the heroic, and the tragic, Sir. Manfred von Göttingen!"

CHAPTER 1. COLD PURSUIT

The sun rose over the snow-capped evergreens surrounding the small town of Adelebsen. In the woods, three men rode their steeds at a full gallop, jumping over fallen trees and dodging low hanging branches. They were dressed in ordinary clothes, wearing bright blues and reds, and one of the three wore a chainmail shirt. Its iron links jangled and danced as he rode, as if each ring were as light as a feather. On his left eye was an eyepatch, under which a long scar trailed across his left cheek - a pagan ritual gone wrong. In their hands, the men carried spears and bludgeons, and on their belts, they carried a hefty sum of florins.

The men rode faster than the frosty wind itself, stopping for no animal traversing the undergrowth. Birds dispersed from the pine trees at the mere sound of the tumultuous beating of horse's hooves. Behind them they heard calls:

"Stop right there you honourless brigands!" They rode faster. The snow and slush were kicked up behind them as they rode; however, they could feel their horses beginning to tire.

"Make for the clearing over there," the man with the eyepatch declared. "We'll have to make a stand, or else they'll catch up to us."

"Agreed," said another in a gruff voice. The third man nodded, for he was mute, and therefore had no ability to make a speech. The three men rode with haste towards the clearing. Their hoods flew in all directions. The mute's hat flew off in the wind, planting itself far behind him in the snow. There was no hesitation; their ill-gotten gains would be more than enough to replenish their rugged accessories. The brigands rode to the clearing until the man with the eye patch came to a halt. He dismounted his horse and clamoured over to his saddlebag, from which he drew a crude bastard sword. His companions did the same, gripping their spears, and keeping their bludgeons and knives close at hand. In the distance, the thunder of hooves echoed through the trees.

"You hear that, lads?" asked the man in the eyepatch. "That is the one thing between us and bein' filthy rich!"

"One last stand, and then we make for Bohemia and leave this wretched tribe behind us!" said the other of the two vocal brigands.

The three men waited in formation, anticipating the thunderous danger in their midst. In a matter of seconds, the band of riders broke through from the foliage and slowed down. The brigands carefully sized them up. There were five lawmen, clad in steel from head to toe, and carrying long lances with razor-sharp heads. They lined up side by side. Their destriers whinnied and began pawing at the icy ground with their steel-toed hooves. The riders' breaths seeped through their visors and emerged like smoke into the chilled air. The man in the middle, their leader, called out.

"Men in formation!" The men lined their horses up perfectly, with little room in between. "Present!" The men tilted their lances. "Charge!"

The five knights rode in unison. Their horses shook the ground like an earthquake. The deadly mass of horse and steel-clad rider approached the three helpless targets.

"Hold!" called out the man in the eye patch. The mute quickly dropped his spear, jumped on his horse, and fled. His money pouch, as well as his blanket, dropped on the ground as he left with haste. The remaining two trembled with fear. The five riders emerged over the hilltop, paving a streak of hoofprints into the freshly fallen snow. Within moments, the knights closed the distance. They could see the whites of the brigands' eyes as they approached. With their lances steadily aimed at the two wavering targets, victory seemed certain. They spurred on their horses in the final seconds of the charge. BANG! The hulking mass of steel and flesh crashed right through the poor men who stood in the way. One of the knights' lances impaled the eye-patched brigand in his good eye, and meeting little resistance, carried straight on through to the other side. The other lay trampled in the snow, bones broken from the mass of two horses having run over him. The men slowed.

"Nice work boys," called out the leader. He lifted his visor. He was a young man of seventeen years. His brown locks poked out from beneath the brow of his klappvisor bascinet helmet. His armour was lined with brass and bore ceremonial engravings with the history of his house, the House of Göttingen. His name was Manfred, and he was the third son of the famed general, Prince Otto von Göttingen. The principality of Göttingen was a small state under the hegemony of the Electorate of Saxony, in the Holy Roman Empire. Although the small fiefdom wasn't particularly affluent, it could certainly hold its own in the face of invasion. Prince Otto von Göttingen was famous for his contributions against the rise of Protestant forces in Bohemia and Moravia. In fact, he was a crusader, like his father, grandfather, and great grandfather: Albert II, Duke of Brunswick-Lüneberg. The Welf dynasty, the dynasty to which Manfred and his family belonged, had mostly consisted of crusaders up until this point. But, Otto did not want Manfred to be a warrior. Although his heart lay with the Teutonic Knights, he feared a deadly fate for his son. Besides, in his old age, Otto believed in diplomacy over bloodshed.

Worst of all, Manfred would not inherit the title of Prince. He was third in line to the throne, and thus, he would inherit next to nothing. Only a small estate in Adelebsen, a minuscule town under the Principality of Göttingen. Thus, it was his duty to protect the town, and Manfred enjoyed actively engaging with the people. He led his retinue often through the woods, hunting for roadside robbers such as the ones they had just dealt with. Manfred was excellent at the craft of skirmishing. Although he had never fought in a pitched battle, he was told tales of the crusades in Prussia and the Holy Land and dreamt to one day join the ranks of those very holy warriors. Unfortunately, there was no such opportunity any longer. Jerusalem was long lost, the Protestants were firmly suppressed, the Mongols of the Golden Horde were overthrown by the Russian Principalities, the Kipchaks posed little threat to the Kingdoms of Bohemia and Hungary, and the Teutonic Knights successfully completed their conversion of the Estonian and Prussian tribes. But still, Manfred dreamt of one day leading an army and defending all of Saxony against foreign invaders. However, for now, he made the best of his duties and ensured that he fulfilled them to the best of his abilities.

"That was one hell of a chase!" he exclaimed whilst catching his breath. "Those tribesmen were fast!"

"It's a shame that such a good lance was wasted on such a brute," said Roland with a smirk as he tried to wipe the carnage off of the bent tip. He wore a short-sleeved red surcoat over his armour with the Göttingen coat of arms, a white castle on a field of blue, which lay atop a golden lion on a field of red. On his triangular heater shield, as was with the rest of the knights, was the same coat of arms. They wore them with pride to ward off enemies and announce their presence. His Pamplona style great bascinet had notches on the side of it, one for each of the men he'd slain. What once looked like a tally now looked like a grid. Roland was Manfred's best warrior.

"I suppose you ought to mark that one on your helmet," exclaimed Friedrich with a lighthearted smirk, pointing at the small indents imprinted by the local blacksmith. "Soon, that blacksmith will have to forge you a whole new helmet!" Friedrich was Manfred's fastest rider and the most chivalrous of all his knights. He memorized the chivalric code from start to finish and based every decision upon it, as well as the holy scripture. He prided himself on his piety. He was considered the perfect knight, aside from his love of the finer things. They say that the clothes make the man. Well, on the field of battle, it could not be truer. Friedrich characteristically wore a bright red, stylish jupon over his armour and a Venetian style great bascinet. The bucket-like helmet blinded him like a mole, but it was the best protection one could ask for. He took pride in the fact that both were made in Italy.

"I hope you didn't get any blood on your jupon," stated Wilhelm, clad in a red, leather coated brigandine suit of armour and a nasal bascinet helmet. He preferred to have more visibility and ventilation in combat, due to his chronic asthma. Although he may not have been the most physically adequate of the five knights, he was Manfred's closest friend and most trusted confidant. His lack of skill was outweighed by his absolute loyalty.

Finally, wearing a Cherbourg style great bascinet and breastplate painted with the coat of arms of Göttingen, was Ulrich. While the others engaged in friendly banter, Ulrich dismounted and began looting the bodies. Ulrich was always the first to finish the job, as he was the most focused and skillful in the ways of combat. However, he also loved coin, and wouldn't hesitate to grab a florin with every passing opportunity.

"Have you found anything?" asked Manfred, after having a good laugh with the other knights.

"Not yet," replied Ulrich. "That is, aside from these coin

purses. The poor youngen who fled left this behind as well."

"How much is in there?" asked Manfred.

"A hefty sum," replied Ulrich, weighing the bags in his gauntlets carefully. He didn't want to take them off, as the snow would surely rust them, and his hands would freeze over like Lake Peipus. "Who should we give it to?" he asked.

"Well... I suppose the men they robbed it from must have already passed. Here, let me take the pouches; I'll find a good way for us to spend the florins while also aiding our citizens," replied Manfred. Ulrich tossed him the purse.

"Should we not divide the money amongst ourselves?" asked Roland. "I mean, we are the ones who caught those scoundrels after all."

"But that was simply our duty," replied Manfred. "This money belongs to the people, not us. It should go to them. Ever since I was young, my father always told me that a good ruler is not the one who is feared, nor the one who is loved, but the one who is so good at their job that the people barely know of their existence. I, for one, am not my father, and I believe that we should let the good people of Adelebsen know that we care about them."

"Don't you think it would be more well spent if you had control over it?" asked Ulrich.

"I think that they should have the right to choose. Besides, we ought to ensure that we are more popular than that damn Pastor Leon. What do you think, Friedrich?" asked Manfred.

"I think that we should get out of this freezing cold, or else we won't be giving money to anyone," replied Friedrich. The group had a good laugh and quickly got to work. They used some sticks as shovels to dig a mass grave, in which they carefully placed the two lifeless corpses. Afterwards, Ulrich piled the dirt back on top of them. Friedrich delivered a short prayer for the two men in Latin, the language of the Catholic Church.

"Domine mi, qui es in caelis,
Beati regnum tuum, et benedicatur in ea,
Hic exhortamur in annis quaterdecies Anno decimo,
Hi homines luere peccata sua, et aures suas in caelum
Hos ut paeniteat ob furta avaritiae
Sed parce eis, Domine, ipsi sciunt quia non bonum,
Haec natio fera misericordia merentur; nam illi non
    possunt videre lumen Dominus,
Domine, obsecro, peccatum hominibus peccata
    eorum:
Amen."

"Amen," the other four replied. They didn't know what it meant, and frankly, they didn't care. But, they trusted Friedrich to send those men where they deserved to go, wherever that was.

"We should leave now before we all join them," exclaimed Wilhelm, wrapping his arms tightly. The five men at arms mounted their powerful steeds and cantered their way back to the town. The road wound like a serpent, weaving its way from tree to tree. All around was the chill of winter. Since the plague hit the town, everything seemed more macabre. Nearly half of the residents had been killed by the disease within the past twenty years. The plague was known for its terrible effects, as it grew buboes in the victim's armpits and groin, and sprouted blood spewing pimples all over the body. How could the good Lord unleash such a thing upon his own creation?

The plague had devastated Europe, nearly killing one out of every two Christian souls. Göttingen was no exception. Its people had suffered at the hands of this terrible disease for decades since it first arrived in 1388. Göttingen was lucky in that regard, as it was quite remote from the rest of the Empire. The disease had first struck German territories in 1348 and devastated its populace until 1350. Adelebsen was struck later than the rest. At least that meant that the church was willing to aid the victims. It sent blankets and food and whatever else charitable nobles and peasants alike could offer.

The five riders returned to Adelebsen. They were greeted by the guards amiably before they made their way into the small town. They rode through the thin streets and sharp turns until they reached the main square. It was quaint and small, but it was filled with busy people going about their daily lives. Many shops were open around the four corners selling vegetables, fish, eggs, milk, and of course, bread. As well, there were goods merchants too, who came from large cities like Leipzig, Hanover, Frankfurt, and Cologne. They sold all kinds of goods, from fine and colourful clothing to farming tools. The horses clipped and clopped on the cobblestones.

From the square, the men could see a tall hill on the edge of town, off in the near distance. On the top of the hill, beside a large field, was Adelebsen Castle, Manfred's estate. It was a tall building and completely whitewashed on the outside. The roof was covered in snow, resembling the thatched roofs of all the houses in the town below. The castle loomed over the town, surveying the landscape far away, and keeping careful watch over its citizens - but, the people of Adelebsen were fine with it. They enjoyed the feeling of safety that the edifice provided. It was an assurance that they were delivered from harm and that their local lords cared about them.

Manfred led his retinue up the hill. Before entering the gates, he looked back over the town. The snow-capped roofs resembled a sea of white. He looked into the streets and saw children playing in thick padded jackets and women collecting groceries and preparing delicious meals for their husbands. Off in the distance, in the fields, he saw most of the village's men toiling away in their colourful garb. They worked hard in the morning, such that they could enjoy ale and food in the afternoon. Manfred knew that they worked for him and that he had all rights to the food they produced. However, he also understood that his people needed protection and that he was one such person who could provide that. Thus, is the fair trade of the feudal society. Not a single florin is spent on taxes, but nobles must have food to feed their valiant warriors.

Manfred hailed the guards.

"I'm home," he called out. The two large wooden doors opened, and two guards came to lead the way and take the horses. The knights dismounted and walked through the small courtyard to the large, fortified keep. The horses were guided to the stables, where they were washed and fed. The men, on the other hand, went straight through the yard, passed the blacksmiths and artisans, and walked straight to the kitchen.

Manfred opened the door.

"Ennelein?" he politely asked. A stout, middle-aged woman made her way to the door with a grin on her rosy face.

"Manfred! What trouble have you and your friends gotten into today?"

"Oh, you know, the usual. Just a few of those damn forest dwellers trying to rob from the travellers of these roads. One of them got away."

"Oh, you poor lad," she said playfully. "Come now, you must be starving! I've just finished preparing some nice cooked rabbit. I think you'll like it," she said. She went into the kitchen where another four cooks were working away at preparing a meal for all of the lord's retainers. Ennelein came back out and put an embroidered tablecloth on an old wooden picnic table, and she laid out five thin loaves of bread. Manfred and his men sat down and began taking off their armour. Ulrich called over his squire, Conrad, to help the men out and tend to their harnesses.

"Good day out in the woods, sir?" the youngen asked, in complete adoration of the grizzled veteran.

"We made quite a profit. We'll make sure it reaches the right hands," Ulrich replied.

"Was any blood spilt?"

"Too much, as always," said Friedrich.

"Just enough," smirked Ulrich, as the group made their way through the yard. Conrad parted with them to tend to his affairs. "Boy, how about you bring us all a pint?"

"Come now, Ulrich, you just had whatever's in that flask of yours," interjected Freidrich. "That elixir won't do you any good."

"Ah, to hell with it. If God doesn't care that monks drink like dogs, he ought not care that I do," Ulrich replied. Conrad, unsure of what to do, left after tending to their harnesses without bringing an ounce of anything.

Ennelein trotted out of the kitchen with a large wooden plate, filled with deliciously spiced rabbit. She also came out with a few sauces. She pointed to a light green one.

"This sauce is made from garlic, all the way over from Wallachia," she exclaimed. Manfred smiled.

"Thank you Ennelein, it looks delicious!" he said.

"Why don't you come and join us?" asked Friedrich.

"I'm alright," she replied. "I already ate some porridge this morning." The five men all took some rabbit with their hands and cut off chunks with their rondel daggers. With their pinky fingers, they served themselves sauces. Each sauce was filled with flavour, ranging from tomatoes to chickpeas.

"Delicious!" exclaimed Ulrich, as he devoured the meat right off the bone.

As the men ate, they watched the artisans work on a new mural that was being painted inside of the courtyard. It depicted God blessing the German nobility. Portrayed in it were all of the local lords and noble friends of Prince Otto. All, except for Manfred.

"Tell me something, Manfred," said Roland. "Why are you getting a mural done without you in it?" he asked.

"It's not my mural. My father is paying for it, and I think it'll look lovely. He just doesn't want me in it because I am not exactly a successor."

"Yeah, why is that again?" asked Wilhelm.

"It's because I'm third in line. My eldest brother, Otto II, is first in line, and if anything happens to him, my second eldest brother, Reuben, will inherit the throne."

"That's not fair; you're a far better warrior and leader than they are!" exclaimed Wilhelm, getting all riled up.

"I know, but I'm not educated in the ways of being a politician. Although father loves to fight, he doesn't want a warrior as a son. Not as long as our estate is in Germany, the most peaceful kingdom in all of Christendom."

"Ha! Peaceful? That's just because the emperor is too scared to do anything because he needs the support of his electors," said Roland. "You know what I think? I think that the Emperor should just invade France already and get it over with. Or at least help out the Teutonic Knights over in Prussia. Maybe we should have warriors instead of statesmen."

"Come on, Roland," interjected Friedrich. "You know that it's unfair to just invade the French. What did they ever do to you?"

"They are Franks; they should be under our rule! They have had power for too long!" replied Roland.

"Settle down boys," said Ulrich. "A lady's about to be in our midst." A fair maiden made her way through the courtyard to the knights.

"Wow, such strong knights in our court," she said playfully. "Speaking of invading France again? If only the tiny town of Adelebsen were more powerful than the entire Kingdom of France."

"Don't worry. If those arschlöchers come looking for Alsace again, I'll go there and deal with them myself," replied Manfred jokingly.

"Wow, and think, I'm married to such a brave warrior!" she exclaimed.

"Come here, Maria," said Manfred, as he embraced his wife. Manfred and Maria had been married at the age of twelve. Maria was the daughter of Prince Goetz of Kassel, a powerful lord governing the state of Kassel, near Göttingen. Prince Goetz was currently 'occupied' by a trip to Sicily. Like all arranged marriages, they had some disagreements. But, overall, they got along extremely well. They were nearly perfect together. The only dispute was that Maria was an absolute pacifist, while Manfred loved war. That's why he never spoke to her about his missions as a man at arms.

The group of six talked at the table, and Ennelein brought out another bread plate for Maria to eat with them. All of the knights loved Maria, as she was kind and funny, and she was always considerate and respectful of the points of view of others. After managing the estate, unlike most other noble ladies, Maria enjoyed going into town and interacting with the people. She often gave alms to the poor and homeless and played with the children while their parents were busy. It was just who she was. Nobody knew why she was so kind, especially as she was of noble birth, but everyone just assumed that she was an exception to the rule.

Adelebsen was quite a religious community. Every Sunday, mass was held in the local church. Those who lived in the estate, however, attended their own separate mass. Although the outside of the building was somewhat simplistic, the inside of the castle church was beautiful. It was covered in paintings, gold and silver, with depictions of biblical tales. In the castle church, there were also a few cells for travelling monks and clergy members. These cells were always maintained at top shape and were often repurposed for any visiting guests. Although the church was within the castle walls, it was not exclusive to anyone. All were allowed to worship within the building, but most peasants felt more comfortable in the town church. It was also nearer to their homes.

The town church was much simpler. It received less funding from the Bishop, and neither of the two churches collected any tithes. The church was funded primarily on donations, and considering that the town of Adelebsen struggled with the plague, they received quite a large sum of donations. However, corruption was much more apparent in that church, as the priest lived a more lavish lifestyle than any other in the town. He was the only man aside from Manfred with enough power to control the town, and that he did. The priest, Pastor Leon, used the church funds to pay for spices from the silk road, which his sons sold in a shop in the main square. As well, the priest was always quick to sell indulgences, to save the souls of sinners.

Manfred could do nothing about this man, as he represented the lord. He knew that the man was wholly unholy, but he did not want to lose the favour of his people - the favour that he had rightfully earned through his good deeds. Instead, he appeased the priest but always warned him not to cross the line. Manfred always considered his primary duty to maintain security and order in his town, and him confronting the priest would do nothing but sow the seeds of chaos. He was disgruntled and upset about the man, but he wasn't in much of a position to deal with him. He simply didn't know how. Until the day came when it was imperative for him to do so, Manfred decided he'd just keep on maintaining peace and justice in the way he felt confident.

"This tastes delightful Ennelein!" Manfred exclaimed. He was happy for the moment, proud of his victory. But Manfred subconsciously yearned for something more. He needed more than just rabbit to satiate his appetite. He needed every troubadour and scholar to know of brave Sir. Manfred's chivalrous exploits. The only problem was that there were no exploits to be found. Manfred glanced once more at the mural, and then took another juicy bit out of the rabbit.

The group enjoyed themselves over the rabbit and, afterwards, indulged in a cinnamon coated raisin loaf.

CHAPTER 2. UNEXPECTED GUESTS

Later that day, Manfred and his knights engaged in jousting practice. It had been a while since they last competed in a tournament, mostly because there was nothing to celebrate. The last tournament that they had been to was two years prior. It was held in Hanover, the capital of the Electorate of Saxony. Manfred was barely old enough to fight, but he still did. He defeated two opponents before being unhorsed himself. Ever since, Manfred loved jousting and mounted combat. The other four knights, aside from Wilhelm, were all older than Manfred and had seen much more combat in tournaments and otherwise. In fact, Roland used to be a freelance, making his earnings through jousting. His excellent skill and prowess with the lance were noted by Prince Otto, which is why he was taken under the Prince's wing and added to Manfred's personal guard.

The men were all trained from birth to use a lance on horseback, but they also trained in other weapons. Manfred particularly loved using his axe, and Ulrich was fairly close to his war hammer. He named her Menschentöter - Man-Slayer.

Roland and Wilhelm practiced using flanged maces. Of all of the single-handed weapons, they were the simplest to use. As Wilhelm often said:

"All you do is whack 'em with the heavy end."

This rule had held true thus far, but the men still trained rigorously in the martial arts of these weapons. All aside from Friedrich. Friedrich believed that all knights should be excellent swordsmen. Although all of the other knights carried arming swords for worst-case scenarios, Friedrich became an expert with a longsword. He loved the idea of knightly duels, and what better weapon to specialize in than the longsword?

The five men practiced hitting straw targets mounted upon old wooden logs. They rode past, attempting to skewer the hey disks with their lances or whack them into oblivion from atop their mighty steeds.

They practiced all day until sunset, at which point they were called inside by Ennelein for dinner. Instead of meeting in the same room near the kitchen, all of the castle residents sat at the long tables in the great hall. The great hall in Castle Adelebsen was a separate building in the courtyard, which similarly resembled the church. However, it was larger than the church and closer to the keep.

The hall was tall, and the wooden beams running across the archway were decorated with numerous banners representing the heraldic sigils of local lords. The flags cascaded over the dining guests.

The main table at the end of the hall was mounted atop a short wooden riser. It was where Manfred and Maria sat, alongside the knightly retinue, their squires, and Maria's ladies in waiting. The chatter of retainers was soon overwhelmed by the sound of drums, pan flute, and lute, as a band began to play in the center of the hall. This band often played at Manfred's dinners, as he paid them handsomely, although they were street performers from the town. As well, there were dancers, who were soon joined by some of the joyous retainers of the castle.

The feast-like meal was soon brought out. It was made up of fresh game from the court's hunters. There was a wild boar, and two large elks, all seasoned deliciously and with large juicy apples in their mouths. They were accompanied by loads of fruits and vegetables and, of course, Ennelein's specialty sauces. As well, there were numerous cakes and loaves to indulge in. Everybody was given a bread plate to soak up the juices; however, it was frowned upon to eat these plates, as they would later be donated as alms by the castle's church.

The meal was festive and joyous, as everybody celebrated another day of successful work. As well, the wines and ales contributed to the mood, resulting in some lopsided dancing by a few of the stable boys.

After the dessert was served, the meal was interrupted by a messenger. The music abruptly stopped. He burst through the doors and headed straight over to Manfred.

"Manfred! Manfred! I come to deliver you a message from your father in Göttingen," he cried out. Ulrich and Roland quickly stood up, blocking his way. Ulrich, being the larger and stronger of the two men, proceeded to pat the man down for any hidden weapons and stripped him of his bollock knife.

"Bring me the letter," said Manfred.

"There is no letter, sir," replied the messenger. "Your father simply told me to inform you to make haste and ride to Göttingen at once."

"By God... that man. Can I at least finish dinner?" asked Manfred.

"He seemed fairly serious sir. I think that there may be news from the Electorate."

"I'll go with you," said Maria, looking at Manfred.

"It's okay. You stay here and be entertained. If it was serious enough, father would have come here himself," replied Manfred. He kissed her on the forehead and rose with his knights. Ulrich gave the knife back to the messenger.

"Thank you kindly," he said. Ulrich gave no response, as he enjoyed his food and didn't like his meal being interrupted. Wilhelm stuffed a lemon bun in his coin purse for the ride over. Friedrich continued to crunch on an apple as he followed the unit down the shallow steps.

The party of six exited the hall and headed straight to the stables, where they mounted their horses and left for the road. It was dark outside, and the sound of bullfrogs grew louder as they rode on. The cold began to get to the men, so they stopped along the side of the road briefly to put on their cloaks.

"Is that Italian too?" asked Wilhelm, as he looked at Friedrich's paisley embroidered cloak. He smirked in response. Roland took a sip of ale from his flask, hoping that it would make him feel warmer.

It didn't.

It was still deathly cold outside, so the sooner the troop got to Castle Plesse, the better.

"How much longer do we have to ride?" asked Wilhelm.

"Only an hour or so," replied the messenger. "But I don't like these roads. It is said that there are wolves roaming around here."

"I'm not afraid of any wolves," said Roland. "If they attack me, I'll kill them."

"With what? A sword?" asked Ulrich with a smirk.

"Well... yes. A sword ought to be a superior weapon to a few claws, wouldn't you think?" said Roland.

"By God, you are stupid. At least you can aim a lance. It's too bad you don't have it on you, or else you could have challenged the wolves to a joust!" he exclaimed, making fun of Roland.

The troop rode on through the cold of night, stopping only briefly once more to relieve themselves of all the ale and wine they had drunk previously. In the distance, on a hill, they could see the candlelight of a tall spire.

"That's Castle Plesse," said Manfred. "I know that tall, spiked spire all too well." The troop rode up to the castle gates. The castle was large, far larger than Adelebsen Castle. The whitewash was glowing in the night sky.

The gates opened wide, and the group trotted their way

into the castle's barbican, through the gatehouse, and into the courtyard. There, their horses were tended to, and the men walked straight to the castle's great hall. As they entered, they saw a magnificent room, filled with murals and heraldry. In the center, the Prince's throne was seated, and around him were pews for his local government. In the chair sat Otto, and beside him, his wife and Manfred's mother, Grunhelda. Before them in the hall were two men, speaking to him. Otto turned his attention to Manfred.

"Ah, my boy, you finally arrived. Come here. Meet these two fine gentlemen. They have travelled far and wide, and I think that you should meet them," said Otto. The two men turned around. One of them was dressed in ordinary clothes, but he was evidently foreign. On his head was a flamboyant red chaperon, and he wore bright blue and green clothing.

The other man was dressed in full armour, with a Cherbourg cuirass masked by a sleeveless white surcoat with a cross on it. He was a tall, older gentleman with red hair. He wore a white cloak with a black cross, and atop his houndskull bascinet were three painted black and white peacock feathers. On his left arm was a horseman's targe, bearing a black cross on a white field. This was the uniform of the Brother Knights of the Teutonic Order.

"Hello," the knight said. "I am Sir Maurits van Melle. I have travelled here from the Duchy of Ghent, in the Kingdom of Flanders. As you can see, I am a Teutonic knight. I was just discussing some matters of importance with your father. Would you care to join us, Sir. Manfred?" he asked politely.

"Greetings, and welcome to Göttingen, Sir. Maurits," replied Manfred. "Of what matters do you speak?"

"I come bringing news from the order. They are preparing for war. I have travelled far, and my destination is Marienburg, in Prussia, to join my brothers in arms and deliver this scholar to them," replied Maurits.

"Yes, I am a scholar indeed," said the second man. "My

name is Renault d'Anjou, and I have been sent by the Pope to evaluate the legitimacy of the order's claims."

"Alright then," said Manfred, "But why must I rush over here in this God forbidden hour of the night and leave my subjects and precious Maria to hear about the missions of these two honourable men?" Manfred was irritated at his father.

"Manfred, I have called you here because these men need help, and the timing of their departure is of the utmost importance. They came to me asking for shelter, and of course, I gave it to them. But as we spoke to each other, it became apparent that they need a guide. They need someone who speaks the same dialects that they do in Saxony and Brandenburg, and someone who knows the way through Germany. You do, Manfred," said Otto.

"So? I'm sorry, but I do not see why I, in particular, must be subjected to such a mission. My duty is to my people."

"Manfred, we all know that you will, unfortunately, receive next to nothing when it comes to inheritance. Besides, you are the most skilled in combat of all of my sons. That is why you are an excellent candidate."

"I thought you didn't want me to become a crusader. Why do you change your heart so rashly now?"

"You aren't going to," said Otto sternly. "Your job is simply to escort these men to their destination and return, not to join them in battle like a fool. Besides, I think that when you come to terms with the bitter harshness of the Prussian wasteland, you'll see why it isn't a good idea for spoiled young lads such as yourself to go off fighting in these senseless wars," replied Otto. Maurits looked at him sharply, but said nothing, for he did not want to get involved. "What say you, child?"

"No, I won't be hauled around like some bodyguard simply to escort this foolish bookworm and his religious fanatic friend. My duty is to my people and my people alone," replied Manfred firmly. He began to turn around until his father spoke again.

"Wait! Before you come to any brash decisions, know that, if you do this, you will earn my respect and, perhaps, a little more land than simple little plague-infested Adelebsen. Besides, I would send you with twenty of my best pavisiers. Ten crossbowmen and ten spearmen. What say you?" proposed Otto. Manfred had to think for a moment. This was his lifelong dream, to join the Teutonic Knights and march off to glory. But, at what cost? What would happen to his town, or his castle, or his wife? Manfred finally made up his mind. He thought for a moment. If he was given men, he could finally command a small army of his own. Was this not his life-long goal? Furthermore, Manfred soon realized that his father could strip him of his lands if he did not oblige. For whatever reason, he was intent on sending him away, and Manfred came to terms with this.

"Aye, I'll do it."

"You will? Perfect!" replied Otto. Maurits, go ahead and make this man a brother of the Order. Perhaps you'll put some sense in that young mind of his.

"Please kneel, brother," said Maurits. Manfred got down on one knee, grinning. He certainly looked forward to fighting pagans in the name of the Empire and Christendom. "I officially dub thee in the name of the father, son, and holy ghost, a brother at arms of the Teutonic Order. Your aid will be greatly appreciated to the order, I assure you."

"Thank you, sir," replied Manfred. Content, Manfred and his men left. Perhaps it was the alcohol in him, or the excitement of becoming a crusader, but Manfred felt on top of the world. Ecstatic, he left the hall after saying his goodbyes, and he and his men embarked on the ride back to Adelebsen.

CHAPTER 3. THE TOY SOLDIER

The next morning was cold and brittle. The maid had forgotten to light the hearth in Manfred's room. He looked around and saw the long, cascading drapes and the decorated mantelpiece. On the mantelpiece sat naught but a single wooden sculpture. It was a small wooden horse, crafted for Manfred by his own father. As a child, Manfred had access to all the toys he wanted. Looking back, Manfred remembered that his favourite was a small toy soldier, also made of wood. He was painted in the black and yellow of the empire, and he was built to be strong and tall. Manfred loved playing with him, all the time wishing that one day he could become him.

Manfred looked again at the wooden horse. He loved it now even more than he had then. It was harkening back to a simpler time. A time without politics or economics but, instead, only chivalry. Although he didn't spend his former years in the church or on a horse every day like Friedrich, or learning to fight every day like Roland, Manfred's childhood was characterized by massive parties and tournaments; the true luxury of nobility. So much for that.

Manfred turned his gaze to his wife. He kissed Maria on the forehead before getting out of bed. He was cold to the touch, as he slept in nothing but his nightgown, consisting of a thin tunic that went down to his ankles. It was blue and embroidered with silver. Manfred took the garb off and slipped on his hose, his shirt, and his belt. Finally, he realized that it would not get any warmer, so he took off his belt, put on his gambeson shirt, and put his belt back on. He left his sword by his bedside. Then Manfred walked over to his window. He opened the curtains and looked out across the town of Adelebsen. It was gorgeous in the winter. The snow on every rooftop glistened and gleaned in the sunlight, and icicles clung onto every roof gutter. The streets were nice and clean, with the sugar-white snow coating the polished cobble-stone. Afar, Manfred could see all the way to Göttingen and beyond, and he could see the rolling hills filled with forest and farmland. It was truly beautiful.

Manfred was happy there. He enjoyed the songs of the birds in Adelebsen, and he loved the grandeur of nature there. Although he slightly envied his brothers, as anyone would do, Manfred was content with his life.

He didn't want to leave.

Manfred came to question his decision. Was it the ale or had his father tricked him? Would he be damned to hell for all eternity for abandoning his people and family? Manfred loathed himself for his decision and wished he hadn't made it, but at the same time, he knew that some inner desire had forced him to say yes. He knew that if he let the opportunity go, he would soon feel the guilt of turning on his own childish dreams. Manfred put on a brave and determined face. It was time to come to terms with reality and himself. He put on his stockings and shoes and began walking down the winding steps of the keep tower. His stomach turned with every step. What would he tell Maria? She had been nothing but good to him, and yet he was turning his back on her. Manfred feared the judgement of his people. He had kept them safe since he became an adult, and now he was leaving?

"What if that last brigand returned, and pillaged the town? Nonsense! It was one man, and I'll have guards here. They'll

keep everyone safe, and they'll keep my family safe."

Manfred descended from the stairs and into the great hall where breakfast lay waiting.

"The appetite of labourers works for them; their hunger drives them on," said Friedrich, who was already there. "I learned that at mass today. You weren't there?"

"A good ruler must be well fed," replied Manfred. "I learned that in school. The teacher said that a ruler must be deprived of all appetites so that he is driven by rationality and not emotion."

"The priest wanted to see you; to bless you before we leave."

"I forgot that today is Sunday. My apologies to the priest."

"Are we really doing this?" asked Friedrich. Manfred paused. He didn't know what to say. He knew that the answer was yes, but he didn't want to say it. He didn't want to admit it. He was scared. He had dreamt of this day all his life, and now that it had come, he dreaded it.

"Yes," replied Manfred sternly. He turned and sat down and began eating his sandwich. Friedrich and Manfred ate in silence. Before digging into his food, Friedrich rehearsed a quick prayer in his head. He thanked the Lord for his daily bread and asked for aid in the journey to come.

The two men ate together for a short while before Friedrich departed. Manfred sat alone. Alone to think, and alone to worry. At that moment, Wilhelm walked in with Sir. Maurits. They were both talking, and ready to eat.

"That was some sermon, huh?" said Wilhelm.

"Yes, indeed," replied Maurits.

"Manfred! You woke up! How's it going?" asked Wilhelm.

"I'm fine," replied Manfred. "Yourself?" he asked.

"I'm alright," replied Wilhelm. He could see that something was wrong. The generally enthusiastic young Manfred seemed withdrawn. "Look. I know that this is a milestone, and it is completely your decision. But I've known you since we were little, and as far as I can remember, you always wanted to become a crusader. I know you, Manfred. You were always made for more than this tiny town; you were made to lead armies."

"Then I guess twenty's a start," replied Manfred with a smirk.

"Look, if you don't feel up to it, you don't have to come with us," said Maurits. "But, your aid would be greatly appreciated." Manfred looked at him and back at Wilhelm. In Wilhelm's eyes, he could truly see the kindness of one friend to another. He understood what Wilhelm was saying and took his counsel to heart. He was right. Manfred wouldn't let any town get in the way between him and his dreams, not even if the town was his home. This was his destiny.

"Don't worry, Sir. Maurits, we will come with you," replied Manfred decisively. This was it. This was his final verdict. No more overthinking things; it was time to focus on the road ahead. It was time to become the wayfaring knight he dreamt of being.

It was time to become a toy soldier.

CHAPTER 4. THE MAP

Manfred and his knights sat in council, with his father, his advisors, and of course, Maurits and Renault. They sat around Prince Otto's dining table, on the top of a short stage in his great hall. In the center was the best map of the Empire that Saxon scholars had to offer. It was a series of dots, with names on them, and lines connecting those dots.

"Ah yes, I have seen maps like these before," said Renault. "Those dots are settlements, and those lines are roads."

"How could one possibly know these things to such proportion?" inquired Ulrich.

"They don't," replied Renault. He pointed to a small line, and a much larger one as well. "See this long line here? This is the one that leads from Göttingen to Adelebsen, while this small line leads from Adelebsen to Kassel. As you know, it is far quicker to travel from Göttingen to Adelebsen, than from Adelebsen to Kassel."

"Right," said Ulrich. "I have travelled those roads many times before."

"Have you?"

"Yes, and I have even gone to Bremen with my own band of mercenaries. We passed Brunswick and Hanover, and we almost reached Hamburg," said Ulrich.

"Wow! I know little of those places, but on the map, they appear far. Were there many brigands along those roads?"

"There were none that my men and I couldn't handle, and certainly none that would stand a chance against our current company," said Ulrich haughtily.

"Well then, is it decided?" asked Otto. "Is this your plan?"

"According to the map, it says that Hamburg is only North of us. We have to go east as well," replied Roland.

"Yes, Roland, but Prussia is North of us, and none of us have travelled east," replied Manfred. "When we reach Hamburg, we will be guided by our map alone."

"So, we will take this precious document with us? That is foolish, to say the least! We would be risking such a precious document, worth many florins," said Ulrich.

"Yes; but is there any other way?" asked Renault. "As long as Prince Otto would allow it, I humbly ask to take the map with us. Surely we could secure it in some chest of some kind."

"I do give my blessing for the map to be taken with you. But, Renault, I would like for you to copy the map onto another paper before you take it, that way you can take the copy instead. I presume that you have no need for artistic sea dragons and mountain giants on your map?" said Otto.

"Yes, you are right," said Renault. "I shall have it copied by this evening."

"Then we should leave tomorrow morning," said Ulrich. "There is no sense in leaving at night. We should see the road ahead of us."

"Agreed," said Manfred. "It will give us time to say our goodbyes as well."

"Fine, we shall leave tomorrow morning. At the break of dawn, we'll meet here in the court of Castle Plesse, where we will sort ourselves out," said Maurits.

"Yes," said Otto. "I will have mustered my pavisier shieldmen by then too." The troop agreed on the timing and decided to spend the rest of the day doing whatever they pleased, that is, aside from Renault, who was hard at work.

Manfred returned to his wife to spend the day with her. The rest of the knights, including Maurits, visited the Red Rabbit Inn, a small tavern where they loved to spend their time when they were not on duty. The night fell suddenly, and a dark blanket was laid across the sky and pelted with bright, glistening stars. Even the sun itself was wary of beginning a new day, for it feared the troubles that lay in wait.

The next morning, the five knights mustered in the courtyard of Castle Adelebsen. They wore their full armour, ready to face brigand and beast along the arduous road ahead. In the yard, Maria came to say her goodbyes. She looked at Manfred with a teardrop in her eye. Both had agreed to stay strong in this moment and had already confided in each other the night before. Their hearts were filled with agony upon seeing each other, yet they both knew that it had to be.

"The Lord giveth, and the Lord taketh away," Maria said in a trembling voice. Her idiom didn't lighten the mood in the slightest. Manfred looked at her.

"Take good care of the town," he said. "I shan't be gone for long. And if I am..." he paused. "If I am, assume that I'll be gone forever." His voice faltered, and he swallowed a hard bite of pain. Maria broke into tears, but Manfred stayed strong. "Form up!" he called out. His four men at arms formed a horizontal line in front of him. Before leaving, Manfred decided to ceremonially entitle each of his men. He turned to Friedrich. "Friedrich, will you be my scout? Do you pledge to be the eyes and ears of the company until your last days, and serve the commanding officer, myself, undoubtingly?"

"I do," he said bravely.

"Ulrich, will you be my left-hand man? Will you ride with me into battle at any cost, and give your life in my name?"

"I will," replied Ulrich.

"Roland, will you be my righthand man? Will you aid me in times of trouble and danger, and save me in the midst of the chaos of battle, even if it means giving your own life?"

"I will," replied Roland. Then, Manfred turned to Wilhelm. Manfred had his squire, Herwig, hand him a banner, newly crafted, with the coat of arms of Göttingen, a grand white castle on a field of blue, which lay atop a golden lion on a field of red. The banner was mounted atop a long lance with a golden head.

"Wilhelm, will you be my bannerman? Do you promise to raise the flag long and high and keep it standing, even in the face of danger? Do you pledge to defend my house's name to the last drop of blood in your God-forsaken body, and do you pledge to fight alongside me until the very end, until that very banner is sliced from the pole and burned in the infernal wastes of hades?"

"I do," Wilhelm said firmly. He looked Manfred in the eyes, and Manfred nodded accordingly. The order was established.

The knights' squires mounted as well and donned their armour. They were dressed in red and blue and carried swords and light lances as well as gambesons, chainmail, jack chains, and brigandine, produced by Göttingen's own smithery. On their heads were simple kettle helms and open-faced bascinets without aventails. Their horses carried the tents and supplies, but these young boys were just as willing to fight as their mentors. They too were trained in the art of horse and foot combat, and when combined with their horses, were quite formidable opponents. Wilhelm handed the banner over to his squire, Thomas, as the role of bannerman was more ceremonial than anything.

The troop was off, and they rode to their first destination: Plesse Castle, where they would unite with their warband and begin the adventure.

CHAPTER 5. INTO THE UNKNOWN

The party arrived at Plesse Castle before noon. They didn't hand their horses off, as they intended to be leaving promptly. There, the two travellers waited, and with them was a small army of ten crossbowmen and ten spearmen. They were in a linear formation. While they wore red and blue clothing and some minimal armour, in their hands were tall grey pavise shields, carrying the black "T" of the Teutonic Order's Sergeants at arms. As well, the master artisan emerged from his workshop alongside Otto with a mysterious crate.

"Open it, son, they're yours," said Otto. Manfred wondered what they could be. He opened the lid to find five white canvas covers for their heater shields.

"Thanks. Now they won't get wet from the snow," said Manfred, somewhat sarcastically. He was disappointed but didn't expect much from his father to begin with.

"No, no!" said Otto. "Open one. See what's on them!" Manfred opened one up, revealing a slim black cross, the cross of the brother knights of the order.

"Oh my, thank you!" said Manfred.

"You may not be a real Crusader, but at least you'll look the part when you get there," said Otto playfully. "Here, open this one," he said, as he gestured towards one stashed away in the corner of the crate. Manfred unveiled it, revealing a beautiful black and yellow cross, as well as the imperial eagle heraldic in the center.

"Wow!" said Manfred. "But... isn't this coat of arms reserved for the Hochmeister?"

"Don't worry," replied Maurits. "You aren't in the order, so they can't really punish you. Besides, it looks too regal to pass up, doesn't it?" he asked jokingly.

"Yes, it absolutely does. Thank you, father," said Manfred.

"Don't thank me, thank the master artisan; it is his craftsmanship," replied Otto.

"Thank you," Manfred said to the master craftsman. Friedrich and Wilhelm followed his example.

At that moment, Grunhelda, Manfred's mother, emerged from the castle. Manfred began to feel a terrible sadness.

"My boy, I'm going to miss you," she said. Manfred felt a stinging pain in his throat, the sort that arises when you feel a terrible need to cry, but simply can't. Manfred wasn't truly sad that he was leaving his mother, but instead by the fact that he felt he never truly had a mother in the first place. In all his memories, he never recollected spending any time with her. No bedtime stories, no family dinners. He was always left alone to play with his army of toys, or train with his teachers. Manfred glanced at his saddlebag, in which he had secretly stashed the wooden horse. He placed his hand over it to calm himself and remind himself of all the good times he enjoyed in that castle.

"I'll miss you too," he said painfully.

He was lying.

Manfred simply nodded at his father, and his father nodded back before Manfred mustered the troops. They quickly snapped into marching formation, and one spearman stepped forward.

"I'm field commander Franz von Plesse, at your service m'Lord," he said in a Lower Saxon dialect, contrasting the High German that Manfred spoke.

"Nice to make your acquaintance. I hear that you have a sturdy group of men?" replied Manfred.

"I do indeed. I would rather fight alongside these men than any other army in the world," responded Franz.

"Good. If you maintain cohesion and high morale, I'm sure that we'll make it out alive," responded Manfred.

"Indeed, sir. I can't help but notice your fantastic mounted retinue as well," said Franz, pointing at the riders.

"Ah, yes. These are my men, handpicked." Manfred introduced him to them.

"Pleasure to make your acquaintance," said Franz, tipping his kettle helmet.

"Formation!" called out Manfred. He looked at his parents and then rode to the front of the column, where he shifted his attention to the road. "March!" he called out. The column of twenty footmen and twelve riders made their way forwards, slowly trudging through snow and ice to their next destination: Einbeck.

CHAPTER 6. RED WITH BLOOD

As the party marched on, they grew tired and weary of the cold.

"Onwards, men. Einbeck is not far now," said Manfred, fearing that his army had already lost morale within a day of the journey.

"I think that you should let them rest," said Wilhelm. "They're tired, and you don't want them to resent you. Not this early at least."

"Fair enough. I'm growing tired as well. Tired and cold. I do hope that we reach Einbeck soon," replied Manfred. "Men, set up tents here; we'll camp until we have our wits about us, and then we'll press on to reach Einbeck before dark." The men scrambled to set up their tents, as did the squires. The troop camped out for a while. The knights took the opportunity to clean off the snow from their armour, and Renault decided to use the temporary cover to unravel the map and ensure that they were on the right track. Friedrich decided to scout ahead and to make sure that Einbeck was close bye. The squires stretched the new canvases over their mentors' shields. The knights truly resembled warriors of the order now. They looked like knights from the days of old, who fought dragons and giants, saving damsels in distress.

Manfred wished that dragons existed so that he could slay one. He wanted to prove to everyone that he was capable of doing so, and he wanted to enjoy some excitement in his life. Instead, this perilous journey would have to suffice.

After a few minutes, Friedrich returned at full gallop. His breath trailed behind his aventail like smoke flaring from a dragon's mouth.

"Manfred! Manfred, I have news!" he shouted. Manfred stood up tersely. "Manfred," Friedrich said as he approached. "Manfred, there's smoke on the horizon in that direction." He pointed in the direction of Einbeck.

"So? It's a village. They must have some cooks or blacksmiths or something. Fear not dearest friend, for it's no harm to us. I see no reason for your panic," replied Manfred.

"No, Manfred. He's right," interjected Ulrich. "At this time of year, smoke should be barely visible at all over the trees."

"What do you imply?" asked Manfred.

"I'm saying that something must be on fire, and I haven't heard of any witches being caught in these parts," replied Ulrich. He looked at them gravely.

"We must help those villagers from the jaws of those ruthless pillagers!" shouted Manfred.

"You can't be serious sir," said Friedrich. "We don't even know how many they have!"

"That's your job," replied Manfred. With that, Friedrich gave no response and simply mounted his steed and galloped away. He knew that this battle would be pointless, and he felt that Manfred simply wanted to wet his sword.

He was right.

The pavisiers formed into ranks and packed up their belongings within minutes. The squires did the same and gave their shields to their mentors. The men began advancing, ready to receive the news from Friedrich. They bravely marched in a column through the woods, eager to spill blood.

Soon, Friedrich returned.

"I see roughly fifteen of those heartless pillagers. I believe we have no chance of defeat, sir," he stated.

"Excellent," replied Manfred. He signalled for his unit to advance with speed, and they broke into a sully.

"How well are they armed?" asked Maurits.

"They are all nothing more than brigands. No horses, no harnesses," replied Friedrich.

"Good, we can charge them," Maurits replied. He was wary of the coming battle. He had seen warfare unimaginable to the men beside him. In 1382, in his youth, he fought for Ghent in the battle of Roosebeke. He despised the French until he got involved in fighting off chevauchee raids by the English on French towns. Soon, he supported the French during the Hundred Years War, and he served in the raid of Blackpool Sands, in which he and 2000 of his comrades faced a crushing defeat at the hands of a local militia. There, he saw the carnage that he had only heard of in stories. The hails upon hails of English longbows were only matched in terror by the foot knights they faced soon after. Although Maurits liked the idea of defending these villagers, he feared for his life and the life of the men beside him.

The army approached the village cautiously. There, they saw the church set ablaze, with people inside. The rest ran about the streets attempting to escape torture and death.

"Form up!" called out Manfred. The men formed a solid shield wall with crossbows behind them. The horses lined up side by side. "Present!" he told his lancers. They lowered their lances. "Charge!"

With haste, the cavaliers, knights, and squires together, charged into the fray. The knights formed the vanguard, and the squires rode behind them, forming a hulking mass of steel and lance. They propelled themselves into the small army of brigands who looted and plundered their way into obliviousness. The ground trembled. The dirt and slush behind the cavaliers flew up like it had been shot out of a cannon. One by one, the brigands turned their heads towards their enemy.

"Run!" their leader shouted, as his men scrambled into buildings and alleyways. Through the main street, the riders charged, massacring all brigands who stood before them. The citizens of the village hid in their houses, and those trapped in the church were aided by their cavalier liberators. Although they had all suffered severe trauma from the smoke, luckily none had died.

The pavisiers formed a schiltron formation in the village centre, locking their shields together like a wall and planting their spears in the dirt like stakes. The crossbows sniped the brigands one by one, while they stood protected by the wall canvased wood. Continuously the brigands crashed into the hearty wall, and continuously they were repelled by slashing spears and bollock daggers.

After aiding the victims in the church, the knights and squires disbanded, ruthlessly hunting down all brigands in sight. Soon, the party had killed them all, with the few survivors running for their lives. The troop had suffered no casualties, as expected, and were thanked by the villagers with extra rations and ale.

"Thank you," said a little girl, who offered Manfred a flower. He accepted it and thanked her. The party partied into the night and enjoyed the ale and rations gifted to them by their hosts. The villagers provided lodgings for each of the men, free of charge, as further payment for the heroic deed. There, the men slept until the next morning when they departed for Brunswick.

CHAPTER 7. BLACK MAGIC

The next day, the party left the town at dawn. They began marching after a light breakfast of bread and cheese. Hungover, they stumbled through the knee tall snow left from a heavy storm the night before, and blood stained the pristine white snowflakes as the wounds of the injured leaked out. No men were lost, however, and morale was still high because of their glorious triumph.

The horses neighed often, releasing frigid spurts of icy spit. They were cold, far colder than the soldiers themselves. Their winter fur was exfoliating, leaving hairy clots in the blood-stained white.

"Where to next?" asked Roland.

"Brunswick," replied Manfred. No response. No man wished to fill their lungs with the bitter cold air, so they kept their mouths shut like vault doors. The troops trudged slowly for half the day until they came across a fallen tree. It was a large coniferous tree with porcupine-like bristles. It was completely impassable as it ran the entire span of the short, uncleared path.

"It's blocking our path," said Ulrich. "We have to move it."

"No, wait," said Manfred. "Look at where it broke," he said, pointing to the stump. There were axe marks. "This wasn't the storm. Someone felled this. It could be an ambush."

He was right.

"You are right," muttered Maurits. "We should tread carefully from here on out." His lips froze. The riders gazed into the wilderness, and the pavisiers formed a marching column designed to combat and ambush. They all clenched their weapons like vices. Manfred dismounted.

"Squires, come help. Everyone else, cover us," said Manfred grimly. The squires dismounted and rushed to his aid. "Lift on three!" shouted Manfred.

The five men lifted and worked their way around the log for a few minutes. The unit lay in wait in formation for an impending attack. The knights began scouting in the woods after a while. They hoped to discover their pursuers before they themselves would become compromised.

Friedrich headed deep into the woods. The snow was no taller than that on the roads, but he did follow a set of child-like footprints. Soon, however, they faded with the fresh snowfall, and Friedrich was left stranded among the endless trees. He looked back to where his camp was, but he knew that he had to continue, to find whoever fell that tree. Friedrich cantered through the woods for a few minutes until he found a small cleared path. The trees seemed to bend into arches around the path, providing a sort of shelter. On the ground, he found footprints again. They were larger and farther apart, but they were footsteps, nonetheless. Friedrich proceeded down the path. He looked over his shoulder. He couldn't see his party anymore, but he felt no need to, for he was about to hunt down their target. He urged his horse forwards through the path.

He continued on until he began to hear singing. The lyrics were faint and foreign, but the song itself was beautiful. The singer sounded like a fair maiden, well trained in the art of song, but Friedrich was more amazed at her ability to sing in those harsh conditions.

Friedrich treaded forwards with caution, following the

voice. The footprints promptly ceased on the ground. Friedrich followed the source of the music on a tangent off of the small path. He emerged upon a small hut. Outside of it, skulls hung, painted in blood.

The music stopped.

Friedrich dismounted his horse and approached the shack stealthily. However, the snow revealed his footsteps. He knew that he was no longer going unnoticed. Friedrich stood tall and marched forwards towards the door. He knew what lay in wait for him. He had heard tales of such creatures in stories, but nobody believed them. Not even peasants were so superstitious that they would believe in black magic. Nobody believed it except for the lunatics who were diagnosed with possession. The church didn't, the nobility didn't, peasants didn't, men, women, and children didn't. They didn't exist, and yet, there one lay in wait for him, huddled in her shack, probably practicing alchemy or eating a child. Friedrich was terrified. He clasped his wooden cross necklace and moved forwards to the door.

He looked around and saw nothing, nobody. He emerged to the doorstep and came to the door. On it was engraved a pentagram, and various other symbols surrounding it, such as a crescent moon, the Aries ram head, flames, and upside-down crosses. Friedrich clenched his cross harder. He began to tremble. The fear overwhelmed him. He slowly raised his hand to open the door. It was locked. He stepped back, and with the pommel of his longsword, he broke the handle. He kicked the door down, and with a wild cry shouted:

"Reveal yourself, you vile witch!"

An old woman sat in the corner tending to a fire. The shack seemed much larger on the inside. The walls were rotten and infested with small bugs and worms. They were lined with shelves carrying leaves, powders, and liquids, all foreign to Friedrich. The fire which the woman tended to harboured a small copper bowl in which there was a sizzling turtle, spiced with ferns from the woods. The woman sat shrivelled over the hearth like a hermit in a cave. A hermit she certainly was.

Friedrich looked at her in wonder. She had no horns or green skin; she looked like a human. But he knew that she wasn't one. Friedrich prepared to strike her. "You have plagued this land for too long. Prepare to die!"

"Wait!" she hollered, extending her left arm. "Why do you wish to slay me thus?" she asked in a foreign accent. The woman strained herself to speak like this. She was old and frail and was unable to act with the spontaneity of her opponent.

"I know you not, woman. But what I do know, is that one of your vile kind released a plague onto this land, and it very well could have been you!" he shouted. He lifted his blade again. "The power of Christ shall vanquish thee!" he shouted, bringing down his blade upon his victim. He cleaved her in half. What remained was no more than a withered husk of a body, expelling blood like a fountain.

Friedrich paused. He took a breath. He was shaken. His eyes were wide with zeal.

"What have I done? Was that a witch, or simply some delusional old hag?" he asked himself. "Why have I ventured into the woods only to find and murder an old lady? I must speak nothing of this. If my comrades inquire as to the redness of my blade, I shall reply with the blood of our ambushers," he thought. Then it dawned on him again. "Scheiser! I still have to track the ambushers!" Friedrich stepped outside and mounted his horse. Like the wind, he galloped back to his party. In the distance, he heard cries of battle.

"No! They have already attacked!" he muttered. He spurred his horse to ride faster. The snow was no match for his horse's muscular front legs. The snow behind him kicked up like a tidal wave. "Onwards, boy. Ride to relieve your brothers!" Friedrich came upon the carnage with haste. He clasped his lance and crashed into the first of his enemies, impaling him like a kebab. He soon noticed that they were not men at all, well, not full-sized men anyways. They were dwarfs. Freidrich had heard of them in tales. He heard that some were born of human parents, and some were born of dwarf parents. But, he knew for a fact that their defining feature was their small stature. He'd never seen one before, but he'd heard about them performing as jesters in the royal court. Manfred's father, Prince Otto, had told Freidrich that they couldn't think any harder than a mule. But, by the looks of it, these dwarfs were well aware of their surroundings.

The small rectangular man lingered on the tip of his weapon for a while, dragging on the ground into his bandit brothers. Friedrich dropped his lance and joined his comrades.

"Friedrich, where were you?" asked Manfred, fighting the small but fearsome warriors from his horse. Axe in hand, he cleaved at the small men on both sides. Friedrich drew his long sword and gripped it firmly. He rode over to Manfred and his horsemen while hacking and slashing on all sides.

The dwarfs were short but numerous. There were many dwarf colonies such as this one throughout Europe at the time. Having been shunned by their communities, they took to the forests to live in peace among comrades of similar stature. While most dwarfs at the time found work in the courts of nobles as entertainment, others were forced to isolate themselves from society in dwarf colonies such as this one. This colony happened to make its profits from banditry.

The battle raged as the cold grew ever more stinging. The schiltron formation was dispersed, and a linear battle erupted between the two forces. It was severely one-sided.

"We have to retreat!" shouted Manfred. The horsemen attempted to break the dwarfs' line to no avail. The dwarfs' ranks were armed fiercely with spears and axes. The riders' horses simply wouldn't charge into the bristling ranks of short, well-armed targets.

Manfred circled his axe in the air, calling for a retreat. His riders followed him, as did the pavisiers soon after. At that moment, a short man stood upon the fallen log and shouted, "Halt!"

The dwarf was clad in chainmail and brigandine and was clearly some source of authority within the half-men's ranks. "They are not the Prince's sons' retinue! They're Teutonic Knights!" he cried out. The dwarf crossbowmen ceased their fire, and the spearmen halted their advance, waiting to rejoin the fight.

Manfred was confused. He was the son of the Prince, but he made no comment on it, for he feared that he would give up his advantage. The dwarf scanned the field. There were about a dozen dwarfs slain, and yet only two of the pavise crossbowmen fell. The rest were either wounded on unscathed, and the riders had received no harm. He feared for his men's safety, and therefore ended the attack.

"My name is Wendel of the little folk.," said he.

"I am... Hans, Hans von Zürich. I am travelling to Prussia," replied Manfred.

"I am sorry for your men," replied the dwarf. "I instructed my men to attack anyone with the sigil upon the shields of your squires," he said, pointing at the shield that Conrad held in his hand. "We hunt for the son of Prince Otto von Göttingen. We received news that he was heading this way."

"And, what would you do with that man if you found him?" asked Manfred.

"Well, Hans, we would ransom him back to his father. He's an affluent man."

"Why would you wish to do such a thing?"

"Because we here are dwarfs. As you know, many of us are born of dwarf parents. I, on the other hand, was born of normal-sized parent, much like yourself."

"So? What does that have to do with Prince Otto?"

"Well, Hans, many of us, like myself, left our homes to live here where we wouldn't be ridiculed. This is clearly imperial land, and imperial land is not taxed. We only pay rent to the

Elector of Saxony himself. But, the Prince still wants to tax us for our residences in Einbeck, despite the fact that we no longer live there. It's simply due to the fact that he can't sell them to any other peasants because the rent is too expensive! Besides, they'd be surrounded by the plague victims who still populate that place!" replied Wendel.

"Actually," responded Friedrich, "I just ended the witch who caused the ailment. The towns should be safe." Friedrich looked content in saying so, having come to the decision to be proud of his handiwork.

"Witch? What witch?" asked Wendel in confusion.

"You little men run about these woods and don't notice the great big shack implanted in the thicket just across those bushes?" Frederick asked with a laugh, as he pointed towards the witch's hut.

"Fool! That *witch* never harmed a fly and certainly didn't cause any plague. You know naught of which you speak. She might be crazy, but she's just like us – different. That plague was sent here for you all to atone for your sins, and that's why we don't have it here in the woods. So, take your plague-infested bodies and move along," Wendel replied. Friedrich didn't believe him. How could God have created such a thing? It simply made no sense.

"Well, we cannot cross with that log in the way," replied Manfred. Wendel gestured to his men, and they came and lifted the log as Wendel hopped off.

"Enjoy your safe passage," said Wendel. "But be warned, we are not the only brigands treading these woods."

"Nonsense!" exclaimed Ulrich. "I have travelled these roads before; I believe you to be spreading farbs. I encountered none of the likes of you!"

"Times have changed, friend," said Wendel. "Tread with caution, for we are still on the hunt."

The party moved along through the dusk, carrying their dead and wounded along. It would be a long and cold march to Brunswick. The night grew dim, but they needed treatment for their injured and Christian burial for their dead.

CHAPTER 8. CHILL OF WINTER

Brunswick appeared under cover of night, hidden between a collage of ice and dead trees. Its lights were lit and looked like large stars in the night. Smoke whistled from the main smithery like a chimney, blanketing the night in soot and ash. The armourers there worked day and night to produce the finest products in Saxony. Göttingen was gone. The world lay ahead.

The party approached the town, stomping through the snow to get there as quickly as possible. Of course, tavern candles were still lit, and the riders rode ahead to book rooms for all of their living. The dead were stripped and dropped off by the plague victims outside of the church. A quick prayer was said, and then all rushed to escape the cold. They went into the tavern, and the men sat around one long table. At the head sat Manfred with his knightly retinue beside him. Beside them were Franz and his men. The guests sat at the end. The tavern keeper approached Manfred and his retinue with a small chest.

"Greetings, noble travellers. How may I help you today?" the tavern keeper asked.

"Please leave us be for just a moment," Manfred replied. "Actually, you know what, how about an ale and a rabbit stew for each man here?"

"Absolutely, my Lord. I will have them ready for you at once," the keeper replied. "You seem to be quite a battered bunch. It may do you some good to connect closer to the Lord."

"What do you mean?" asked Franz, somewhat impatiently.

"Well, good sir, in this chest I present to you a fragment of the true cross! The very cross which Jesus spilt his blood on. I'll let any man touch it for a single florin."

"Piss off, you damn profiteer. Get us our stews hastily now or we'll be off," replied Manfred bitterly.

"Forgive me sir, but perhaps you would wish to ask your men if they are interested?"

"How much was it for the rabbit stews and ales?"

"Let's call it a total of twelve florins."

"Good. I'll give you twelve when they come, and not a penny more. Off with you." The tavern keeper scurried off with his wooden chest. Franz and Manfred sat in silence. Most men refrained from speech, with only a handful of quiet conversations emerging. When the ale and stew came to each man, the clamour of wooden spoons and bowls fostered more mingling, and soon the tavern sounded like a market square. Franz decided to speak.

"They were good men," said Franz. "They didn't deserve to die so young."

"We should go back and kill those damn halflings," said Roland.

"No, we were outnumbered, and already lost men; we cannot afford to lose any others," replied Manfred.

"Sir, it pains me to say this, but we'll have to replenish the ranks in order to maintain proper formation," said Franz.

"What do you mean?"

"We need two more crossbowmen. We have their armour; we just need to pick up two men. Hunters would suffice."

"I will not drag around hunters with me and feed them as I do my soldiers. We will recruit real warriors. Mercenaries." Manfred looked around. He scanned the tavern, but only saw drunks and homeless escaping the cold. "We will find no decent men at this hour. Come, we should get some rest and recruit a more decent type in the morning."

"Decent type?" asked Ulrich rhetorically. "I think you've been hidden from the real world for too long, my Lord. No mercenary will have the decency of your courtly folk."

"Really? And what experience have you with mercenaries?"

"I was one, remember?"

"And you would not say that you or your men would rape and pillage in the way that you would speak of, right?"

"Well, m'Lord, I've changed. But the truth is, that we were not courteous folk. We stole and pillaged all we wished until we got hired. And when we got hired, most jobs were dirty work for some criminal. We fought no gallant wars, the most gallant it got was robbing robbers. I assure you; you will not find a mercenary fit to serve a Prince."

"Well then, Ulrich, will I find mercenaries fit to serve a general?"

"If it is the soldier type you look for, you are in the right place. But if you want warriors, hardened warriors, we should instead travel to Magdeburg. There, they train warriors, marksmen, men at arms, you name it. It's on our way, and we can certainly spare the time. Sir, trust me, we rely on our men."

"My men."

"Yes, sir."

"Fine. We'll go. I'll check the map with Renault in the morning, but I am certainly willing to follow your plan," said Manfred. Franz agreed, and the group reflected on the matter in their rooms over the course of the night, or what was left of it. The wounded had a chance to recover, and the tired had a chance to sleep. However, in the morning, they were far from battle-ready.

CHAPTER 9. CHILL OF DEATH

The next morning came swiftly. The town roosters woke the party and returned to their cage-like coups. The men were tired and unfit to march, but they had to press on. After a quick breakfast of porridge at the tavern, the troop donned their armour and began the strenuous march to Magdeburg. The march was long and arduous. Winter raged around them. The map showed no distances, leading to uncertainty among the trailblazers.

Tired, they marched on through the woods until the trees faded, revealing endless stretches of farmland. They were covered in snow and ice, and little grew aside from weeds and pine trees.

"We should find a place to rest," said Wilhelm. "The soldiers are tired and unable to march. We could surely find a farmhouse or something of the sort."

"I agree," replied Manfred. "Friedrich, go find us a lodging. Until you return, we will travel this long and rugged road towards Magdeburg." Friedrich rode forwards with haste. However, within minutes, he returned.

"Manfred, good news!" he called out. "Over there, over that hill, there is a crossroads, and there is a small town." Renault scanned the map.

"Yes, you're right," he replied. "It is the small town of Helmstedt."

"We should wait there until the cold subsides," said Manfred. He led his troops to the town. It was small and quaint but buried under heaps of snow. The houses were cold and dark, and no sign of life was visible. The unit marched through the town in search of life, anybody, but they found none. They headed over to a large wooden barn where they all rested and ate holes in their provisions. It was a ghost town. Not a single soul was in sight. Instead, there were stray rabbits and dogs. No smoke emerged from its roofs, and no candles were lit. Something had happened there, but none of the men were inclined to find out.

The barn was a suitable resting place. It provided shelter from the cold and space for the wounded to lay while re-bandaging their wounds. The men sat and recuperated well into the evening, and the troop rested there overnight. Outside, a frigid storm raged. Sleet and hail smashed into the barn walls. Inside, the men lay trembling, waiting to fall asleep and deal with the terror in the morning.

In the morning, the bitter cold remained, but no storm raged. Instead, however, the barn doors had been smashed to pieces by the harsh conditions. The roof of the barn had been struck by a large tree. Manfred looked around, dazed and tired. He scanned his men. Some had purple fingers, others purple lips, some had both. The blood slowed in their veins, frozen from the night before.

"At least they're rested," said Ulrich.

"They can't continue like this. They need more time," said Wilhelm.

"We don't have time," replied Maurits. "We need to get to Marienburg as soon as possible."

"We cannot wait like this; we need to move quickly," said Renault. The party looked at Manfred for a verdict. He eyed his men and saw no more than a group of tortured men:

beaten, bruised, cold, and broken.

"We have to continue," said Manfred. "If you can't make it, or if you want to turn back, feel free. But if you are able to march all the way to Prussia, join me. You are free men, and free to leave you are, but I will certainly not abandon these men, and I believe it is our duty to ensure their arrival. Those able should join me, but those who wish to stay here and rest like cowardly maggots can do so at their leisure. Just know that, by nightfall, you will all have starved to death and frozen among the pastures that surround us." The men looked at him. Franz stood up.

"Not all of us can come. Certainly, less than half are even fit to make the journey. Men, I have known you for ages. I would gladly fight and die by your side, and I certainly hope you feel the same towards me. But it is not our job to freeze in vain. The injured, tired, and cold will stay. If you wish to come, rise now, but know that there is no more turning back," he said.

There was a death-like silence. Not a single man moved. The air seemed to thin, and time seemed to stop in its tracks. Not a man was willing, but one. A crossbowman arose.

"I will join you," he said. He was young, and his face was pale, contrasting his dark purple lips. However, he was uninjured and deemed himself ready. He gazed at his comrades, prompting followers. Two spearmen arose and said nothing. They were followed by three more crossbowmen and another two spearmen. They rested on their shields and bundled themselves in their cloaks, but they seemed fit enough. Manfred looked at the remainder. They were weak and scathed and looked like veterans on a battlefield. Manfred understood their fear.

"Fine. Four crossbowmen and five spearmen. What an army. The sick and wounded will be escorted home by my squires after some more rest. I will leave you all half of our rations. Use them well," said Manfred. With that, he ordered the remainder of his troops into marching order. The seven riders and their army of nine infantrymen began the second leg of the journey to Magdeburg. They trudged forward through the snow with cloth wraps over their faces. They made their way through the icy wasteland to the town.

CHAPTER 10. THE BARD

As they moved through the icy wastes, the veil of white began to retreat. On the rarest of trees, some saw flowers beginning to bloom. In the fields, the glistening ice gave way to blotches of slush. The air was still deathly cold, but an ember of hope burned in the hearts and minds of the soldiers. The walk was long as the roads were broken at points and required the men to dismount and lead their horses through deep puddles and slippery ice patches. To the joy of the men, they came upon a crossroads where they saw footprints in the frosty mud.

"Travelers must have come here," said Manfred. With glee, the men rejoiced, as they knew that with travellers would soon come civilization. "But we must be wary, as those could be brigands just as well as good Christians. Stay sharp, and do not let up your guard," he ordered. The men knew that this was true, but they couldn't help but feel that their arduous journey would soon be filled with much more ease.

The unit marched with haste towards the large town of Magdeburg. They sang songs and chants to make the walk more bearable, as they all wanted to arrive in good time.

"There once was a man named Farmer John,
He loved to tend to his crops,
But then one day a big storm came,

And all of his cattle dropped!
There once was a bandit named cow thief John,
He loved to collect cattle,
He rode all day till he was sent away,
And was hired to fight in battle!
There once was a soldier named Spearman John,
He was strong and fierce and tough,
He fought his way to the end of the day,
and decided he'd had enough!
There once was a man named Old Man John,
He was a hermit that lived in a cave,
With a blade and a cane, he'd just sit there all day,
Until the Lord sent him to the grave!"

"That music is not fit for a band of honourable crusaders," said Maurits. "I think that we should show you how it's done." Renault pulled out a lute from his bag and proceeded to play. The two men began to sing a beautiful rendition of "Palästinalied." When the two men finished, the troop cheered for them. Manfred looked in astonishment at the amazing music that he had just heard.

"Where did you learn such music?" asked Wilhelm.

"When I was a child, I loved to visit the cathedral in Antwerp and listen to the monks sing. It was beautiful. When I joined the order, I heard this song for the first time. It is the order's anthem," replied Maurits.

"And you, Renault. How did you learn to play the lute like that?"

"In France, performers such as myself are quite common. That is why I switched my ways to serve the church. I learned to play in school," replied Renault.

Renault proceeded to play another song. With it, he sang along. It was a tavern tune which he had learned in Occitania.

"In the streets of Marseille,
Among the ales and wines,
Sat a beautiful wench whom I did wish to know,

So, I trotted on over,
To make her my lover,
But in my visage did her wine swiftly go!
Oh, oh, if only I'd known,
That she had her own lover, and was wedded to another!
So, I leapt to my feet,
And returned to my seat,
And I played cards with a man who was soon to be beat,
I played a good hand,
Then he got me banned,
And scowled in anger and called me a cheat!
Oh, oh, if only I'd known,
Swapping cards below the table,
Was considered illegal!
So, I soon left the tavern,
And returned to my cavern,
And I sang about places that I've never been,
Then my neighbor did shout,
To quiet the noise down,
And came to my door with the biggest club I've ever seen!
Oh, oh, if only I'd known,
That the man was a killer,
And I was a poor singer!"

The soldiers cheered. They loved the song, and they sang it loudly and continuously throughout the entire rest of the journey to Magdeburg. Over the horizon, the town emerged. The sprawling town made noises loud and intertwined before the settlement even reached the sight of the troop. When the unit arrived over the ridge facing the town, they were astonished at its size. It was large and walled and was bustling more busily than Constantinople itself. The people were affluent and wore bright reds, yellows, blues, and greens on their shirts, pants, and dresses. The streets were spotless. The local latrines and cesspits were cleaned daily, creating no stench in the streets but the manure of untrained livestock.

"This makes things a little more complicated, doesn't it?" said Franz.

"No, it doesn't. We'll visit a tavern and hire a troop in no time. Imagine how many taverns there must be," replied Manfred.

"Manfred, that would be a mistake. We want these new men to be loyal to us, not their own group. We should split up and recruit a certain amount of men individually, and then chose the best of the lot," interjected Ulrich.

"Alright then, how many do we need?" asked Manfred.

"Eleven men," replied Franz. "Spearmen would be preferred, but crossbowmen would also be appreciated."

"We would be lucky if we found fighters, would we not?" asked Wilhelm. "We are a small unit, so we should find the best fighters."

"I don't think that show fighters would be subservient to me," replied Manfred. Nobody questioned his authority. "But," he added, "Good fighters may serve us well, especially if we're taken by surprise."

"Sounds fine by me," said Ulrich.

"Well then, it's settled," said Manfred. "I will divide my money into seven. The seventh group, our loyal soldiers, can help themselves to meals at a tavern of their choosing. The rest of us will split off and recruit the two best soldiers we can find... who will accept our coin, of course." Manfred took a few florins from his purse and divided them into seven. The riders took them and soon split into groups to discover their future companions.

CHAPTER 11. THE BULL

"Ulrich, come with me, I could use your advice," said Manfred with a beckoning gesture. Ulrich joined him, and the two began riding into town to look for new recruits. "Where should we look first?"

"To be honest, I don't know. This town is foreign to me, and it's people I do not know."

"Well, how did you recruit your own band of mercenaries?"

"I first served as a lowly sellsword. Then, I was recruited in an old tavern where many of us ruffians used to waste our days away, and I was hired into the troop. From there, I worked my way to the top. When I recruited men, I looked no further than ale houses and bars, but, looking back, I'm no longer confident that they are our best option, especially considering our destination."

"Hmm. I see your point. However, I do believe that we should take what we can get. We just need to find the best of the bunch, well, the four best, and then we can civilize them... just as my father civilized you," Manfred said playfully.

"Fine then. We can start with a tavern, but if we don't find the right men, we must move on. We have until tonight to find proper fighting men, and we need to ensure that our recruits are the finest. You have the coin; we just need to see who'll accept it."

"Agreed."

The two men rode through the streets until they found a large, but quaint, alehouse. From the street, the two men peered inside. The decor was spartan, and the tables looked run down. There were a variety of guests, but they were all men, and all of fighting age.

"I believe we have found our destination," said Ulrich with a smirk. The two men tied their horse's reins to the trough outside. Beside their barded destriers were six more horses of fighting size with minimal equipment. Some were armoured, and most were scarred from arrows and pikes. They were tough animals and had surely seen much violence, but they were calm and patient like well-raised children. "We don't want more riders," said Ulrich. "We should locate the mercenaries with spurs and rule them out. They'd only cause us trouble, as Franz needs men he can command. Our knights are better trained than any sellsword criminal with a horse."

"Alright then, how about you lead the way then? Locate the best group from which we can hire," replied Manfred.

"Yes, sir," replied Ulrich. Ulrich walked through the door and held it open for Manfred. The two eyed the various groups sitting at the tables. No doubt the tavern's purpose was solely for hiring mercenaries. Above the bar was a green shield, and on it, in gothic script, was a scroll reading "The Bloodied Blade." This was the name of the tavern, which was immediately understood by both of the knights. Ulrich began to survey the various groups. First, he set his eyes upon the riders. Their spurs made more noise than the drunks beside them. The drunken lot was clearly lacking discipline. Beside them were men with the most flamboyant garb he'd ever seen. Either they were expensive or hadn't seen a day of combat in their lives. None of those groups seemed capable. Then, Ulrich turned his eyes to the fourth table. It was secluded and shadowed in the back corner of the pub. The men there were already in armour and seemed battle-hardened. They were most likely deserters.

"Manfred, you see those men over there?" asked Ulrich.

"Yeah, they seem scary. We should hire them."

"Well, maybe. They do seem tough, but there's no way any mercenaries could get such equipment by simply selling their bloodshed. They must be deserters."

"What if they're just really good at their job?" asked Manfred, with a fairly leading look.

"Fine, we can speak to them, but do not express haste of any kind. We must test them first, discover who they are, and what their plans are."

"Alright," replied Manfred. The two knights walked over to the four men sitting at the distant table. There were enough seats for both of them to sit down. The mercenaries ate in silence.

Before Ulrich and Manfred could even sit down, one man asked,"Can I help you?"

"Yes," replied Manfred. "I am looking to hire some mercenaries to aid me in escorting two men to Prussia. I have thirty florins here in my purse. Are you interested?" Ulrich gave a glare of distress to Manfred. He had just disobeyed the entire plan.

"Wait," replied the mercenary captain. "Who are you?" he asked.

"I am Sir. Manfred von Göttingen, son of Prince Otto von Göttingen, and beside me here is my loyal companion, Sir. Ulrich."

"Right, well I'm Bertolf," he replied. "Are you some kind of noble?"

"Yes, indeed, under the Imperial Electorate of Saxony."

"Damn nobles, always thinking you can buy your way through life. I won't take your filthy money, nor will any of my men," replied Bertolf.

"Wait," said Ulrich. "With this coin, you could buy your way into any brothel, bargain as much as you like, and upgrade your equipment. Imagine what a man like yourself could do with a suit of armour like this one."

"Why would I work to perpetuate your damn corrupt system, instead of happily continuing to eat my eggs and porridge, which are currently getting cold right on the damn plate in front of me?"

"Any man can be bought. Besides, imagine all the business you'll get once people hear of your grand adventure to the North," replied Ulrich. Bertolf looked around at his men who replied with expressionless faces. They, frankly, couldn't care less.

"I'll tell you what. If you can out drink me, I'll join you for all of those precious florins. I need a good drink, and more importantly, I need an employer I can trust. What do you say?"

"Deal," replied Manfred, jumping in. He was known to be a capable drinker, but Manfred was more used to drinking wine, not ale. "I'll buy as many pints as needed."

"Alright, let's get to it," said Bertolf with a smirk. Manfred went up to the bar and asked for an open tab. The bartender reluctantly agreed under one condition, that they wouldn't be so intoxicated that they'd start a fight. Manfred agreed.

The centre table was cleared, and all the other mercenaries gathered around to watch the showdown. Manfred and Bertolf looked each other in the eyes. Manfred was determined to defeat his opponents. Two pints were placed at either end of the table. Once one was finished, it was to be refilled before they downed the second one, and so on, until one of the two drinkers couldn't drink anymore. At that point, they'd lost. Ulrich called out:

"Three, two, one, drink!" The two competitors finished pint after pint. The race was heated and messy. Ale was spilled on the floor; other ale was vomited out. Both drinkers had a tough time. They poured ale down their throats like babies sipping breastmilk. They voraciously gulped down the bitter liquid. Slowly, both men grew drunker and drunker. Manfred grew dizzy and couldn't see properly. Eventually, after four and a half pints, Manfred missed his mouth entirely. He was out. Done.

He had lost.

Slightly disappointed that they'd lost, and slightly relieved that they wouldn't hire those lowly brigands, Ulrich rushed to the aid of Manfred. He helped him out of the tavern, keeping his balance. As Manfred began to vomit again, Ulrich rushed him into the alley beside the tavern. There, they rested. Manfred, bent over, vomiting out a large amount of alcohol, was completely incapacitated. However, Ulrich soon heard footsteps behind him. He turned around to see the four mercenaries standing in front of them, weapons drawn.

"Have you changed your mind?" he asked.

"Ha! You didn't think we'd let you walk away with those florins, did you?" replied Bertolf. It couldn't be.

"You backstabbing, evil little worm!" replied Ulrich. He drew Menschentöter, his trusted war hammer. He had no shield or helmet, leaving him vulnerable to the enemy's attacks. "Come at me, you runts!" he shouted, standing in front of Manfred. The four charged at him, but the ally was thin enough that he could essentially fight them one at a time. The first was Bertolf. He hacked at Ulrich with his large bardiche axe to no avail. Most strikes were blocked either by Ulrich's left vambrace or his war hammer, and the strikes that landed avoided his head. Then, Ulrich plunged himself forwards, trapping the shaft of the bardiche in his armpit. Boetz dropped the polearm and hastily drew his rondel dagger. However, he was too late, and Ulrich swung with his war hammer right under the brim of his kettle helmet. The crow's beak of the hammerhead tore right through Bertolf's cheeks, and the spike on the end broke his nose. Then, with another strike, this time with the hammerhead, he smashed

Bertolf's jaw. It flew across the alley and shattered on the side of the tavern. Before confronting his next opponent, Ulrich heard shouting from behind the brigands. The flamboyantly dressed mercenaries in the tavern had come to rescue the two knights. Altogether, there were fifteen of them. They formed a wall of bristling halberds and pikes. As they aimed their polearms towards the thin alley, the brigands had nowhere to go. Their options were to either die by a wall of steel or die at the hands of a knight. Two of them charged into the pike wall to no avail. The sharp points penetrated right into their brigandine armour. The last man was quickly slaughtered by Menschentöter. Once the criminals were dealt with, Ulrich sheathed his war hammer and approached the band of mercenaries who saved his and his master's life.

"My name is Ulrich, at your service," he said, bowing down to them.

"I know your name," a man in the center of the line replied. He was well armoured, as were the rest, and he wore affluent black and yellow clothing. Upon his Burgundian kettle hat were the black and yellow horns of a bull. "We heard your conversation in the tavern. We knew it wouldn't end well. We've hated those damn scoundrels for years." The man spoke in an accent, almost French, almost Latin, but not quite either.

"Well then, I'm glad you saved our lives. How may I repay you?" replied Ulrich.

"Well, you could give us those coins for a start," he said. Ulrich looked surprised and taken aback. "Then, you could let us accompany you to Prussia. We are here because we wish to be in your service, sir. My name is Leon von Uri."

"We would be grateful to acquire your services, Leon, but we don't look for so many. Our commander can only lead another eleven men, and we have already sent scouts to hire two for each of them as well."

"Well, you're in luck, as I am quite capable of commanding my own men. So, now that that's out of the way, what say we sober your friend up, and take those coins, huh?"

"Fine. We are indebted to you, and this is the least we could do." Ulrich took the coins and handed them to Leon. "So, where is Uri? I don't recollect this as being a town in the Empire."

"Well, my friend, we are from your Empire, but we're not German. We are proud Swiss, mountain men of the south. We travelled here after fighting off the Austrian invaders. Now, we are soldiers without work, so we have travelled the country in search of those in need of our... talents. However, nobody needs fifteen men, and those who do won't hire anyone but native Germans. That's why we decided to save your life."

"Well, I'm certainly glad you did," replied Ulrich. The men returned to the tavern, and upstairs, they washed Manfred in cold water until he was sober enough to ride his horse. The troop returned to the tavern in which the pavisiers enjoyed themselves. The group united and conversed, and booked rooms for the night, awaiting the arrival of the other questing knights.

"So," Franz asked Leon, "what brings you to Magdeburg?" Leon lowered his articulated bevor.

CHAPTER 12. THE BLACK KNIGHT

"It all began a few years ago," replied Leon. "My men and I were all simple folk. We lived in the mountains and tended to our mountain goats. We lived in a small village looking over the city of Uri. Our symbol is the bull, which is why I wear horns upon my helm. Anyways, one day a messenger was sent from Austria. He wore the Habsburg coat of arms, but we didn't know any heraldry, as we had no use for it when farming. So, the messenger first went to Uri. We saw his caravan, but we didn't think much of it before they came to us, as many travellers go to and from the city. As he came, however, we knew that something wasn't right.

He marched to the doorstep of our town hall where we were all summoned by our mayor. As we sat, staring at the ordained altar, waiting for the messenger to open those tall wooden doors, we knew that something was going to happen. We sat, and waited, and when the man entered, he did so with pride. He marched up to the front and presented to us all. *'Good News.'* he said. *'You are all now Austrians.'* Enraged, we killed that man, and prepared for a fight. When the rest of Uri heard of what had happened, they all took up arms and rallied to us. The city provided an excellent defence. We trained ourselves and equipped ourselves with arms and armour bought by the canton. Soon, the rest of Switzerland joined us. Uri, together with Unterwalden, Schwyz, Ticino, and Bern, was ready for its defence. However, after a six-month process of preparing, the Austrians sent only a few hundred knights. We had thirteen hundred men. Through forest and mountain, we ambushed them. We fought with our pikes and halberds and sent them back to Austria. In defence against their campaign, we had employed a scorched earth tactic. Our farm was scorched, along with many others in the region. It is for that reason that we have abandoned the profession of farming. Soon, we decided to search for employment. As we speak German, we decided to move into Germany, but we had to stay away from the South - in fear that the Austrians would find us and hunt us down like dogs. So, we headed North, up through the Palatinate, east through Saxony, and we ended up here, in Brandenburg, when we finally got a job."

"What was the job?" asked Franz.

"When we arrived at Brandenburg, we didn't first come to Magdeburg. Instead, we had to pass through Helmstedt."

"We did too," said Franz.

"Right, and you probably saw that it was abandoned. But, when we first arrived about a year ago, it wasn't. It was a quaint small town that managed most of the fields around it. In the main tavern, they housed many travellers who came across their crossroads. We were some of those very travellers who needed a place to stay. So, we spent a few florins on ale and food and went to bed in some of their rooms. The next morning my friend Wolfe and I walked down the stairs to have some breakfast. When we got there, the bartender looked quite startled to see us and quickly fished around in his pockets to find something. He was a short and stocky man, surely of Southern build. I gave him a puzzled look as I had no clue as to what he was doing. Hastily, he pulled a small slip of paper out of his pocket and handed it to me. Unfortunately, I can't read, so I asked him to, and he read

'Greetings fine mercenaries, and welcome to Helmstedt. I hope you found your stay pleasant here. Before you all head on your way, I require something of you for which you will be rewarded greatly in silver and gold. My name is Sir. William von Lappwald, and I am in great need of your services. I fear that my daughter has been kidnapped and is being trapped in a keep somewhere in the nearby Bartenslebener forest. I fear for her safety, and I have no knowledge of who or what has taken her. Please meet me behind the barn as soon as you receive this message - there is no time to waste.'

Upon hearing this message, I was finally relieved that there was someone who was willing to hire us. Wolfe and I decided to help the man, but first, we had to take all of our men and belongings and enjoy our nice porridge and sausages. After breakfast, we donned our armour and held our polearms, and in marching formation, we headed down towards the barn. When we got there, I quickly peered around to see if anyone was present. Surely enough, I came across an elderly gentleman, alone, dressed in fine garb, and sleeping against his horse while holding his cane. I approached him, noting that he did have a sword at his hip.

'Hello?' I asked, to wake him up. He grunted and kept sleeping. However, when I said it again, a little louder, he hopped on his feet as startled as a housecat. *'Fear not, I am here to serve you, remember?'* I said. He responded with a friendly visage, and we soon got to work. He explained to me how his daughter was promised to another local knight, but instead, she loved her own man. Her father was lenient enough to let her marry him, as he was a God-fearing Christian still. Unfortunately, the knight she was promised to became angry, and, dressed in black garb to hide his identity, stole her before she could marry. The next day her father came to the tavern looking for men like us. Apparently, nobody showed up with our talents, except for us. He must have seen us the night before, but we were probably too drunk to be

approached. Anyways, he promised us ten florins. Five before the deed was done, and five after. It was a good deal, to say the least. So, we got right to it. He pointed us in the right direction, and we were on our way. Sure enough, upon approaching Bartenslebener forest, we found the keep. It was tall and crooked and round and had a spire at the top sharper than any in the east.

We approached the building in formation, knowing that one knight, although powerful, could not defeat our block. We advanced with caution, but nobody was there, not even a bird. Naturally, we kicked open the door, which was perhaps too easy, and we marched up the stairs. There, that's when we saw him. At the top of the spiralling staircase was a knight clad in black armour, wielding a black shield, black mace, and black horned greathelm. One by one we advanced on the fiend, but nothing was to come of it. Our pikes were too long for him to reach us, and his armour was impenetrable. So, I did what I had to. I charged the man with my halberd, hooked his horns with the crow's beak, and I tore him off his balance, into the central shaft of the tower. His bucket-like helmet plunged him into the depths below. The man plummeted to his death, and the fair maiden was finally saved. Once we were sure of his death, we cut of his head to present to the noble. We also salvaged his armour and distributed the untailored parts among ourselves. The rest, alongside the corpse, we gave a Christian burial, so that the lord could send him to hell.

Afterwards, we returned to the tower to rescue the maiden in distress. We kicked open the upper door, but inside, to our surprise, the lady sat freely upon a bed weeping. Beside her was a scroll. We couldn't read it, but it looked official.

'*What's wrong?*' I asked.

'*You killed him,*' she replied meekly under a veil of tears.

'*Exactly, we killed him; so, you're safe now.*'

'*No, you don't understand.*'

'*What don't I understand? That man kidnapped you and*

prevented you from marrying the man you love!'

'No! You have it all wrong,' she cried out. *'He's the man I love. He rescued me from being married to my father's choice, and now he's hired you, murderers, to come and kill this man. You butcher!'* she called out. It was at that moment that we realized the wrong that we had just done."

"Wait a minute; you're saying that, if you could have, you would have helped her go against her father's wishes?" asked Franz.

"Of course! I don't know how you Germans do it, but in Switzerland, our women are strong and responsible and can make decisions for themselves," replied Leon.

"Well, in Germany our women are our equals too, but the father is still the patriarch of the family. He knows what's best for the family!" said Franz irritably.

"With all due respect, to hell with the family. How can one serve their kin when living a life of torment?" asked Leon rhetorically. "Anyways, back to our story. She hated us, and we knew it. We couldn't accept the evil man's pay. Instead, we decided to help her. We devised a plan.

Later that day, we returned to the old man behind the barn, where we agreed upon. He seemed glad to see us, and we played the part. We happily presented the head, but to the old man's despair, it was not the head of the black knight. Instead, it was the head of the intended husband, who we had also killed after our conversation with the maiden.

'We don't want your money,' we said, after dropping the head at his feet. *'But what we do want are clothes, food, and your daughter.'* The old man obliged at sword point. We also cut off his ring finger for good measure.

After that whole ordeal, we went on to Magdeburg where we have been finding a few jobs here and there. The maiden is with us; we trained her to be a fighter, clad in her ex-lover's sable armour. She used to be called Mary actually, but now she goes by Freya. She says it's one of your ancient pagan gods."

"Have you seen that old wretch ever since?" asked Franz.

"No, fortunately not. But, if we ever do again, I'm sure that I'd slay him on the spot. Or, better yet, we'd watch Freya do it," replied Leon with a chuckle.

"You are a good man, Leon," said Franz. "Although you may not adhere to our customs, I look forward to commanding my men alongside yours. You are part of something greater now. As you can see by my men's shields, you are now brothers at arms of the Teutonic Order."

"I'm honoured by your words. I think that you too have good morals and that we will work well together in the field. Our men can easily work hand in hand to defeat any foe that comes upon us," replied Leon. The two men cheered and resumed to drink and party with the rest of the troop, awaiting the return of the questing knights.

CHAPTER 13. THE LION OF MAGDEBURG

"Where will you go, Friedrich?" asked Roland.

"I don't really know to be honest," replied Friedrich. "Perhaps we should look around and see what opportunities we might find. What say you?"

"I agree. I certainly hope that I get to fight them. That would certainly be a good gauge of skill, don't you think?"

"Roland, Franz needs men that he can lead on the field, not some duelist. What use have we for them?"

"That's bollocks. We are constantly in danger here in towns, on our own. Having some skilled fighters might prove their worth. Besides, by the time we get to Prussia, all of our hired companions will leave. Honestly, we're supposed to too, but I fear that Manfred would wish to retain us."

"I will remain by his side as a loyal knight should, no matter his orders. He's a good man. Hot-headed, but good," replied Friedrich. "I do, however, understand your point about needing duelists. We can't rely on the skills of our companions, for we could easily be mugged by bandit groups along the road."

"Good. Then we should fight them," remarked Roland cheekily. The two knights rode through the streets until they began to hear music and cheering in the distance. They rode forth to see what it was, and to their liking, there, in the main square of the citadel, was a tournament.

"By God, we've been blessed," said Roland staring at the lists.

"Fine, go and enlist. You won't be bringing anyone back, though," said Friedrich.

"What do you mean, you aren't coming to joust?"

"Of course not! I might be fast, but I'm no jouster. I'll find something else to do."

"Fine then, I'll be off," said Roland cheerily. He jumped off his horse and headed straight to the lists to give his heraldic and name and await his placement. Friedrich headed off in a different direction. Behind the spectatorial building was a string of shops, and from behind there, he could hear a clamouring of another kind. He heard the bashing of sword against steel, and then he knew that he should uncover what was going on in the hopes that it would lead to suitable recruits. He rode his steed behind the buildings revealing an alley. There, two men in gambesons and wearing gauntlets partook in combat with their arming swords and bucklers. Like grasshoppers, the two of them jumped about, eyeing each other and maneuvering their blades and shields to attempt to target their opponent.

Around the small wooden arena were about twenty men placing bids and cheering on their favourite competitor. Then, all of a sudden, one of the fighters leapt at the other like a lion. The other guided the blow away from himself, but it grazed his arm. Despite his thick gambeson, the sword cut through like butter. He retaliated with a strike from below, but his opponent had already jumped out of the way. As Friedrich approached, the two continued for minutes, before the wounded man lost too much blood and fainted. The crowd erupted with a roar. Half were enraged, and the other half looked as though they had just won the lottery. "Hoorah for

Leopold!" a man cried out. He was clad in a full suit of armour, and upon his head was an open-faced bascinet. His tabard was ordained with a black lion on a white field. The man was a knight. He also, judging by his position, was the judge. Friedrich approached him.

"I'd like to duel your best longsword," he said. The knight gave him a wayward look.

"Nobody here will fight you."

"And why's that?"

"None of my fighters have armour like yours. You'll cut them all to bits."

"Fine then, I'll fight your two best. I just need to hire two men to take on a journey with myself and a unit of soldiers. We are headed to Prussia, and we need the best men money can buy to take us there."

"Ah, so you want a master on the battlefield, and in the arena?" said the knight, chuckling.

"Well I'd certainly have the coin to pay off such a man," replied Friedrich. The man laughed.

"Show me what you've got," he replied. Friedrich pulled out his coin purse and showed him the florins that Manfred gave him. "By God, that's a lot of coin."

"It is. Now point me to the two men who will receive it."

"Look no farther," said the man.

"What?" replied Friedrich. He was surprised as the man seemed too old to fight well, and he seemed comfortable in his current job.

"I'll go with you, and I'd certainly beat any of these men here."

"Fair enough. But, how may I know you to be as good as you claim to be, good sir?" asked Friedrich. He may have been noble, but he was no fool.

"Fight me."

"So be it. I challenge you to a duel."

"Cut the scheiss; just fight!" replied the man. On his

bascinet, he unhinged a houndskull visor, and from behind the stockade, of all the weapons there, he chose a poleaxe. It was the staple weapon of the knight. Its brutal head had three attacking faces. In this case, they were an axe head, a maul comparable to a meat tenderiser, and a thin spike which protruded from the weapon's top end. He then offered any of the weapons to Friedrich, who chose a two-handed mace. He figured it would act somewhat similarly to a longsword. He was wrong.

Before the fight even began, members of the crowd began placing bets. Friedrich faced his opponent in the eye, and his opponent did the same. Then, Friedrich took a swing. He missed. The old knight stepped aside with ease and knocked Friedrich's helmet with the butt of his weapon. Friedrich took another swing, this time along a horizontal axis. Although the swing did land, it was caught by the wayward knight, who then proceeded to rip the weapon out of Friedrich's hands with the force of a horse.

"You cannot defeat me; I am the Lion of Magdeburg!" he cried out through the breaths of his helmet. Friedrich drew his longsword and began to half-sword with the tip facing forwards.

"Now this is a fair fight," he remarked. This time the wayward knight struck. He thrust the butt of his poleaxe into the cuirass of Friedrich, and then he brought the hammer of the axe down upon Friedrich's head. Friedrich was knocked back, but he soon after propelled himself off of the stockade and into his opponent, forcing him to let go of the shaft. It fell to the floor with an obnoxious clunk.

"Alas, the two men faced both with sword in hand!" cried out the lion knight while unsheathing his blade. The two men jabbed at each other to no avail, until Friedrich eventually lunged into a thrust. The lion knight caught the blow, however, resulting in an interlocking of blade and gauntlet. The men shoved at each other for a great deal of time before

Friedrich's arms gave up and he was nearly caught and sliced behind his knee.

"I yield! Mercy!" he cried, and the old man stopped. The two men sheathed their blades, raised their visors, and embraced, as was customary.

"You endured well, friend," said the man.

"As did you, for I have finally met my superior," replied Friedrich. "Tell me, what is your name?"

"My name is Sir Ernst Meyer, Lord of Colbitz. I am known to many, however, as the Lion of Magdeburg."

"An impressive title well deserved, friend. So, I take it you'll be coming with me?"

"That would be correct," replied the knight.

"Well, have you a mount?" asked Friedrich.

"No, I don't. I cannot use my trusty poleaxe atop a horse," replied Ernst. The two men collected their belongings, Freidrich mounted, and they both travelled towards the lists, where Roland should have been. However, they found no Roland, so they continued on to the tavern, where they met up with the troop, their new Swiss comrades, Wilhelm, Maurits, and Renault.

CHAPTER 14. THE HORSE AND THE HORSELORD

After the group split up, Wilhelm headed off on his own into the town. He hadn't really thought of any good places to hire new recruits, so he figured that he'd wander around for a bit and try to see if he could find anyone. He asked a few people:

"Do you know of anyone who might be looking for a job, I mean, who knows how to fight?" But people mostly responded by either shaking their heads or walking away to disassociate themselves from him. Wilhelm rode through the streets looking for anyone, anything that might prove useful. He rode through the cobblestone streets observing the bustling trade, expert craftsmen in their shops, and merchants selling spices, bread, and vegetables. As he rode, he eventually came across a man standing in the middle of the road. He looked angry, and people avoided him. His horse, overburdened, seemed weak and underfed. As Wilhelm observed from afar, the man revealed a stick in his hand. It was decorated with precious stones and engraved by artisans. Then, the man ruthlessly raised the stick and struck his horse. The horse whimpered.

"Damn horse!" he shouted. "Useless!" Then he raised the stick again. Wilhelm couldn't bear the sight. He rode at full speed towards the man. Dust from the streets kicked up into the air. Civilians cleared the way and watched as the knight rode at Godspeed. With his mitten-like gauntlet, Wilhelm grabbed the stick clean out of the man's hand.

"Take that you reprobate!" Wilhelm cried as he did so. Confused, the man looked around and saw the knight with his stick.

"Give that back you lout!" he cried.

"No, I won't. In fact, I should take your horse too."

"You thief. I'll beat you for this," replied the man.

"You'll beat me? Really? With what?" Wilhelm taunted while shaking the stick in the air.

"Why'd you take my stick, you scoundrel? That baton is all I have left."

"You can't treat your damn horse like that. He's clearly starved and abused."

"Who are you to say that? It's my damn horse, and I can do with it as I damn please. Now give me that stick and piss off."

"I'm not giving it to you so you can just beat that poor beast even more."

"Yeah? Then I'll report you to the guards."

"For what, doing their job?"

"For stealing my stick and assaulting me."

"Assaulting you? I didn't touch you."

"Yes, you did," replied the man.

"When?"

"Now!" The man leapt forwards and tried to wrestle Wilhelm to the ground. It didn't work. Wilhelm, in return, began hitting the man with the stick.

"Stop that," he yelled.

"No."

"Stop that; I yield. Isn't that part of your code of chivalry?"

"To hell with chivalry," said Wilhelm as he continued to beat the horse beater.

"What do you want from me?" the man asked. Wilhelm

stopped. He looked around at the ring of spectators which had formed.

"I want you to direct me to a mercenary. Not any mercenary, but the best damn mercenary in the Goddamn town. Understood, you damn lout?"

"Fine," replied the man. "There's a man, he's a hun, slit eyes and all. I'll take you to him."

"A Hun, like, from Hungary?"

"Yeah. I'm sure you'll like him."

"What's a Hun doing all the way here in Germany. Why doesn't he just run off with his Kipchak brothers."

"He's no Cuman, he's a Mongol," said the man. Wilhelm looked distressed. He'd only ever heard of those devilish men through tales. He heard that they ate babies and breathed fire.

"Fine then, take me to him. Better have him on our side than against us," said Wilhelm. The man led his horse forwards, but it stubbornly resisted. "Leave the damn horse; if he won't move now, he won't move when we're gone either." The two men made their way through the streets to the edge of town. It was clearly a poorer neighbourhood, a ghetto of sorts. In the ghetto, there were beggars and money lenders. The horse beater nodded to one, who nodded back, revealing a black kippah on the back of his head. The two men moved on through the ghetto and eventually ended up at a small house. It was above a bakery. Wilhelm dismounted and put on his helmet, fearing the worst. He kept his mace at his side and his shield on his back as well.

"Ready?" asked the beater.

"For what?" replied Wilhelm. Without a word, the man opened the door and pushed Wilhelm inside. The man followed and kept the door open. It became the main source of light. Inside the house, there was little lighting aside from a few candles. A man sat meditating on a central carpet in front of a wolf totem.

"Excuse me, are you the Mongol I've heard so much

about?" asked Wilhelm.

"Depends on who's asking," the hefty asianoid replied, while keeping his eyes closed.

"I want to hire you. You can join our troop and come with us to Prussia."

"Prussia? No. I'm not going back," said the Mongol.

"Excuse me?" Wilhelm began to get frustrated. He just wanted the Mongol to comply. Who in their right mind wouldn't accept such an offer?

"I'm never going back to those wretched crusaders."

"You don't even know how much I can offer you. I have thirty florins in my pouch right now which can all go to you."

"I'm not for sale, goodbye," the man said, keeping his eyes closed.

"Everybody has their price," replied Wilhelm. The Mongol rose to his feet and opened his eyes. He was dressed in bright green and red and wore a typical fur hat. He looked at Wilhelm, twirled his long and thin moustache, and said:

"Get out, or I'll force you out."

"Clearly you haven't heard of the German ways of hospitality, half-man."

"Don't call me that!" the Mongol yelled as he drew his sword. The horse beater ran out of the house, picked up his stick, and ran away.

"Don't call you what, half-man?" said Wilhelm. He was trying to bait the Mongol, to test his steel and try to convince him to join the troop. Wilhelm didn't want to have to find another recruit, and he certainly didn't want to let Manfred down. The Mongol swung his dao at Wilhelm with two hands, but it did nothing. It just hit his coat of plates and glanced off. Wilhelm, in turn, pulled out his mace and shield. "Fine then, prove your worth, scum, before I offer you my irresistible florins." The Mongol grabbed his shield and prepared for a fight. Wilhelm swung at him, but the Mongol blocked the mace with his round shield. He then shoved Wilhelm down the steps leading up to his home. Wilhelm clonked his way to the ground and quickly got up. Wilhelm began to feel short of breath. It was an asthma attack. He stumbled to find his footing on the unkempt icy cobblestone. "I'll kill you, savage!" he muttered. Wilhelm was no longer playing. He was hurt. Hurt and angered, and he'd unleashed a rage never seen before by him. Wilhelm was determined to end his foe. The Mongol ran down the steps and fiercely swung at Wilhelm with all his strength, but his dao sword simply couldn't apply enough force to injure Wilhelm through his thick, protective armour. Wilhelm gave a rageful laugh. "This is for all the good Christians you've slain." Wilhelm smacked the man with his mace, landing a flanged tip straight into his rib cage. He heard a distinct crack echo from the impact. Blood trickled from his chest. The Mongol looked at him warily and then looked around. Both duelists heard footsteps. The town guard quickly swarmed in and encircled the two.

"Drop your weapons!" cried out the captain. Both men obeyed. Their weapons were picked up by the guards. "You're both in a lot of trouble, gentlemen," said the guard captain. "Dueling out in the open air in our great town? You ought to know that duelling is illegal, at least here. Guards, take them to the keep, we'll sort things out once they're detained." A few burly guards tied their hands behind their backs and escorted the two trouble makers towards the keep of the town. They passed merchants and beggars and every sort of citizen one might expect. Everyone was enthralled by the spectacle. Children threw a few handfuls of dirt at the men, but when one was inclined to pick up an old vegetable, their father stopped them, warning them that they'd use it for fertilizer.

Upon reaching the keep, Wilhelm and the Mongol were held in two small cages. As he rested, Wilhelm's asthma subsided, relieving him of his discomfort. The two sat in silence for a while. Neither willed to speak with the other. So, they just sat there, awaiting trial, separated by a few iron bars.

CHAPTER 15. THE CHURCH

"Where should we go?" asked Renault. He had never recruited anyone in his life. Even Maurits was assigned to aid him once Renault had come pleading for help from the order in Ghent.

"Well, I don't really want any scoundrels in our entourage. Between you and me, I think we already have enough sinners."

"Alright then, in what direction do you propose we go?"

"Perhaps the order may have a church here or something of the kind. We should look for a church and ask the priest for directions if there is one."

"Why couldn't we just ask a common pedestrian?" asked Renault.

"I don't know, I thought that a priest might have a better sense of where religious buildings are. Besides, what peasant would want to help us?" replied Maurits. The two men rode in search of a spire, a cross, or anything of the sort. Soon, they found a small house with a cross on top. The house was a church, but not much of one. It was rugged and in shambles and looked as though it could only seat about twenty people.

"Well, I suppose we might start here," said Maurits. He dismounted and lead the way. Renault followed, holding the reins of the horses and tying them to a trough outside. Maurits knocked on the door. The door was small and frail and moved every time Maurits gently struck it.

"Who is it?" asked a voice from inside.

"It is Sir. Maurits van Melle, Brother Knight of the Teutonic Order and defender of the Catholic faith." The man opened the door.

"You must always be careful in times like these," the man said sheepishly. He was a small frail man who wore the robes of a priest. He invited the two men inside. The church was extremely small. It sat a limited number of worshippers, and the altarpiece was a crude wooden carving of a blood-red Jesus being tortured by devilish Byzantine Romans.

"Quite an altarpiece you have there," said Renault.

"I'm sorry, I didn't quite catch your name, sir," replied the priest.

"I am Renault d'Anjou, emissary of the P..." Maurits cut him off.

"He is the emissary of the Prince of Anjou." Renault looked at him with wonder, but Maurits knew that they had to keep a low profile, especially when looking for combatants for hire.

"Interesting, can I help you, fine gentlemen?"

"Yes, actually," replied Maurits. "I was wondering if there happened to be any Teutonic Church here?"

"Unfortunately, there is none," replied the priest, shaking his head in gloom. "What business must you attend to? If it is money lenders you seek, there is no need for a crusader bank. Our lenders here are shrewd but rich and would be happy to loan you large sums of money. If only those rascals discovered the glory of the New Testament."

"We seek no money lender," replied Maurits. "We wish to recruit capable fighting men of good, decent, stock. Do you know of anywhere where we may find them?"

"You won't find many mercenaries of good stock here or anywhere, knight. Perhaps you could try searching in the town hall where they train the guards. Now, if you don't mind, this is a house of peace. Enough talk of bloodshed."

"I'm sorry, father," said Maurits.

"Our hour of prayer will begin shortly; would you wish to join us?"

"Unfortunately, we have little time, Father. Perhaps we could pray on the road," said Renault.

"Yes, indeed," replied the Priest. The two men left and headed for the keep where they would try to recruit some town guards.

CHAPTER 16. FREEDOM

Both Wilhelm and the Mongol could see through the iron bars at each other and through the bars into the main hallway. They sat in silence, angry at each other for possibly causing their execution. Wilhelm sat in a corner and took off what bits of harness he could. It was uncomfortable, and the air was thick.

"This is your fault," said the Mongol.

"My fault, what do you mean? If you hadn't attacked me then we wouldn't be in this mess," replied Wilhelm.

"I wouldn't have attacked you if you'd just left."

"Well, I would have left if you had at least listened to what I had to say. I went through a lot of trouble to find you, hun. The least you could do would be to process the sum that I'm offering."

"I said I don't want your money," replied the Mongol. "I would never return to Prussia."

"You say return as if you've been there before, but I know the truth. I know that you're from Hungary."

"I am."

"Ha! So, you were lying!"

"No, I wasn't. The Teutonic Knights were called to crusade against the Cumans there and in Bohemia. Unfortunately, they mistook me for one, captured me, and took me to Marienburg. I was able to escape, so I came here, far from all my troubles. That is, until you arrived."

"Well, why weren't you in the East with the rest of your kin?"

"I fled from the horde too. As a young man I fought in the Golden Horde, but no longer. I saw what they did to their prisoners, turning them into meat shields. But I couldn't escape across the border to Novgorod, so I had to instead head south through the White Horde, to Hungary."

"I see. Well, you've been dealt a scheiss hand if I do say so myself."

"You, too," replied the Mongol.

"What could you possibly mean by that?"

"What leader sends their most incompetent knight alone to find a recruit in a foreign town."

"You know nothing; shut your mouth."

"Am I not right?"

"My Lord, Manfred, is young and haughty. He may make some foolish decisions, but he's got the heart of a lion and the soul of a stag. I would follow that man to the end of the earth."

"Well, obviously, that is what you are doing. You know, why do you even seek Prussia?"

"We are escorting a papal emissary there. He will decide on whether or not the pope should aid the Teutonic Knights."

"Well then, you must fail."

"Excuse me?"

"Those crusaders are terrible people. They torture innocents in the name of your lord."

"They defend the borders of Christendom from pagan invasion! You know nothing! Shut your mouth before I come over there and slit your throat, half-man."

"If you succeed, the entire east might fall to German rule."

"Good! Let those damn Poles and Lithuanians experience some civilized order for once. We bring order to those chaotic lands. Once they fall, perhaps Moscow is next? Who knows, Mongol. All I know is that I have a duty to serve my Lord, and this is my Lord's mission."

"You are a fool if you believe in those tales of Jesus and God. God doesn't exist."

"And you, what do you believe in?"

"We Mongols believe in nature. Our gods exist on earth as forces, not entities."

"Sounds foolish and cryptic. There is one true creator and saviour, and when he returns, he'll cleanse the earth of you and your heretic kin," replied Wilhelm. At that moment, the doors of the hall flung open. Through them came two guards, followed by Maurits and Renault. "Sir. Maurits! I'm over here! Save me!" shouted Wilhelm. Maurits looked over, seeing Wilhelm trapped in the dungeon. He turned to the guard.

"For what reason is this man imprisoned?" he asked.

"I heard he was fighting that damn Mongol in the streets. He's here now awaiting trial," replied the guard.

"Well, I fear he can't wait for that," said Renault. "Look, he was fighting a Mongol, right?"

"Yeah."

"Isn't that what our glorious crusaders do every day?"

"That's true."

"And besides, he was probably attacked. If acting in self-defence, shouldn't he be freed?"

"I guess so. Here, let me ask the bailiff. You two men have paid handsomely for your two pavisiers. I'll return the favour."

"Actually, before you go," said Renault. "It looks as though we'll need two crossbowmen as well."

"Fine, I'll ask the recruits. Can you pay?"

"Absolutely. In fact, for your troubles regarding my friend here, let me tip you with a few extra florins."

"Much appreciated. I'll see what I can do," the guard said, winking. He walked over to the bailiff and whispered something in his ear. The bailiff shook his head. Then, the guard offered him a florin, and the bailiff obliged. He walked over to the cell, opened the door, and unlocked Wilhelm's chains.

"You're free to go, lout," the bailiff said. Wilhelm rose to his feet and put his armour back on. Then he collected his weapons from the bailiff and reunited with his two companions. They walked forth for a bit until they reached a small corridor. They moved down and reached a thick wooden door that was locked. On the inside, they heard men training in drills and fighting.

"Wait here," the guards said, as they opened the door and crept inside. Renault turned to Wilhelm.

"What in God's name happened?" he asked. Wilhelm recited what happened from his own point of view. He included the horse beater, the rude Mongol, but skipped the conversation in the cell.

"That's what happened, and I think any of you would have done the same in my position."

"No, Wilhelm, we wouldn't," replied Maurits. "We have to keep a low profile here. We don't have that much time, and we don't want anyone to know what kind of money we have. Nobody can even know our mission, understood?"

"Yes," Wilhelm replied. "But understand that we are helping you, not vice versa, Maurits. We are the ones escorting you for free."

"After I liberated you? Consider our debts paid," said Maurits. The guards returned with four men. They carried supplies and were all armed with pavise shields and either spears or crossbows. On their shields and clothing, they carried the colours of Magdeburg, green, white, and red.

"Thank you for agreeing to join us, friends. We have a long and arduous adventure in front of us, so ensure that you are well-rested at the tavern that we will sleep in," said Renault.

"Thank you, sir," replied one of the four soldiers. "We are poor folk, and the coin you have generously given us will supply our families for years. We are happy to serve you in combat."

"You are gracious gentlemen. I think you'll get along well with your commander, Franz. Come, let's go and meet him," said Maurits. "Thank you, guards, we'll be off." The seven men made their way back to the tavern to meet up with the rest of the group. They were surprised to see an army of Swiss mercenaries sitting with Manfred, Ulrich, and the rest of the unit.

"We bring some more recruits," said Maurits.

"Welcome, friends. Help yourselves to some ale, on me, and we'll retrieve our things and find our rooms once the other knights arrive. I look forward to meeting you all. Please, take a seat and feast with us," Manfred said. The four men sat and mingled with their fellow pavisiers and met Franz.

"Where are Roland and Friedrich?" Wilhelm asked Manfred.

"They haven't returned yet. Hopefully, they will be back soon," Manfred replied. "Tell me, how was your adventure?"

"I'll tell you mine once you explain how fifteen Swiss ended up in our troop," Wilhelm replied playfully. They shared their stories into the evening and awaited the return of the two other questing knights. Friedrich returned promptly after with his new knight Sir. Ernst Meyer, the Lion of Magdeburg.

CHAPTER 17. THE JOUST

Roland happily trotted off on his horse towards the tournament lists. He was excited. He hadn't jousted in the lists for a long time. He was eager to return to his old ways for just one day. Just once he might claim a trophy again and relive the glory of his past competitions. He was a damn good jouster, and he knew it. Roland approached the lists.

"May I help you?" a man said at the front desk. He sat by a map of all the heraldic sigils in Brandenburg. Above him were four shields. One had a bow and arrow. One had crossing swords. One had crossing spears. One had a horse and rider.

"I am here to enlist in the tournament, sir."

"May I have your name, please?"

"I am Sir. Roland."

"I meant family name; this tournament is only open to nobles."

"Of course," Roland said. He wasn't a noble in that sense of the word. Sure, he was a knight, but he was no lord or baron. "I am Sir Roland von Göttingen, son of Prince Otto von Göttingen, Prince in the Electorate of Saxony."

"Ah, a Saxon," replied the man. "You are free to enlist; I just need to see your heraldry."

"Of course," Roland replied. He looked at his shield and quickly tore off the Teutonic canvas liner, revealing the lion and castle sigils of Göttingen. Roland was careful not to reveal his affiliation with the order as Teutonic Knights weren't supposed to fight for sport.

"Right, that checks out, sir," the man replied. "What event may you be competing in on this fine evening?"

"I would like to joust," replied Roland eagerly.

"Are you sure?"

"Yes. Why not?"

"The Duke of Pritzwalk has been on the field for hours on end defeating any challenger. On the last bout, he unhorsed his opponent!"

"I'll face him," replied Roland. "I bet I'll score five points on the first run."

"Ha! Good luck, friend. You're free to go there right now. There's not a single challenger ready to face him. If you miraculously defeat him, you may take the field and win as many bouts as you wish. Alright?"

"Fine by me," replied Roland. He rode his horse into the stadium. The audience consisted of peasants and nobility alike. In the middle, there was a long wooden fence dividing the two sides. His opponent, Pritzwalk, stared at him with determination through the eye slit of his early frogmouth helmet. On his horseman's targe was the black hound on a green tree on a field of white of Pritzwalk. His helmet was adorned with colourful black white and green dog ears and ribbons. His armour was blackened like sulfur in the night.

"We have a new contender!" cried out the herald. His band played a small tune on their horns and drums. "Hear ye, hear ye, for Sir. Roland von Göttingen dares to face Duke Helmuth Pritzwalker. Place your bets now and wait for these men to be lanced." A group of three squires and pages came to give Roland his first lance. "There will be three passes in this bout," said the herald. "Knights, are you ready?" he cried out. Pritzwalk nodded his head. Roland did the same.

The daughter of the Prince of Magdeburg stood up from

her seat. She held out her arm with a handkerchief. It was beautiful. Adorned with flowers and floral patterns.

"Come, let us celebrate the coming of the season of rebirth - Spring." She raised her arm, ready to drop the handkerchief. As she did so, trickles of rain began to emerge from the heavens. The frosty ground grew ever so slightly moist with the droplets of water. Roland closed the visor in his Pamplona great bascinet. His surcoat grew moist. Pritzwalk leaned over, eyeing his opponent. Both fighters steered their horses into position. Pritzwalk's white destrier pawed the ground, while Roland's simply exhaled a cloud of mist into the frosty air. Time began to slow. Both men eyed the handkerchief. The princess raised it slightly higher, and then dropped it. At the release of her fingers, the two knights spurred their horses on. Both destriers leapt into action and rode at full gallop towards the centre of the stadium.

"Huzzah!" Roland cried; lowering his lance. Pritzwalk did the same but said nothing. Pritzwalk was tired after facing so many men, but he still had fight left in him, and his skill was still unparalleled. The two riders crashed in the middle. Roland struck Pritzwalks' cuirass, earning him three points. But, Pritzwalk, at the same moment broke his lance on Roland's shield, earning him four. The crowd cheered eagerly at the amazing pass. Disappointed, Roland slowed his horse and reached out to grab another lance. Once he felt it in hand, he quickly couched it and awaited the second signal. Pritzwalk did the same, keeping a keen eye on his opponent. This time, Roland had a plan. He hadn't come prepared for a joust, so instead of a horseman's targe, he carried a heater shield. He knew it was larger and would thus be easier to hit. This time, he lowered his left arm slightly, revealing his chest which would only award his opponent two points.

"On your marks, gentlemen," cried out the herald. Both men returned to their positions. The lady raised and dropped her handkerchief again. The two men were off, charging at

Godspeed towards one another. Pritzwalk struck his lance on Roland's chest, gaining two points, but Roland broke his lance on Pritzwalk's helm, awarding him four points. Roland was delighted that he was now in the lead. However, his delight was soon to be tarnished by a judge's call.

"Hear ye, hear ye," said the Herald. "Our Lady of Magdeburg has awarded Pritzwalk a point for his excellent horsemanship in this last pass. Our knights are now tied." Pritzwalk raised his lance in thanks. Roland was enraged. He had to win this last point. Both knights renewed their lances and returned to their starting positions. The lady raised her arm once more. When she let go of the handkerchief, the two knights hurtled towards each other. The horses galloped, but Roland decided to prove his worth. He caught the handkerchief on the tip of his lance mid-flight and then broke his lance by striking the handkerchief adorned head on Pritzwalk's shield. Four points. Pritzwalk aimed for Roland's shield, but the sudden detour that Roland took instead exposed his vambrace. Pritzwalk broke his lance on it, awarding him a total of only two points. The crowd erupted in cheer, for a new champion had just entered the arena. Roland had won, and he basked in the glory of his victory. After handing their lances to the squires, the two knights met in the middle of the field to speak with one another. Roland raised his visor, and Pritzwalk took off his helm and held it at his side.

"Congratulations on your most auspicious of victories," he said.

"You were quite an opponent," replied Roland. "I don't think I have ever faced such a skilled man in my life."

"Friend, I have never been defeated before in my life. I commend you, for your skill trumps mine in absolution. Tell me, how has one such as yourself become such an excellent warrior, Sir. von Göttingen?"

"Please, call me Roland. I never received training. My

father was a jouster, as am I."

"Your father being Prince Otto?" replied Helmuth.

"Uh... right. You know Prince Otto?"

"Of course. He is good friends with my father."

"Ah, I see. Well then, we should be friends as well," replied Roland.

"Yes, we should. What are your plans after your victory? Celebration? Or will you stay to fight more opponents?"

"I fear I must leave. Would you come with me?" asked Roland.

"Absolutely, we can celebrate together," replied Helmuth. The two knights rode to the lists where they received their rewards of five florins per bout won. Helmuth received quite a large sum more than Roland. The two men then made their way to a high-end pub. There they indulged in wine and good food and discussed the tournament.

"So, how come you have no retinue, Sir. Roland?"

"I could ask the same for you, Sir. Helmuth."

"It's simple, really. In Pritzwalk, my father still rules, and I have yet to inherit anything. So, when I ran away, I had no ability to order anyone to come with me. How about yourself?"

"Wait, wait, wait, you ran away? Why?"

"I couldn't stand it there in that boring old town. I needed to escape, compete, explore Christendom."

"Well, if exploring is what you're after, how would you like to join my comrades and I on an adventure to Prussia?"

"Ah, so you do have a retinue."

"Well, if I'm to be honest, I'm not the son of Prince Otto. I serve his son. I'm part of his retinue. I only mislead the herald to enter into the tournament."

"I see. And I can also see why you competed and not him. Well, on the matter of an excursion to Prussia, I will comply under one condition."

"Alright, what is it?"

"My father has sent a man to watch over me and bring me

back. He's been following me for days, and I've noticed that he's been conversing with some serious lowlives. I fear for my safety, Roland; will you aid me in trapping and slaying this scoundrel?"

"Is he not following his father's orders?"

"I fear he is also plotting on robbing me and then returning me in a cage. My father is a brutal man with brutal desires, and his rule over Pritzwalk is what he values most overall."

"Enough to kill his own son? That's outrageous!"

"No, it isn't. I am a bastard; well, I was. My father was supposed to marry Princess Maria of Rheinsberg. He loved her, and his parents arranged it. Everything was perfect until one God-forsaken night. He and his friends were drunk at a tournament. Guests had come from all over. One such guest was my mother, a widow at the time, whose name was Princess Emilia Dömitzer. My father slept with her, and nine months later I emerged, ruining everything. I came before the wedding of Maria and my father, and thus the priest would not wed them. He forced my father to marry my mother instead. Now, my father hates me. He sees me as no more than a successor and would use any excuse to kill me. That's the real reason why I left."

"I understand. I will aid you, and then you must come with us for time is scarce."

"I give my thanks," replied Helmuth.

CHAPTER 18. THE HOUND AND THE HAWK

After an hour of drinking and eating, the two men departed.

"So, do you have any idea of where your stalker could be?" asked Roland.

"Yes, I believe I have discovered his tavern room," replied Helmuth.

"Then I suppose we'd ought to teach that bastard a lesson. What say you?"

"I'll make sure he never reports to my father again," Helmuth replied.

The two men rode through the streets, plotting and planning their method of attack. Finally, after a few minutes, they reached their destination. It was a large tavern filled with mercenaries. Roland looked around and realised that it was the tavern in which the troop was staying. When the two knights entered, Manfred stood up.

"Look, men, for our long lost companion has returned with another recruit. Hoorah!" he shouted.

"Hoorah!" a few mercenaries replied, lifting a pint in good cheer.

"Greetings Manfred. I must warn you that I'm on a

mission to aid this knight. He will join us shortly after," Roland replied with urgency.

"Fear not, good Roland. Do you not see the surplus of soldiers under our command?" Manfred said drunkenly while pointing at his unit of mercenaries.

"Manfred, why is it you drink so much but can never handle your liquor?"

"Come now, we have good reason to celebrate."

"Yeah? And what's that?"

"Ulrich and I are alive! And those fine gentlemen over there have agreed to join us. All of them!" Manfred exclaimed with excitement, pointing towards the Swiss.

"Okay, look. We need this man. He's the best jouster I've ever seen, and he cannot return home. I will aid him, and then we may converse some more."

"Well then, farewell on your quest, Roland, and may God be with you!" cried out Maurits, also drunk. The unit returned to their conversation and their food, while Helmuth and Roland made their way upstairs to the rooms. They entered into a small wooden corridor with rooms on either side. They were numbered and were all locked.

"Do you have the key?" asked Roland.

"No, but I do have my gauntlet," replied Helmuth playfully. They went up to room thirteen. There, they unsheathed their swords and strapped on their shields. Helmuth promptly kicked down the door. "Have at thee scoundrel!" he shouted. Inside, a large man jumped to his feet and reached for a messer. The long, curved blade was thick and bulky. As he embraced it, Helmuth entered and began to fight him. Both were well trained, but the man was clearly swifter and more precise. Then, Roland entered the fray and shoved the man into the wall. He dropped his messer and held up his hands. He had sustained a broken nose, and he knew that he could not beat a knight in full armour, much less two.

"Tell me why I shouldn't end you right now, fiend," said

Roland.

"I was only following orders, Sir. Helmuth."

"Don't call me that now. Call me master, fiend. Beg for your life," said Helmuth. "I should chop off your head and send it to my father, but instead I'll wound you, and you can send him the message that I'm gone, and I'm never coming back until he dies, when I can rightfully ascend to the throne." Helmuth then proceeded to draw out his rondel dagger. He grabbed the man's hair and popped his eye with the blade. The man wailed out in pain.

"You devil! You monstrous beast!" he protested. Thick red blood gushed from his eye socket.

"Be grateful that I didn't kill you, lout!" Helmuth shouted. Then, with the pommel of his dagger, he beat the man in the stomach. He fell to his knees, struggling to catch his breath.

Roland turned white. He didn't know what to think. Surely this was better than death, but such brutality? The two knights left the man to his own devices and returned to the hallway.

"What in the nine hells was that?" Roland asked tersely.

"I had no choice. He gave me no choice."

"No, no more of that," Roland replied. "You're a tournament knight, act like it. If you're to join our troop, you had better shape up. Brutality only if necessary. Or else we're no better than the scoundrels we mame."

"Fine. I'll remain like a tame dog. But on the battlefield, I'll show no mercy."

"Good, that's what we expect. Now come and meet your boss," Roland said, ushering Helmuth downstairs to the main hall.

"Manfred, this is Sir. Helmuth Pritzwalker, heir to the throne of Pritzwalk. He is an excellent jouster, and he is willing to join us on our mission to Prussia."

"Excellent," replied Manfred. "Sit down; have a drink. We'll be up early tomorrow." The men sat down with their comrades and enjoyed a delicious feast, after which they all found their rooms. The new unit consisted of thirty-seven battle-ready men. They were prepared to brave the rainy season on their way to Marienburg.

CHAPTER 19. MOONLIGHT

That night the tavern was quiet. The men took up nearly all the rooms, and they were sound asleep as they knew that a long day lay ahead of them. The slight chill of the night wafted in as the tavern door crept open. A pair of footsteps creaked through the main hall to the staircase in total darkness. Not a single soul was witness. A man, light-footed as a mouse, climbed the stairs on all fours. Not a sound was made. The man stalked through the hallway. At his hip was a longsword. In his hand was now the hallway candle. He sifted through the rooms, carefully eying the numbers on the doors. Finally, he arrived in front of his destination. The man put out the candle. He clenched the hilt of a longsword that rested at his hip. Then, when nobody arose from their slumber, he released the weapon and pulled out two small needles. They were lock picks. He tampered with the lock until... thud! The handle on the other side of the door fell like a hammer on an anvil. All remained asleep, except for one. A startled Ernst rose to his feet. He heard the door unlock. Hastily, he rushed to open the window. The pale moonlight lit up his queen bed. He then grabbed his longsword. Still, in pyjamas, he prepared for a fight.

The intruder slowly opened the door. To his surprise, the room was lit with the cold, white light of the night.

"Scheiser!" Ernst cried, as he leapt forwards. He swung his blade and held it in front of his opponent. His opponent struck back, and his quillon interlocked with Ernst's guard. "Who are you?" Ernst shouted. The two men struggled to break free from the bind.

"Don't you remember me? It's Abelard. You, my friend, owe me a large sum of money! You didn't think you could just whimper off to some far-off land and leave your troubles behind, did you?" The men finally broke free. Abelard thrust, but Ernst parried, and he responded with a strike upwards from below. That too was swept aside, and the men returned to their fighting positions.

"I'm not escaping my troubles. I'm helping a group in need," replied Ernst. "I've been paid. You can take it. All of it. I received a whole ten florins."

"I don't want your money anymore. I've already missed my rent by a week because of you! Now the town is after me!" Abelard slashed at Ernst, but Ernst dodged out of the way.

"So, what do you want?"

"Your head on a stick!" Abelard once again cut downwards from his left shoulder, but before he could follow through, he was run through by another blade. Someone had impaled him from the back. Abelard dropped to his knees revealing Ulrich, blade bloodied, eyes cold with the permanence of death.

"You should be more careful, lion," he said.

"You're right. Why do you think I'm here? Not a single goodbye was said to me. I'm nobody to these people."

"I thought you were the Prince of Colbitz. What about that?"

"I lost that title long ago when I slept with the Prince of Magdeburg's daughter."

"Well, I'd call you a liability if you weren't such a good fighter. Tomorrow, tell Manfred of what happened here."

"Yeah, sure thing," Ernst said. Ulrich began to leave. "Wait, can I repay you? Of everybody else here, you're the only one who woke up and came to my rescue."

"Yeah, these walls are pretty thick, huh?"

"I think I have something you want," said Ernst.

"What could that be?" replied Ulrich. He really didn't want anything. Ernst leaned over and reached into his bag where he put his hand on a book. "I don't want your book. I hate reading. Consider us even."

"No, please; I think you'll like it," Ernst replied. He handed Ulrich the book. "Open it, I think you'll find there's more pictures than words." Ulrich opened the book. On each page, it showed different duelling positions. It was a fighting manual.

"You're a fight instructor?" asked Ulrich.

"Yes. How do you like my work?"

"I'll put it to good use," said Ulrich with a smile. "Now we should get some rest, we have a long day ahead of us. Go to sleep."

"I will. Good night, Sir. Ulrich, and thank you." Ulrich left and returned to his chamber, where he secured his book into his saddlebag.

CHAPTER 20. BLOOD AND IRON

That same night, Manfred and Wilhelm conversed in their room.

"These past few days have been crazy, haven't they?" asked Wilhelm.

"I agree. Just a week ago I would have killed for this opportunity. Now that I have killed for it, I'm doubting my decision," replied Manfred.

"Don't worry. We'll make it there, and once we get to Prussia we can rest until the summer so that it'll be easier to get back."

"That's true. To be honest, I think we've endured the worst of it. At least the worst of the snow."

"I hope so too," replied Wilhelm. He paused. He remembered how different the two of them used to be. How much Manfred changed. "Hey, Manfred, do you remember those three brigands who we hunted down in the woods near Adelebsen?"

"Hah, yeah. That was quite some chase, wasn't it?"

"What do you think the third guy is doing right now?"

"I wonder. I bet he's back with his tribe somewhere, enjoying a nice warm hearth while his stomach is full from boar or something."

"I think he's probably dead somewhere. If he was too scared to fight us, he mustn't be very competent alone in the wild."

"True. What happened to us?"

"What do you mean?"

"We've become killers. You almost killed a man for insulting you, and I just forced half of our men to march all the way to Brunswick for nothing. I called them cowards for being injured! Who have I become?"

"You're right, Manfred. We have changed, for the better or for worse. I think it's the road. Once things lighten up, I'm sure we'll get back to normal."

"I hope so. I can't wait to get back, honestly. I miss Castle Adelebsen, and I miss Maria."

"Yeah, I miss the Red Rabbit," Wilhelm replied with a smirk. "Don't worry. We're going to make it back. Before the solstice, you'll be back home with Maria, and I'll be out playing ball games with the other knights. Our lives will go back to normal; I promise."

"But, will they? Men have died for this mission. This stupid mission. God! What kind of idiots were we to accept this quest? No reward, no honour or valour to be found. We're just going to die like flies out here!"

"No, we won't, because you won't let us. You've led us this far. Every decision you've made has gotten us farther, Manfred. You are a good leader. Don't fear the spilling of blood."

"That's the thing, Wilhelm. I don't, and I never have. Some call me fearless, but sometimes I just think it's stupid."

"No, Wilhelm; it's what makes you an individual. That's what gives you an edge over your opponents. You have the Goddamn heart of a lion. Be proud of it."

"Thank you," replied Manfred. "I just hope we all make it."

"I know. I do too. Take a rest tonight, Manfred. Tomorrow is a new day."

"Tomorrow I'll have to be brave again."

"Then don't be General Manfred tonight. Be yourself. Think like yourself. Think of Maria, you deserve a break."

"I'm so tired of having to be this heartless villain. I've ran more people through with my lance in the past few days than I have in my life. I'm just sick and tired of having to be so ruthless all the time. Is there no more place for humanity? For chivalry?"

"You are the strongest man I know. It is thanks to you that we aren't dead at the hands of some midgets, and it's thanks to you that those villagers were saved. Yes, it was a gamble, but you still saved their lives."

"Thanks, Wilhelm, you've been nothing but good to me."

"No, thank you. Without you, I'd probably have been in some boring old peasant house trying to make ends meet by tilling a farm. You and your father rescued all of us from the gutter, and you pulled us out of that boring town. Because of you, we get to see the world."

"Well, because of me, the world will have a chance to kill you," Manfred smirked.

"That's for God to decide."

"Good night, Wilhelm."

"Good night."

CHAPTER 21. THE SHEPHERD

The next morning the unit all came down to the main hall of the tavern for breakfast. They flooded it like rats. They were all given porridge and bread, paid for by Manfred and his seemingly infinite florins. As the men ate, they chatted loudly amongst themselves. Outside, the moist air gave way to sparse droplets emerging from dark grey clouds. Manfred sat and ate his porridge with his knights. With them sat Ernst and Helmuth, as they were now part of the contingent and, therefore, had to engage in comradery with their fellow knights.

As Manfred finished, he picked up his bowl and went to the bar to return it. Ernst followed him.

"Sir. Manfred?" he asked.

"Yes, what is it, Ernst?"

"Last night, a man broke into my room," replied Ernst. He proceeded to explain all of the events that transpired. Manfred listened intently, but he was slightly irritated by the fact that their new recruit had already become a liability.

"Look, Ernst," he said. "You are a good fighter, but I will not tolerate any debiting or foolery on our mission. Do you understand?"

"Yes, Sir."

"I will continue to employ you, but you must understand

the gravity of these actions. Discipline is key; that's what my teachers always said."

"Yes, Sir."

"You are dismissed," Manfred said sternly. Ernst walked away in shame. Escaping his past mistakes was truly his reason for joining the troop, not the money. No goodbyes, no belongings to pack, Ernst truly had nobody worth befriending in Magdeburg. He dreamt of escaping his errors, travelling the world, and relieving himself of his mistakes. He planned on living his old age by simply working as a duelling coach for some nobleman or selling one of his books for a multitude of florins. Now, he had the florins, and what better place to teach rich noblemen than a state run entirely by warmongering knights? Ernst was given his golden ticket, and he wasn't going to mess it up. Not this time. His past was behind him. No more money lending, no more loaning, no more gambling, stealing, adultering, running illegal fight pits, or anything of the sort. He was free. Now, it was time to comply with Manfred's demands. Ernst had to prove himself to Manfred to ensure that his plan would work out smoothly.

He had to be obedient.

Manfred returned to his men. He whispered and asked Ulrich about the book, to which Ulrich replied by giving an entire description.

"Yeah, Ernst gave me one of his manuscripts. It must be worth a lot as it's quite hefty, and the illustrations are as lifelike as the ancient busts of Italy. To be honest, they have more depth than your mural," he said. Manfred laughed, remembering that stupid mural back in Adelebsen. Just the thought of that mural used to make his blood boil. It used to make him feel like he'd disappointed his father, but no more. Manfred didn't plan on pleasing his father any longer. When he returned, he promised himself that he would declare his prominence and take what he rightfully deserved. He was a ruler, not a follower. Manfred finally understood his purpose.

He didn't have to be the wolf he'd become, but he didn't have to be the sheep he once was either. Manfred was to be the shepherd. This journey was his choice, his action, and it was time to own up to it. No more pitying himself. It was time to make the best of his journey and enjoy Prussia when they arrived. Furthermore, Manfred made plans to enjoy himself a little more.

"Thanks for your description, Ulrich," he said. Then he stood up and shouted, "Attention, men!" He looked around. All fell silent and stared at him. "Men, we have toiled and laboured through snow and ice to get here. Our new friends have endured adventures as harsh as ours. We, friends, have battled dwarfs together, saved villages from plunder, and yet we are still able to win tournaments and kill assassins." He looked to Roland and Ulrich. "Men, I thank you all dearly for your support. Now, as you can see outside, it is raining. Yes, not snow, rain. That means that spring has come, friends. The roads will be easier, and the air will be warmer. And, best of all, we'll move faster. So, I propose that we stop for a few days at our next destination." He looked to Renault and asked him for the next destination.

"It's Potsdam, Sir," replied Renault.

"Exactly! We'll take a few day's rests at Potsdam," Manfred announced.

"Wait, Sir, if I may interrupt," said Helmuth.

"Go ahead man, speak your mind."

"Potsdam is a tiny town, but only a day's march from there lies Berlin, capital of Brandenburg. I believe we should rest there instead," Helmuth proposed.

"How do you know this?" inquired Manfred, still upon the table with full attention of his thirty-six peers.

"I live in Brandenburg. My former estate was in Pritzwalk, a town both North of here as well as Berlin."

"Ah, well then, Sir. Helmuth von Pritzwalk, we will rest at Berlin," announced Manfred. The group cheered, for they knew that games, brothels, ale, good food, and music waited for them in Berlin. They were excited to see the city as most had never even been to one before. With high spirits, the troop marched out into the drizzling downpour and stood in a long linear formation. The cavalry led the way, and the army began to move. Behind the horses was Ernst, and behind him were the pavisiers lead by Franz. Behind them were the Swiss, divided into three rows of five, led by Leon, Wolfe, and Freya.

The unit stepped in mud and puddles, but they were delighted to feel no more sting of frost on their lips and fingertips. The leaves and flowers upon the trees began to sprout from their branches, and the grass beneath the layers of slush and ice began to force their way through. The fresh scent of dew returned to the air, overpowering the foul stench of the cold. Happily, the army marched while singing songs of taverns and soldiers and the streets of Marseille.

CHAPTER 22. VENISON

By nightfall, the unit had come across no town nor village. Not a single soul was seen on the road, and Potsdam was nowhere to be found. Friedrich had scouted ahead multiple times, but he still found nothing but continuous stretches of muddy road.

"We'll camp here for the night," Manfred directed. The soldiers tiredly set up their camps, dreading the night to come. The camp was less than spartan. The men laid on a thin carpet, vulnerable to sticks and rocks of all kinds. The soldiers began by clearing the ground while the knights started a few campfires. Once all was set, the men gathered around the hearths and ate portions of their rations while listening to jolly music performed by hardened soldiers. There was no alcohol. They couldn't risk it, and it was expensive, far more expensive than a few kegs of water.

As the evening trudged on and the sun tucked itself beneath the horizon, the misty drizzle that once filled the air turned into a thunderous downpour. Although the soldiers were already fast asleep in their canvas tents, the wind and rain wisped through the camp in spurts, chilling all it touched. Cold and wet, the horses shivered through the night. As the raindrops drained between the seams of the canvas lining, they plunged into puddles of mud, soaking the carpets and flooding the campfires. Quickly they fizzled out, leaving nothing but cold black ash in the morning.

The next morning came with the call of wolves in the distance. They were harmless but left a testament to the looming dangers of the wild. The men started to pack their things and ate hearty breakfasts of bread, meats, and cheeses. Most clothes were laid out to dry, and the chainmail armour would have to be carried instead of worn to reduce the possibility of rusting. The ground was wet and muddy, turning the campground into an ankle-high swamp. The men begrudgingly drained out their clothes, drowsily, and cold. However, the new day came bright and warm. The sun soothed the horses as they shook off the droplets in their fur from the night before.

"That was one crazy storm," said Leon to Wolfe.

"I know, I wonder what the knights will do. Do you think they'll let us stay and dry out our clothes for a while?" replied Wolfe.

"I think not. They seem to be quite intent on marching with haste, so I fear they will spare us no time until we reach Berlin."

"Well then, it had better come soon," replied Wolfe. The two men returned to their breakfast and drank some water from their canteens. Manfred sat at his fireplace with his knights, eating breakfast, and reminiscing.

"Alright, men. That was one hell of a storm. I was not expecting that," he said.

"Me neither," replied Roland. "I'd left some clothes on the floor, now I'll have to throw them away."

"Don't be so brash," replied Ulrich. "A good day in the sun will return them to normal."

"I think we should give the men a chance to recuperate and dry their belongings," said Manfred. "What do you think?"

"It's too wet here; we have to go someplace else," replied Ulrich.

"Well, when I scouted ahead, I saw nothing close. We won't make it to Potsdam before lunch," said Friedrich.

"We appear to be in a tight situation," said Manfred. "I wonder if we could find some clearing of some kind, or if there's another town nearby." Renault opened the map and surveyed their surroundings.

"The City of Brandenburg is just north of us," he said. "Perhaps we should go there."

"It's not directly on our route, is it?" asked Manfred.

"It doesn't seem to be, but it may be close. I don't think it would be too far of a stray from our course."

"Fine then, I'll scout around and see if it is near to us," said Friedrich.

"Alright, you go, and in the meantime, I'll have the men finish their preparations." Manfred said. Friedrich set off on his journey with haste. He knew that he had to be quick so that the group could plan out their next actions. He trotted through the woods until he began to see smoke on the horizon. He rode further, and there it was, the city of Brandenburg. He identified it by its banners which carried the red eagle. He'd learned about that coat of arms from his schooling back in Göttingen. Although he wasn't nobility, he was acquired by Otto at a young age. It was ever since he had shown skill with a horse. He was once an altar boy in the common church in Göttingen. Even now he longed to return. He remembered the smell of incense and wine that was constantly looming inside, and he remembered the beautiful music sung by the choir. He also remembered Father Leon, the priest. Although he was friendly, Friedrich was also aware of his corruption. He had learned of it at a young age when he was sent to collect silk from a trader from Italy. The man had said that those cloths had travelled all the way from Bactria. Friedrich's one grievance with Manfred was that he never truly confronted Pastor Leon for his deeds. He never truly called him out for his corruption. Perhaps it was fear of the Lord, or fear that he would lose the favour of his people, but Friedrich always knew that, whatever the reason was, it wasn't worth it. Friedrich aspired to be a chivalrous knight and a devout Christian, not some indoctrinated slave to the church.

That was tested once. Leon was always a friendly man, but once, he'd gotten a little too friendly. Friedrich felt the man's old shrivelled hand on his thigh, but he immediately knew that he was not to be messed with.

"No!" he cried out, but the man didn't relent. He called it out again, but it was to no avail. As the man made his advances, Friedrich finally felt the lord's power surge through him, and he picked up a bread knife and stabbed Leon's arm.

That's why he left one day. He pulled the knife out ruthlessly and ran to the stables where he mounted his horse and rode away. He knew how to ride a horse because he often helped the church's stable boy with training the horses. That is where he met his horse. He met him as a boy, and he recalled how everyone always called him "boy" and "buddy," but never Friedrich. That's why he did the same to his horse. It had no name, but he was truly Friedrich's closest friend.

Friedrich rode from the church as fast as he could, but when he turned around, he realized he was not running from anyone. He slowed down and rode to the woods. He had no money, no food, and he didn't want to steal or gamble. In his robes, he rode into the woods until he came across a party. He knelt in the bushes and saw Prince Otto with his falcon and hounds, as well as a few retainers, on the hunt. They were moving through the woods slowly until a man told Otto to stop.

"This is far enough," he said. From his saddlebag, he pulled out a long metal rod in a wooden casing. He gave it to Otto, who looked at it intently. Then, the man poured black powder into one end and rammed an iron ball down the other. He then instructed Otto to point and pull the trigger. Otto did so, and at that moment the loudest noise known to man was heard throughout the woods. The explosion pierced the air, as well as a baby reindeer. It was grazing innocently in the fields before it was impaled by the smouldering ball of iron. Otto looked content with his shot and handed the fire stick back to the man who tucked it into his bag once more. Then, Otto went over to claim his prize. As he knelt there, alone, he spent time cleaning out the shattered iron ball from the reindeer's corpse. As he did so, he was left vulnerable.

Friedrich looked around, and he spotted the reindeer's mother emerging from the woods. Immediately, Friedrich mounted his horse and charged to save the Prince. He emerged from the foliage, jumping over a stream towards the Prince. He looked alarmed and stood frozen. His men tried to stop Friedrich from approaching him, but Friedrich kept riding. He reached the prince just as the doe did. He grabbed the bread knife and planted it in the doe's eye. It fell to the ground, and then got up and attempted to run before the hounds caught it and brought it back down. Gruesomely, they tore its flesh to pieces. Friedrich felt regret for taking its life, but he had to save the Prince, no matter how many deer he'd killed.

"You saved my life," the Prince said. "I must repay you."

"Sir, I need no pay."

"No, please, you must have followed us for a reason."

"I... I have no home," Friedrich said. He felt ashamed to ask for such a thing, but he had no choice. He chose not to discuss the priest's assault as he realized that he would be found guilty. Otto agreed to add him to his retinue and train him as a knight. As they returned to Plesse together, they passed Adelebsen and the wretched priest. The priest stayed quiet about his arm, as he knew that Friedrich was protected now. From then on, Friedrich was trained to be a knight, and was sent back to Adelebsen to be a part of Manfred's guard.

Friedrich gazed over the hill at Brandenburg. He said a quick prayer atop his horse, for he felt that this city was a blessing to the unit. Then, he returned with haste to give Manfred the good news.

CHAPTER 23. BAPTISM IN FIRE

The sun began to fade over the treetops surrounding the town of Magdeburg. As the bartender began packing up, a rough knock barraged the door. The bartender shouted:

"It's closed. Come here tomorrow; there's two for one rabbit stews." The knock continued, and this time it grew even louder. The bartender looked woefully at the drunken mercenaries who still infested the main hall before the door burst open. A single ray of sunshine illuminated the green shield above the pub reading "The Bloodied Blade." In the doorway stood a single man dressed in well-embroidered clothes. His shoes were pointy, but not as pointed as his extravagant hat. Upon his mouth was a bandana, for he was a mute and, therefore, did not have the ability to make speech. He stood and said nothing, observing the men in the tavern and the tavern keeper. Then, he croaked and raised his hand, gesturing for his men to enter. A swarm of ten well-armed peasants entered the building, and the mute made his way over to the bartender. By his side was another man. They both shared identical stitched scars on their right cheeks - pagan rituals. The bartender gave a look of pure and pale fear, and the aroma of urine was laced into the air.

"We're looking for a band of six knights and a scholar," he said. Behind him, more henchmen piled in. They dropped a large sac on the floor, and their comrades got the attention of the mercenaries inhabiting the tavern. Then, they released the string holding the sac together, and the bag crumbled, revealing trinkets and riches beyond compare. The mercenaries gazed in amazement. The bartender stared silently, for he hadn't seen any group that met that description.

"I've seen nobody of the sort," replied the man. The henchman slammed his glove on the table.

"Look, we've just searched nearly every Goddamn inn in this Goddamn town."

"Many travellers pass here daily, sir, but if anybody were to come matching this description, I'm sure I'd notice."

"You haven't seen any knights? Or even a scholarly Frenchman with a large hat?"

"I did see two knights just yesterday, but they travelled with no scholar, to my knowledge. They had a drinking competition, and when they lost, they got into a fight in the alley just out there. They killed four men."

"Describe them to me," the henchman said. The bartender put his hand on the table and leaned in.

"One man was big and burly and had painted armour. The other was young and had brown hair, and his armour was embroidered and decorated all over with etching," he replied. The henchman looked to the mute, who nodded slowly.

"Tell us where he was going."

"That'll come at a price," the bartender replied, looking at the treasure on the floor of the hall.

"We're saving it."

"For what?"

"Our army. Now, tell us. We need to find those men. They butchered two of our tribesmen."

"Tribesmen? You're a pagan?"

"Yes. And you know what? Those two men that were slain were this man's brother and father. He had to leave them to try to get us, or else we'd have had no idea what happened to them."

"So, you not only want me to help a heathen, but also a sodomite? No way," the bartender said. The mute took a bread knife and jammed it into the man's hand, pinning it to the counter. He screamed in pain.

"Now, tell us where they were going!" the henchman yelled.

"Alright, alright. They are headed to Prussia. They came here recruiting because they needed more men to escort them," the bartender replied. The mute slammed his head onto the knife, impaling his eye, and then tossed an old eyepatch onto the table. His brother had worn it before he was impaled through the other eye. The mute turned to the pile of riches and nodded to one of his men. The man began to speak.

"Alright, you drunken bastards," he said to the mercenaries. "These riches here have been accumulated over decades for our tribe. But, because of some murderous knights, the gods compel us to give up our dreams of raiding the prosperous Bohemians and instead pursue those bastards to Estonia. So, do you wish to join us? If you do, these riches await you, if you don't... well... this tavern is going to burn with you in it." The mercenaries looked at each other, and then they scrambled for the riches. As they fought over the mound of gold, the henchmen left the tavern and made their way into the streets, uniting with a much larger army of scoundrels, including many dwarfs, mercenaries, and pagans.

The mercenaries followed soon after, and the mute and his men poured oil on the outer wall of the tavern. Then, he dropped a lit candle on it, burning the inn, its residents, and the shrieking bartender. The mute mounted his steed. The flames quickly engulfed the tavern and blazed embers into the grey-blue night sky. As authorities showed up, the army quickly marched away. Although they left a trail of obvious suspicion, they went unchallenged, as no man wished to get in their way. That was, until they were halted by the citizens of the town. Groups of militiamen poured out of their homes to help fight the fire and confront the scoundrels.

"Halt! You damn brigands have no right to burn down our beautiful town," a man said, leading the militia. Then, a dwarf made his way to the front.

"My name is Wendel, leader of the Dwarfs of Einbeck Forest. I assure you that we come not as foes but as friends."

"Hah! A puny little half man wants to get away with arson? You lot had better surrender now or the guards will come here and give you a good sentence. The gallows are all strung and ready, waiting for bastards like you."

"We here have quarrel only with those villains who have done us wrong, and you should too. Are you not tired of paying unholy rent fees? Aren't you tired of submitting your will to these nobles? They throw lavish tournaments and expect you to praise them as they brandish their butchering skills, waiting to exact their violence on you! Who do they think they are, killing us without remorse or repentance, and receiving no punishment? They have no right! We decide our own fate! Brave men and women of Magdeburg, take note of my words, for we will not submit to these villains who seek to suppress us! Rise! Take what's yours! And follow us to Marienburg where we can exact revenge on our evildoers! Follow the mute to victory!"

The crowd fell silent. They didn't know what to think. He had merit in his words. Then, a man made his way through the crowd. He had freed himself in all the commotion. He was a Mongol. He was starved and beaten, but he was more courageous than the rest.

"He speaks true! I will join them, and you should too," he said. Then he began to chant. "Mute! Mute! Mute!" The crowd joined him. The army of about forty became a force of hundreds. The streets broke into riots. Stores were being looted, and blood began to spill.

"Take up arms!" the henchman cried. "Fight for your

freedom! These men are not appointed by God! They're appointed by blood! Your blood! Fight to reclaim what's rightfully yours!"

The fire began to spread, and the town guard began to form lines to attempt to push back the revolters. They fired arrows and bolts into the crowd, and they formed walls with their pavise shields to attempt to contain the rioters. The guard and the militia clashed in a violent uprising. It was bloody and brutal. The guards' lines had to withdraw, leaving many to be stranded and beaten by their former citizens. Many guards also dropped their shields and tore off their surcoats, joining the rioters. The town was in chaos. The blue night sky turned red and black from all the smoke and fire. It eventually engulfed the entire city.

The keep was besieged until morning when the peasants were finally let in across the moat by two defecting guards. The Prince of Magdeburg was slain, along with his guard, while trying to hold the stairwell. His daughter was defiled and butchered, and his sons died attempting to hold the invaders off. The mute watched from across the drawbridge. The flames of the town reflected in his eyes. His sheer bloodlust seeped through his visage as he observed the massacre. A hidden grimace tied his cheeks together beneath his smoke-filled bandana. The bodies were dumped out of the tower and into the moat. Then, the mute gestured for his men to move on into the town. Soon, the entire town was razed and plundered by the murderous onslaught, and the army of peasants began their march to Prussia, to follow the knights hot on their heels. The force was well supplied from their campaign and well equipped as they looted the fallen guards. The horde was ready for battle. With the cries of liberty in their hearts and bloodlust in their minds, they trekked forth into the rainstorm. Lightning struck down trees, and the rain seeped into their clothes, but the men were too hyped to head back. Nothing lay for them at home. Their women and children were with them, and their homes were destroyed by themselves. Now, they had no choice but to raid and plunder their way to wealth. The zealots advanced with freedom in their hearts, and the mute led his force onwards through fire and rain to their target, Potsdam.

CHAPTER 24. FIRE AND BLOOD

Manfred led his men to the City of Brandenburg. They walked through pastures upon pastures of farmland until they reached a new environment. They found themselves walking among lakes and rivers, winding their way over the hill and bridge to reach the city. As they approached, over the brim of the hill, they finally observed its true magnificence. It stood tall, and more importantly, it was vast. Like a sea of stone and wood creating small tufts of smoke and ornamented by the occasional spire. There was no keep - the entire city was a fortress. It was walled with large stone earthworks with battlements and all. Uncontested, it lay prominent among the crossing rivers and placid lakes. It was truly magnificent.

The troop made their way down the hill towards the nearest entrance. To enter the city, they had to cross over a thin bridge, guarded by imperial guardsmen. The unit approached.

"Greetings, good gatekeepers," said Manfred. "I am Sir. Manfred von Göttingen, and this is my loyal retinue. We beseech entry into your beautiful citadel."

"Greetings, sir. Unfortunately, you won't be allowed in. You and your men can go no further as a group. Your weapons exceed the carrying laws, especially your swords, and you are simply too large of a group to be added to the population," replied the guard.

"Oh, no. You see, we are only visiting. One night, perhaps an afternoon, and we'll be gone."

"I'm sorry, Sir. You may not pass. Feel free to settle down in any of the fields nearby," the guard said, pointing to various clearings. They all looked soggy and loaded with dew. Manfred turned to his men.

"Alright, boys. Let's turn around. We'll have to set up camp outside the city," he said. Then he turned back to the guard. "Wait a minute. If we may not enter here, may we enter Berlin?"

"Yes, you may. The laws are so stringent here as this is the capital of the great Electorate of Brandenburg. Thus, we must keep the Elector and his loved ones as safe as possible. You must understand."

"Of course. We'll be on our way." Manfred turned around and galloped to the new front of the column. They marched out into a field where they set up camp. There, men laid out their clothes to dry, hung up their chainmail on wooden stands, and practiced their fighting skills. Ulrich turned to his new fight book and began practicing the moves.

"Care to fight?" Maurits asked Manfred.

"Alright. Let's see how a crusader fights," he replied. Both men put on their helms ad drew their swords. They sparred late into the day, and the group ended up having a late lunch at their various fire pits. The Swiss drilled their formations relentlessly, and the pavise crossbowmen took this downtime to go hunting for some wild animals. Friedrich took the time to scout ahead and see what lay in store next. When he returned, he remarked that he found both Potsdam and Berlin and that if they had just continued on the main road for slightly longer, they would have reached Potsdam. He spoke of the magnificent fortresses that scattered the land there. It was a shame they had to miss the sight.

That night, the men ate well and slept early, anticipating

the late nights to come in Berlin.

That night, Manfred couldn't sleep. He stepped out of his tent into the chilling night air and sat by the fire. The weather was nice, dry. The sky was pelted with stars. Manfred looked over to the city where light still emerged despite the ungodly hour. He sat down at the fire. He looked into it and saw nothing. He didn't expect to see anything. If the Lord were to speak to him, he would probably do so in person, as he would know that Manfred disliked how encrypted and theatrical religion could get. He hated politics and diplomacy for that same reason, and that's why he loved war. He didn't want to kill anyone, not any innocent at least, but he loved how simple and straightforward warfare was. There was no scheming or plotting, only men attempting to best each other in a game. A game with high stakes.

Manfred gazed into the distance. All was silent except for the bullfrogs and crickets that lurked in the dark. Wolves howled at the moon in the distance. Manfred sat with glazed eyes, nearly falling asleep on his wooden log. He stood up, stretched his legs, and decided to head back in. That was, until he heard a noise off in the distance. He heard bells, powerful bells, like the bells of a church. He looked into the distance. He heard screams coming from the direction of Potsdam, and soon a blaze of smoke lit up the night sky. It was under attack.

"Wake up men! We have a job to do!" he cried out. The men who stayed asleep were either kicked awake or were awoken by showers of freezing bucket water. The unit arose from their slumber and hastily packed up their camp. After about twenty minutes they all stood in formation, ready to march out. Nobody dared question Manfred's decision.

It was too late for that.

Manfred looked out again, looking at the flames. He looked at the gates of Brandenburg, from which a sizeable force also expelled itself, crossing the bridge and entering the sea of farm and lake.

"Let's get moving," he called out, as he mounted his horse. Beside him, his knights emerged. Together, the unit marched towards Potsdam, clad in armour, and ready for battle.

CHAPTER 25. ATTERO DOMINATUS

The army of revolutionaries were halted in their march to Berlin. There, with the Havel River on their left flank, and a thick wood on their right, they stopped near the farmstead of Teltow. In those very fields, the army was to face off against their enemy. They stood fast and began making preparations. Light cavalry was sent to scout ahead, and soon enough, they brought back reports that the Berliner army was approaching. Although it was half the size of the revolutionaries, their ranks comprised of trained soldiers. As the night carried on, morning soon broke, and over the horizon, the Berliner line emerged. Drums beat, horns blared, a battle was soon to fall upon the countryside of Brandenburg. The black bear upon a white field was hoisted high above the countryside, waving in the grey of night. Berlin sent no emissary. They were going to destroy this army of revolutionaries and leave no quarter.

The lines formed. Across the field, soldiers taunted each other. Then, as the sun emerged over the horizon and the sky turned a bright shade of red, the battle commenced. The Berliners sent in a preliminary wave of crossbowmen. With few skirmishers, the peasants returned with what they could - slings, javelins, some light crossbows, and some hunting bows. The Peasant skirmishers were annihilated. They emerged across the field revealing a series of earthworks and palisades constructed by the peasants. They shot down into the enemy line, taking large casualties. Then, as the veil of bolt pelted the pavise shields of the revolutionaries, the mute emerged from a hidden trench. With his mounted sergeants, they charged into the lines of crossbowmen. They swarmed the crossbowmen like locusts, sparing no man. The entire crossbow contingent was skewered and trampled. The Berliners responded by sending in their knights and mounted men at arms, but it was too late.

A large cavalry battle ensued in the center of the field, and soon after, the lines of infantry began to close in. The peasant forces simply outnumbered the Berliners. They charged the enemy with ferocity, creating gaps in the line and pooling through them. Both sides fought hard, but the balance of power soon began to tip in the mute's favour. His men pressed the attack, chasing them back across the fields. Then, once the knights were all unhorsed and defeated, the mute ordered his cavalry charge their left flank. The Berliners were enveloped and trapped, and the force of the cavalry sent them sprawling into the river. Their armour weighed them down, causing many to drown. It was a massacre.

As the battle ensued, drums were soon heard over the other side of the river. The Brandenburg army had arrived with Manfred's retinue. The mute saw him, and he saw the mute. Manfred and his men also laid their eyes upon the horde of dwarfs.

"It's that damn brigand!" he exclaimed. His men formed a pike wall. The Berliners tried to retreat across the river, but it was too deep. Both sides had to find a viable way across. The Brandeburgers looked back, eyeing a bridge at Sacrow.

"We must hold the bridge!" the commander cried out. He and his knights rode for the bridge to establish a foothold. They raced the enemy mounted sergeants there. Manfred and his knights followed the Brandeburgers into battle, and his infantry trailed soon after. The knights formed a massive arrowhead formation and charged their way across the bridge. They had beaten the enemy cavalry, but the battle was far from over. The mute ordered his cavalry to charge into them, but the sergeants were simply not equipped to fight the mounted men at arms. They were routed, and the mute fell back to his infantry. Manfred Swiss pikemen quickly set up formation at the front of the bridge, and the Brandenburger crossbowmen joined Franz' unit in pelting the enemy.

There were enough crossbowmen to tear holes in the peasant infantry. They simply couldn't break through the pike formation. Eventually, the mute called back his men. They fell back to the field as they realized that they had no hope of taking the bridge. Near the farmstead of Wannsee, the marauders made their final stand. They returned to the system of trenches, retrieving longbows and slings, and the dwarfs attempted to set up some infantry lines. The trenches couldn't be charged by horses, as they were guarded by stakes driven into the ground.

The knights would have to dismount. The sun rose high in the sky, and their armour glistened as they advanced. Supported on the flanks by their sergeants at arms, the knights advanced to the palisade to strike down their foe. The battle raged fiercely, but the knights were simply better equipped than their counterparts. Manfred charged the line, breaching the dwarfs, and making his way into the system of trenches. His retinue followed, with Maurits, Ernst, and Helmuth as well. They shuffled through the trenches, slaying all in their path, until they came across Wendel.

"Ah, yes, if it is Hans. Or should I say, Manfred! You thought you could fool me?" he exclaimed.

"You deserve no more than death. What man slays the child of another just to spite him?" Manfred replied. He leapt forwards and struck with his battleaxe. The two struggled in the earthworks until both had resorted to grappling. Manfred threw the little man to the ground, unsheathing his rondel dagger. "You should have finished me when you had the chance!" he cried, as he planted it firmly into the stout man's heart. Manfred returned to his feet. He looked around. Only the banners of Brandeburg remained, flying high in the sky.

"Manfred, we won! We won, Manfred!" Wilhelm shouted. They climbed out of the trench and watched as the remaining shambles of the brigand army ran for the hills. Friedrich stood and said a prayer. Maurits joined him. By their feet was the mute, impaled by Friedrich's longsword. He had blood on his jupon, but he didn't mind. He was just happy to be alive.

The men regrouped with their belongings and walked toward the general's tent. There, his men were collecting loot from the battlefield and burying the dead. Manfred and his men cheered, for casualties were minimal, but Leon made no noise. He knelt over the corpse of Wolfe. The Swiss gave him a proper burial, and Maurits said a prayer in his name. The rest were just relieved that they weren't slain on that field.

CHAPTER 26. BAND OF BROTHERS

Manfred and his four knights approached the main tent. They entered and found four generals and their bodyguards discussing what had happened.

"Greetings, lords. My name is Sir. Manfred von Göttingen. Today, my men fought alongside the forces of Brandenburg."

"Ah, yes. I saw your knights clearing the trenches. And were those pikemen yours too?" asked one of the four men. He was a large man with a grey moustache that curled at the sides of his lips.

"Yes, sir."

"Well then, you have served us well and we dearly thank you for it. Brandenburg offers its hospitality."

"Thank you, sir, but I came to let you know why they attacked."

"No need, son. They came in revolt against the nobility. We've just received news that they were Magdeburgers. They razed their own city and came here to spark a larger revolution. That's why we couldn't let them reach Berlin. The walls may have been more tactical, but we don't want them sparking any more trouble here."

"But, sir, their leader and those dwarfs came for us. We encountered them before. That mute was a pagan who we caught robbing. Those dwarfs wanted to capture me and ransom me to my father, Prince Otto von Göttingen."

"Wait, you are the son of Prince Otto?"

"Yes, sir."

"We crusaded together. Send him my regards. What are you doing so far from Göttingen?"

"My men and I are on a quest. We are tasked with escorting a papal emissary to Prussia."

"Why, that's quite far away. Come, I will give some men to escort this emissary the rest of the way. You must return to your father; I'm sure he's worried for you, and I can't let you put yourself in harm's way."

"It's okay, sir. I plan on staying there for a bit."

"Ah, a true crusader, like your father. If you won't let my men escort this emissary, I will escort you there with my personal retinue. We cannot risk any more troubles like these."

"Sir, we'll be fine."

"I'm not giving you a choice. Your father was a good man, and a great commander. I won't let his son throw his life away over his pride. You did good in that trench, but it was risky. I wouldn't advise it anymore. If you've made so many enemies and you're only at Berlin, you're sure to be dead by the time you reach Marienburg. Come, I'll join you," the man said.

"Thank you, sir. May I know your name?"

"I am Sir. Leopold von Wustermark, knight of Brandenburg." Leopold said goodbye to his generals and told them to inform his family of his decision. Then, he and his men travelled with Manfred and his retinue towards Berlin.

The walk was solemn and silent. Unlike how Manfred had imagined, there were no cheers of victory or parties to celebrate, there was instead grief for the fallen. They didn't have to die, but those men stole their lives like ruthless marauders. Manfred felt rage. He wished he could have slain the mute himself.

The troop reached Berlin with anticipation, but unlike

their prior fantasies, not a single man looked forward to pitt fights and brothels. Instead, the unit went to an inn. They drank their sorrows away among cheery minstrels who sang of their glorious victory. It was depressing. It was a fine inn, however. It was large, and the walls were surrounded by art. They met the new Brandenburger retinue. It consisted of ten knights and twenty spearmen. The unit was large now, nearly seventy men. They all drank together and ate in silence, only breaking the chilling still to discuss the horrors of battle. It was far worse than any other fight they'd been in. True battle was not all glorious counter-charges; it consisted of hordes of people piling onto one another to bat their enemy to death. The soldiers remembered the mud, and how those who feel suffocated in it. They remembered the dwarfs being cleaved in two, and the peasants who looked like pincushions after each volley. The thoughts were unappetizing.

The unit ate and drank their way into the night. Then, they piled into their rooms and slept. In the night, Franz suffered terrible dreams. The night terrors burdened him like a curse. Over and over, he relived the terrible suffering brought upon his men. He saw the deaths incessantly playing in his mind like a show put on just for him.

The unit slept in silence.

CHAPTER 27. INTO THE WILDS

That same night, the remaining peasants, brigands, and mercenaries gathered in the woods. There were only about seventy of them remaining, some injured, some mentally disturbed from all the bloodshed. They all gathered, and the remaining "officers" bickered amongst each other as to what to do. They sat around a campfire, challenging each other's' ideas.

"I should lead," a man said. He was black-haired and had a well-trimmed neckbeard. "I fought the hardest of all these fools. Who of you were even there when the mute first began? I followed him all the way from Brunswick. I should be his successor, not any of these pretenders!"

"No, I should lead," said another. "I am the last questing warrior of his tribe. It was our tribe that funded this rebellion, and our gods who told us to chase after those corrupt knights. It is by the gods that we should form our new nation." Many more contenders staked their claims and fought for hours. They debated late into the day, some even fighting each other like savages. The group grew hungry. A peasant man stood up.

"Why don't we just disperse into Berlin and take up normal lives again?" he asked. There was no reply. Soon, many more stood up with him. Just as they were ready to leave, the Mongol rose to his feet.

"I'll tell you why. You abandoned your lives. You dishonoured your God. You have been marked by blood and war, and you know nothing of the streets of Berlin. Tell me, what was your trade?" he asked.

"I was a blacksmith," the man replied.

"Well then, blacksmith, tell me how you will acquire food in Berlin. Do you know of any smitheries ready for hiring? Or will you start one yourself with your own anvil and hammer? That is, if you can afford them. People of Magdeburg and mercenaries and brigands, I speak to you not as a Mongol but as a man. A man who, like you, threw away his life to be free from oppression. Our lives here may seem hopeless, but I assure you, I have a plan. Follow me to victory, or follow these pretenders to defeat," the Mongol announced.

"What is your magnificent plan, pray tell?" asked the tribesman.

"We have no chance at confronting the forces of Berlin, and we have already lost the strongholds of Potsdam. I say that we exact our revenge another way. We know the destination of those Teutonic knights and their pikemen. I know you all know them well, for they slew many of your, nay, our brethren on the field of Teltow. We know that they ride for Prussia, and we know that the Teutonic knights are at war with the Poles. I say we take a shortcut to Prussia. We can move through Poland, explain the situation to the Polish nobles and acquire their favour, and ambush those sorry sons of bitches in the Tannenberg Forest. What say you?" he cried. The crowd cheered. "What say you?" he cried again, even louder. The crowd cheered once more. They began to chant:

"Mongol! Mongol! Mongol!" and they discarded the other candidates. The Mongol had their support.

"Come, men. We must hunt and rob travellers for their food and wealth if we are to survive, so let us make haste. Furthermore, we need shelter for the night. Come, let us get to work on building a shelter for us all, and tomorrow we can feed ourselves. Friends, our bellies will ache today, but I assure you, tomorrow we will feast on whatever your God has granted us," the Mongol said. The horde and the remainder of the women and children all collaborated to build a large shelter, as well as bows and arrows for hunting and robbing. Every man was trained in longbowmanship by the Mongol, who himself was an expert archer. As well, he had the remaining mercenaries form a personal guard unit of about ten men. He was in charge now, and this was his horde. With one single goal in mind, he swore to exact his vengeance on Wilhelm and his fellow knights, and perhaps kill as many Teutonic knights as he could in the process.

The next morning was damp in the forest. The horde arose to the sound of farmers in the fields. They continued their practice with longbows, and they shared the water that they had collected the night before in buckets. Soon, sorties were sent out. They sent some men to hunt and others to guard various small roads and bridges. Unknown to the city of Berlin, the Diedersdorf Forest was now under the absolute control of the horde.

The Mongol and his men patrolled around the camp, policing things and waiting as game was brought in for cooking. One large fire was made. The horde didn't fear to gain the attention of the Berliners through the smoke, as they knew that the Berlin garrison wasn't strong enough to vanquish them with ease. Instead, it was a stalemate. Neither side intended on attacking one another, so they coexisted for the day. At noon, the sorties were called back.

Various exploits were also piled up as a few travellers had been robbed by the horde's longbowmen. With spoils and food, the horde was now content once more. Although the conditions were less than favourable, they continued to try to make the best of things. They were a society of warriors now, refugees of their own design, and fugitives in their own fatherland. They had to accept that.

There was no escaping the fact that their primary goal now was to intercept that convoy, and all decisions of the group had to work towards that goal. The Mongol also sent out sorties to recruit more brigands and mercenaries to the cause using the spoils they reaped.

Come nightfall they had received a total of twenty more soldiers ready to fight and learn how to shoot with a longbow. The horde rested under the shelter once more. The next day, they would have to get moving in order to beat their enemy to Prussia.

CHAPTER 28. THE MOLE

In the dead of night, Manfred arose in his sleep. This time, it wasn't a bad dream or sleep apnea, but instead, a large thud was heard on the door. Wilhelm woke up in his bed as well but stayed there while Manfred approached the door. Behind his back, he kept his rondel dagger at the ready, and he opened the door only partially, revealing a tall, thin man with a fair-haired beard. Upon his chest was a dark blue coat of plates; upon his head was a kettle helm with cheek plates, and on his hands were a pair of demi gauntlets. In his hand was a longbow, and upon his back was a makeshift quiver made of rabbit hide.

"Greetings, m'Lord. I come in peace," he exclaimed. Manfred eyed the man with suspicion.

"Who are you?" Manfred replied.

"I am Gustafus Haraldsen, sir. I come as an informant."

"An informant of what?"

"The peasant army; it still exists."

"How? Both Wendel and the Mute are slain."

"Yes, but a new man has taken power, a Mongol," Gustafus said.

"How do you know this?"

"I was part of the army."

"Excuse me?"

"I was part of the army. The mute's army. Wendel's army," Gustafus said. Manfred raised his dagger to the man's throat.

"You stood on that field, watched that carnage, and did nothing?" he exclaimed.

"I'm doing something now, aren't I?"

"Well, you haven't done much. All you've done is given me another senseless fear. Your forces are destroyed, depleted, and will never rise again."

"That's just it. The Mongol, he's devised a plan."

"Then quit stalling and tell me this plan so I might thwart it!" Manfred exclaimed in frustration, lowering his dagger.

"I will do it for a price."

"Price? What price? I have you surrounded, every room in this inn has a man of mine in it. There is no escape for you."

"I need no gold, sir. I am wounded, and I need treatment. In the woods, we have no medicine or alcohol," Gustafus pleaded. "Please, sir. If you take me to an infirmary, I will repay this debt by consistent espionage."

"Show me your wound, soldier," Manfred said. The man lifted his left sleeve. It was bandaged, and blood was pooling into the wrappings, turning them a dark shade of crimson.

"It's infected, sir," the man said. "I need to sterilize it or something."

"I'll tell you what," Manfred replied. "We'll pour alcohol on it and disinfect it and treat it properly. I'm sure that Franz knows how to make a splint."

"No, sir. It mustn't be treated, only sterilized, or else my comrades will find out," Gustafus replied. Manfred agreed. He brought Wilhelm with him, and both carried their rondel daggers. They went to the main hall of the tavern and asked the bartender for a pint of schnapps.

"That'll be expensive mate," the bartender said sleepily.

"I know," replied Manfred. "It's worth it." Wilhelm pinned Gustafus down with his arm outstretched, and then he turned to Manfred.

"Are you sure we can trust this Swede?" he asked.

"If not, we're losing nothing by it," replied Manfred. Gustafus unwrapped the bandages. He bit down on an arrow to brace for the pain. "Are you ready?" Manfred asked. Gustafus nodded. Manfred carefully began to tilt the pint. Gustafus grew scared, but he fought his fear and stayed still. Then, the first drop hit the wound.

"Ah!" Gustafus cried out. He screamed with pain. He attempted to wrestle himself free, but Wilhelm held him down. Manfred continued. The schnapps filled the hole where an arrowhead once was, pooling, and mixing with the thick red blood. They continued the procedure until the pint was empty, and then they wrapped some fresh bandages on top.

"Alright, Gustafus, it's time to speak up."

"Yes, sir," he replied. He whimpered from the pain, but he tried to fight it.

"Come on, man, you have to be back before sunrise."

"Alright, I'll tell you everything," Gustafus replied. Gustafus explained the entire plan, to go to Poland, to ambush the men, and exactly where the colony was hiding. He was then released. Wilhelm turned to Manfred.

"Are you sure we can just release him like that?"

"He stuck to his promise; I'm sticking to mine," Manfred replied. They watched as the man trudged his way across the field once more, sneaking back into the woods. Then, the two returned to their cabins and engaged in a long and hearty slumber.

Manfred dreamt terrible dreams – the kind depicted in plague chronicles. He relived the slaughter on the fields of Teltow. His mind became infested with skeletons, dancing about, taunting him. They asked him to join them. They shrouded themselves in flames, bore weapons, and fought amongst each other, resorting to tooth and bone to break the enemy. Manfred, scarred by the massacre he had witnessed, felt all the horror in his sleep. It reminded him of the lives that were lost. The dreams plagued him like a curse, deep into the night.

CHAPTER 29. HUNTING FOR WOLVES

That morning the troops all gathered in the main hall. As the soldiers ate their barley soups, Manfred stood up and called their attention.

"Men, I know that yesterday was tough. We lost many good men, including the beloved Wolfe of the Swiss Brigade. We must remember those men and cherish their memories," Manfred said. Then, he changed his tone. "But, the time for lamentation is over. We have a mission. We are all soldiers here, and this was likely not your first battle nor your last, though possibly your bloodiest. Men, another battle is on the horizon. Those brigand bastards are still hiding out in the woods. I know that you have all suffered greatly at the hands of that rioting horde, but we now have them on their heels. We must find them and catch them before they reach Poland, for if they acquire the favour of a noble there, we may face a far tougher challenge. We must summon the garrisons of Berlin and Brandenburg. Leopold, we need all the men you can muster. Friends, we will smoke out those cowards and end them rightly. We deserve revenge for our fallen. We deserve justice. For Wolfe!"

"For Wolfe!" the unit cheered in unison, repeating it multiple times until it engrained itself into their minds like a zealous rage. With zeal and fervour, they chanted. Manfred and his guard sat back down and began to make plans with Leopold.

"Manfred, you have my full support in this matter. If what you say is true, I will muster as many men as I can. I fear another pitched battle, considering our losses from the last one, but I will do all I can to keep these lands safe."

"Thank you, Leopold. I believe that we should split into two groups. Leopold, Wilhelm, and I can go to Brandenburg to acquire their support. Ulrich, I entrust you with Roland, Friedrich, Maurits, and Renault. The rest of the men can stay here," ordered Manfred.

"Understood, sir," Ulrich said. Immediately, he stood up and began to vacate. His men soon followed. Manfred and his men stayed a small while longer before they left. Before they left, Wilhelm paused.

"Wait, Manfred. Isn't Helmuth a noble from Brandenburg?"

"Yes, why?"

"Perhaps he could help us."

"You are right. Good thinking." Manfred ordered Helmuth to come with them. Together, the three men rode off back in the direction of Brandenburg.

The group rode through the battlefield of Teltow. The clean-up crew was still working away at the mass graves and looting the dead, scavenging for florins, weapons, and untailored armour. The trench also remained unfilled. It evoked the cruellest memories in Manfred. His raid, hacking through man after man, and of course, the slaying of the dwarf. Manfred felt no pride in it. He knew the man's plight, and frankly, he also found his father to be guilty of injustice. Manfred and his group rode across the farmers' fields, back into the lake pelted countryside of Brandenburg City. The lakes surrounded them like puddles of blood. The trees loomed over them like the hands of the dead, reaching up from their graves. The men looked around, calm, but disturbed. As they approached the bridge that led to the city, the guard willingly let them pass. The horsemen clopped their way across it with a serenity unattained before. The city seemed peaceful, rested, and completely ignorant of the occurrences that had passed the day before. Nobody seemed to mourn the dead, nobody cried on the streets for their fallen heroes. The soldiers of Brandenburg seemed to have passed silently, unknown to all but their own fallen brethren, and the ones who remain had to carry the burden of knowing that they too could have taken their brothers' place.

Manfred felt the chill of death.

"The people seem unscathed by the events of yesterday," Manfred said to his men quietly.

"That's the trouble with soldiering, son," replied Leopold. "We die so that they don't have to care about whether we live or die. Life isn't like the stories of old. Soldiers mustn't soldier in search of heroism or glory or honour, but instead, they must fight for what they truly believe in, protect who they love, or else, what is it all for?" The four men rode over the cobblestone streets. The horseshoes on their horses' hooves struck the stone, creating a rhythmic percussion. They headed for the keep.

It was a short and stout building. It didn't need to be fortified, as the city itself was a giant castle. The men made their way through to the gates.

"Who dares enter the Keep of Jobst von Luxembourg, Elector of Brandenburg, and Contender for the Imperial Throne?"

"It is General Leopold von Wustermark," replied Leopold. Without hesitation, the guard quickly realized that he had almost denied entry to the Elector's righthand man.

"My bad, Sir. Leopold. It's been a long day. Please, follow me," he said hospitably while leading Leopold's horse. Once dismounted and inside the complex, the men made their way up the main stairwell to the Elector's office. Leopold knocked on the door.

"Come in," an elderly voice said from inside. Leopold opened the door. Inside were two men standing around a table with a detailed map of the empire. The older of the two began to speak. "Greetings, Leopold. Before you begin, I would like you to meet my cousin, King Sigismund of Hungary. He arrived yesterday after our skirmish. I hope you could adequately explain this heroic defeat." Leopold was astonished. Perhaps the most powerful Christian king in the East was right in front of him. Immediately he bowed down, and his companions followed.

"My Lord, I am humbled by your presence," Leopold said.

"Don't be a grovelling worm. I hear you are an excellent general and an even better retainer. Rise to your feet; you deserve as much respect as me. So, tell me, what happened in these fields?" Leopold stood, but his compatriots remained kneeling.

"My Lord, a peasant revolt came to our doorstep and took Potsdam. We had no choice but to unite with Berlin and vanquish those heretics."

"Good," replied Sigismund. He turned to his cousin. "You mustn't let any such revolts happen within your domain. I'm glad you acted in accordance with Berlin. We need to consolidate allies if you are to run for election."

"Yes, cousin," replied Jobst. "So, Leopold. I thought you had left. What brings you back?"

"Sir, we know of a colony of survivors. They are hiding in the woods just East of here. With more men, we could smoke them out and slaughter them all. Or else, we fear they may ally with the Poles and ambush us on our journey."

"Ambush you? Why? What use do they have for you?"

"I hear that their leader, a Mongol, has a grudge against this company of noble knights. It is up to us to stop them and ensure that the papal emissary arrives in time," replied Leopold.

142

"What is the mission of this emissary?" asked Sigismund. Manfred rose to his feet.

"He is sent to observe the Teutonic Order and see if the Pope should declare a crusade on the Poles and Russians," he said.

"That would be quite favourable to Hungary," said Sigismund. "If we had Teutonic neighbours, they might aid us in fighting against the Cumans. I will give you my retinue, as long as no word of my participation is said. Understood? If this all falls apart, I wouldn't wish to stain the honour of Hungary with another Nicopolis."

"Forgive me, my Lord, but what happened at Nicopolis?" asked Manfred.

"Oh, you should have seen it. It ought to have been before you were born, youngen. It was quite a sight. The banners of England, France, Germany, and many more from across Christendom united with my people to wage war on the Ottoman cur. You see, back then, they weren't so large as they are now. Wallachia, Bulgaria, and Serbia all had their own kingdoms. But on that fateful day, all hope was lost. I tell you, knights are becoming a thing of the past, Manfred. Fight hard in Germany while you can, for when the Ottoman akinji cavalry comes to Europe, we will all be out maneuvered, and outflanked. Only our hussars will be a match for them. Anyways. Fight like a lion, defeat their men once and for all, and do not get my men killed. Take the day!"

"Yes, sire," said Manfred delightfully.

"I too will give garrison reserves," Jobst said. The party, content, returned to the main square. There, they united with a small force of twenty men from the garrison, and a retinue of one hundred Hungarian hussars. They were a numerous force of light cavalry. Manfred, scrutinizing them carefully, found their clothing to be quite odd and foreign. Their tall brimmed hats seemed almost ridiculous to the German knights. Furthermore, their shields were exotic and intriguing

– the type of weaponry only found in artistic manuscripts depicting far off magical lands like Sindh and the Orient. And yet, the fighting force looked colourful, like a horde of European nobles dressed in festive attire. The Germans found their garbs to be quite pleasant, nearly harkening back to the olden days when tournaments were held more often, and nobody had to fear the spread of the plague. From the scores of riders, one of the tall, Slavic warriors rode forwards.

"My name is Jogaila Galicianov. I am the commander of the king's royal retinue."

"It will be a pleasure serving alongside you," said Manfred.

"For me too. Just promise me one thing."

"What is it?"

"Never ask my men to give mercy. They slay all enemies before them. If their charge is stalled, we will all die."

"I understand. Your wish is granted," Manfred said. Leopold also returned with his retinue of another fifteen billmen. The large force exited the town. Out of windows flowers were thrown to them. They were praised as heroes, marching out to war to save their lands. As they crossed the battlefield, they no longer felt vulnerable and distraught; instead, they were filled with confidence, and were eager for the fight to come.

CHAPTER 30. THE BEAR OF BERLIN

Ulrich and his followers approached the Prince's residence. It was a castle perched upon a hill in the center of the city, known as Prenzlauer Berg. The castle looked over the entire city like a watchful eye. The city itself was vast, and it took nearly half an hour for the men to reach the castle. The front gates were guarded by two well-armed guards. They stood on the other end of a long drawbridge, which prostrated over a deep moat. The group assembled before the guards.

"We come to speak to the Prince," Ulrich said.

"He can't be seen in his current state. What is your business?" asked one of the guards.

"The army that Berlin so valiantly defeated yesterday has regrouped in the woods. We have a formidable force with us, and we would like to see if the Prince had any men to spare."

"Any men to spare? Ha!" the guard replied.

"Look," interjected Roland. "We don't have time for this. We need men soon, or else this mission might fail, and more Germans will be killed protecting these lands. If you don't let us through when we're done with those brigands, I swear to God I'll come back and slay you myself."

"Oh, is that a threat?" asked the guard. His colleague called out above himself to the walls.

"Patrols! We need assistance!" At that moment, another six crossbowmen rushed to their location and pointed their crossbows directly at the knights. Roland unsheathed his sword halfway. The guard raised his poleaxe.

"Wait!" Maurits cried out. "Stop. We are not your enemy, nor are you ours. Let's all just calm down here." The guard maintained his position and Roland did as well. All froze, eyeing each other down. Then, a man shouted from the walls.

"What seems to be the full, Hans?" he asked the guard. The man was dressed in ornate clothing, fit for a king.

"These men are threatening me," Hans replied.

"Well, what do they want?"

"Sir," replied Ulrich. "We come in peace. We simply wished to speak with the Prince."

"Well, let's lay down our weapons. Shall we?" the man said. He gestured his hand, resulting in the lowering of the crossbows. Hans returned his poleaxe to the ground, and eventually Roland resheathed his sword. "I am not Prince Frederick, for he is gravely ill. I am his son. Will that suffice?"

"Absolutely, my Lord," said Ulrich. The group was let inside, and they were seated at a picnic table where they were served apple infused water and some sweet bread.

"My name is Siegfried Hohenzollern, heir to the throne of Berlin. What are yours?" Siegfried asked. The group each introduced themselves. "Now, what brings you here to speak with me?"

"The army that was defeated yesterday is greatly weakened but has regrouped in the woods. We have a large army waiting and men recruiting from Brandenburg and Wustermark. Are you willing to put a few men under our command to aid us in this raid? It will rid your lands of those brigands. We assure you of our success," said Ulrich.

"Why would you and your men take particular interest to crush these remnants of resistance?" Siegfried asked.

"Our friend Renault here is a papal emissary. We are escorting him to Marienburg Castle in Prussia, so that he may decide on the validity of the Teutonic Order's claims of declaring a crusade."

"Really? How exciting! Please do show me your papal seal." Renault pulled the stamp from his bag. On it where the crossing keys and crown of the Pope. "Quite extraordinary indeed," Siegfried said.

"Please sir, will you aid us? I assure you that your men will be treated as ours, and that victory is certain. Under our command, there will be no chance of defeat," Ulrich pleaded.

"I do not doubt your competency in commanding," said Siegfried. "But I have another proposition. I am a man, and my entire life has been spent learning the ways of war. I would not wish to drain Berlin's reserve army anymore. Instead, I propose that I personally join you, alongside my retinue knights."

"That sounds excellent, sir," said Ulrich.

"Also, I wish to command your forces. I believe these woods to be on my father's soil, and these men pose a threat to my land and my land alone. I will lead your men to victory," Siegfried said.

"Sir, I don't know if..."

"Don't reject this offer, soldier. It will only be uttered once," he said. Ulrich looked to his compatriots. None wanted to pass up the opportunity.

"Fine. You may lead us," said Ulrich. "But we must attack this afternoon once we reunite with our comrades at the Inn."

"Sounds like a plan. This will be fun," Siegfried said cheerfully. The group waited around a bit until Siegfried and his knights armoured themselves. They and their squires came riding out into the courtyard upon their destriers. Their horses were ordained in exquisite armour, and their surcoats were gilded and decorated with the black bear of Berlin as well as the black and quite quarters of the house of Hohenzollern. There were seven knights, each in their own set of armour. Siegfried's armour was the most splendid, however. It was gilded and fluted and even had an early form of plackart armour, which hung from globose cuirass by a brightly decorated red leather strap. Upon his back, a black and white cape cascaded down to his saddle. "Do you like it? It was all designed and smithed in Milan," he said with a smile. Upon his Milanese Armet Helm was a fantastical plume of black and white, as well as a sculpted bear, snarling at all foes who dared to face him.

"Very impressive," said Maurits. "You wear that into war?" he asked.

"Of course. How else will my men know who I am?" replied Siegfried. His knights were armed with their own individual armours, and jupons and surcoats covered their upper harnesses. Upon all of their heads were wolf rib bascinets, allowing for tactical sight and breathing on the battlefield. The unit rode back to the tavern where they awaited their compatriots' arrival.

CHAPTER 31. THE PLAN

The hussars arrived at sundown. They set up camp in the fields before Berlin. Once complete, Manfred rode through the sea of white canvas to the gates. He and his riders rode together to the tavern. The doors opened, and through it walked Manfred and his men into the room. There, he saw his band of soldiers and met their Berliner reinforcements.

"Sir. Manfred, I presume?" asked Siegfried.

"Yes, it is I. I expected Prince Frederick to be older," Manfred replied.

"I am not him, for he is ill. My name is Siegfried, his son."

"Excellent. I am elated to see that you will join our ranks, Siegfried."

"Actually, sir, I have been promised the role of General of your men. I hope this won't spur up too much trouble, will it?" asked Siegfried.

"Who promised you this?"

"Your comrade, the man with the painted armour."

"Ulrich?"

"Yes, that's the one," replied Siegfried.

"Then I will speak to him about this. Will you excuse me for a moment?" asked Manfred. He made his way through the crowd to where he saw Ulrich. Ulrich was sitting at a table. In front of him was Gustafus. "Reporting more news?"

"Yes, sir. The Mongol has made plans to leave tomorrow," replied Gustafus.

"Good, because we attack tonight," Manfred said. "Will you excuse us?" Gustafus left. Manfred turned his attention to Ulrich, who knew exactly what was about to happen. "What exactly did you promise this Siegfried?"

"I told him that he could lead the army. It's his land so it made sense," replied Ulrich sheepishly.

"You are not one for games, I know this, so I will say this plainly. He will not lead this army; I don't care if he leaves. But if he does, he will be forever known as a coward by his people. Do you understand?" Manfred asked harshly.

"Yes, sir."

"Now, I'm going to go over and tell him the news. Stay put and get whatever else you can out of Gustafus. Understood?"

"Yes, sir," replied Ulrich. Manfred made his way back over to Siegfried. When he looked over, however, he saw Siegfried and Jogaila already arguing. Manfred quickly stepped in.

"Men, what seems to be the fuss?"

"This, this fool!" exclaimed Jogaila. "He wants to control my men. They are light cavalry! They cannot charge a bunch of trees!"

"They are horsemen!" replied Siegfried. "They will charge if I want them to. Do your job!"

"I will not fight for this man," said Jogaila.

"Stop!" shouted Manfred. "Jogaila, you still control your hussars, and Siegfried, the only men you control are the ones you bring to the battle. Be that fifteen or fifty, that's what's fair. Understand?"

"I will leave your army then," replied Siegfried. "And I will outlaw it from this city."

"If you leave us, you will be known as a coward," said Manfred. "Besides, when did you last win a battle for your city? I'm sure that your enemies would love to point out your incompetence in battle. Charging into a forest with light cavalry? You are no general. Follow me, and you will return a hero, got it?"

"Fine," replied Siegfried. He stormed off back to his men.

"That man is a fool," commented Jogaila. Manfred just looked at him and then returned to his men. Around a table, the commander sat. There was Leopold, Jogaila, Siegfried, Franz, Leon, and of course, Manfred. Gustafus also sat there, providing them with information. They sat at the table, and with a blank sheet of paper, Gustafus drew a map of the battlefield from his memory. The council observed the map and began formulating a plan.

"We need to draw them out," said Franz.

"I agree," replied Manfred. "Can you do that with a hail of crossbows?"

"Of course."

"Then, we will need to charge them by surprise," said Manfred. "We need fast horsemen. Jogaila, if your hussars hide in the trench system that these men dug, can they quickly charge out and rush their longbows?"

"It seems doable," said Jogaila. "But we will need a cleared landscape; at the last moment, Franz, your crossbowmen will have to scatter," Franz agreed.

"Alright," said Manfred. "Now, we will need a commando force to go in and burn down their settlement. We could loot it too. Leopold, I was hoping your men could do this? My men and I could join you, alongside Gustafus, to lead the way."

"Yes, Manfred. But what if he leads us into a trap?" asked Leopold.

"I won't," replied Gustafus, still at the table. "But we should evacuate the women and children. They had no choice in this and have done no wrong."

"Fine," replied Leopold.

"Look, if he does lead us into a trap, we can have Siegfried and his knights to escort them away and keep an eye on us. If anything happens, they can get the attention of Leon, who will be waiting with a pike block to close off the rear of the forest, ensuring that the only escapees are noncombatants."

"I will be there," replied Leon.

"I want a more active role," said Siegfried.

"Would it help if I gave you my knights as well? There's no point in keeping horses in the forest," said Manfred.

"Alright, that'll do," said Siegfried contently. The plan was set; the men were ready. Under the cover of darkness, the men marched out to the fields of Teltow, facing the Diedersdorf Forest. The Swiss and Berliner contingents made their way around the back. The hussars descended down into the forest, keeping a watchful eye. Slowly, Gustafus led Leopold and Manfred's contingent into the woods, and they crept through the foliage, ready to strike. All were in position. All were quiet.

The Swiss sounded their horns once they were in position. Franze's pavisiers sounded theirs as well and advanced to the forest, hailing the unsuspecting revolutionaries with a storm of bolts. Immediately, the peasants leapt to their arms, equipping themselves with longbows and spears they came out to fire upon the crossbows. Then, as most of the fighting men left the forest, the hussars charged out from the trench, and simultaneously, the knights converged in to evacuate the noncombatants and make ruin of the horde's supplies. The hussars charged down the longbowmen with speed and efficiency, and the spearmen were not formed up well enough to raise a valid defence. The allied force was winning the battle.

Through the foliage, Manfred and his men stormed the camp, killing guards and directing the women and children towards the Swiss. Those who protested were slain, the knights had no time to lose. Finally, once the battle was finished and not a soul remained, they set fire to the encampment. The buildings erupted into flames, and all was set ablaze. Soon, the wind picked up, carrying the inferno to the trees. Within moments, the entire forest was set ablaze.

Through the smoke and fire, as the men were leaving, Manfred saw the Mongol. Without telling his comrades, he charged. The Mongol responded in kind and leapt forwards through the veil of smoke and ash. The air thickened. None knew where Manfred was.

The two were alone now.

Manfred attacked him with his axe, but the Mongol was now wearing armour and wouldn't be defeated as he was before by Wilhelm. They clashed for minutes, axe hitting shield, sword hitting armour. Eventually, the two were both beginning to suffocate from all the smoke. Manfred lifted his visor.

"Manfred! Manfred!" Wilhelm cried from the fields. He turned to his comrades. "I'm not waiting any longer, I'm going to save him." He marched forwards into the inferno. The heat boiled Wilhelm in his armour, so he tore off what he could and left it on the field. He rushed in. There, near the hearth, lay Manfred. On the ground he was cooking in his armour, shield still strapped to his arm, unscorched, untouched. Wilhelm quickly ran to him and picked him up. As he looked around, he saw no Mongol, no man, not a soul by Manfred. The steel burned Wilhelm's flesh as he pulled. He tugged with all his might until he was weak, and then kept tugging. He pulled and pulled, with metal burning into him. Choking on the smoke and ash, he kept pulling. His asthma flared, constricting his airways which were already infested with the thick, black smoke.

Finally, Manfred was out. Wilhelm laid him down on a bed of grass, and then he himself fainted beside him. The two laid there, and their knights came with stretchers to bring them back to Berlin. Wilhelm's last sight was the night sky. He gazed at the stars and swore he saw one form a cross. Then, he faded.

CHAPTER 32. HUNTING FOR MEN

Snowflakes rested upon Manfred's visage. With the little energy he had, he opened his eyes. He stared up at the winter sky, watching the snowflakes fall, for he had no more energy to do anything else. He saw as branches glided by, floating in the air. The air was cold, frozen, a harsh return to the weather once passed. Manfred was swaddled in blankets and cloaks and was being carried on a stretcher by two pavisiers. Eventually, one of them looked down. His face was swaddled in cloth. Startled, he got his friend's attention.

"He's awake!" he shouted with glee. His friend turned to him with disbelief, then turned to the body. He saw the eyes glancing up at the sky.

"He's awake!" he, too, shouted loudly for all to hear. He unwrapped his face cloth and shouted again. Eventually, the caravan stopped. Three knights rushed over. Ulrich ordered the men to step aside.

"He's alive! I knew it!" shouted Roland.

"It's a miracle," said Friedrich. The stretcher was lowered to the ground, and Friedrich said a quick prayer praising Jesus. After he was finished, Maurits said another as well, asking for the preservation of life and health for Manfred. Manfred was dazed. He heard little of it, and little in general over the sharp ringing in his ears. He was hungry, extremely hungry, as if he hadn't eaten for days. Then Manfred remembered what happened. The Mongol, the fire, all of it until his blackout.

"Where are we?" he muttered softly.

"We are in Pomerania, on the road to Gryfino. There we can get you to a doctor. Luckily, the winter cold has preserved you. Your burns cover your entire body, so you mustn't move, but luckily none of your wounds were infected as you were still in your armour when Wilhelm extracted you. Your face is fine too, thankfully, you lifted your visor before succumbing to the heat," replied Ulrich.

"Wilhelm? He saved me?"

"Yes, he did," replied Ulrich softly. He looked down. Manfred knew what that meant.

"I'm sorry," he muttered under his breath. Nobody heard him. The ring in his ears was replaced by a painful sting in his heart. He felt guilt, genuine guilt. If he only hadn't been so stupid as to follow that Mongol, none of this would have happened.

"How... how did he... pass?" asked Manfred feebly.

"His burns were exposed. As he lay in the grass beside you, it must have gotten infected by the dirt. He succumbed to disease," replied Ulrich.

"When? When was this? For how long have I been... asleep?"

"This was three nights ago," replied Ulrich.

"We have ensured that you stay hydrated over the past days, but we couldn't make you eat. We should rest here, set up camp, and cook something," said Friedrich. Manfred was starving. He nodded in compliance. As the group warmed around a robust fire, they explained what had happened thus far on their journey. They noted that they would soon reach Prussia, at least that's what their map said. In reality, they were only halfway. Manfred no longer felt a vicious hate for his foes, but instead a pang of guilt; a realization that his recklessness cost a life. He thought upon Wilhelm's words in the tavern, how he said that he wasn't trained for this, so he need not feel guilty. Manfred instead took ownership of his actions. He knew full well what he was doing and what he was risking. He wasn't trying to exact revenge on a foe, he was trying to save his friends from future repentance. Manfred did it for his companions, and instead, he risked their lives.

"So, tell me," said Manfred. "Has anything interesting happened in the past few days?"

"Well," replied Roland. "We were attacked by wolves."

"It's okay, Manfred. Don't worry about anything; just rest," said Friedrich, as Ulrich scolded Roland in the background.

"No, no, I want to hear this story. It will... take my mind off things," Manfred croaked.

"Are you sure? It isn't very interesting," said Ulrich, attempting to dissuade Manfred from indulging Roland.

"I truly want to hear it, interesting or not. I care about the lot of you, so I want to know how things have been," Manfred said. He looked at them with despair in his eyes, forcing Friedrich and Ulrich to capitulate.

"Fine," said Ulrich. "It all began two days ago. To leave the Berlin area we had to leave through a long strip of forests and meadows. The Bernau, I think it's called. We were walking through, trudging and stumbling on. Our horses were cold, we were cold, and snowfall had only just resumed. All day we marched that path to Eberswalde until Wilhelm made a noise."

"Wilhelm was still alive?"

"Yes, alive, but very ill. He asked for food and drink, and when we gave it to him, he consumed it like a lion. So, we continued our journey, feeding him along, until we realized that one of his bandages was leaking. It had left a long red trail in the snow. It was fine, nobody fussed about it, but we were concerned about Wilhelm's health. We realized that we had to rush for Eberswalde. Friedrich scouted ahead and informed us that it was in fact on an off-road, trailing off of this one. Thus, we decided that it would be faster to go in the woods by horse and let the rest of the group catch up to us by foot. We rode through the woods with Wilhelm close in hand, but night fell sooner than we had expected. We brought a candle with us, so slowly we threaded through the woods. Within moments, we reached a pond. It was large and roaring with waves. We couldn't cross it; we would have to go around. We began to circle the pond until we heard a howl from out in the forest. We thought nothing would come to us, that nothing would even dare to harm us.

We were wrong.

Soon, the number and volume of the howls amplified, but we had to still move slowly to avoid injuring our horses. Then, Wilhelm's horse got spooked. With no rider on it, its reigns freed themselves from my hand, and the horse galloped off into the darkness. All we heard after that was the cry of a horse in pain. It had been caught. We urged our horses to speed up, but that wasn't possible. So, we dismounted, protecting our steeds. We formed a ring around Renault and the horses. Maurits, Roland, Friedrich, Helmuth, and I all stood with our lances raised as pikes, forming a wall with our backs facing the pond. We saw the glint of canine eyes spotting us from among the trees. The mud below our feet started to sink. That's when the wolves came out; they attacked us but couldn't get through our wall."

"They got through to me, though," said Roland. He raised his vambrace. "Check it out; I have dents from the teeth and everything!" he said, pointing to a few small dents.

"Mind your tongue," said Ulrich. "Anyways, the wolves attacked us, but we fended them off. Then, we had Friedrich ride ahead and take Wilhelm to the town, but he passed along the way. Okay? The end," said Ulrich, clearly scarred too from the loss of Wilhelm.

"I'm sorry for bringing it up; if I had known that it would include Wilhelm I wouldn't have asked," said Manfred.

"It's okay," replied Friedrich. "You deserve the right to know how he went. It was peaceful, I assure you. I buried him by a tree along the way, and I carved a large cross into it so we might identify it on our way back. I still have his mace, if you want it." He presented it to Manfred. Manfred accepted it and held it tightly.

"All you do is whack 'em with the heavy end," he said painfully, quoting Wilhelm. The four of them paused in silence, mourning their loss. After a few hours, Manfred felt well enough to continue on his horse. Covered in blankets, he rode as best he could, but he was still in no condition to ride fully. His wounds were tender and coarse and occasionally stuck to his tunic and trousers. Ulrich and Friedrich gave him support as he rode, balancing him on his horse, and ensuring that he did not faint. The party marched through the evening to Gryfino, Pomerania.

CHAPTER 33. MAN-SLAYER

By the evening, the unit came across a long bridge which led the way across the East Oder River. On the other end was Gryfino. Hastily, the four knights rushed ahead, attempting to reach an infirmary as quickly as possible, and the rest marched across in search of an inn. The four knights entered the gates and immediately asked the guards for help.

"Sir," said Friedrich. "My friend here is in dire need of a doctor, where might we find one?"

The guard turned to him and politely said:"It is at the corner of third street and center avenue." He pointed right down a wide street, leading straight to the city center.

"Your city is organized like a grid?" asked Friedrich astonished. The guard quickly explained how the Polish Duke Barnim I organized the city into rows and columns like the roman cities along the Danube. After receiving the explanation, the group rushed to the doctor. Sure enough, they came across a large building with two stories that held many ill and many injured. They made their way through the halls until they reached a desk, where a scribe documented all visitors and patients. The group registered Manfred and sat down awaiting treatment. Apparently, there were only two doctors.

"Thank God we made it," said Ulrich.

"Gott Mitt Uns," said Friedrich, forming the prayer hands motion.

"I wish Wilhelm could have seen a doctor too," said Manfred in a mournful, solemn tone. Ulrich turned to him with inquiry.

"Funny you should say that," he muttered under his breath. Unfortunately, all still heard.

"Excuse me?" asked Manfred. Friedrich and Roland shut their mouths like vault doors.

"I'm just saying, you still haven't even taken ownership for Wilhelm's death."

"He was my friend. Why are you saying this?"

"And still you don't say it. Don't you realize that this is all because of you?"

"Don't do this, Ulrich."

"It was no Mongol nor fire that killed Wilhelm; it was you. Your own stupidity."

"Ulrich, do you seriously think I don't know this? That I don't feel guilty every day for my mistake? That I don't wish it was me instead of him?"

"Oh, don't give me that hooplah. It wasn't a mistake. It was intentional that you followed that man into that infernal hellscape, and the truth is that, if given the same scenario, you would do the exact same now too. Why? Because you are no more than a stuck-up child. You are unfit to rule and unfit to lead men."

"Ulrich, remember who you are talking to. I am your commander," Manfred shouted.

"Not anymore," said Ulrich in a soft voice. He got up and walked out. Manfred was left in the waiting room with just Friedrich and Roland, neither of whom said a word, and neither of whom rushed out after Ulrich. They just sat there, the three of them. They looked at one another and then looked down. They understood Ulrich. Who could blame him? But did he have to be so ruthless with his words? They sat pondering in silence until the door flew open once more. Ulrich returned and slammed a coin purse on the table.

"This is the remainder of the coins that you gave me for recruiting. The Swiss didn't accept it all, so I kept the change. I haven't spent any of it - I haven't gotten the chance to. I was going to keep it, but then I realized that I don't want your filthy florins," he shouted. Manfred looked at him, exhausted.

"Keep them. You'll need them."

"Damn you!" Ulrich shouted. He looked at the three of them all seated together like cold sheep. "And by the way, Wilhelm was not killed by a Mongol or a fire, but instead by this. The three of you worshipped Manfred like a god, and even after Wilhelm's death, you persist in your loyalty. Why? Is this all for Otto's spare florins? Or is this out of some sense of duty? This man has done nothing for you! You just grovel at his feet, perpetuating a Goddamn corrupt system. Those peasants who we just killed had a better sense of justice than the two of you. Manfred is no god, he deserves no respect, he has done nothing but fail us all! I'm done, and you should be too." Friedrich sat in silence, but Roland stood up. He couldn't take this internal strife.

"Ulrich, don't go," he pleaded. "Don't head back without us; just finish the journey. Have some loyalty for your comrades. Don't let Wilhelm's death be in vain."

"Head back? Oh no. Adelebsen will never see my face again," Ulrich said. "Nor will you." He snatched the coins and returned outside. There, he slipped onto his horse and galloped away into the town. Nobody followed him. Nobody had the will, nor the energy, nor the courage.

Not even Manfred.

CHAPTER 34. LEECHES

"The doctor's ready to see you," said the man at the desk, as he pointed down the hall. There, at the end, a woman stood in a long black gown. On it, there were numerous blood stains. Her sleeves were rolled up. Roland looked at her and then back at the man at the desk.

"Are you sure she can help our friend?" he asked. The woman spoke from the end of the hall.

"I just successfully amputated a man's arm. I think I can handle it," she said confidently. She gestured for the men to follow her up the stairs and into one of the side rooms. Manfred looked around. On one side there was a stained-glass window that displayed a blurry view of the street, displayed in red and green. The doctor saw Manfred staring out of it. "It's a stupid window, I know, but the church funds this place, and it was extra material from their own construction."

"It's okay," he replied. "I like it." The doctor smirked. She cleared a table that was in the room and rolled out a long white tablecloth.

"Lie here for me," she instructed. Then, she turned to Manfred's companions. "Can either of you explain what happened?"

"He's burned," replied Friedrich.

"Where, and how long ago?" she asked.

"All over, and four days," replied Friedrich. The doctor turned to Manfred. Out of a drawer, she pulled a root.

"Chew on this," she said. He put it in his mouth and began chewing. "Good, now take off your shirt, shoes, and hose. I have to examine the wounds." Manfred took off those pieces of clothing and gave them to Friedrich and Roland. As he took them off, his burns stung, as the threads of cloth that were once stuck to the wounds were ripped off. Some scabs opened, but little blood came out. The doctor asked Friedrich and Roland to leave the room. Slowly they exited and returned to the waiting area. "Luckily, your burns have only come in splotches," the doctor said. She pulled out some ointment and began to apply it to the wounds. "How exactly did you get them?"

"I'm a knight," Manfred replied.

"Well, I figured as much by your sword," she said, looking at his sword and belt.

"Yeah," Manfred said with a chuckle. "Anyways, I was fighting this murderous Mongol, but all around us there was fire."

"Well, that sounds like an unfortunate place to be in. You are lucky that you made it here on time," she said.

"True. I passed out from heat exhaustion, and the floor must have heated my armour up so much that it began to burn through my aketon. My friends threw it away when they retrieved me. They told me that the fire had burned right through it at parts."

"I'm still glad you had it on you or else you wouldn't have survived. No matter how burned your wounds can be, they can still be infected. So, how did everything catch on fire?"

"Well, it was in a battle. We had set fire to an enemy camp, but it was in the woods, and the wind carried the flames to the trees."

"Oh my. That's quite unfortunate."

"Well, I suppose we brought it among ourselves. We made

sure to evacuate the women and children before setting any ablaze." Manfred paused. "Most made it out alive."

"You attacked women and children?" the doctor asked in shock. She stopped applying the ointment.

"It was for the right cause. Their husbands and fathers and brothers were attacking Berlin. Please, don't stop treating me, I can't die here, I must return to my family," Manfred pleaded.

"Don't worry," she replied while continuing to treat the wounds. "This is a hospital; we take all patients, no matter who they are. But that doesn't mean that your sins are absolved."

"Yes, doctor. I will be sure to go to the church to ask for forgiveness once I am healed."

"That may be a while, Manfred. There is a black burn on your left arm. Don't move it," she said tersely. She reached for a cream that she applied to the blisters. It was cold and thick. Then, for the black burn, she sprinkled some herbs. Manfred cried out in pain. He bit down harder on the root, which slightly numbed his body. Afterwards, the woman used a small glass to pour lukewarm water into the black burn's hole. The water became charred and murky. She drained it with a towel and then pulled out a metal scalpel. She looked Manfred in the eye.

"Manfred, I won't lie to you. This will hurt... a lot," she said. Then, she reached for the burn. Manfred trembled in fear. She began cutting away the charred skin. Manfred screamed out in pain. It was too much; she stopped and hastily strapped him down to the table. Once he was secure, she continued. Manfred cried, and his wound bled. The blood was a charred dark red. Pieces of blackened skin floated in it as it poured out. She collected it in a bucket. Beneath the layer of charred skin was a crispy, white layer. Once all of the black skin was removed, the doctor wrapped the wound in a bandage. Manfred was still screaming in agony. Then, the doctor placed two leeches below the burn, to draw out any infected blood, or any blood with dissolved charcoal in it. Manfred fainted from the blood loss.

CHAPTER 35. THE CEREMONY

Manfred slowly opened his eyes. To his joy, he was no longer in the hospital room, strapped to that wretched table. To his despair, his arm hurt now more than ever. Manfred sat up. He was wrapped in wool blankets inside of his tent. He got up and stepped outside. He saw Roland and made his way over to him.

"Roland. Where are we, pray tell?"

"Oh, Manfred, you're awake."

"Why are we camped here? Did the city guards not let the army inside?"

"No, no. Apparently there were no inns in the city. For obvious reasons, few travellers come by here, and when they do, they can rent straight from the Duke."

"Ah, I see. Well then, where is Friedrich? When shall we leave?"

"It is midday," replied Roland. "We were waiting for you to awake. The doctor said that you must rest. I think a day is enough."

"I think so too, so tell me where Friedrich is, and we can get moving."

"Right this way," said Roland, leading the way. Together, the two made their way through the camp. Many empty barrels were used for gambling and playing chess, and many men sang shanties by the hearth. The rations were also open for lunch, and soldiers ate voraciously. The two approached Friedrich, who was speaking with two other men. They wore long white robes and carried necklaces with crosses on them. One of the two men, the elder, had a shaved head and carried a staff with a cross on the end of it. Manfred approached.

"Friedrich, long time no see," he said playfully.

"Ah yes, the lord commander has awakened. Feel rested?" asked Friedrich.

"Indeed, and ready to get moving. What say you?"

"Actually, I have just been conversing with these two fine young gentlemen. They come with a group of missionaries. They too travel to Marienburg, so perhaps we could move together?"

"I like this idea, Friedrich, but will they not slow us down?"

"But is it not our responsibility to protect these men? We are Teutonic brothers at arms now, are we not?"

"Fine. We should discuss this with Renault first, however. I feel that the pope may take precedence over some pilgrims," replied Manfred. The two agreed, and the five men headed over to discuss with Renault. Maurits and Renault were singing songs around a hearth with other men. Manfred and the others approached.

"Renault, how goes it?"

"Well, thank you. How about yourself? I heard that you screamed in pain in the hospital room. It sounds like it was a vicious procedure."

"Well... well, yes. I suppose it was."

"Alright then, what news have you?"

"We are ready to get going. I don't suppose you'd mind if we travelled with this group of missionaries, would you?"

"I believe it to be in both of our best interests," Renault said. Maurits stepped forward and looked at the two men. He turned his attention to the elder.

"What church are you from?" he asked. The bald man

167

spoke.

"We come from the Teutonic Church in Vienna. We are Austrians. We travel north to spread the word of God."

"Well, I hate to mention it, but the word of God happens to already be spread there," Maurits replied with suspicion. "Tell me, Teuton. What is your rank in the church?"

"I don't suppose it is any of your business, brother knight," replied the man. Maurits looked at Friedrich.

"Have you told him why we head north?"

"No," Friedrich replied. Maurits looked to the missionary.

"I am no mere brother knight," he said. "I am the Summus Marescalcus of the Dutch Chapter, Grossgebietiger of Military Affairs for the Order, and Marshal of the Teutonic Order. You are the escort marshal, correct?" Manfred, Friedrich, and Roland all became confused.

"I thought you were just a knight," said Manfred.

"No, I am who I say I am. Renault here is my squire. We travelled without guard to hide our identities. If Polish spies found out who we were, they would have killed us before we even reached Göttingen."

"But you let me raise an army," Manfred said in a confused voice.

"I trusted you, Manfred. The situation called for it, and you responded, as any capable commander would. Besides, our troops didn't carry Teutonic flags. Anyways, we were instructed to follow this path and meet up with the real papal emissary, this man before you. Inside the city there should be an army of Brother Sergeants at Arms," replied Maurits.

"Yes, he is right," said the man. "I am Sir. Augustus Abelard of Danzig. A crusader force of two hundred lies within this city."

"Wait, so there is no Papal emissary?" asked Friedrich.

"Yes," replied Renault. "I am no emissary. There is none. The papacy hasn't condoned the order for hundreds of years, and our newest war is the most controversial."

"Manfred," said Maurits. "You and your men have served us well, but you have no more obligation to aid us." Manfred had to think. There was no more reason for him to go north, but the whole reason why he left in the first place to experience life as a crusader. He had to make a decision quickly, before the Teutonic knights left.

"If I come with you, will I be knighted?" he asked.

"You are already a knight," replied Maurits.

"I know, but I mean knighted as a Teutonic Knight."

"Why would you want that?"

"I come from a long line of crusaders. I wish to join them."

"Manfred, you are not your father."

"So? My father is a coward now. I wish to be a Teutonic Knight. Will I be knighted?"

"Manfred," Maurits said. Then he paused. He reflected upon his adventures with Manfred, and what he knew of the boy. "Manfred, if I knight you, you will be obliged to return to Marienburg with us."

"I understand," Manfred replied. He turned to his comrades. "But I charge no debt to you. You are free men, free to lead Franz back to Göttingen."

"Manfred," said Friedrich. "I will stay with you to the end. One of the pillars of chivalry is loyalty, and that is one thing I can adhere to." Friedrich turned to Maurits. "If Manfred is knighted, I wish to be too," he said.

"I'll come too," said Roland. "I still haven't met my match." Maurits observed the three young knights.

"You have all proven yourselves more than worthy. So, I ask you this. Kneel before me, all three of you." The three knights complied. As Ernst and Helmuth were walking, they saw the three kneeling before Maurits. They quickly ran and knelt too, knowing exactly what was going on. "Ah, I see we have some more recruits," said Maurits with a chuckle. He trusted the men to obey the laws of the order. He heard their stories and knew they had nowhere to go. He understood their dedication. "Please, repeat after me: I do profess and promise obedience to God and the Blessed Virgin Mary and to you, Brother Master of the Teutonic Order, and to your successors, according to the Rules and Regulations of the Order. And I will be obedient to you, and to your successors, even unto death." All five of the knights said the oath. With his sword, Maurits tapped all five upon their shoulders. Then, he raised the blade into the air. "Aid!" he cried. The group followed. "Defend!" he cried, and the group followed. "Heal!" he cried. All five repeated those words. Once the ceremony was complete, Maurits sheathed his sword. He looked at the five men and said: "Rise Brother Knights." He whispered something in secret to Renault who ran to their tent and retrieved a box. "In here, I have five mantles, one for each of you. Wear it at all times, in life and battle. Protect it with your sword and shield as you would defend the faith."

"Yes, Marshal," replied the knights. One by one, he bestowed the pristine white mantles upon the five men. On the left shoulder was a black cross.

"Thank you, Marshal," said Manfred.

"No, thank you. You and your men have brought me here. Without your help we could not have made it," replied Maurits. "Now, release your mercenaries, for Prussia lies ahead." Manfred agreed. He was overwhelmed with joy. He had done it. He finally became a crusader.

If only Wilhelm was there to see it.

Manfred stood up on a log.

"Friends. You have served me and my comrades well. Swiss pikemen, I thank you for saving my life at the tavern. Leon, you will always be remembered. I give my condolences for your loss once more. The only one of them I knew personally was Wolfe. He was nothing but a good and honourable man. Franz, I give you a choice. You may come with us and lead our retinue, but I give you an equal opportunity to return to Plesse. Choose wisely, for colder roads lie ahead. I thank you all for joining us on this journey. I wish you all profitable futures. Thanks be to all of you. I send you off now with pain, for this release seems premature, yet our escort for the future has been here the whole time. Goodbye friends, farewell, and Godspeed!" Manfred cried out. He stepped down from the log and returned to his tent where he began to pack his belongings. Franz came to him.

"Sir, I have made a decision with my men," he said.

"Go on dear friend, speak your mind," replied Manfred.

"Please do not forget that this journey has been arduous and treacherous, and we are all lucky to have made it this far."

"I understand. I do not think any less of you."

"I give my thanks, sir. My men and I have families, families who need us."

"Yes, I too know the pain of separation. I wish Maria was with me here, now."

"Then why not return with us?"

"I have to first make a name for myself. Would you be so kind as to do me a favor?"

"Yes, lord. Anything."

"When you return, can you send for Maria?"

"Of course, what would you have me say?"

"Tell her that I love her. Tell her that she is the best woman a man could ever know. Tell her I miss her. That I have every night. And... tell her that I will be gone for a long time. I am a crusader now. Tell her I will return once the battles are won, and once the heathens are conquered. Tell her that I will fight until I can no longer. And please, tell her that I will return with the most badass battle wounds," Manfred said with a chuckle. A single tear formed in his eye. Perhaps it was the cold, perhaps it was the pain of the burns, but Manfred knew that it was his last ounce of humanity. He was a warrior, and a warrior was all he was. He finally realized that nothing lay in store for him back in Adelebsen. He had grown akin to the road in a demented, sadistic way. He was a prisoner of his own passion. He craved glory, and now that he was on the brink of it, he wouldn't stop until he had it.

He finally understood what it was like to be the toy soldier.

"I will be sure to tell her all of those things, Lord. I will have them written immediately."

"Thank you, Franz," said Manfred. He gave a salute. Franz gave one as well.

"Godspeed, Manfred," he said. He left the tent and returned to his men. Manfred finished packing his belongings and followed Maurits to the main square in Gryfino. As he crossed the bridge, he looked into the water. There, he swore that he could see Maria's face, smiling at him. The tear still lingered.

CHAPTER 36. DANZIG

In the main square, the army assembled into ranks. There were spearmen, voulgiers, crossbowmen, mounted sergeants, allied men at arms, peasant levies, Swedish longbowmen, and of course, ranks upon ranks of Teutonic Knights. The army was large, two hundred men. All of the knights wore the same uniform as Maurits, without the peacock plume. The soldiers were mixed. Some units dressed in grey and carried a "T" shape on their surcoats. Others had the coats of arms of allied lords. Together, they formed a powerful sight. Manfred and his knights followed Maurits to the front of the force. Upon the stockade, where the gallows usually hung, Augustus and his squire put on their own armour. Augustus too was dressed like Maurits, feathers and all. He stepped forwards to present to the crowd.

"Catholic men of Germany. Men of Christ. Today, we finally return to Prussia, to defend our brothers against the Polish scourge. With us, we have Sir. Maurits, the Summus Marescalcus of the Dutch Chapter, Grossgebietiger of Military Affairs for the Order, and Marshal of the Teutonic Order. Cheer men. Gott Mitt Uns!" he cried out. The crowd chanted the same words back to him. Like a zealous horde, they marched out of the city. They sang songs such as "Palästinalied." Maurits and Renault conversed with the two men, and Manfred and his four knights rode in unison with the allied cavalry. They were a mix of sergeants and knights, but they seemed to be a formidable force. Together, Manfred and his men conversed. The group rode to Danzig. It was a Prussian-owned city, one of the largest in the North. The road was long and arduous. The settlements they passed were small and sparse. Through wood and field, they rode. Occasionally, they received messengers from Prussia or from allied kingdoms such as Pomerania and Livonia. As they headed north, the cold seemed to simplify, despite the coming of spring. Every morning the group prayed, every evening they prayed, and before and after every meal they prayed.

The army marched all the way from Gryfino to Danzig within a week. The city lay on the Martwa Wisla river, a complex series of currents that created a large irrigated region. Around the city, there was plenty of farmland, most of which cultivated wheat and barley. Finally, the group reached the city wall.

"Halt!" Maurits called out. The unit stopped. Manfred and his men waited patiently for further instructions. This was the first City that they would stay in since Gryfino and the second that they had seen in days. The first they had seen the day before. Gdynia it was called. It was a port town, and it was nowhere near large enough to support such a large army. Finally, Maurits returned from the gates. The portcullis was raised, and trumpets blaring, the army entered the city. The group marched through the streets until they reached a small fort within the city. From the walls of the fort hung long banners, each with two white crosses, and a golden crown upon a red field. Besides those were other banners of the Teutonic Order, with a black cross on a white field. The army entered. The fortress sat upon the river. In the back, there was a tall keep made of wood and stone, and from the keep protruded a small room with a pulley system to unload ships. All cargo went through the fort. The army settled in the main courtyard before being instructed by the unit to go to separate rooms. Maurits came to Manfred.

"Maurits, this is a beautiful city."

"I'm glad you enjoy it. Tell me, I have no retinue of my own. Would you men be willing to join me?"

"Of course," Manfred replied.

"Good. Then, come with me, I will show you to your rooms," Maurits said. The knights dismounted and handed their horses off to a few page boys. Then, they followed Maurits up the spiralling stairs that led to the walls. Once they were upon the walls, they looked out. They could see the entire city and beyond. The landscape was flat until it reached a border of woods. In the distance, they could see a large, red castle. "Do you see that castle?"

"Yes, what is it?" asked Manfred.

"That is Castle Marienburg, the jewel of Marienburg, the capital of Prussia and the North. That is where we will venture off to tomorrow. The rest will stay here, for I hear the castle is already overloaded with men."

"Wow, it looks amazing!" exclaimed Roland.

"Tell me, Maurits. Why is the castle red? Why is it not white like our castle back home?" asked Friedrich.

"That is because it is constructed with bricks. We decided not to whitewash it as it is a symbol. The red colour comes from the clay, native only to this region. So, we decided to show it off. This is our home, and we are proud of it," said Maurits patriotically. The six knights and Renault walked down the walls to a guarded hallway. In the hallway, there were rooms on either side, and Maurits assigned one per man. Manfred walked into his with his belongings. It was small but gorgeous. The windows were covered in stained glass, and the walls were painted with beautiful murals. After a long week of marching, Manfred went to sleep.

CHAPTER 37. THE RED CASTLE

Manfred woke up with a startle. Outside, battle horns blared. He heard shouts of men in combat and the clanking of steel against steel. Manfred rushed to his sword and shield and burst out of his room in his nightgown with a holler, ready to face any invaders. But, to his surprise, there were no foes to be seen. In the courtyard, knights fought with full contact, shoving each other into the wooden rails that surrounded the arena. Most of the fighters were crusaders, some were allies. The mane with the trumpet called out.

"Wake up all! Today is yet another bright and cold day here in Danzig. Breakfast will be served in the meeting hall as our dining room is still under renovation," the man said. The guests and soldiers slowly went down for breakfast in their own time. Manfred waited for Friedrich and Roland, and the three of them went together in their casual attire. No aketon, no coif. Only the luxurious and colourful clothing that Manfred was once used to. The three made their way downstairs. Their stomachs rumbled. As they entered the hall, they were behooved by the glorious plethora of food items. From boar to quail eggs, they had it all. After two full weeks of travel, breakfast was welcome. Their tasteless rations were nothing in comparison to the magnitude of delicious food that they beheld. They ate around a large round table. The room was a conference room, where delegates were to stay if they were to visit Danzig or Marienburg. At the table, many delegates sat. There was a group from Sweden, some from various German states, there was a group from Denmark, from Milan, Florence, and even a group from Muscovy. They all sat and ate, conversing in German and Latin, and enjoying the delicious feast. Finally, when most had finished, a man entered the room. He was a stocky man, with a curled moustache and a bright red and gold feathered cap. Around his shoulders was a mantle with the black cross of the order. The man spoke with a Thuringian accent.

"Greetings all, and welcome to the great city of Danzig. Many of you have travelled far, coming from lands to our North, our South, our West, and even the near East. I thank all of you for coming. For those of you who will be joining our crusade, there will be a caravan leaving for Marienburg in one hour. For our honourable delegations, we will be travelling there as well, but we have hired stagecoaches to bring us there. I hope you all enjoyed your stay, but do not despair, for our new destination, Castle Marienburg, will exceed your expectations. My name is Lord Heinrich von Plauen, and I am one of the Hochmeister's many commanders. I am personally charged with protecting the lands surrounding Marienburg. If you have any questions, feel free to ask. Do not rush your meals, we won't leave anybody behind," he said cheekily. Heinrich left the room.

Later that day, the caravan reached Marienburg. The tall red castle was magnificent in scale and architecture. It was the largest castle any of the five knights had ever seen. On the walls lay banners carrying the black cross as well as the Hochmeister's cross. Over arches and doorways, there were shields upon which a heraldic of a red castle was displayed, for it was the coat of arms of Marienburg. On one side of the castle was the Nogat river, a calm and tranquil body of water. Two other sides were also surrounded by a shallow lake, creating a dreadful marsh-like area. The caravan followed Maurits through a gatehouse and across a long bridge that spanned the full length of the river. The gatehouse was armed with two portcullises and was pelted in murder holes through which bolts and spears could be launched. The caravan eventually made it into the second gate, placing them inside the main courtyard of the complex. Despite the name, this place was no mere castle, it was a colossal fortress. A citadel for military purposes only, and a haven for the order. It was clear that this edifice was the center of operations for the order in all of Livonia. What the building lacked in splendour it made up for in sheer efficiency. It seemed simply impenetrable. Maurits stopped the caravan there as the soldiers all mustered into the yard. Maurits began giving units directions in regards to their lodgings. Many units were sent outside of the castle to settle into military camps.

While they waited, the five knights climbed the stairs and strolled along the walls, taking in the view. As they turned the corner, the true face of the order was revealed. A sea of tens of thousands of military tents infested the farmlands. A massive army was assembled, and for what? What was being planned which required such a large sum of men? Surely the Poles couldn't match such a force? Manfred decided to inquire. He returned to the yard where most of the units had been directed away. He approached Maurits.

"Maurits," he said. "Maurits, I have seen the army assembled in the fields. It is vast, so vast. Too vast," he said with a chill in his voice. "I thought that you and your knights fought to defend your lands, not conquer your way to Karakorum."

"Manfred," Maurits replied, "There is no scheme at hand. There is information that I have been informed of which you are not yet aware of. You should follow me to the meeting of the high command soon. They will call one once they are aware of my presence."

"They?" asked Manfred.

"The generals of the order. Now that I have arrived, we must plan a conquest," Maurits said. "We will begin our preparations this evening."

"How soon will this campaign be?" asked Manfred.

"It is unknown," replied Maurits. He continued to muster units, and Manfred returned to his men. Later on, after waiting for nearly half an hour, they were called to discuss with the high council. Maurits led his men up the stairs. "When you enter the discussion hall, you mustn't make noise," he said. "You are my retinue. Just, vote for whatever I propose, and remain silent and courteous."

"Of course," replied Manfred. His men all gave signs of approval. Finally, once they reached the fourth floor, they entered into a hallway. At the end were two large doors. Two brother knights opened the doors and let the group in. As the door creaked open, all heads were turned to the group. The room was a large, ovular amphitheatre, which sat nearly thirty men. Manfred and his group sat together in the back, and Maurits descended to a seat that was saved by his comrades. The room was decorated with murals of angels and biblical stories. There was also much silver and golden embroidery. In the center, above the Hochmeister's throne, was an old bronze pagan plate with a cross hammered into it. It was a symbol of Prussian dominance in the region, a testament to the Order's bloody past. Below the plate, in a large wooden throne, sat the Hochmeister, Grand Master Ulrich von Jungingen, facing all of his retainers. He sat like a king, like an emperor, with splendour and might. After sorting out his documents, Maurits approached the audience. Master Ulrich arose from his seat and joined the audience to see the proposal.

"Greetings all," said Maurits. "For those of you who I am not yet acquainted with, my name is Sir. Maurits van Melle. I have travelled from Ghent in the Netherlands, but I come with a plan ready. I believe that we have the forces to rival the

179

enemy's."

"Nonsense!" some of the officials cried out. Others hushed them, trying to save Maurits.

"As I was saying, we have the manpower. We need to strike hard and fast before the Poles can retaliate. We should campaign into their land. Conduct chevauchee raids on their towns and provoke them into a premature battle. Without the help of their Lithuanian comrades, they will be unable to respond. We have an army now; we should use it!" Maurits cried. Then, another man stepped forwards.

"Although you all already know me, my name is Sir. Werner von Tettingen. Unlike our Dutch friend here, I have a plan that will work. We need to wait for more men to arrive. Those Lithuanians will assemble their armies faster than we expect. I believe that we should instead bait them into attacking our lands. We can burn our crops, starve out their campaign, and make a stand here at Marienburg," the man declared.

"That will not work," replied Maurits. "Our land is too small to go about burning crops. We will need those crops if we are to last a siege. We will have no time to prepare. Harvesting season is long past. If we follow your plan, we will all starve."

"Well, that's better than wasting all of our men for your stupid campaign," replied Werner. The two men looked at each other with disdain.

"Settle down," announced Master Ulrich. Both men sat down, and Master Ulrich took the stage. "We will vote on the matter. If you wish for Maurits' plan, raise your hand. If you do not, keep your hand down. Now, all in favour of a lightning campaign, raise your hand." Manfred and his men raised their hands, as did a few more officials, but it clearly wasn't enough. "Well then, that settles it. We will all live here until Autumn, it seems," Master Ulrich said. He dismissed the congress, and the officials all left and piled into the hall. Maurits, angrily and silently, showed the group to their rooms. They were all near each other. The men settled in their cells aimlessly and restlessly. Comfort was now a stranger to them, even after just two weeks of hardship.

Later that day, Maurits called them to his side once more. They were called to the war room - a top-secret cell behind the Hochmeister's office where he and his generals planned for war. Manfred and his men were to wait in the office with the other guards while the officials conversed. Maurits entered the cell. There, around a large wooden table, were another four men. First, was, of course, the Hochmeister. Next, at his side, was Sir. Werner von Tettingen. To his right was Sir. Albrecht Unterwalder, Komtur of Elbing. On the opposite side of the table was Sir. Heinrich von Plauen. Maurits joined the ensemble to discuss the war.

"Greetings, Maurits. I know that this is not the plan you would have wanted, but I believe that this is what must be done. We must keep the order in one piece before we attempt to expend all of its military might on one foe. What if we were to fail? What then? I hope you can understand," said Master Ulrich.

"Yes, Grand Master," Maurits replied. "But I must confess, the last time I saw you I didn't think you were soft enough to fall for the rhetoric of this diplomat!" Maurits said firmly, pointing to Sir. Werner.

"Now, now. Fear not, Maurits. I know that we have our differences, but in this room, we do not look for what is best for ourselves, but what is best for the brotherhood. In this case, it is defending our towns and cities from raids," said Master Ulrich.

"Yes, indeed," said Albrecht. "Elbing is under great threat. I have reached out to our brothers in the Livonian Order, and they have agreed to send troops to my aid. However, lord, I do wish for you to command them to send more. They need no defence. We know that it is the Poles that we should fear, not the Lithuanians, and certainly not the Russians. You only have authority over their branch of the order."

"I see your predicament; however, I believe that they should keep their troops there. We can make do with what we have. We should fear the Lithuanians with guile and suspicion for I fear that they may launch an attack on their front as well, perhaps even their main campaign. Furthermore, Novgorod and other Rus Principalities could easily join their anti-crusader pact. I think that our men are fine where they are," replied Master Ulrich. "Now, moving on to diplomacy. Werner, have you sent an ultimatum?"

"Yes, lord. I asked for all Polish land up to the Province of Warsaw. If they deny our agreement, which they will, we have a perfect casus belli in the eyes of the lord, do we not?"

"Yes, indeed. You are cunning, friend. I am glad that you are on our side and not theirs," Master Ulrich said. Then, he turned his attention to Maurits. "Maurits, I know that you disapprove of this plan, but we wish to use your knowledge of war to its fullest potential."

"Yes, lord. I will follow you into battle."

"No, no, not just that. How may we make this campaign completely unbearable for those Poles?"

"As Werner said, we could use scorched earth tactics. But that won't be enough to dishearten them - the distance is too short. We must also harass them on the road. We should cut off their baggage trains with speed. It is known in the west as 'hit and run' tactics."

"Ah, yes, I knew that you would come in handy. I give this plan my full support. You may appoint any commanders you wish."

"Sir, I would prefer to conduct these raids myself."

"Maurits, we cannot risk you. Despite your efforts, we all know that a large battle will come, and when it does, we mustn't let them reach Marienburg. That is why we need you. You must guide us on the battlefield, show us how to defeat their Tatar mercenaries."

"They take savages as mercenaries?"

"Yes, and worse. I hear that they have Turks and Persians, and even Africans."

"I don't believe these tales. They may have Georgians and such, but men from the east? Only a fool would believe such a thing."

"You are right, Maurits," said Heinrich. "I know that you don't fear this enemy, but we mustn't underestimate him. We will always be outnumbered by him, so why not use the fortifications of Marienburg? Why not hold a siege?"

"Our rations wouldn't last," said Maurits.

"They would, we could import from Germany and the Kalmar Union, as long as we maintain our roads to Danzig."

"And how would we do that?"

"We would have to begin building earthworks to connect the two fortifications now," replied Heinrich. Maurits was skeptical.

"I don't believe that we would have the time. We would have to sally out and meet them in the field. I know that you love sieges, Heinrich, but we all have experience. You do not, and I don't believe there to be any substitute. One day, if you lead an army of your own, I hope that you learn from our victory over these Poles," said Maurits harshly.

"Alright, then. Maurits, you will have to appoint your commander. Everybody, this council is over. Let us leave in secrecy," he said. The five men exited the cell and entered the room. Then, Maurits had an idea. He knew just the man, just the puppet to do his bidding on the battlefield. A good commander, and an even better man at following orders: Manfred.

"Manfred," he said. "Would you like to be the new commander of the first light horse brigade?"

"Of course!" Manfred replied with glee. Never before had he been in control of so many men. An entire brigade! That was nearly four thousand men - and all were apparently mounted, sergeants. Maurits returned the men to their rooms, and he told Manfred his plans in private. For the next three months, Manfred would have to train and learn the ways of large-scale mounted combat. But he was a good learner, and within weeks he was ready for the battlefield. Manfred became used to warding off raids and sacking small border villages. He was an excellent commander, and a fearless one. The banner of Göttingen, a white castle on a field of blue, which lay atop a golden lion on a field of red, was waved over the heads of the merciless cavalrymen. Manfred was officially a commander, a field commander, and for months, he patiently awaited this large battle of which the Generals spoke.

CHAPTER 38. THE RAID

For two long months, Manfred and his men raided and plundered, and rushed to the aid of the occasional village. Maurits was dead. He was slain not by Poles or brigands, but by a tumour that festered in his abdomen. The doctor had said that he died of natural causes, but there was nothing less natural than a growth of such magnitude; a golf ball. It blocked his waste from exiting his body, leading to two full weeks of excruciating pain and sickness. In the last few days, he refused to eat or drink anything. That was his end. Starvation. Not a Pole or a brigand, a tumour that forced him to starve himself to death. Manfred mourned his death, but it helped numb the stinging pain of Wilhelm's passing. He only longed to see Ulrich return or to return himself to Maria.

Every day, Manfred woke up, ate a communal breakfast in the grand great hall, and then rode off with his men. They followed missions based on the order's espionage and made sure to leave no survivors. Manfred was proud of his work, as were his men. This day, on the sixth of July, the scouts brought back some different reports. An informant, dressed like a common peasant, dashed up the staircase of the castle. He brushed past the guards and rushed to a large wooden set of doors. In his office, the Grand Master Ulrich was stamping seals of diplomatic letters, urging nobles to join the cause. All of a sudden, he heard a frantic knock on his office door. Startled, he missed the wax.

"Who is it?" he called.

"It's a scout," replied one of the guards.

"Ah, yes. Let him in," he said. The guards opened the door, and the informant rushed inside. Barely catching his breath, he held his knees. Then, he gave his message.

Manfred ate his breakfast ferociously. It was delicious, and he was hungry. He and his men conversed with glee, discussing previous raids and defences, and their victories and spoils of war. Friedrich showed off his new silver cross necklace. All was well until a page boy ran to Manfred's side. He whispered something in his ear.

"What is it?" asked Roland.

"The boy says that the invasion has begun. We are to report to Master Ulrich immediately; we must prepare at once," replied Manfred. All five knights stopped their meals abruptly and hastily made their way to the office. Manfred led them across the walls. Where icicles once hung, were dry, hot machicolations. The warm summer air breezed in through the ramparts, and a calm breeze rushed into Manfred's face. In his belt was a letter tucked. It was Maria's response to Manfred's message. He held it dearly. He knew that he had to return to Adelebsen someday, but only once the war was over. It was time to put on a brave face, as preparations had to begin. He opened the office door with force.

"Ah, Sir. Manfred," Master Ulrich said.

"Hochmeister. How goes it?" Manfred replied.

"You've heard the news have you not? This is no time for pleasantries. Our scouts have reported astronomical numbers, nearly forty thousand will soon cross the border. We need you to begin raiding their baggage train. We must choke them, weaken them, and then destroy them on the battlefield. Understand?" Master Ulrich asked. Manfred nodded. He understood exactly what to do, and he also understood the gravity of his mission. This was no petty raid. His next actions would discern the outcome of the war. He marched out with pride, wearing a poker face of masterful construction. His men were eager. He was not.

He wished to return to Maria in one piece.

In front of the castle, a small town had formed among the military tents. Lowlives and local women had come to live there and interact with the boisterous soldiers. There, the army amassed. Manfred summoned all four thousand of his riders. They formed into a large square formation on the large grassy meadow between the two rivers. Manfred rode along the front line and said his speech.

"Men of Christendom. Good fighting riders of Christendom. I call to you now in your Lord's hour of need, for today, we fight the scourge of God; we fight those who oppose his divine hand. Let us lay waste to these infidels and destroy their baggage. We will claim their belongings, steal their horses, rape their women, slay their porters, and fester diseases within their food and water. What say you men?" he cried. The horsemen cheered with barbarous hate. Their zealous eyes displayed the sheer disgust towards their enemy. Like savages, they chanted as they rode off to war. Gradually, the square disintegrates into a thin line, as the army rode through the Tannenberg forest to intercept a supply chain.

After one and a half days of riding, Friedrich returned with his team of scouts.

"We saw them," he said. "They have reached the Vistula river. They mustn't have a map, because they crossed at the first bridge they found, and they are now heading west to Znin."

"Excellent," replied Manfred. "How many are there?"

"It is a large caravan. They have few guards, and all are on foot. They carry horses with them as well."

"Why would they do that?"

"Extras I suppose. They also take with them large

stagecoaches, undoubtedly filled with supplies."

"Of course, what else could be in there? Good work Friedrich, we must now make haste to Starogard, for we must intercept them before they reach a settlement. If they are heading towards a town, they must have men with them," Manfred said analytically.

"I suppose so," replied Friedrich. "But, then again, they seem to be lost. It would make no sense for their caravan to march to Znin, while their army marches in another direction."

"Anyways, we need not fret. Let us ride with haste," replied Manfred. He gave the order, and the army swiftly rode across the river westwards. They followed a road down to Starogard, and soon, they saw the caravan. It was in the late afternoon. Quickly, the army followed them to a clearing, where then they emerged from the forest. "Form up!" Manfred called. His subcommanders had their men form into fighting positions. Together, the group formed a giant wedge. In the distance, on the horizon, Znin was in sight. The soldiers of the caravan halted and quickly tried to make preparations. "Charge!" Manfred called out. The light horsemen advanced. They started with a trot. Then, as they gained speed, they shifted into a canter. Finally, they rode at full speed towards their targets. Like a pack of wolves, they prowled the field, and finally, they converged on their enemy. It was no battle.

It was a slaughter.

Manfred and his men made quick work of the caravan. Undoubtedly, there were many more in the region, all attempting to carry rations and supplies to the large army that had just trespassed into Prussian land. By sundown, the raid was over. Manfred and his men plundered the caravans, taking the best horses and cutting the rest loose. The army shared the wealth of the stagecoaches. Oddly enough, there weren't many goods inside of the wagons aside from food. So, they ate, and they set up camp, for they had travelled far.

188

There was no way that they could safely return to Marienburg under cover of darkness. So, they set up camp on the sight of the fallen. They gave the dead burials after looting them, and a Teutonic priest came to say a quick prayer for the fallen on both sides. The night dawned with speed, and the men were soon fast asleep after yet another victorious raid.

CHAPTER 39. NEVSKIY

That night, Manfred couldn't sleep. He felt the stinging urge to go to the bathroom, so he did. He stepped outside, and by the hearth, he took a leak. He looked around and saw his scouts carrying torches. Manfred opened a bottle of wine and began to drink. Distant canine howls pierced the ringing silence of the night. For minutes, Manfred just sat and pondered and drank until he could drink no more. He looked around once more before returning to his tent. Again, he saw naught but the torchlight of his scouts; however, he could also make out a figure in the woods. Manfred grabbed his sword from his lodging and soon approached the figure more closely. He could see its eyes in the pale moonlight, and soon, he could make out the figure of a little girl. Her silver hair was unbrushed, and she looked wildly at Manfred as if she was looking for him, as opposed to vice versa. Manfred approached, but she quickly scampered off into the woods. He looked around, but his scouts were too far away. Manfred quickly followed her tipsily. His vision was somewhat blurry, but he felt he mostly kept his wits about him.

"Little girl, little girl, why do you run? I have no will to harm you. You are safe," he shouted. She laughed and stopped.

"I know," she said in an innocent voice. Manfred was taken aback.

"You are quite a queer little girl, aren't you? What is your name?" he asked kindly.

"I am Isolde," she said happily.

"Well, I am Sir. Manfred."

"I know, Manfred," she said. Then, she began running once more. Manfred followed her again, thinking that she was now trying to play a game. The light of the moon and stars illuminated the path before him as he ran, ensuring that he had stable footing at all times. Manfred chased the little girl until he could no longer see her.

"Isolde? Isolde? You shouldn't run off into the night like that. If you're unlucky, beastly monsters may come for you! It is said that Odin' Army, a wild cavalcade of ghastly hunters, reave the Northern stretches of Christendom. You wouldn't want them to snatch you up, would you?" he called out. He was now lost. He looked around for a little while until he saw something. His face grew pale with fear. Illuminated, freshly burned into a tree, was a flaming pentagram. Manfred drew his sword. He no longer felt like playing games. "Isolde? Come out now! Stop playing games," he shouted in a commanding tone. Instead, a bush opened for him like a door, calling to him, telling him to enter into the thicket.

He looked around and saw nobody but the dark and jagged trees. He walked inside, and behind him, the branches shut once more. He found himself stranded in total darkness. "What be this witchcraft?" he asked with fear. A small candle illuminated. Around him now he saw the inside of the thicket. The branches knitted together to form walls. In front of him was an old lady. "Are you a witch?" Manfred asked. She was dark-skinned with black hair, and she wore the garb of the Roma peoples. The lady was a gypsy. Manfred had heard of Roma. He was taught a few unflattering tales of their kind in Bohemia and Hungary. He never expected to see one. In fact, he hadn't seen a dark-skinned person before in his life. He grew up with stories of their pagan rituals and thievery. Never had he expected to find one, much less as a witch. Isolde opened her eyes to look at Manfred, but both of her eyes were blind.

"I can see you," she said.

"How?" Manfred asked.

"I sense your presence, Manfred," she said.

"How do you know my name?" he asked.

"I already told you that I know," she replied. Manfred paused to think for a moment.

"You are Isolde?" he asked in shock.

"I am," the lady replied. Manfred was frozen with fear.

"You have undertaken quite the journey," the woman said.

"How do you know my name?" replied Manfred.

"I know you, Manfred. I know your wife and your friends. In fact, I spoke with Wilhelm just the other day," she said.

"What are you, some kind of soothsayer?" Manfred asked.

"Not yet," she replied. Manfred fell silent, as did she. She then reached into a bag that lay beside her, and she pulled out a book.

"How do you expect to read? You are blind," Manfred said.

"I may be, but you are not," she replied. She handed Manfred the book. Manfred examined it. It was a thick leather book, bound with intricate lacing, and lined with brass framing. He looked at the cover. In large golden letters, it read: *The Saga of the Shepherd Knight.* Manfred was intrigued. Beneath the title was the coat of arms of Göttingen. Manfred was shaken. Slowly he turned the first page. It read:

Manfred, the Shepherd Knight,
Dread of dwarfs, slayer of witches, feller of axes, ghost of
*   the east,*
and butcher of tyrants,
Turned to the first page of the book.
He read of his future, of his shortcomings and failures
Of his triumphant victories,
Of which there were none.

He read of his death,
At the hands of a bloodied blade,
Which suited him best,
A bread knife,
In the arms of the man who had harmed him most.

The script ended. All other pages were blank. When Manfred finished reading, the book burst into flames, but he remembered the words well in his head. Then, Isolde began to cackle.

"What is this black magic?" Manfred asked. He held his blade to the witch.

"I am no magician; I simply know what the spirits allow me to," she said. Manfred loosened his grip and then brought his sword back down to his hips.

"Am I to believe this prophecy? That a mighty witch slayer is to fall by a bread knife?"

"You may believe what you wish," replied the witch.

"You said you spoke to Wilhelm."

"Yes."

"How is he?"

"I mustn't say."

"Why?" Manfred asked angrily.

"I mustn't say," Isolde responded. Manfred held his blade to the witch's throat once more and pressed just hard enough for a single drop of blood to trickle out and slide down the fuller.

"You will tell me, wretch," he said.

"Wilhelm has given you strength, I see," she replied.

"What do you mean?"

"As you entered you shook. Now you stand as a true man."

"Well, to quote your prophecy, I am the Shepherd Knight, and therefore Wilhelm was one of my sheep. Shepherds don't like to lose their sheep, do they?"

"He was more than just a sheep, wasn't he?" asked the witch.

"He was none of your concern. Now, tell me what you know of him or I swear that by God I will run this blade through your wrinkled old neck."

"I see you have taken akin to the prophecy," the woman said. Manfred grew red with rage. He had had enough. He launched the blade into the neck of the woman. Unlike a magician of any kind, she just sat there, motionless, blood streaming from the gaping hole in her esophagus. Cold and lifeless she sat, staring at the ceiling. Then, at that moment, Manfred heard a thudding outside. He looked for an exit but there was none. The thudding grew louder. He heard yells in an indiscernible language. Finally, axes broke through the foliage, releasing into the enclave the bright daylight. In Russian, the rescuers conversed with each other. They hacked at the wall and finally made a hole large enough for Manfred to escape. Finally, once he was out, and was about to walk freely, he heard the knocking of arrows. He looked around, and four men armed with composite bows had their arrowhead pointed at him. They were druzhina, armoured from head to toe in tegulated plate and lamellar armour. Their faces were covered by veils of chainmail that hung from their Norse and Byzantine-inspired helmets. Their teardrop shields bore sigils of Jesus, Mary, and highly ordained crosses. They were colourful, wearing all sorts of reds, greens, blues, and yellows. In total there were about twenty warriors, all with horses; freed horses from the raid.

"Who are you?" Manfred asked with confidence. A druzhina with a steel mask walked in front of Manfred. The archers lowered their bows. Their arms were tired from holding the position for so long, and with steel vambraces on. With a long cavalry sabre, the druzhina forced Manfred onto his knees.

"Your worst nightmare," it replied in a terse, low, and sickly voice.

"Why are you capturing me?" Manfred asked.

"We are not," the druzhina replied. "We wish to work for you against the Lithuanians." The druzhina now spoke in a slightly higher voice with a strong Russian accent.

"Where are you from?" Manfred asked.

"Narva," the druzhina replied. Manfred, no longer feeling threatened, rose to his feet.

"Would you show me your face?" he asked politely.

"No."

"If we are to collaborate, I need to know what you look like."

"I need you to guarantee that we may work for you first," the druzhina said.

"Sure, I suppose. I see why not. I would just have to register you into the Teutonic payroll and..."

"Niet! We will not be catalogued by crusaders. We will go undocumented, and paid out of your pocket. Understand?"

"Yes," replied Manfred in fear of losing his head.

"Now, what is most dear to you that is on you?"

"Why?"

"Just answer the question," the druzhina said. Manfred thought for a moment. He didn't know whether or not to tell the truth. However, he decided that he shouldn't risk it, so he chose the most convincing option: the true one.

"It is this letter," he replied, taking the letter from Maria out from his belt. The druzhina took it.

"Why is it important?"

"It is personal."

"Good enough. It is to ensure that you do not have us all killed when we follow you back to your men, German."

"You know that they will be looking for me by now, right?"

"That's why you will pretend to love us, or else we burn the letter. Understand?"

"Yes," replied Manfred. Then, as the druzhina gave the letter to one of his colleagues, he did something surprising. He lifted his helmet instead revealing the face of a woman. She

195

had long red hair - typical of the Rus.

"I am Boyar Katerina Nevskiy, a distant granddaughter of the Great Nevsky."

"The Great Nevsky?" Manfred asked in a confused voice.

"Yes, Alexandr Nevsky."

"Ah, I have heard tales of the demon. No wonder you wished to hide your identity."

"So, you know of his genius victories against the Germans and Swedes?"

"Genius? You must mean cowardly. That man was a villain in all regards."

"Look, there is no time for this. We should go to your camp," she said. Manfred complied. The druzhina gave him a horse, and he led Boyar Katerina to the camp where various search parties had been scrambled. The men were joyous to see Manfred's arrival. They were also joyous to see the addition of some more light cavalry. The group began to pack promptly, and by the end of the day, they had reached Marienburg. Manfred shared the prophecy and the story of the girl and the bush to no one. Instead, he told a story of a pack of hungry wolves and the noble druzhina that saved him from them.

CHAPTER 40. GREEN WOOD

On the morning of July 10th, 1410, the German army marched out from Marienburg. After a day's march, the army set up camp at Allenstein, where they met up with an additional force of seven thousand men at arms of the Livonian Order. In total, the army was constructed of roughly thirty thousand. They first encountered the Polish army at the Vistula river. Both sides stared each other down, neither side wanting to cross the river with such vulnerability. Instead, the Polish army headed east to overcome the river. The German army paralleled their motion. They expected to face a force of forty thousand. In reality, with their Bohemian, Ruthenian, Moldavian, and Tartar mercenaries, the Polish-Lithuanian forces amounted to nearly fifty thousand. The next day, the army set out again. They sang Christian battle songs such as Palastinalied and others. With high morale, they marched, for they knew that despite the enemy's numbers, the Germans had more knights, more cannons, and the favour of God. Manfred and his outriders acted as scouts, surveying the land for enemies and plundering enemy supply lines. Occasionally small skirmishes broke out between the two forces, but they resulted in relatively low casualties. Both armies knew that the enemy was near. By the fifteenth, the armies had sufficiently scouted each other out to know the exact forces that they were facing. It was on the field between Grunwald and Tannenberg that the Germans chose to make their stand. Both sides fought for God, both sides fought for the defence of their own land and people, and both sides believed that victory was imminent; however, only one side could march away victorious. The two armies amassed on the field facing each other. While the German army stood atop the hill in broad daylight, surveying their opponents, the Polish-Lithuanian army instead sought refuge under the cover of the forest. For hours they stood. Envoys were sent, but neither side wanted peace. From the top of the incline, the Germans looked down upon their foes. With forested land outlining the confines of the battle, there would be no ambushes. No hidden forces. All cards were on the table.

On the top of the hill, the commanders organized. Manfred was one of many, and they all briefed in private. They had superior artillery, so it was their decision as to when the battle would begin. They had all the time they needed. The generals gathered in the central tent where Master Ulrich had a map of the battlefield drawn. Around the table were Manfred, Master Ulrich, Werner, and Albrecht.

"Alright, men," said Ulrich. "Remember that, today, we fight for God. He is with us, and thus, we mustn't fail him. I have already sent an emissary with two swords to Jogaila to mock him. He won't accept a duel, but I will propose it anyway. Now, in regards to our strategy, we need to come up with a way to use our cavalry to full effect. Our estimates show that we have seventeen thousand knights and men at arms, ten thousand pavise infantrymen, one thousand crossbowmen and bombard crew, and of course, Manfred's four thousand rough riders. Any suggestions?"

"I have one," said Werner. "I believe that we should charge them with full force. We should rush them. They have missile superiority, but we can advance under cover of our bombards."

"No," said Albrecht. "Our bombards are too inaccurate. We cannot fire overhead of our own soldiers."

"Besides, our cavalry cannot charge into a forest. That would be suicide," added Manfred.

"Well then, how might we lure them out?" asked Master Ulrich.

"I have a plan," Manfred said with confidence. "We could fire our bombards at them to lure them out. Once they are vulnerable, we could use the hill to propel a heavy charge to demolish their ranks."

"That is a good plan, but we don't have enough knights to span their entire army. We will have to keep our knights at the flanks and focus our infantry on them," said Albrecht.

"Do they not have cavalry to counter ours?" asked Werner.

"No," replied Master Ulrich. "They only use mounted sergeants and skirmishing cavalry, such as their Mongols and Lithuanian mounted crossbows."

"Well then, we can crush their cavalry, surround their infantry from the flanks, and take the day," said Werner. It sounded too good to be true, but he was right. That plan would certainly be enough to break the Poles.

"I agree," said the Hochmeister. "Werner, you can take the left flank. Your knights will be charged with ensuring the safety of our crossbowmen and bombards until the flanks are closed. Albrecht, you must charge their left flank. Your men must push through whatever defence they hold, for we must envelop their center. They have more infantry than we do, and that includes dismounted knights. Finally, Manfred, I want you to aid Werner's knights. Guard his extreme left flank and ensure that our crossbowmen go unscathed. They will be instrumental in pelting down their infantry. I will hold the center and order the advance once you have all broken their cavalry. Do we all agree?"

"Yes, sir," replied the three generals in unison. They all

made their way to their stations. As they looked out over the army, they were all shocked by how many men had amassed upon the field. No commander had seen anything like it before. Manfred and Werner walked together to the bombards. There, upon the left flank of the hill, they awaited the Hochmeister's orders. As they sat atop their steeds, they conversed.

"First field battle?" asked Werner.

"No. Why?"

"You look scared," Werner said. He was right, Manfred was slightly pale.

"I'm not," said Manfred, putting on a brave face.

"Fear not. God is with us. Today we defeat the infidel."

"Everyone says this, but I know the Poles to be Christian."

"What true Christian would fight the army of the Lord? Look, I know you feel fear. I can smell it like a wolf smells blood. But, do you see all of your cavalry here? What would they think if their own commander trembles? Fear not, Manfred. I care not for your sanity, but for our victory today. After today, throw up if you have to. We will have won already."

"Kind words," Manfred said playfully.

"I know. Some call me a poet," Werner replied with a smirk. Both laughed, but both also trembled with the fear of impending doom. Between the leaves of the trees, they saw the glistening steel of their enemies and the red banners of Poland and Lithuanian nobles.

"I fear not for my life, but I fear for my wife, Maria. I must return to her alive," Manfred said.

"I understand. I too have a wife. I fight for her today. If the Poles win, they will kill her and my children."

"Isn't Tettingen far from Prussia?"

"They don't live in Tettingen. They live within the walls of Marienburg. They won't survive a siege. At least, my unborn daughter wouldn't."

"I understand," replied Manfred. He felt for Werner. Werner may not have been the brightest, but Manfred still respected him as a man.

"You see that banner?" asked Werner. Manfred looked across the field. Mounted high upon a shaft was the banner of Topór, the white battle-axe on a red field.

"Yes," replied Manfred.

"That is a Polish banner, but the men below it are Lithuanian. I believe that Duke Jan of Topór is leading the Lithuanian right."

"Is he a good commander?"

"Yes. I have fought him many times. He deserves the honour of leading the right flank. To the Lithuanians, the right flank is usually the vanguard."

"Well then. We will have to be swift," replied Manfred. The two fell silent as they just realized what was to come. The attack would come first from their side. They knew, but didn't want to acknowledge, that they would be the first in danger. So, they said nothing. The army waited for hours. Finally, they saw the Hochmeister's emissary return with both swords. He had a word with Master Ulrich before Master Ulrich called up a priest. The priest came in front of the army, and all bowed to pray. He muttered a prayer that could not be heard all the way on Manfred's flank. Then, the Hochmeister's banner arose over the war tent. The battle was to begin.

"Fire!" Werner called out immediately. At that moment, the fuses were lit. Two gigantic bombards launched a deafening volley upon the unsuspecting Polish-Lithuanian army. Within seconds, the German's heard the horn blast of war. The Polish lines advanced from the trees, revealing a long line of red and silver glistening in the hot summer sun. Manfred and Werner parted ways. As Manfred rode through his ranks, he could smell urine, sweat, and fear.

"Fear not, men. Look to your sides and remember who is beside you, for in the battle, we will not know friend from foe.

Today we ride into heaven!" he shouted.

"Gott Mitt Uns!" the army cried, as they erupted into a violent war. Like a plague, the sounds of the zealous chanting crossed the sodden field. The crossbowmen promptly advanced at Werner's command. They marched towards the Polish lines, ready to pelt the Poles with a storm of bolts. However, the Lithuanians promptly responded with a charge on the right flank, as expected. The banner of Topór flew in the wind like a flying dragon. They rode with speed, far faster than any knight. The crossbowmen ran for their lives to escape the onslaught of horse and rider. Many were shot down by mounted crossbowmen. By the time that Werner and his knights responded with a counter charge, it was too late. The crossbowmen were decimated, and the remainder fled the field.

"Defend the bombards!" Werner shouted as he led his men into battle. Manfred followed the charge on the left flank, aiming to envelop the oncoming cavalry. Both sides thundered towards each other. The Lithuanian crossbow cavalry cleared the way, revealing their lines upon lines of mounted sergeants. The ground shook. Manfred led his men into battle with eager zeal. As the sides converged, they saw the whites in each other's eyes. With a voluminous crash, the two sides smashed into each other. Many horses in the front-rank broke bones from the impact, especially on Werner's side under the heavy weight of the knight. Werner's knights rode through with ease, slaughtering sergeants and Tatars left and right. Manfred's unit, on the other hand, was stalled. Manfred ran his lance through the first man. To his right, Roland did the same. Then, Manfred drew his battle-axe and hacked and slashed his way through the front lines. The battlefield devolved into chaos. Horse and rider flew in every direction. Werner's knights stormed through the enemy and rode straight to the line of infantry, leaving Manfred and his men stranded against the Lithuanians. Manfred saw the bannerman of Topór. He rode to him, axe in hand. As the two met, Manfred sliced. The flagpole was decapitated, as was its bearer. Then, Manfred set his eyes upon Jan Topór himself. Topór was a large man, with a large falchion in hand. His onion top hound skull bascinet was painted in the red and white colours of his house. Manfred rode fearlessly in his direction. As he closed the distance, Topór saw him and countercharged. The two met in the center of the field. Topór swung his falchion with might. As Manfred attempted to block with his axe, the haft of the weapon was cut in half. The axe head tumbled to the floor. Topór swing finally landed on Manfred's bascinet. He had broken the hinge, and Manfred's klappvisor tumbled to the ground as well. It was trampled and caked in the dirt. Manfred's face was now exposed, and it revealed his fearful expression. His head rang like church bells, and he felt queasy. Without hesitation, Manfred drew his arming sword and returned to the fight. He couldn't think; it hurt. He could only remember his training. Topór and Manfred took a second pass at each other. This time, both extended their arms. Topór aimed for Manfred's exposed visage. Manfred, on the other hand, aimed for Topór's horse. It was the Pole's only vulnerable point. As the two converged for the second lime, Manfred stuck his blade deeply into the horse. It skidded and tumbled over into a pile of dead bodies. Topór was launched into the fray of destriers. Manfred, weaponless, dismounted. He picked up a sergeant's lance and held it firmly, casting his heater shield aside. He squared down his opponent. Then, Topór charged at him. Manfred thrust with the lance. Although it didn't pierce Topór, it held him at bay. The two circled for a moment, and then, Topór was struck down by a lance. The bearer of this lance was Roland.

"It's a shame that such a good lance was wasted on such a brute," he exclaimed sarcastically. Then, he rode off with mace in hand to fight off some more Lithuanians. Manfred pounced upon the fallen Topór. He pulled out his rondel dagger and held it to the man's eye slit, but just before he stabbed, Topór lifted his visor.

"Mercy!" he cried. Manfred paused. The two looked each other in the eyes. They could see the humanity in one another. Manfred cast the dagger aside and quickly drew Topór's arming sword. Then, he rose to his feet once again. Topór arose as well, unarmed, with arms raised.

"Retreat!" Manfred ordered. Topór obeyed. He was given a horse by one of his men, and then the Pole ordered a tactical retreat. The Tatars remained, and were slain by Manfred's rough riders. Friedrich dismounted and came to Manfred's side.

"Why did you let him go?" he asked.

"He was not a bad man," Manfred replied.

"He tried to kill you!"

"He was following orders. These people, they only fight to protect their land. So why do we kill them?"

"They are attacking the Christian faith itself. It is not chivalrous," said Friedrich.

"Well, if chivalry is the answer, I believe it to be chivalrous to grant a man mercy when he asks for it," said Manfred. Friedrich paused.

"I suppose so," he said. The two looked at each other and then smiled. They smiled not because they had almost died, but because they still saw some form of humanity left in one another. "Good," Friedrich said. Manfred looked around and re-horsed himself.

"There is still a battle to be won," he said. "Follow me, men; follow me to victory!" he cried. The remnants of his rough riders charged into the center of the field. There, the left flank was held at bay by a unit of Russians. They carried the banners of Smolensk. Without crossbowmen, it seemed impossible for the German's to breakthrough. The right flank was nowhere to be seen. They had been stalled by a countercharge of Polish knights. The Smolensk infantry was now Manfred's prime target. "Charge!" he commanded. He charged with the rough riders that he had left, of which nearly half had perished. Manfred's druzhina branched away from the mob, firing arrows upon the Smolensk infantry. That branch became a large flanking maneuver that split the force into two halves. Manfred was content with this decision as it would result in an envelopment. His forces crashed into the Russian line. A hard-fought skirmish ensued. Manfred and his knights circled the fray, picking off any fleeing enemy Russians. After an hour of combat, the right flank had finally pushed through, but it was unable to flank the line as Polish reserves had been sent forwards. A stalemate began as both sides pushed for ground. Teutonic knights dismounted to meet their enemies on foot. After hours, under the scorching heat, the heavily armoured knights began to tire. With one final push, the Hochmeister charged with his own personal guard into the fray. "Rally men!" Manfred cried. "The Hochmeister fight on our side today!" However, no progress was made.

Within moments, the Lithuanian cavalry returned, once again led by Topór. He saw Manfred, and out of honour, he redirected his charge towards Werner's contingent. Surrounded, they were destroyed. Werner rode out to join Manfred and his men. The roughriders, isolated, retreated to the center of the field where the last stand was made. The German battle line was completely unfurled. Squires and porters joined the battle. The Order was on their last limbs. Then came the final straw. Jagiello led his personal guard towards the Hochmeister's knights. The charge was simply too much to bear. The Hochmeister was unhorsed. After a few short moments of fighting, he was slain, struck down by four Polish infantrymen who finally stabbed him through the eye slits. When Manfred saw that the General had fallen, he knew that all hope was lost.

"Retreat! Retreat! Run while you can!" he shouted,

"Manfred, no; you vowed to stay by the Hochmeister's side!" Friedrich exclaimed.

"I will not stay here and watch my men die," said Manfred.

"What are you doing? Have you lost all honour?"

"To hell with honour," Manfred replied. He led his army away from the battle, back into the Tannenberg forest. Upon seeing his evacuation, Albrecht retreated as well. Albrecht led the dismounted knights and infantrymen to the camp where they tried to encircle the wagons into a makeshift fortress. Friedrich, appalled by the breaking of a vow, decided to leave Manfred and join the remnants of the order. He disappeared into the camp, and Manfred continued on without him. No goodbyes were said; there was no time. All was lost. Manfred led his men to the only refuge he could think of, the final defence of the Teutonic Order: Marienburg.

The defeat at Grunwald was forever known as one of the greatest defeats in the history of the Teutonic Order.

CHAPTER 41. MERCY

Under cover of dark, Manfred and his outriders rode through the woods. Only two thousand remained. All was calm and well until Manfred heard a stream in the distance.

"We will have to go either east or west. I have no map," he said.

"Will that not slow us down?" asked Helmuth.

"It will, but we cannot cross the river. It is too dangerous," Manfred replied. At that moment, Manfred heard the thunder of hooves in the distance behind them. "Run!" he cried out. His small army raced forwards towards the river. However, once they reached it, there was no escape. The rough riders turned around and charged forth into their pursuers. They were the very same Lithuanian cavalry that they had faced earlier that day. The charge was futile. Under the numbers of the horde, the army crumbled. Werner was unhorsed and captured. Only one hundred riders remained. Encircled, Manfred surrendered, as he didn't want to waste any more lives. He and his men were forced to dismount, and out from the darkness emerged Topór once again.

"I see that your act of mercy has not served you well, has it?" he asked.

"Not particularly," replied Manfred with a melancholy

smirk.

"What is your name, young knight?"

"Sir. Manfred von Göttingen."

"Well, Sir. Manfred, I have been sent by the King to bring him your head on a plate."

"Then take it, and let the rest of my men be."

"Manfred, I'm afraid that I cannot do that."

"Don't kill them, they're innocent," Manfred protested. "All they did was follow orders, my orders. I am the one to blame for our stubborn resistance. Take me, not them."

"Fear not, Manfred. I do not intend to execute you, although your plea for death was quite compelling."

"Why won't you just kill me? Those men don't need to die. They don't deserve death. It is because of me that two of my closest friends are dead and another left. I deserve death more than any of them."

"Well, Manfred, how could I tell my children that I killed the man who allowed me to return to them?" Topór asked. Manfred fell silent. "All I ask for is my sword back; I quite liked it."

"Of course," Manfred said. He drew the sword and presented it with his head down like a squire.

"Stand up. I give mercy to knights, not peasants," Topór ordered. Manfred arose with the blade and presented it in the same way. Topór took the blade and sheathed it back into his scabbard. "I will have to slay your men. Don't worry, I will let you keep your personal retinue."

"What? Why? They have done no wrong. They only followed orders."

"They are all Catholic crusaders," Topór replied with zeal. Manfred thought for a moment.

"Not all."

"Not all? Who here isn't a crusader scum? Point them out. And yet I fear that you would lie to my face despite my clear act of chivalry."

"There are twenty Russian druzhina. They are not Catholic, German, nor crusaders," Manfred replied. Topór looked skeptical, but even he had to admit that they had done little wrong.

"Fine, they can live. But, Manfred, you have reached the fullest extent of my mercy. If I see you again on the battlefield, I will kill you."

"I understand," said Manfred. He then proceeded to mount his horse. Roland, Helmuth, Ernst, and Werner followed his example, as did the Russians.

"Oh, and Manfred, one last thing," Topór added.

"Yes?"

"If King Jagiello asks for Manfred, tell him that he died here today among his men."

"Of course," Manfred replied with a solemn head nod. He rode off with his men, ruing the day that he might encounter Topór again. As he looked back at the forsaken souls, he felt guilt, but he also realized that he had to return to Maria. He looked over his shoulder one last time and saw the first execution. He saw the silhouette of a sergeant decapitated. He looked onwards towards Marienburg. He rode around the river and went North. He and his men had to ensure that the lives of the fallen were not in vain. Manfred said a prayer for Friedrich and the sergeants as he rode. He didn't know if Friedrich had received a Christian burial, but Manfred hoped that he did. He knew that it was what he would have wanted.

CHAPTER 42. GHOST OF THE EAST

The twenty-four riders reached Marienburg at midday. They were exhausted, as were their horses, but they were just happy to return alive. Manfred felt the dread of losing Friedrich, and it revived the same sorrow that he had felt upon hearing the news of Wilhelm. Manfred wanted to think that Friedrich was still alive, but he couldn't. How could he? Surely not a single man survived in that mockery of a fortress. Friedrich was dead; there was no silver lining. As Manfred approached the gates of Marienburg, he saw the doctors and surgeons working hard. Plenty of injured filled the inner courtyard, and plenty of dead filled the rivers.

"Good Lord," he muttered to himself.

"It smells like old meat," Helmuth said.

"Watch your tongue; those are the dead of which you speak," said Ernst solemnly. The riders all rode past the gates and into the courtyard where their horses were attended to. First thing before all, Manfred walked over to a blacksmith to fix a new visor to his bascinet. As he spoke with the smith, he saw Heinrich exit the inner walls to greet Manfred and his men.

"Manfred, old friend, lord am I glad to see that you made it!" he called out, extending his arm for a handshake. Manfred reciprocated. He hadn't known Heinrich for long, despite what the recent epithet implied, but he felt comfortable around him. He seemed to be a reasonable man, ready to put his life in front of his mens' at any time.

"I am sure glad to return to the safety of these walls," Manfred replied.

"Yes, I'm sure you are. The returning men have trickled in from the Tannenberg, telling tales of the horrors of battle."

"They are deserters are they not?" asked Manfred.

"No, not deserters. Well, technically yes, but I prefer the title: *sane people.* You see, there comes a point in a battle when it is futile to continue the fight, and I see that these men knew exactly when that point was."

"Friedrich held the line. He joined the remaining men when they tried to make a final stand."

"And what of them?"

"You have heard no news?"

"No, I have heard none of any last stand."

"Then, I suppose they must be dead. All of them. And the cowards here that seek aid from your doctors are all too ashamed to admit it because they don't want to remember that there was another option," Manfred said with quiet rage. His blood began to boil. The thudding of hammers against anvils continued to set his mind on fire. It was still hurt from the falchion strike.

"Manfred, I think you need some rest. Come inside," Heinrich gestured. At this point, the Russians branched off, and Manfred and his three knights marched through the halls. On either side, he saw defences being set. Hourds were being built along the walls of the castle. The gatehouse was being filled with sacks of rocks, and quivers of arrows and bolts were set along the battlements.

"I see that you are preparing for a siege," Manfred said.

"When the first men returned to this castle, the first thing they shouted was that the Poles were coming. I know that

Marienburg is their next target, but I will not give it up with ease."

"How can we last a siege? We have no food stores. We will run out within months!"

"Manfred, the lord is with us. Besides, we have enough men to stall their siege."

"Stall? Stall for whom?"

"I have sent word to the Livonians. Hopefully, they realize that now is not the time to be frugal with men. If Marienburg falls, they will be next."

"That is welcome news."

"Indeed."

"So, how many men do we have?"

"The garrison has 3,000 of my personal men. If we add the survivors of Grunwald, well, we have received five hundred so far. I would expect another one thousand."

"Has Danzig not sent men to aid us. Hasn't Konigsberg?"

"Konigsberg and Danzig sent all of the men they could to Grunwald. All that remains is a collective 200 sailors."

"That is disappointing. Does the Holy Roman Empire not wish to preserve us?"

"By the time they even muster an army, it will be too late."

"I see," replied Manfred. "Well then, how can I help?"

"I won't risk you and your men on setting up the hourds; the scaffolding is far too dangerous. Instead, would you work with the armourers to distribute proper equipment to all?"

"Of course," replied Manfred. He and his men returned to the blacksmith where his visor was nearly completed. The blacksmith came to Manfred in a hurry.

"I'm sorry Sir, but our standard-issue visors use two side hinges. Could we just give you a standard-issue helmet instead?"

"No, that helmet is important to me. On it, engraved, is my family history."

"I see sir, what would you have us do?"

"Show me the helmets that have been looted from the battlefield," Manfred said. "We can look for parts there." The blacksmith took him to a large storage room where old equipment and captured armour was stored. Manfred browsed a collection of twenty helmets. Some were too outdated; others had the wrong hinge type. Not a single klappvisor was in sight. Then, a particular helmet caught Manfred's eye. It was a Cuman face mask. It was painted a ghastly white, and the moustache was in gold. Manfred pointed to it. "Can you put that on my helmet?"

"That? You will look like a barbarian."

"I will look like death himself. Can you do it?"

"Of course, sir," replied the blacksmith. They returned to the smithery, and within moments the process was complete. Manfred donned his new helmet. It smelled of war, but he loved it. Manfred also received a new battle-axe. Swords were of low supply as they took far longer to make. It was time to get to work. Throughout the day, Manfred spent his time equipping the soldiers with the standard-issue equipment. Mere sergeants and serfs were armed like knights, with full Cherbourg cuirasses, pauldrons, gauntlets, and hound skull bascinets. It was magnificent. Heinrich's predictions were right; by nightfall, two thousand more combatants emerged from the woods, nearly half of which were ready to fight again. As Manfred looked over the battlements, the red banners of Poland and Lithuania appeared above the treetops.

Quivering, he muttered "Gott Mitt Uns."

CHAPTER 43. THE WEASEL

On the twenty-sixth of July, the Polish army finally amassed in full force. Manfred and his men had regularly sent out raids to infect the enemy food supply and burn the fields around them. The food stores had only enough for two months, but by Heinrich's estimates, that was all they needed. All the while, Polish catapults, cannons, and trebuchets pelted the walls with massive boulders, forging large holes, but killing few. The castle was undermanned, and thus, the forces were too spread out to be targeted. On July thirtieth, a Polish emissary approached the gates.

"Who goes there?" asked a guard, petrified.

"I am a representative of King Jagiello. I wish to negotiate the terms of your surrender," the emissary replied.

"Open the gates," Heinrich instructed. Reluctantly, the guards complied, letting the single man inside the outer courtyard. His horse was not tended to, no porters came to his aid. He was unarmored and vulnerable, but the Germans had no intention of harming him. Perhaps terms were the best option; would the Livonians really come to the rescue?

"Greetings, General Heinrich."

"Greetings."

"I bring word from Great King Jagiello."

"Yes, you have made that quite clear."

"May I come inside?" the emissary asked. It was customary to be hospitable, but Heinrich didn't want him to learn the interior of the castle, in case of invasion.

"No. Speak now or return to the abyss from which you came."

"Fine then. I see that you wish to get right down to business. King Jagiello orders you to leave your castle, and all nobility will be spared and ransomed."

"And the rest?"

"They will be executed like the dogs they are."

"You dare to step into my court and offer the terms of my men's execution? Are you a fool? I would slay you right now if I wasn't trained in diplomacy, you weasel. Return to your king and say that if he wants the castle, he will have to kill every last man, woman, and child. We will never surrender, we will never back down, and every last one of us would rather die than see this patch of dirt under Polish rule. Listen to the boulders smashing against our walls. Listen. Any one of them at any point could come right down upon you and you would die just like the rest of us. After you desecrate the temple of God, you ask for twisted repentance? I think not. I will not leave this castle outside of a body bag. So no, I will not surrender, I will not let you into my home to survey the interior and eat away at our food stores. I will not waiver. Understand?" Heinrich asked in a rozen rage.

"Yes, sir," replied the emissary, in a timid voice. He grew pale, and the stench of urine festered around him. "I will leave you now in peace." The emissary hastily mounted his horse and scampered off into the Polish camp. The barrage continued. The cannons erupted with satanic roars, instilling fear into the hearts of the defenders. But they held on. With limited food, they continued unwaveringly. Rats, dogs, cats, all were carefully added to the rations of the starving defenders. It was harsh. Every day they held mass in the inner courtyard, praying that their scouts would bring back news of Livonian support. Everyday, Manfred and Heinrich were saddened to hear that not a Livonian soul was on their way. So, they prayed. That was all they could do. They prayed and awaited their impending deaths.

CHAPTER 44. THE LION, THE EAGLE, AND THE RAM

For two weeks, the defenders held strong. Polish sappers attempted to tunnel below the walls; however, the Germans launched their own counter tunnels. Some of the Polish tunnels were successful, destroying parts of the outer wall, but they were quickly replaced by piles of rubble and wood. The counter tunnels intercepted many, but not enough. They were undermanned and undertrained. Even worse, every day they received bombardments in heavy numbers, but on this day, that was not the case. In the early morning, the barrage stopped. The Poles had run out of cannonballs and boulders. Upon hearing the silence, cheers of Gott Mitt Uns erupted with glee. Men dropped to their knees to thank the Lord. With a boost of morale, the defenders kept their poker face against the enemy. The next day, the Lithuanian contingent withdrew. The Polish and Moldavians still outnumbered the Germans two to one, but the Order finally had a fighting chance. Manfred carried out more raids, stealing ammunition and infecting rations. Manfred and his spies found that many Poles were disheartened and low in morale, which was far from the case of the Germans. Heinrich gave speeches at dinner, ensuring that reinforcements would come. The Holy Roman Empire had sent the Order money, for they could not muster any army on time. With the money, the German army expanded by another five hundred Bohemian and Moravian mercenaries. The mercenaries had to land at Danzig and sneak their way through the Polish encampments to Marienburg. They were welcomed hospitably by the Germans, as with them they brought supplies and ale.

After another week, the Germans still held out. On the eighteenth of September, Heinrich came to Manfred with the broadest smile upon his visage.

"There is hope," he said.

"That's hard to believe. My belt has already been tightened past the smallest loop. What could possibly relieve the dread of starvation?"

"A Livonian army," Heinrich said ecstatically.

"A Livonian army?" Manfred asked, as his expression turned from solemn to elated.

"Our scouts reported an army of five hundred knights. They are coming to our aid."

"Five hundred isn't very many."

"It's enough to threaten the Polish camp."

"That is welcome news, Heinrich. We must drink some Bohemian ale and party."

"No. If our scouts have this information, the Poles must too. They won't abandon this siege; they will try to win a swift victory and use the fortifications to repel the Livonians. One last battle," Heinrich said sternly. Manfred nodded.

"One last battle," he replied. Manfred walked out onto the walls where he saw men training, praying, and repairing wounds. Heinrich followed.

"Good men of Marienburg!" Heinrich announced. "I come with good news, a Livonian force rides to relieve us. Frugal as it may be, it is still hope." The army cheered loudly. "However, we must maintain our iron will. The Poles will soon unearth this information and launch one final attack. Reinforce the gates, boil water, and load sacks of stones, for we will have to face them at last. Today, we either reap victory or tomorrow, we face St. Peter like true, fearless men. Gott Mitt Uns!" he cried.

The army began to repeat those words as well. Shortly after, they got to work. All men rushed to their stations, and all horses were kept safely locked away in the stables. From the walls, the men threw caltrops, and they buried caltrops and arrowheads in the rubble of the collapsed walls. As well, they set fire to the surrounding trees so that they couldn't be used as screens for enemy archers. Finally, the soldiers collected large sums of water from the river and uploaded them upon the battlefield, creating a soaked marshland to slow down the Polish advance. They were ready for battle.

The castle was prepared. All men stood at their stations for the entire day, armed to the teeth like knights. The crusader army stood unwaveringly under the scorching summer sun. Finally, in the afternoon, they heard the sound of Polish battle horns. A clumsily assembled horde emerged from the encampment, pushing two large siege towers as well as a set of ladders. On their right flank, the Poles advanced a battering ram. Attacked from all sides, the Germans held their posts, ready to hold off the onslaught of Polish soldiers.

Manfred held the center wall with his knights. With an iron will, he waited for the siege tower to approach. However, as it made its way across the field, it slowly sank in the marshland.

"Fire!" Manfred commanded, and all of his men pulled out crossbows from behind the battlements. They rained death upon the Poles as they slowly trudged through the marsh. The siege tower became stuck in the mud. As it sank, it swayed, tilting from side to side Eventually, as the Poles pushed, the front right wheel continued to sink into the marsh, digging deeper and deeper, while the other wheels were all clogged by the thick wet mud. Soon, the tower stopped moving and the entire tower fell over, crushing men below. The Poles hastily mounted their ladders upon the walls. "Hold the walls men. No surrender. No quarter!" Manfred cried.

"No quarter!" his men shouted. As the Poles scaled the ladders, the German defenders poured stones and boiling water upon the attackers. Men fell back into the marsh, but eventually, a few men gained a foothold on the walls. Vicious fighting ensued. Some men were thrown off the walls, others were slain and fell where they stood.

Ernst launched himself into the enemy lines fighting as viciously as a lion. Manfred and his knights followed. Axe in hand, he chopped and hacked at his opponents. However, he saw Ernst fall to the ground. A Moldavian billhook had pierced his left knee, rendering him incapable of walking. Manfred tried to protect him, but it was too late. He had already begun to bleed, and he couldn't move. There was no escape.

Eventually, the overwhelming horde of Poles took the walls, shoving Manfred and his men to the stairs. At the last moment, the Russian contingent made their way to the front line and forced their way through, ferociously balancing out the odds once more. Katerina seizes Ernst, and she and her druzhina cautiously escorted him down the stairs and to the inner courtyard to receive medical attention. The fighting was horrid, killing many, and trampling the wounded.

After a few more minutes, the German forces began to crack under the pressure of the Polish horde. Manfred looked around. The outer gates had been breached by the ram, and the right wall was taken by the other siege tower. Heinrich saw Manfred and his men making their stubborn stand and knew that their efforts would be in vain.

"Retreat to the inner walls!" Heinrich ordered. Manfred complied, leading his men back in through the inner gate. Once most of the men came through, the portcullis was slammed shut. Rows of crossbowmen stood behind it and upon the walls, launching wave after wave of bolts upon the attackers. The Polish made distance from their enemy. The heat of battle slowed, and an exchange of arrows and bolts filled the air. Through the storm of metal and ash, the battering ram made its way to the front gate. Polish peasants were forced to push the ram. All of them were shot down by German crossbows. Once the first wave was shot, the second wave pushed the ram, and so on and so forth. Finally, the ram reached the gate. Before it struck, King Jagiello rode onto the field and demanded a ceasefire. Heinrich complied as he wished to hear what Jagiello had to say.

"What bloodshed," Jagiello said loudly. "What bloodshed has been brought to your soil, and what bloodshed shall follow if you do not capitulate. Surrender the castle, and the survivors will be free to go."

"How can you ensure our safety?" Heinrich asked.

"I give my word," Jagiello replied.

"I will not trust a man who lets his own peasants die to push a damn ram."

"That is the nature of warfare, is it not?"

"No, it doesn't have to be," Heinrich replied. Then, he turned to his men. "Archers, fire!" The exchange continued, slaughtering many of the exposed Poles. The ram slammed into the portcullis, creating the foulest crash. The sound of the impact echoed in the ears of all and cut through the incessant twanging of the losing of arrows. All hope seemed lost. There were simply too many. But Heinrich was not ready to surrender. In the distance, Manfred saw smoke emerge atop the Polish camp. The bold red banners of Poland were set ablaze. Manfred watched in astonishment as the white eagles were engulfed by flame.

"They're here! The Livonians are here!" he cried ecstatically. King Jagiello turned his head and watched in horror as his camp was overrun with Livonian knights. He had lost. The King of Poland was defeated. The German army erupted into a cheer of Gott Mitt Uns. They fell to their knees once more to thank the Lord as they watched the reluctant Polish retreat. They had won, but at what cost? Manfred surveyed the battlefield. As the Poles fled, they revealed a screen of fallen men: Germans and Poles alike. The sight was horrid and gruesome. Manfred walked over to Ernst who lay upon a stretcher. When he talked to him, he didn't respond. Manfred felt his hands; they were cold. He knelt to say a prayer.

Later that evening, the Livonians were greeted gleefully, and a banquet was held with the remaining rations to celebrate the end of the siege. The war was not over. During the Polish invasion, many fortresses had been left unmanned and were thus claimed by the Poles. They would have to be taken care of. However, with the new Livonian support, as well as promised aid from both Hungary and the Holy Roman Empire, all hope was not lost. Manfred and his men rejoiced and also mourned the loss of Ernst. Death had become normal now. Each passing affected them all less and less, to the point where now it was all but a slight feeling of sorrow. Manfred still felt grief for the dead on both sides. He knew that they both fought for their homelands and their gods, both of which were ethically correct according to his teachers. However, Manfred celebrated with his men, for he had every intention of going home.

CHAPTER 45. THE JOURNEY

Manfred, Roland, Helmuth, and the Russians all gathered in the inner courtyard of the castle. It was the morning of September thirtieth.

"You have served me well, Manfred. But I understand that you must return to your family. You will be missed," Heinrich said. "You fought valiantly during the siege, and I'm sure that you did all that you could at Grunwald. Thank you," Heinrich said.

"I hear that you are to be crowned Hochmeister for your valiant commandership," replied Manfred.

"Well, let's just hope that I am just as decent of a diplomat," Heinrich replied with a chuckle.

"I wish you and the Order luck."

"As I you. Godspeed, Manfred," Heinrich said.

"All hail the Hochmeister," Manfred replied playfully. With that, he and Roland were off, ready to return to Adelebsen with their new comrades. The Northern German farmland and forest were far less treacherous in the Autumn. Manfred returned upon the road by which he came. Before travelling to Berlin, he made one stop along the way. He went to the town of Eberswalde where Wilhelm was buried. He asked the locals for directions, and there, in the graveyard, was a cross upon which Wilhelm's helmet sat. His Venetian great bascinet still had blood stains on it. Manfred knelt down by the grave and shed a single tear. Then, he laid down Wilhelm's mace. He said a prayer for Wilhelm. Manfred finally had the strength to accept Wilhelm's passing. He was gone, and there was nothing he could do about it. All he could do was celebrate his life. Manfred reflected upon the good times they had together. Then, he stood up, and without a word, got back up on his horse to ride to Berlin.

When passing Magdeburg, the town was not large anymore. It was now a small town built upon the ruins of the previous one. The sheer destruction of the fire was insane. Manfred and his men set up camp near there and set up their own campfire. As the night fell the group talked in peace and harmony. There were no bandits or insane one-eyed revolutionary pagans. They were alone in the woods, safe. Before going to bed, Manfred decided to confide in Roland.

"Roland, do you want to know what really happened that night?"

"What night?" Roland replied.

"The night when I walked alone into the woods and was attacked by a pack of wolves. The night when I met the Russians."

"What more is there to say? I find it odd that you walked alone, but I suppose that with all this killing it's hard to sleep."

"Well, there were no wolves."

"Oh?"

"That night, I think I met a witch."

"By God! What happened?"

"Well, I followed this little girl into the woods thinking that she was lost. I wanted to guide her away from our army. But then she disappeared. Instead, I felt a strange urge to enter into a bush, so I did, and then I saw this old woman. She claimed to be the little girl."

"So what? She was probably crazy."

"Well, I told the little girl my name, and this old woman knew it without me telling her."

"So? She probably just overheard it."

"You don't understand. She gave me a book."

"What was in it?"

"It said my future. It called me a feller of axes and an eastern ghost."

"Like your helmet."

"Exactly!"

"So? What's the issue?"

"She said that I would be stabbed to death by someone holding a breadknife, and that I would bleed to death in the hands of the person who had done me the most harm."

"So, someone will shank you and then hug you? I don't get it."

"I don't either. I don't know what to do. I fear my own destiny."

"That's no destiny. To hell with destiny. You are Sir. Manfred the Great, killer of Poles and commander of horsemen. You forge your own destiny. I think that either you were dreaming, or that book was a load of hooplah."

"Really?"

"Yes. If you ask me, don't worry about it. She probably just made a few lucky guesses."

"Alright then, if you say so," replied Manfred. He wasn't satisfied. The prophecy itched at his mind like a parasite. But he didn't want to plague Roland anymore.

"Good night, Manfred," Roland said.

"Good night," Manfred replied. The two dozed off into a hearty slumber.

CHAPTER 46. THE WHITE CASTLE

Over the horizon, Manfred and his riders saw the tall Castle Plesse. He was excited to return to his home in Adelebsen, but Plesse was on the way. He thought he'd return the map to his father and say a fake hello to his mother. They rode slowly towards the tall castle, but the banners had been knocked off the walls. They didn't hang anymore where they once were; the white castle on a blue field over a golden lion over a red field cascaded the walls no longer. Instead were long black banners, the banners of death. The flag of Göttingen flew at half-mast. Manfred approached the castle with caution. As he approached the gates, he kept his visor on. He wanted to surprise his father, as obviously he thought that Manfred was killed at Grunwald. He approached the gates.

"Who goes there?" asked a guard from on top of the gatehouse.

"Tell Prince Otto that I wish to meet with him," replied Manfred.

"You haven't heard the news?"

"No, what news?" Manfred asked.

"Otto is... dead," the guard said slowly. He looked down at his feet. Manfred was shocked. Never in his wildest dreams did he expect this.

"How did he pass?" Manfred asked, lifting his visor.

"He caught the plague."

"What were his last words?"

"He asked for his son, Manfred, but his son was already dead as well. He died at Grunwald as a glorious crusader, but we spared Otto the news. It would have troubled him too much," the guard said. Manfred grew numb. He felt no rage nor sorrow, he simply felt nothing.

"Who is in charge now?"

"His two sons, Otto the Younger and Reuben, have divided the land."

"I wish to see them," Manfred commanded.

"What business do you have?"

"It is of high importance," Manfred said.

"And what is your name?" the guard asked.

"Manfred," Manfred replied. "Sir. Manfred von Göttingen, third son of Prince Otto von Göttingen, Count of Adelebsen, and Brother Knight of the Teutonic Order," Manfred said. The guard went pale. Immediately, he stumbled to the gatekeepers and instructed them to open the doors as quickly as possible. Together, the two men heaved the door open with haste. When Manfred entered, the guard bowed his head in solidarity.

"Welcome home, Manfred," he said hospitably. Manfred rode his horse inside with pride. He dismounted and handed his horse off to the porters, as did his fellow riders.

"Show me to my brothers," Manfred ordered. The guard complied sheepishly, rushing him into the great hall. Inside was a grand feast. There, in the hall, Otto II and Reuben sat upon Manfred's parents' thrones. They drank wine and ate fine pork. In the corner, a band of troubadours played a jolly tune. As Manfred stepped inside, the music stopped. All of the court retainers turned their attention to Manfred and his men. "Excuse me if I am interrupting your party, but I wish to speak to my brother," he said. Manfred's brothers looked as pale as ghosts. They realized that they had made a grave mistake to claim his father's land, and they knew that Manfred was now seeking revenge.

"Yes, yes. Everybody clear out," Otto II said.

"Yes, please do," said Manfred sarcastically. He marched up to the thrones. "So. Who told you that I was dead?" Manfred asked.

"We just assumed..." Otto II muttered.

"You just assumed what? That you could assume my death and strip me of my proper inheritance?"

"Well, to be fair, this never was your inheritance. You are the third in line."

"You dare to tell me this while you split the wealth like a gang of brigands and party over my father's grave? This is no time for celebration!" Manfred shouted.

"Calm down, Manfred."

"Calm down? How can I calm down? What have you done with Adelebsen? Where is Maria?"

"We claimed Adelebsen, as we thought you were dead."

"You what?"

"We replaced Maria, as she is a woman and therefore is unfit to rule."

"And who did you place in her stead?"

"Well, the priest seemed like the most valid candidate."

"THE PRIEST?! WHICH PRIEST?!" Manfred asked in pure rage, dreading the answer that would seek to emerge from his brother's foul visage.

"P...P... Pastor... Pastor Leon," replied Otto II with the highest form of terror. Manfred said nothing. He took off his gauntlet and slapped his brothers with it, both of them, across the right cheek.

"I challenge you both to a duel."

"A duel?"

"Yes; trial by combat."

"With both of us? At the same time?"

"Yes. I will slay you both, take what's mine, and butcher that damn Leon."

"Fine then. I suppose we must accept," replied Reuben, standing up confidently.

"Wait, wait," interjected Otto II. "Is there no other way to get around this?"

"Otto, you are just like father: a coward," Manfred said sternly. He marched out of the hall. "I will return. When I do, be ready." Manfred stormed out of the hall with his Russian entourage. Their next destination: Adelebsen.

CHAPTER 47. THE GOLDEN LION

The twenty-three riders returned to Adelebsen. They were welcomed amiably by the guards.

"What happened when I was gone?" Manfred asked one of them.

"A whole lot," he replied. "Since you left, Maria has been in charge. She's a good ruler. She found a way to lower rent, and she even found a doctor to come and help fight the plague here."

"But I hear that she is no longer in charge," Manfred said.

"That is true. Prince Otto II gave that title to Pastor Leon, as they both claimed that a woman couldn't legally rule."

"Well, can women rule?"

"I haven't seen any law prohibiting them from positions of power," said the guard.

"Well then, is Leon any good?"

"No, he has raised taxes and he follows your brothers' every corrupt command. Not to mention that our tithes all go to the government now, the government being him. But, what can we do? He represents the pope, and we cannot go against the will of the pope."

"Where is he?" Manfred asked.

"Probably in the castle, sir."

"And Maria?"

"Probably there, too."

"Excellent. Don't inform them that I am here," Manfred said with a grin. He and his riders made their way into the town. As they passed through the narrow streets and sharp turns, they formulated a plan. Finally, Manfred knew what he would do. As they passed into the main square, Manfred first headed to Leon's sons' textile shop; however, upon arrival, they noticed that it no longer existed. "Of course, Leon must be using tax money to keep his sons afloat," Manfred said gruffly. They rode up the hill to the residence. Manfred lowered his visor and gazed back upon the quaint little village. It didn't deserve the plague or the corrupt pastor, and that was why Manfred wanted to defend it. He rode into the residence. Upon seeing his armour, the guards recognized who it was. Franz came out to greet him, but he put a finger over his visor indicating that his identity must be kept a secret. As their horses were tended to by Manfred's retainers, Manfred and his men made their way into the great hall. There he saw Leon and his sons lounging around, listening to music. In the corner, Maria was meeting with disgruntled citizens. Before she could see him, Manfred marched up to Leon.

"Who are you?" the old priest asked. "What do you want?"

"I am Sir. Reinholt von Danzig, and I come to inform you that you are being stripped of your priesthood," Manfred said in a stern voice. Leon was startled and worried, for if he lost the authority of God, there would be no reason for the people to follow him.

"Why should I believe you and your barbarian friends?" Leon asked. Manfred fished into his saddlebag and pulled out the seal of the Teutonic Order, awarded to him by the Hochmeister Ulrich von Jungingen upon his ascension to commandery. The seal was legitimate, even Leon couldn't deny it.

"Pastor Leon von Adelebsen, you are officially

excommunicated for your crimes against God's children, having stolen money from the people to fund the business of your own sons. Your crimes against the Church will be compensated through execution. I will give you thirty seconds to repent," Manfred said, drawing an arming sword from his scabbard. The Priest was so frightened that he could think of nothing but to try and flee. However, Manfred caught him and shoved him back onto the throne. One of the priest's sons fled. As the Russians tried to stop him, Manfred ordered them to let him go so that he could spread the word. Leon began to cry. He didn't pray to confess, he just shouted:

"No! Not me! Why?"

"Now, face your execution, heretic!" Manfred shouted. He ran his sword through the pedophile. He embraced him closely, feeling all the joy of ending the vile worm of a man. Leon grew cold. But, as he did so, Leon's second son became angry. He grabbed a breadknife and rushed at Manfred. About to stab Manfred up the aventail, Roland stepped in the way.

"To hell with destiny!" he shouted as he grabbed the blade and stabbed the son with it. Maria, in shock, hid behind a couch. However, when Manfred took off his helm, revealing his familiar face, she began to stream tears of joy. She came and embraced him. He embraced her as well, shedding a single tear.

"I thought you were dead!" she exclaimed. The two held each other for a long moment. The Russians began to usher the guards in to clear the body. Manfred and Maria enjoyed a meal together, prepared by Ennelein. He told her of his journey, the tragic deaths of Wilhelm and Friedrich, and the desertion of Ulrich. He told her everything. Maria and Manfred were overjoyed to see each other. "Well, after all that trouble, you must be happy to be alive! Thankfully, you're back home, so you can finish all of this fighting," she exclaimed.

"I'm not done yet," Manfred replied, with a slight grin on the corners of his mouth.

CHAPTER 48. THE LAMB

Maria, Manfred, and his riders arrived at castle Plesse. Once more they were welcomed into the castle and led to the great hall. Manfred marched inside with his men, setting his eyes upon a large crowd and a ring formed with benches.

"Surely the Prince of Göttingen could establish a more suitable ring," Manfred mocked.

"I will slay you, brother. You wish to come here and usurp what is rightfully mine? I will not tolerate this within my princedom," replied Otto II. Manfred marched into the ring to speak with his brothers, as did they.

"Look, I acted brashly," Manfred said in a hushed tone. "I do not wish to fight you. We can avoid this if you just grant me Adelebsen. It is rightfully mine."

"You rightfully own nothing. Do you dare return, prodigal son? Why don't you go back to your wars and fighting, and let us politicians govern as we rightfully should?"

"Is there no way to avoid this fight? I do not wish to slay you, but I will if I must."

"Well, on the contrary, I quite look forward to ending you," replied Otto II, lowering his visor. It was a hound skull bascinet, ordained with the family history much like Manfred's. Reuben wore a similar suit of armour, but instead of a cuirass was a coat of plates.

"Well then, I suppose that if there is no other option I will fight. But answer me one thing, if I win, will I become Prince of Göttingen?" Manfred asked.

"Sure, if you win; and if we win, we will own Adelebsen again."

"Fair," Manfred answered. He slammed his visor shut. His haunting visage installed fear into his foes like an eastern phantom. Manfred drew his arming sword, as did his brothers.

"Wait!" Maria cried. "It's not worth it, Manfred. I would rather lose Adelebsen than lose you," she said wholeheartedly.

"I cannot leave Adelebsen to these fools. They have already done enough harm by installing Leon as a Count. Over my travels, I have realized that I must take what I am owed. These fools are no more qualified to rule than you or I, so why should they? I fight not for myself, but for you and all the good citizens of Adelebsen," Manfred replied.

"Enough chatter, let's finish this!" Reuben exclaimed. He leapt forwards, swinging at Manfred. It did nothing but glance off of his armour. Then, Otto II stabbed him, but Manfred easily knocked his blade aside. Then, Manfred crushed the pommel of the blade into Otto II 's helmet. He tumbled to the floor. He was not unconscious, but he didn't want to fight any longer. Manfred left him to be. Reuben swung at him again, once more achieving nothing. Manfred half-sworded his blade nearly all the way up Reuben's aventail. Reuben's hands shot up, and his blade fell to the floor with a heavy clank. "Mercy!" he cried. Manfred granted him his mercy after easily defeating him but then he came to terms with what is right.

"I do not want Göttingen," Manfred said. "I will continue to rule Adelebsen, and you two can split the rule over Göttingen fifty-fifty with my wife, Maria. She is a better ruler than I, and the people here deserve a good ruler, for once." His brothers looked at him in awe. How could he be so gracious to them? Being the conniving men that they were, they gladly accepted the offer. "Oh, and by the way, my residence in Adelebsen will be the new main castle of Göttingen, not Castle Plesse any longer. I couldn't bear to be so far away from my wife," Manfred said. He exited the ring and embraced his wife, sweaty as he was. The two were relieved and content, finally. Manfred and his men returned home to restore order to the town. Together, he and Maria told the town of Leon's breeches of canon law, and the reasons for which the supposed emissaries came to execute him. The people trusted Manfred and Maria, just as they always had. They too were not content and relieved that Leon was gone, for, despite his power, he was a terrible ruler. In honour of Manfred's return, the castle held a feast. But, instead of indulging in the fine food among his retainers, Manfred had no music play, for it was still a sad day. There was death, and Prince Otto's fatality was not long passed. Manfred invited all to the banquet, not just his court retainers, giving the people all the same foods that he would normally eat. In truth, there was not much difference between his food and the common food, but after such a heavy season of taxation under Leon, the people were happy to receive a free meal. Despite the solemn mood, it was a joyous occasion. In their hearts, the people knew that this was a restoration of a peaceful age, nay, the introduction of greater age. Manfred ate his chicken.

That evening, Manfred decided to see his father's grave. It was not six feet below like many of the peasants. Instead, it was placed prominently beneath the church of Plesse Castle, in the crypts. Manfred descended with his guards. As he entered the room, he saw the grave. It was a large stone box, and the lid had a life-sized effigy of Prince Otto. The master artisan had done a fine job with this work. It portrayed Otto in full harness with his hands in the prayer position. Manfred wept over his father's grave. He looked at it, and then told his guards to leave.

"I wish to be alone," he said. As the guards left, they shut the doors to ensure Manfred's privacy. Manfred began to speak to his father. "Father, I hope that I have finally proven my worth to you. I know that you value war very little, but I served the nation just as you did. I fought the Order's enemies just as you did, and most importantly, we won. The last time I said goodbye to you was because you wanted to get rid of me; ship me off to the North from where I would never return. Well, surprise, I'm back," Manfred said. He looked at the grave. Then, from the corner of his eye, reflecting in a droplet of tear, Manfred saw a man in the corner. He turned around. "Who are you?" he asked. The man was cloaked in a brown cowl that hooded over his face. In his left hand, he held the seal of Topór. "You have come to kill me, haven't you?" Manfred said. The man advanced. From his cloak, he drew a bread knife.

"Duke Jan of Topór and the Mongol send their regards," the man said. Then, he violently slashed at Manfred.

"Help!" Manfred exclaimed. Manfred tried to block what he could, but the knife cut his arms in the process. Two guards rushed in and knocked the assassin out of the way, and Manfred stumbled onto the effigy of his father. In his father's arms, he bled. The guards quickly seized the assassin and took him away, and wrapped Manfred's arms, but Manfred began to fade. Maria and Roland came running down the stairs.

"Manfred? Manfred!" she shouted. She mounted him up upon the effigy as it was the only table-like surface nearby. "The doctor is coming soon," she said with tears in her eyes.

"I love you," Manfred said, in great pain. "Don't let my brothers have Adelebsen."

"Don't say that. You will fend them off yourself when you get better," Maria replied. The two embraced for a moment. Manfred grew colder. Finally, the doctor arrived. "Help him!" Maria cried. The doctor rushed to his aid. He hastily bandaged the scars further.

"He should be okay, as long as the wounds are not infected," the doctor said, applying pressure to the lacerations. Thick red blood poured out of Manfred's arms, but the doctor kept on adding layers of bandage upon bandage. Manfred looked around at Maria and Roland and his guards and the doctor. He didn't feel fear. He wasn't afraid of death. But what he did know, was that destiny was certain, and he was certain that destiny would bring him together with Maria again. Manfred clutched onto the letter that was still tucked away in his belt, and then he looked up at the ceiling. Upon it was a mural of the coat of arm of Göttingen, the white castle upon a blue field above the golden lion upon a read field. Manfred felt joy, as it reminded him of Marienburg. He thought of the last stand and the relief he had felt after the battle, and he thought of Ernst. Then, he thought of Friedrich, and then Ulrich, and then Wilhelm. Last, he thought once more about Maria. Finally, Manfred closed his eyes, releasing one last tear.

The letter floated to the ground.

INTERLUDE

"Wait, wait, wait," interrupted the king. "What in God's name are you doing? I hired you for at least a Fortnight longer. This story had ought to continue. Don't end it prematurely."

"My King, fear not, for the tale of the town and its people still continues on. As you well know, after death, the world just continues on, as if nothing had happened at all," replied Walter.

"But, my father died of illness. This brave warrior couldn't have been assassinated; he could have fought him off!"

"My King, he had no weapon."

"So? He's a great warrior!"

"My Lord, one must have a weapon to fight. Even the greatest warriors can be killed. Even the most untouchable people."

"So, you're saying that I could be killed?"

"Oh no, but everybody loves you, my Lord."

"Well that's a load of shite. A rebellion rages as we speak. Not to mention, Somerset is struggling still in France. Many people would have my head!"

"Then perhaps you ought to listen to what happened after Manfred's death. You see, a warrior king doesn't fix many of their country's problems when they die. Similarly, with Adelebsen, when Manfred was gone, few people were left to adequately protect the town."

"Really?"

"Well, like you said, after your father died, he left you in charge, which prompted a rebellion! Not to mention, the lands he once conquered are being retaken as we speak."

"But it's just one man who is gone."

"But that man was an inspiration to his soldiers and a master tactician. With him gone, how could they fight as well as they had before? Anyways, my King, are you aware of the tale of Sir. Percival?"

"Believe me, you've bestowed it upon us far too often for me to forget."

"Excellent, as it will become important in the story to come," replied Walter.

CHAPTER 49. SIR. PERCIVAL

Maria opened the first page of the Tale of Sir. Percival. As her eyes scanned the ink-cluttered page, she couldn't help but avert her attention to the embalming of her husband right below her feet. In the crypt, below the Great Hall, Manfred lay motionless and still with his guts half poured out. His murderer sat tied to a chair in the room next door.

"Who sent you?" asked Roland in a tranquil yet vicious tone. He was tired from the grand adventure, weakened by weathering, and yet, there were still toils to deal with. Manfred was dead, yet his troubles lived on.

"I made it pretty clear to him," the assassin replied, nodding his head towards the room next door. Roland replied with a look of disgust. One of the guards came and hit the murderer harshly across the cheek, such that small droplets of blood poured from his lip. Just as the pooling red liquid splattered against the stone tiles of the crypt's floor, Maria's tears moistened the pages of her archaic manuscript. She cried in agony for her loss. She was no hardened warrior, but instead, a gentle soul caught up in the violent mess. She felt no vengeance, only grief.

"I said... who in God's name sent you?" Roland asked.

"Even if I told you, you can do nothing about it," replied the murderer, half choking on his bloodied esophagus.

"I haven't got all day; spit it out," Roland said, drawing his rondel dagger. Upon seeing the blade, the assassin was jolted with horror. The realism of his situation hit him like a tidal wave.

"Fine, I'll talk, just don't cut me."

"Oh, I'll cut you however many times I like. I just won't kill you."

"You're a brute, you know that? You and all of your men. All you do is hurt people and say you're doing good."

"You just stabbed a man to death; you shouldn't be talking."

"At least I stabbed a bad man."

"You stabbed an innocent man."

"Innocent? He was a Teutonic Knight. He fought for an evil cause, and he deserves no pity."

"Enough. Just speak."

"Fine. I was hired by Topór."

"Topór? I thought that man was long gone? How did he know where we live?"

"The Mongol came to him. It was a rainy night in the siege camp near Marienburg. The Mongol came with a group of brigands who said that they had information on one of the German commanders. Topór let him in, spoke with him, and then slew the barbarian."

"He killed the Mongol?"

"Of course. That's what those Hun dogs deserve," the assassin said, spitting blood on the ground.

"So, you attacked the red castle?"

"No, I wasn't there."

"Then, where were you?"

"I was a local hunter."

"Well then, how long have you stayed in Adelebsen?"

"Not long, only a few weeks. I ran into your friend along the way."

"Really? Who?"

"He goes by the name of the Sable Knight."

"Really? Does he go by any other name?"

"He calls himself that because he painted over his cuirass with black paint. His real name was Ulrich; I believe he worked for Manfred."

"He did. What did you do to him?"

"Nothing. I simply asked for directions to Göttingen and came on my way."

"And what is he up to?"

"He's now in a mercenary group. They call themselves the Knights of the Maunch. They hunt for raubritters."

"Ha! Ulrich hunts for robber knights? What a joke. I would think he was one if I didn't know any better. You'll have to procure better lies than the ones which have slipped from your morose tongue, fiend," Roland said, brandishing his blade.

"I speak the truth, you must believe me," the assassin replied, squirming in his chair.

"Why should I? For all I know, everything you've said is a lie. I'm not exactly one for murder, so I'll tell you what. Do you like games?"

"N... no."

"Well, I do. I love games. In fact, to me, killing's a game... nay... an art."

"I would agree, I am a..."

"Shh, now. I'm speaking. Since killing's an art, I think I'm going to paint a pretty picture."

"Please, don't."

"I think I will. It will be of you, with your head on a pike, right outside of this manor's gate. How do you like that?"

"I'm telling the truth, I swear it!"

"You expect me to believe that you came all this way for a few coins?"

"Not a few coins; I was forced to. Topór said that he would burn my village to the ground if I didn't bring to him Manfred's head."

"Well then, you're not exactly a professional, are you?"

"No, sir."

"Tell me one last thing... how did you get into the crypt?" Roland asked. The assassin grew pale, gazing at the men guarding the entrance. They replied with brutal glares. Then, as the murderer's lips quivered, they slowly unleashed a wicked sound.

"I paid the guards," he said slowly and softly. Roland, taken aback by this, turned his attention to the guardsmen.

"These damn guards?!" he shouted, unleashing a fury unlike any other. The guards now trembled, for they knew that they couldn't fight their way out of this. "That must have been a large sum of florins!"

"It w... was, sir," replied one guard, swallowing a large gulp of fear.

"You killed this man," Roland said to his silent audience. Roland then stormed out of the room and called for reinforcements to imprison the guardsmen as well. Then, from the end of the hallway, Roland turned back to the three subdued perpetrators. "Come tomorrow, you'll all be hung."

CHAPTER 50. RELEASING THE SHACKLES

Maria turned the old, yellow pages with vigour as if she had entered a trance. This was the one refuge she found from her life, the life that had so drastically turned for the worst upon her husband's acceptance of one, simple task. She lamented in silence, with a heavy heart. Her sadness was unbearable. As she read of the valiant Sir. Percival, she couldn't help but be reminded of her courageous and hot-headed husband. It was the only book she wanted to read; the only book in the manor's library that she would read, for it gave her a slight glimpse of what once was. Eventually, snapping her out of her trance, Roland entered the hall with rozen rage.

"What troubles you, good knight?" she asked, for she was the only person inhabiting the room.

"Oh, my lady. I thought the hall was empty. I apologize, for I shall rant elsewhere."

"No, please. I don't mind. Tell me what plagues your mind."

"No, my lady, you mustn't be troubled with such things; not in this time of great sadness."

"Roland, we must stick together now that Manfred is gone.

I'm sure that his brothers will come like hounds for this town, and we have no legal means to defend it."

"What do you mean? You were his wife; can't you hold the town?"

"Of course I can, legally, but the church would have it that only men can hold lands."

"That must be false; I have heard of dames who hold lands all across Europe."

"Well, those dames either have living husbands or hold royal blood. My blood belongs to Kassel. I fear I must retire there in the face of Manfred's brothers' aggression."

"My lady, you can't. We cannot afford to give up Adelebsen. The people need you; you are a superior governor to Manfred's brothers. He would die before he'd let his lands fall into the hands of his brothers."

"He did," Maria said sorrowfully. "Tell me, why are you angry? What brought you here?"

"It's nothing, my lady."

"It is certainly something, or else you wouldn't plague yourself with it."

"Fine. It was the guards. The assassin paid them off to gain entry to the crypt," Roland said. Maria was shocked to hear it.

"Well then. This is saddening news. I would have them banished."

"Banished, my lady? Not hung?"

"Of course, not hung; we are running a town, not a slaughterhouse."

"My lady, these men must pay for their crimes."

"For their greed?"

"For their disloyalty. For their treachery. For their murder of your husband."

"You can't truly believe that they knew he would kill Manfred."

"What other role could he have played? I will see to it that they're hung tomorrow at noon."

"No, I order you to have them banished, stripped of lands, titles, and possessions."

"My lady, they will be hung."

"Remember who you are speaking to," Maria said sternly. "They will be banished." The two made eye contact for a period of time before Roland gave in.

"Fine, my lady. Banished they shall be," he said, leaving the room in disdain. Maria was disheartened that she had now gained tensions with a man who she thought of as an ally. Soon afterwards, Maria vacated the hall as well. She approached Franz, once the commander of Manfred's infantry, and now the captain of the town guard. Franz sat in the courtyard, eating a radish stew. As Maria sat down beside him, Ennelein brought another bowl for her.

"May I be of service to you, m' lady?" he asked.

"Franz, you have been highly loyal to my husband and me, and I will be forever indebted to you."

"Thank you, m'lady."

"I'd like you to call off my plans to return to Kassel," Maria said abruptly. Franz paused.

"You wish to stay here?"

"Yes, I have changed my mind. I cannot let Manfred's brothers take hold of this town."

"Well, how do you plan to hold it?"

"I don't want bloodshed. I never have and never will. I will settle this diplomatically."

"Well, if it's diplomacy you're after, I don't see how I can be of much aid to you."

"Franz, I need you to prepare the guards, just in case."

"My lady, you can't seriously be considering..."

"I am. If it comes to it, this town must hold. Kassel will come to our aid, I know it."

"Well then, I suppose I'd better get to work," Franz said, finishing his stew.

"I'm grateful for your service," Maria said.

"Don't thank me, thank my men," Franz replied, heading off to round up all the off-duty guards. Eventually, he and twenty men approached the training field. They were surprised to find the Russia druzhina already brandishing their skills with mounted lance and bow. Boyar Katerina had her men train every day with fitness and martial activities as rigorous as the training of knights. Their martial prowess was matched only by the cold steel they swung in their hands.

"Sir. Franz," Katerina said, dismounting from her steed. "What brings you here?"

"Lady Maria wishes to stay."

"Really?"

"Yes. She has informed me that Kassel will bolster her claim. I certainly hope that she can solve this politically, as our town is in no fighting condition."

"From what I hear, it once was."

"Yes, yes it was, back when Manfred ran it with his knights. Now, we have nobody."

"Nobody but seasoned war veterans and elite Rus warriors," Katerina said with a smile, swinging her sabre about as if she was facing an opponent.

"You and your men are well-trained warriors."

"Of course, all druzhina must be."

"Well, I wonder if we could train with you?"

"Of course," Katerina said. From her saddlebag, she pulled a birch bark scroll. On it was a diet, exercise routine, and sleep schedule for her warriors. Franz looked at the paper and smirked.

"These men won't last a day without bread."

"Bread makes your stomach soft. Only meat and vegetables can build strong warriors."

"Did they teach you this when you trained in Neva?"

"They taught me this in kindergarten," she replied with a laugh. The two units practiced with each other for the extent of the afternoon. They practiced their marksmanship and military drills, preparing for a battle in the streets. God forbid it would ever come to it.

CHAPTER 51. UNWANTED GUESTS

On the morning of October 5th, three days after the death of Manfred, one day after his funeral, a long line of riders approached the town. Leading the way were Manfred's brothers, Otto and Reuben. Behind them rode their heralds, ladies and gentlemen of the court of Göttingen, minstrels, and retainers. The retinues of soldiers that they brought with them were small but intimidating. Reluctantly, Maria let them into the town. She received them in the great hall, not with a feast, but instead a reception of Gregorian chants and light snacks.

"Welcome to Adelebsen, Lords."

"I was hoping to be invited to my own brother's funeral," replied Otto, impatient and disgruntled.

"How dare you? You would walk into my court unannounced like some invading foe and insult me in front of my courtiers, only for the ends of spiting me after the death of my murdered husband?"

"You are right. We are no invading force, but instead, a force hoping to reclaim our lands. It is the least you could do after the death of our beloved brother," Otto replied. Reuben stood by him like a dim-witted escort.

"You had better give it to us, or we'll execute everybody here," Reuben said loudly.

"Well then, that was quite brash," Maria said without fear. "Roland, please show Reuben to the pheasant tartlets such that we adults could discuss these matters?" Roland stepped forwards.

"How dare you call me a child!" Reuben cried.

"You are a child. When your brother was defeated in combat, you shot up your hands faster than a jackrabbit. You deserve no respect."

"You can't have Adelebsen; it's ours," replied Reuben.

"Yours? So, what, you and Otto will split it down the middle? How in God's name are you to share it?"

"We need not be questioned by the likes of you," Otto II interjected. "Just make the announcement and be done with it. I presume you've already made plans to return to your home in Kassel? Your father must be longing to see you. I hear that you haven't visited him once since his return from Sicily."

"Well, he has seen me. He came to the funeral, and in fact, he is here in the court right now," Maria replied. Her father, Prince Goetz emerged from the crowd to stand beside his daughter.

"I am here, as are one hundred and fifty of my finest soldiers. I would be happy to advocate for my daughter's claim in the Imperial Court if that is your wish," Goetz said menacingly.

"We will do nothing of the sort. This town belongs to my father's dynasty, the Göttingen dynasty," Otto said, unintimidated.

"What is worth more, this town or your men? There is no need to bicker over this land. My daughter was his wife."

"When my father died, Göttingen didn't pass on to his wife, but instead to us, his sons."

"But Manfred had no sons, nor daughters for that matter. The town goes to Maria, it's what he would have wanted."

"Don't say that; you didn't know him. We may have squabbled, yes, but we were brothers. Blood is, and always has been, more solid than marriage. The judges know it, the priests know it, and every court from here to Hispania knows it. You have no claim. You can either leave my town, or I'll kick you out," Otto said.

"Otto, there is no need to shed blood," Maria stated. "We can solve this like nobles, without barbarity."

"You lost the right to say that when you decided to usurp our hold. Go back to Kassel. This is our town, and we will defend it to the last man," Otto replied.

"Defend it? You don't have it," Maria replied.

"Do you really think that when faced with the decision of you and me, your guards won't drop their spears and run?"

"They will not. I trust them. They have served me well."

"So well that they let murderers into your crypt?" Otto asked. Maria was shocked.

"How did you know?"

"I have eyes everywhere, my lady," Otto replied with a grin. Maria paused.

"Leave now, and never return," she said, stricken with emotion. Goetz eyed the two brothers as they stood.

"You would not receive us? We have travelled far," Otto said. "You may hate us, but you have no quarry with our courtiers."

"Fine," replied Maria. "The courtiers may sleep in the guest house. The brothers can sleep in the crypt with their father and brother." Roland nodded and escorted the brothers to the crypt where they set up beds of straw and linen sheets. Afterwards, the two brothers set out into the town to discover the place. Surprisingly, it was the first time that they wished to visit the place in detail. On their way out, they noticed that the mural depicting the family had been painted over with whitewash. Otto understood that Maria hated him, but he wouldn't let that keep him from Adelebsen.

CHAPTER 52. RHUBARB

After dinner alone, Maria prepared for bed. She was solitary in her chamber, as she had been for months. Before it was bearable, for she at least had the hope of Manfred's return. Now, the weight of troubles that Manfred left behind began to bear down upon her like the stone of a mill. As the days passed, she felt her kindness fleeting like the leaves outside her window in the Autumn breeze. She began to loathe the stress she felt. How could she single-handedly maintain her grasp upon this town? Her father could only fight her battles, both literally and metaphorically, for so long. Maria had to develop a plan. One without bloodshed or sin.

"Warm milk before bed, m'lady?" asked Maria's attendant, Ennelein

"Yes, please," Maria replied with a warm smile.

"You must be quite troubled, m'lady," Ennelein said, as she placed the glass in front of the dame.

"My troubles are mine alone, sweet Ennelein. I couldn't think to place my burdens upon your shoulders."

"It would be no trouble at all, m'lady. I know it must be lonely in this room all by yourself, so I thought I might keep you company. You know, just somebody to talk to."

"You have served me long and well, Ennelein. Tell me, what do you suggest I do?"

"M'lady, you wouldn't take advice from a servant..."

"Enne, you have aided me with trivial dilemmas in the past, and I call upon your wisdom once more. What should I do?"

"Well, m'lady, I have little experience in the world of politics, but I can say that I can see where your troubles reside. When I was little, my father used to tell me tales of his time living in the woods as a charcoal burner. He told me of his experiences like a father would to a son, for he had no male child, and instead, he had to make do with what the Lord gave him. He told me of snakes that roam the forests of Saxony. One such snake is the viper, a demonic creature with poison so deadly it kills a man to the touch. One day, when my father and his comrades were watching the kiln, he felt a tingling around his ankle. He looked down, and there it was. The devilish serpent replied his look with a keen stare of his own, haunting my father forever onwards. Immediately, my father jumped up, faster than a rabbit. His comrades drew their messers and began hacking at the sly beast. First, one man cut off the end of the tail, but the snake kept crawling. Then, the next man cut the snake a few inches closer to the head, but the serpent continued. One after another, each man hacked at the beast until the animal was only a quarter of the length it had before; however, it continued to wriggle, threatening all of the burners huddled around it. Finally, my father took a shovel and decapitated the animal, slicing its head clean off. Only then did the snake cease its villainy."

"What do you wish to say with this tale?"

"M'lady, if you want to kill a snake, you have to cut off its head," Ennelein said solemnly. Maria gazed at her in disbelief.

"You would have me murder a guest in my own home?"

"I would have you serve the Lord's justice."

"Who are you to propose such a thing? Who has put these thoughts in your head?"

"My husband spoke to Roland yesterday while cleaning his

horse. Roland had informed him of your dilemma. M'lady, you can't give up the town. Those boys will never stop until either you are dead or they are."

"Enne, this is madness! How could you conjure such an image? I would not have it."

"M'lady, I apologize for speaking of it. I will return your glass to the kitchen at once," Ennelein said as she exited the room.

"Enne, wait," Maria said, brought to madness by the stress that clung to her like an anchor.

"Yes, m'lady?"

"How would you do it?"

"How would I do what?"

"You know... cut the head off the snake?"

"Well, m'lady, no plan has crossed my mind just yet," Ennelein replied. She turned around to leave before she made any decisions that she could regret; however, an inexplicable force returned her to the room. "Rhubarb extract, m'lady."

"Rhubarb extract? Isn't rhubarb the vegetable that I find in my stew?"

"That's only the stalk. The leaves can give your throat an itch, or even worse, it can bring great illness."

"Enne, if you did it, it would have to be tonight."

"I know, m'lady. The extract is the juice taken from many leaves. Together, they would surely slay a man in his sleep. I apologize for planting these sinful thoughts in your mind, m'lady. I must retire."

"No, Enne, not yet. I ask that you bring some wine for our esteemed guests. Mix the wine with whatever you wish."

"My lady, you would have me murder them?"

"It is your choice, Enne. I can't order it; my spirit would not allow it. Instead, I give you permission to do so if you so desire," Maria said, plagued by thoughts of death and fear. Ennelyn slowly left the room. As Maria sat to ponder, she immediately regretted her decision; however, she could not leave her room anymore. What if somebody was to hear chatter in the halls? Maria trusted Enne with her life, and now, she also entrusted her with the lives of her guests. Only time would answer her fears now.

CHAPTER 53. CANDLELIGHT

The next morning came with a startle. A boisterous thud on the door woke Maria from her deep slumber.

"M'lady, something's happened. We need your attention immediately," the guard said, patiently waiting outside of his lady's chamber. Maria peered out of her window, seeing a dark night sky.

"For heaven's sake, what's the matter? It's the middle of the night," Maria said loudly at the door.

"I apologize, m'lady, but it's about your guests," the guard said. The memories of the night prior hit Maria like a tidal wave.

"By God, what has been done?" she asked, opening her door with a jolt.

"They're dead; both of them. We found them laying on the crypt floor with blood spilling from their throats."

"Were they alive when you found them?"

"They were, but not a word came out of them. Before we could carry them to the doctor, they passed, one after the other," the guard said solemnly. Maria, now filled with regret, began to tremble.

"Take me to them," she said. The guard nodded and escorted her down the spiralling staircase to the doctor who lived in the town. Accompanied by a team of guardsmen,

Maria rode, clothed only in her nightgown and cloak. Finally, they reached the small infirmary. It was quaint. Like the small cubic lodgings beside it, it sheltered beneath a thatched roof and supported itself on pillars, lifting a section which protruded slightly onto the street. It was the only building in the town with a lit candle inside, aside from the blacksmith's shop, which remained lit at all times. Maria dismounted and headed indoors. Her guards followed, making sure that nobody saw them enter. As soon as they stepped inside, they saw the two bodies, exposed, and cut open like fish. Blood pooled everywhere, slipping through the cracks of the old wooden table. The doctor hunched over them, taking samples from their stomach and mixing those samples with other chemicals.

"How did they die?" asked Maria, trying her best to hide the plot which plagued her mind.

"I don't know yet," replied the doctor, fixated on his glass vials.

"Why not, pray tell?"

"Madam, the matching of chemicals is difficult, and the one that these men ingested seems to have been plant-based, making it even harder."

"You will address her as your Lady, doctor," a guard said in a booming voice.

"It's fine," interjected Maria. "I don't care how he addresses me, as long as he finds out what killed these men."

"Shall we launch an investigation first?" asked the guard.

"You haven't already?"

"No, we await your command. We thought that perhaps you may wish to inform the other guests first."

"Yes... yes, you're right. We shall wait until dawn when all rise, and then we shall break the news. We can question them each at that time," Maria said, concealing her deceit. It burned her like poison, lying, but she couldn't do anything but lie. Even if she went to an imperial dungeon, Ennelein may face even harsher punishment. Maria had to keep Enne safe from all of it, as she only had played with her mind, ordering her to kill the men. "Where is my handmaiden?"

"At the manor, I suppose," the guard said.

"Well then. Let's return to our sleep, we have a long day ahead of us," Maria said. The guards escorted her back to the manor, ensuring her safety from similar fates. The night was cold and dark. The trees swayed around the party as they rode through the streets. Cobblestones beneath their hooves made a boisterous clopping, cutting like a knife through the still of night.

Maria watched the homes and stores carefully, examining the details as they became enlightened by her brightly shining lantern. They were not tall, only two floors high, with roughly carved wood and a smooth layer of whitewash. The wash in the night like phantoms paving the way, guiding Maria back to her home. This was perhaps the last time she would ever see it. The sight, the smell, everything that made her home her home. Come sunrise, it would be gone, all of it, and the peaceful still of night would be ruptured by the foul stench of death.

Maria rued the day that blood would seep into the recesses of the cobblestone, and she promised herself that that day would never be of her own doing. But, had she already failed? Was that a promise that she simply couldn't keep? As Maria returned to the manor, she took note of all that she could. In her room, once the door was closed firmly, she began to hastily pack her belongings into old, unused chests. Her clothes were already kept in a chest at the foot of the bed. Maria hastily stashed away her mirrors, self-maintenance kits, perfumes.

Maria scoured the room for any trinkets left by herself or her husband. She cleared the mantlepiece, stashing the thumbnail paintings of her and her husband. Beside it sat a wooden horse. It was small and crude, like the toy of a child. It brought no memories to her, other than the cognisance that her husband valued it greatly. She tucked it into her coin purse, making a promise to herself that she would leave it atop Manfred's tomb. At the moment, the stone coffin had no lid. Instead, like a ghoulish mummy, Manfred lay exposed for all to see, rotting like a foul demon, and evoking memories like an undead beast. Maria wished she could have seen his effigy once it was carved, for it would be the lid that finally sealed him. Instead, she would have to visit once this ordeal was over, if it would ever be over, or else she could speak with him once again in person.

Maria cached the horse like buried treasure and placed her hand on the doorknob. Then, it came to her. She could spend one more night in the manor. A few more hours of slumber. Nobody else knew about the murder, nobody else of importance. In the morning, she could return with her father to Kassel. It would seem less suspicious, and she would have a chance to inform Roland, Helmuth, and of course, Franz. Would Ennelein come with her? Maria decided that she would ponder this decision when the sun was out, when she would be in a better state of mind.

Maria returned the horse to the mantlepiece and lay the trunks adjacent to each other. Before returning to her slumber, Maria gazed out of the window. Through the window, she could see the town once more. Small flickers of lights from the watchmen danced in the dark. Maria felt a storm of sorrow swirl inside of her like a torrential rainfall. Her heart ached, not for Manfred's brothers, but for Manfred, for his desires, and for his company. She failed him. Because of her brash decision, she made his dream of saving the town impossible. Of course, his brothers could no longer take the town, but some other Göttingen noble would claim it. Their wives perhaps, or worse, some outsiders from Münster or Leipzig.

Maria was saddened by her superfluity. With tear-soaked cheeks and a heavy heart, Maria's consciousness faded into the realm of the unconscious. Her thoughts now danced freely in her mind, manifesting themselves in dreams unlike any other. Maria fell fast asleep.

CHAPTER 54. THE RED AND WHITE LION

Prince Goetz of Kassel, Maria's father, rose to the sound of a proud rooster. The man rose to his feet immediately, with the discipline of a soldier. He was an older gentleman, with grey hair and a stiff upper lip. The barren waste that was his hairless head was rivalled by his robust silver beard, whose curls seemed to flow from his chin like a babbling waterfall. His pyjamas, although mostly undecorated, bore his family crest: the red and white striped lion on a field of blue. He belonged to the house of Hessen. His dynasty dated back as nobility for centuries, but instead of calling himself 'von Hessen,' he preferred the title, 'von Kassel.' He thought it more adequately reflected his interests. Goetz was a simple man. He cared naught for the luxury and pomp and circumstance which came along with nobility. Although he wasn't about to donate all his gold in alms, he was also not the kind of man to throw parades after any minor political victory. This man cared for one thing, if anything at all, and that was his children. Maria was his eldest daughter, and thus she was married first. He had two more children, both failures in the eyes of the masses. His second eldest was Helena, but she preferred the name, Lena. She, like her brother, was yet to be married, mostly due to her obsession with doing male activities. As a noble, she was entitled to engage in whatever she liked, and to her, that meant jousting, duelling, archery, horsemanship, hunting, and a whole list of other male duties. According to Goetz, Lena would never be married, which is why he gave up years ago. Ever since, she has trained to become a tournament knight, like Roland, but instead of a freelance, she would work for her father and brother, if the time ever came that he would inherit the estate. Her brother, Augustus, maintained the valuable and esteemed tradition of being a drunk since the age of eleven. Now, at the age of fifteen, the boy was yet to be married, and did nothing but party, drink, eat, and sleep with the wenches who sell themselves in the brothels. He was the exact opposite of his sisters, two high achievers. It wasn't wholly his fault, though, as most of his life was spent endure the mental torture of being blamed for his own mother's death. She succumbed to mass blood loss when giving birth to him. To make matters worse, Augustus suffered from hemophilia. His father, Goetz, used to tell him that it was his curse for making his mother bleed to death. Augustus championed the irony like a rainbow coloured albatross. Goetz regretted his harsh treatment of the boy, now that he saw what it produced. On that day, his birth, Goetz embraced his wife one last time before she was escorted by her midwives to the birthing chamber. His last words were:

"You've gotten two out, just one more to go." They knew that Augustus would be a boy from the blood testing, so Goetz was content to stop producing once they had an heir. Now, he would trade the boy in a heartbeat for his wife again. Some things never change, and this was the reality of Maria's dysfunctional family. Goetz hated his son but still would die for him. He would die for any of them, and that is as true as the truth can get. Kassel was little over a day's ride from Adelebsen. Did Maria visit during the entire time of Manfred's quest? Not once. She dreaded the dinner time arguments, the verbal abuse flying across the manor and the constant barrage of:"Why don't you visit more often?" If there was a hell, she imagined it to be Kassel. Now, it was her new home. That morning, Maria came into her father's room to tell him the news. She told him of the murder, but not of her part in it, and with a cautious grin, she explained that she needed to return to Kassel. With the slightest of smirks, Goetz embraced his daughter.

"No assassin can get to you, my dear," he said. "Have you issued an investigation yet?"

"No, father."

"Don't worry, Maria. I will bring my finest head-hunters. They will get the job done in no time. Within a week the assassin will be drawn, quartered, and hung in the town square - you'll see," Goetz said in his exuberant tone. It was one semitone higher than his normal tone, which was a whole octave higher than his tone of anger. The bison-built noble began to pack his things. "Oh, and Maria..."

"Yes, father?"

"Don't inform the guests yet. I will have my men do it; I can't risk you being stabbed by some shisha-smoking porter. Only tell the people you trust the most," Goetz said in a stern voice. Maria contemplated her plan of action.

"I have to gather my henchmen at once," she said, storming from the room like a plough horse.

In her quarters, Maria assembled Franz, Katerina, Roland, and Helmuth. One by one they came in, wondering why they were brought here. Franz assumed that some scheme was at play and that he would soon have to assemble his guards in defence of the town. Together, they came before her, all curious to hear the news.

"What information do you wish to speak so urgently, pray tell?" said Roland.

"Roland, I've gathered you all here because the brothers Göttingen are dead, slain at the hands of some slippery assassin, most likely crawling within our walls as we speak. Although they were my rivals, to say the least, they were of noble blood, and thus this crime cannot go unpunished."

"M'lady, whoever did this is on our side," said Franz.

"Our side? There are no sides when playing with a wild killer such as this," replied Maria.

"My lady, we mustn't act rashly. If you call an investigation, it is doubtless that the Emperor will catch the scent of the pie we are cooking. Perhaps it is best to remain tranquil until your position is less... suspicious?"

"Suspicious? You wouldn't have the audacity to think that I..."

"Apologies, my lady. I meant no disrespect. Nobody in this room, in this castle, or within the walls of this town could even conceive of the notion that you would commit this... act."

"Good. But your argument is valid, and it is for that reason that I will return to Kassel. Franz, you are to act as Lord Regent when I am gone. Katerina, I believe that you will serve him well. But, first, you and your druzhina must escort our guests back to their respective castles. Roland and Helmuth, you two will accompany me on my return to Kassel."

"Forgive my intrusion, my lady, but why do you entrust this important task to just two knights, as opposed to your father's retinue?" asked Helmuth.

"Helmuth, Roland, you two are my finest lances. I must remain undetected, invisible to the manhunters and assassins that may lurk in these very woods. Even these walls have ears, and to all of you, I entrust this information of utmost secrecy. You two must escort me in the case of any brigands, or those devilish tribesmen which I have heard so much about."

"Yes, my lady," said the two knights in unison. The plan was set. Everything was ready. As a gentle breeze wisped through the window, the five allies knew that the winds of change were blowing, and although the sweet autumn air pronounced naught of the sort, all breezes reflect violent storms in the distance. A new age was to dawn on the town of Adelebsen. The red leaves that stuck to the walls of the town like wet paper marked the coming of spilled blood and sharp tongues. They could not fight their way out of this one. Whether Maria killed the brothers or not, the team had one goal: to keep Adelebsen in the hands of the deserving.

CHAPTER 55. GOTT SPEED

All guests, workers, and the poor were invited to eat breakfast at the castle. It included a wide array of fruits, vegetables, and meat pies, as harvesting season was in full swing. Maria sat at the main table. Beside her, where Manfred once was, was an empty seat. Nobody had the audacity nor the coldness of heart to claim the centre chair as their own. Breakfast was a joyous occasion, a distractor from the work to come. All enjoyed it, and extra portions were made for the guards on watch duty. Once all had eaten and satiated their hunger, Maria rose to make an announcement. With her silver spoon, she tapped her goblet.

"Friends, we gather here on a joyous occasion, for this is truly a mingling of two communities; however, you may notice that two of our valued guests are not with us today. Last night, Sir. Otto von Göttingen and Sir. Reuben von Göttingen were assassinated, poisoned most likely. As the Lady of this town, it is my responsibility to ensure that we are all safe from harm. It is for this reason that our guests from Rosdorf and Friedland must return immediately. At midday, our very own elite cavalry will escort you back to your homes. I, myself, will return to Castle Löwenburg in Kassel, where I will remain until a full investigation is completed, and it is safe to return. I will leave Adelebsen in the hands of my trusted righthand man, Commander Franz von Plesse. I know this may be difficult for many of you, as I understand that some of you may have made friendships with Reuben and Otto, but we cannot hold a funeral until the investigation is complete. Until then, their bodies will remain in Adelebsen for further examination. With that, I hope you all have enjoyed your breakfasts," Maria said, taking her seat once more. The crowd erupted into panicked conversation. The shocking news was not broken gently, and to many of them, they doubted the security of their social status now that their employers were dead. As to be expected, some guests began to speculate, preemptively accusing Maria of vengeful murder.

In the courtyard at midday, everybody gathered to join their respective caravan. Maria and her two bodyguards made plans with her father to meet him at Castle Löwenburg. They decided that they would take the road along the Fulda river, while Goetz and his retinue would instead return through Staufenberg.

"When we arrive, I will order at once that my head-hunters come to this God-forsaken town," Goetz said. "You would be pleased to meet my finest. He goes by the name Adolf Ratzinger, but I doubt that it's his true name. He's an outlaw, just like you will be soon," Goetz added.

"I give my thanks for your support, father."

"Well, I once had one of my three children married. Now, none of them are. I suppose that, when you return, we can begin to plan another marriage."

"Father, I don't think I'm ready to..."

"Don't you want some young stud? Currently, you are the stadtholder of Adelebsen. You can get whatever husband you wish in the region. I will send a message to all the local Lords with unwed firstborns."

"I'm not ready. I loved Manfred."

"Manfred was a political marriage. You can learn to love again," Goetz said before mounting his horse. "I'll see the three of you in three days. Don't be late," Goetz said, rearing his horse in the most masculine way possible, before galloping off with his men at arms to the front of his caravan. Off they marched southwards, in the direction of Dransfeld. They were followed out of the vicinity of the manor by Katerina's forces, leading the guests from Rosdorf and Friedland. Rosdorf was on the way to Friedland; thus, they could travel in unison. Finally, Maria, Franz, Helmuth, Roland, and their squires remained in the courtyard.

"I suppose this is goodbye, for now," Maria said to Franz, giving him a hug.

"I suppose so, my lady," Franz replied with a nod. As Maria hugged him, she slipped a piece of paper into his belt. Finally, the five travellers mounted their steeds, ready to ride towards the Fulda River.

"Goodbye, friend," Roland said. "When I return, drinks are on you," he added with a smile.

"Only if you bring some sweets from Kassel," Franz replied with a hearty laugh. Helmuth nodded before the five departed. Off they were, just as Manfred's party had left the town nearly a year earlier. This time, however, there was no Manfred. The five travellers made their way west towards the Weser river, which split at Hann Münden into the Fulda and the Werra. As the travellers left, Franz reached for the note. He held it in his hands for a moment, curious as to what it could say. He knew Maria reasonably well, having spent half a year in the town; however, Maria passed no note to Roland, who she had known since her marriage at the age of twelve. Franz paused, brain swelling with confusion and curiosity, but also fear. He feared what was to come - he feared that Maria really was a murderer. He felt no sadness for the death of the two brothers; in fact, the news brought him a slight moment of exuberance. But, now that the crime had to be paid for, it seemed risky at best to be close friends to a killer. A killer of nobles no less. Franz slowly unfolded the paper slip, clutching in its hands.

Then, he peered down at the paper like it was an ancient scroll, unearthed for the first time - the only scroll of the most ancient civilization on earth. Franz couldn't bear the suspense. He quickly read the paper. As he read the short message, he began to wonder what was next? The message said one short clause:

I did it.

Franz, shocked and dismayed, tore the paper to bits and burned the bits in the nearest candle as he made his way back to his room. In the barracks, he lay upon his straw bed, watching the ceiling like a play. What was to be done? Then, Franz's imagination gave birth to an idea. He was a warrior, not a politician or an assassin, but he would certainly scheme before he, his men, or his friends would be put on trial. The death of Manfred ached his heart like a scorching blade. Franz could only imagine what would become of Maria if found guilty, or worse, if Roland or Helmuth or Katerina were believed to be accomplices. Franz loved Katerina. Not in the way that one loves a friend or a pet, but like one loves a partner. He found her charming and witty, and he found her martial fortitude impressive, to say the least. He was not very attracted to her physically - she was not a conventionally attractive woman, but he did certainly love her. He had never expressed it, and he didn't know if he ever would. Instead, he was happy to see her leave to escort the guests back to their homes. Although it pained him to separate himself from her, he thought it was safer now, so that she could invade a murderer in the castle. But now, with an imminent investigation, her absence could be seen as suspicious. Franz had to protect her, Maria, Roland, and even Helmuth. All of them. He would gladly put his life before theirs in an instant. He had lived for forty years, and in those years, he had experienced a good life. He had fun, he experienced adventure, he explored the world of the German folk. His comrades were now well paid and well-fed. Now, he didn't have much more to live for, aside from the prospect of one day living a life with Katerina at his side. She was of similar age, perhaps a half-decade younger, and she seemed available, although she hadn't shown any signs of interest in anyone. Franz was ready to risk it all for his peers. He devised a plan.

CHAPTER 56. BATH HOUSE

The road to Kassel winded along the Fulda river, bending every which way until the quaintest of settlements was to be seen. Time and again the travellers passed such farmsteads with woe, for in any one of them could be some disgruntled Friedlander, or a big brick of a Rosdorfer who'd had too much to drink and too much practice with a knife. The group dared enter none of them, for they were instead intent on reaching their destination in one piece. The road was surrounded by a tall, orange forest, filled with creatures both great and small, all going about their daily business with little attention to the steel-clad horse and rider. Deer emerged in packs like bees, swarming the trees, grazing upon the tall grass that had grown over the course of the summer. The riders rode with comfort, for they were in no real rush; however, they also rode in silence. None of them wanted to discuss the murder any further. None of them wanted to unveil any information the likes of which should never be unveiled. All except Roland. A man of little care, Roland decided to break the silence with characteristically bold and unforgiving words.

"You know, if those usurpers were to have laid a hand on you, my lady, I swear, I would have butchered them like fresh swine," Roland said, taking a long sip from his flask of only God knew what.

"You flatter me," Maria replied in a sarcastic tone. As the riders rode, the silence resurfaced for a while. As Maria thought, the darkness of her actions haunted her further. "Tell me, Roland, when you were on your journey, did you ever take a bath?"

"No, I suppose not my lady."

"Hmm... were there bathhouses for you to do so?"

"I suppose so... what do...."

"And Manfred? I don't suppose he took any?"

"No, my lady, I don't suppose he did. May I ask wh..."

"Your men, any of them. Of all of your twenty men, did a single one decide to make use of a bathhouse?"

"No, my lady, but why do you wish to know this? It can't come as such a surprise."

"No, it doesn't," replied Maria. "If I had gone on that journey, I wouldn't have lasted a day."

"Come now, don't say that."

"No, really. I would have run home the second I saw blood."

"Is this about you wanting to take a bath? Just because we wouldn't do it doesn't mean you couldn't take one."

"It's not just the bath, Roland. You warriors are a special breed. You are something I am not; you have something that I don't."

"Warriors? You must mean killers. What we have that you don't is a sword and an absent conscience."

"Well, well yes. How do you do it? How can you run a man through like that?"

"Excuse me?"

"How do you kill a man, maybe two, maybe three, maybe a whole wagon full, and wake up the next day like nothing ever happened?"

"My Lady, I don't think you want to know."

"Well I asked, didn't I?"

"My Lady..."

"Don't do that, Roland."

"Do what?"

"Say *My Lady* like that. It's not you, or at least it's not who you were."

"What's that supposed to mean?"

"You and Manfred went off on that quest and returned like different people. Before, Manfred would never have the gall to confront his brother like that. And you, you wouldn't bat an eye at a wench until you were piss drunk."

"I would not."

"But you would. It's the truth, and we both know it. You're what, twenty at least? Maybe nineteen? And you're not married yet? I get it, you and the others wanted to have fun. It's fine. It's just that you've evolved now. Manfred did too. And I'm here, the exact same as a year ago, not having gone on that journey, trying to deal with the messes of entirely new people. I just don't know how to handle all of this. You're so courteous now; it's great. You call me *your lady* all the time, and I really do appreciate it. But, honestly, would you have called Manfred *sir*? No, of course not. You two were friends, stronger than links in a steel chain, and yet I was his wife, and I only really knew him for a day. One damn day," Maria said with grief. She began to weep as she rode. From Roland's saddlebag, he pulled out a handkerchief and offered it to the maiden. Helmuth did the same, but she refused both and carried on riding.

"Maria, you knew Manfred the best of all of us, there is no doubt about it. You're right, I have changed. I used to be a wreckless imbecile who injured men for sport like a hooligan on a horse. I was no brave questing knight, and I'm still not. But, your husband brought me as close to it as I'll ever be. That man had made us legends."

"Well, now Freidrich and Wilhelm will be nothing more than just that - legends."

"That wasn't his fault. They chose to sacrifice themselves,"

273

Roland replied, comforting Maria.

"Roland, I know that he was a good man. But, tell me, was he a good leader?"

"Well, just like you said, he changed. He became the best commander I've ever known. My Lady, Manfred's death has had its impact on all of us, but I can see that it has troubled you the most. I believe that the best way to relieve yourself of trouble is to drink," Roland said with a smile, offering his flask. Maria slowly accepted, hoping that the alcohol would soothe her pain.

"To Manfred," she toasted.

"To Manfred," Roland replied. Maria poured the sharp, bitter liquid down her throat. In the distance, the party set their eyes upon the small village of Scheden.

CHAPTER 57. THE KNIGHTS OF THE MAUNCH

The thunder of hooves echoed over the fields of Hanover. Leading a V-shaped formation of knights was a man clad in black armour from head to toe. In the distance, cries for help echoes across the farmland like the sound of war trumpets. The Sable Knight was grand in stature. While his men behind him held their lances firmly, the black combatant swung his war hammer about like a wild barbarian. Upon it was engraved: "Menschentöter". The seven knights carried white shields with grey maunch heraldics on them, representing a lady's sleeve, the ultimate symbol of chivalry. Their leader scanned the horizon through the eye slot of his Churburg great bascinet and set his eyes upon a faint image in the distance.

"Over there!" he cried in a gruff voice, pointing his war hammer in the direction of the turmoil. "There seems to be about three of them."

"We'll slaughter those damn highwaymen like pigs!" exclaimed the knight riding to his right-hand side. The men rode forth, through the fields of wheat, making for their target.

Upon the road lay a wounded merchant, whose comrade held him. Above them stood three fierce men-at-arms, raubritters, who had no regard for life outside of their own.

"Damn Jews," one of the brigands said, shoving one of the merchants aside. "You know you ought to be rid of Christendom. You bring bad luck." He spat on the wounded man. They searched the wagon of the two poor men, pocketing whatever coin and precious metal they could.

"Oy, do you hear that?" one of them asked.

"I think there are horses coming," replied another. They looked in the direction of the sun, and from the radiant light came the silhouette of seven steel-clad riders.

"Run," the third man said, slinging a sack over his shoulder and mounting his steed. The two others followed suit. A chase ensued, as horse and rider kicked up dust behind them; however, the brigands' poor workhorses were no match for the bold warhorses of their pursuers. Soon, they were caught up to by the silver riders. In a sweeping motion, the three men turned to face their foe, fearlessly charging into them like noble knights. Unfortunately, although knights they may have been, noble they certainly were not. With a crushing blow, the leader was knocked unconscious by the Sable Knight. His deputies unhorsed the other two and sent them scurrying for the tall grass.

"Let them run, those honourless brigands," the Sable Knight said. He raised his visor, revealing the face of a grizzled, middle-aged knight.

"Sir Ulrich, what shall we do with the florins?" one of the knights asked.

"We take half and give the other half back to the merchants," Ulrich replied, taking a sip of water from his flask. The knights looted their fallen opponents until they saw another smoke signal coming from a farm a few kilometres away.

"Sir, there seems to be another robbery ensuing. Their gang probably found some more Jews," a knight said. Ulrich looked in the distance.

"Alright, you lads go, and I'll return the florins to that poor merchant."

"What's the matter, getting too old?" asked a knight with a chuckle.

"No, it's just the last time I gave you trinkets like these, I saw them in a brothel the next day," Ulrich replied with a hearty laugh. The knights set off once more, and Ulrich returned to the merchant who sat upon the road, still trying to bandage his comrade. Before handing over the money, Ulrich decided to pocket a little more for himself. "Right, here you are," he said, handing a large sack to the man.

"Please help me, my brother's dying," the merchant replied, holding rags upon a large gash in the fallen man's chest. Ulrich stayed atop his horse and dropped the sack to his feet.

"I don't do medicine," he said in a low voice.

"Please, he will die if you don't help. Just give him some water," the man said, desperately trying to hold onto what little life his brother had left. Ulrich tossed his flask to the man and turned his steed around. As the man gave the drink to his brother, he shouted at Ulrich. "Hey, don't you leave. That's not all those brigands took, not even half."

"We Knights of the Maunch have to make a living too."

"So, you steal from us? You vigilantes are all the same," the merchant said angrily.

"Perhaps it would do you well to show some respect," Ulrich said. "I just saved your life. Most men 'round here wouldn't show your folk an ounce of mercy."

"I will give you no gratitude until you come and help my brother. Just hold him until I get alcohol to pour on him."

"I'm far better at taking lives than saving them," Ulrich said, spurring his horse onwards into the distance. He rode into the sunset like a folk hero, making his way to the direction that his comrades left in.

He followed the farmland roads, making haste with his obedient steed. He rode for a few minutes. With his visor up, the fresh, autumn air rushed his face and tickled his stubble. He slowed his horse to a trot for a moment. He decided to let it have some rest. After a few minutes spent recuperating, he gave the animal an apple and spurred it onwards once more. He rode along the road, watching the farmland pass by. The rolling hills ascended and plummeted off into the distance. The bright green of freshly cultivated land contrasted the faint blue sky.

As he rode, he came across nearly thirty travellers on the road. They garbed themselves in long, white gowns. Some bore red crosses on their backs. These people were self-flagellants. These people whipped themselves, travelling from town to town, in the hopes of receiving help from God. To them, they wished to imitate the suffering that Jesus faced in order to receive the Lord's sympathy. For this reason, such travellers were common in the times of the Black Death. Now that it was long gone, these morbid self-torturers were not a common sight to the lands of the Empire. Ulrich was no longer filled with the pleasantry of the Saxon landscape.

In a low voice, some of the travellers hymned Gregorian chants while others gave prayers to the Lord above. The long line marched slowly. Blood trickled down their backs, revealing a rough grid of bright red scratches. Ulrich pulled the reigns of his horse, bringing the beast to a halt.

"Tell me travellers, why do you bring such ailment to yourselves? The plague is long gone from here; you have no more reason to fear God's wrath," he stated. As he approached, he noticed the people's skin was pale, like ghosts. The wraith-like figures continued on without acknowledging his presence.

An old woman, no taller than four feet, stepped out of the line, revealing herself, and hobbled her way over to the grizzled knight. She was dark skinned and wore foreign clothing. Ulrich found her presence strange. He hadn't expected to find any Arabs or Moors in Hanover. She stayed in the centre of the road as if to slow the man down and slow he did. Ulrich came to a halt with his horse. "Tell me, wretch, have you seen six wily knights with white shields?" he asked, knowing full well where they were. He wished to make contact with the woman because something drew him to her. It made him interested in knowing who she was, and where she was headed.

"Good day, Ulrich," the woman replied. She looked at the knight through her blank white eyes, reaching deep into his soul like a demon from the abyss.

"How do you know my name, hag?"

"Do you call all women hags? If you wish to know my name, it is Isolde."

"Well then, Isolde, who sent you to me? What business do you have with me, Sir. Ulrich von Göttingen, the Sable Knight?"

"I have come to warn you. Three of your comrades have reunited with the earth, and the fourth is soon to follow. If you do not return to your home with speed, all the forces of nature will ensure that that man is gone, and there is naught you can do."

"You speak in tongues. Speak plainly now, or I will cast you dead with this here instrument of death," Ulrich said, resting his war hammer upon his shoulder like a lumberjack's axe.

"Ah yes, your precious Manslayer."

"You know the name of my weapon as well?"

"It's engraved on its side."

"You have good eyes for a blind woman."

"You have poor manners for a knight. You can redeem yourself, Ulrich. Be the knight you were born to be. You kill with a passion; use it. Slay the wicked and restore justice. You may have forsaken your own destiny, but the destiny of your friend is yet to be determined."

"Why should I listen to you? I don't believe in magic, there are no witches."

"Well then, if you won't listen to me, maybe you would prefer a more scholarly source. A book perhaps?" Isolde asked. From her vicinity emerged a great mist. Within moments it engulfed the areas, giving a stench of putrid sulfur. Ulrich's horse whinnied, bucking about like an angry bull. Finally, all faded to tranquillity. The world reverted to its origin, but one thing had changed. In his saddlebag, beside Sir. Ernst's fight manuscript, was a new book. On its spine, seeming burned into the cover was spelled the title: "The Tale of Sir. Ulrich von Göttingen." Ulrich got chills. He had never believed in witchcraft, but this was undeniable. Like a ghost, the old hag was gone, vanished into thin air. Ulrich, after looking around, opened the book to the first page.

CHAPTER 58. OUT OF THE OVEN

The next morning, Ennelein rose to the sound of chirping birds. In her abdomen was terrible guilt. She had served her master well, remained loyal and obedient, yet Maria fled off to Kassel without her. Enne sprung to her feet, ready to start the day. She had no time to sit and sulk, for the matron would soon come to usher her to her chores. Enne gazed around the cold, dark room, wondering if things could have been different. Should she have poisoned the guests? Enne turned to God for answers, kneeling before a small altar carved from wood, depicting Jesus on the cross. Enne prayed, meditating with her thoughts, letting her doubts ruminate into terrible terrors. What if the guards remembered her? What if they accused her? Enne got dressed, clothing herself in a long dress-like garb which cascaded down to her ankles. Atop it, she wore a typical sleeveless tunic to help brave the chilly morning air. As she stepped outside of her quarters, into the courtyard, she began to tread atop the bulbous morning dew. She thought she might check on her Lady's quarters before setting about her daily activities, just in case she had left anything behind on accident. Enne made her way up the spiralling staircase and into the quarters, brushing past two guards. One of them was one of the watchmen for the crypt two nights prior.

"Excuse me," she said, making her way to the tall wooden door.

"What business do you have here? The Lady's away."

"She is, so I didn't think it would still be guarded."

"Franz' orders. As regent, he wanted the room to be watched at all times. Nobody goes in or out. Nobody gets past me," the guard said in a brutish voice.

"Well, somebody did two nights ago," Enne said, cheekily jesting the idea that she was of any guilt.

"Scamper off before I send you away with blood spilling from your lips. You could have just as easily killed those men. Nobody else came into the crypts."

"Well then, why don't you arrest me?"

"Maria made sure that you're protected."

"Well then, I suppose my lips won't have blood coming from them after all."

"Maria's gone," the guard said sternly, eying Enne with an intimidating look. Enne turned around, but just before she left, Franz came by, pacing through the halls like they were military barracks. When he saw the young maiden cast outside like an evicted peddler, he came to her and the two bull-headed guardsmen.

"What's the meaning of this?" Franz asked.

"You said that nobody was to enter," the guard replied.

"This girl is an exception," Franz said, gesturing that she entered. He turned to her. "Something's waiting for you inside."

"Thank you m'Lord," Enne said, briskly walking past the guards into the room. As the door creaked open, Enne laid her eyes upon a small piece of parchment carefully laid upon the bed.

"It was under the pillow before," Franz said in a mild and calming voice. Then, he vacated the area, returning to his busy work. Enne immediately sat upon the bed and opened the message. She could not wait, for her anxiety was getting the better of her. But, as soon as she realized that it was from Maria, and that it had been hidden under the pillow, Enne turned pale. Hastily, she scrambled to read the letter from top to bottom in a matter of moments. It told her how sorry Maria was for putting such a decision on her, and how she intended on making things right. Enne scoured the message for details, but there were few. There were, however, instructions. With sound mind, Enne decided to follow them to the minute detail. With great haste, she scurried out of the manor, dashing past the guards and other attendants of the residents. Franz watched her leave out of his office window, gazing upon her as she descended into the town. She soon became lost to him, unreachable. Out of sight, and out of mind. There was no smile on his face, for he felt guilty to have orchestrated such an ordeal. Instead, he pondered what to do next.

CHAPTER 59. BROTHERS AT ARMS

Enne ran through the streets to keep her hosts from waiting. They must have been waiting for days if the letter was written by Maria. But it wasn't, and Enne was surprised when she traversed through the woods that, instead of a bold army of men at arms from Kassel, she found three dismounted horsemen. They were lightly armed and carrying the red and blue of Göttingen upon their clothes and shields. Enne watched from a bush before emerging to introduce her presence. She observed as they sat together in silence beneath a tree, eating apples like children. They were nearly as young as children, with clean faces and lean figures, for they were only teenagers. After thinking for a moment, one man, a man with particularly dark hair and pale skin, opened his mouth to speak.

"I wonder where the wench is," he said, as he rose to his feet to feed his horse. It was a pale white horse, whiter than snow, contrasting the man's raven-black hair. It stood beside three other horses, two with horse coats, one without.

"Who cares," replied another. He had red hair and green eyes, completely foreign to Germany. He spoke in a foreign accent. The slightest buds of a goatee sprinkled his chin like dandelions in a field of grass. "She's a damn murderer, and if she never comes, at least we won't have to go all the way to

284

Hanover. Franz told us to wait here, so that's what we'll do."

"Have a heart," said the third. He was a tall man, long and slender like a spruce tree. "Imagine if you were in her shoes. She must be terrified."

"She'll be even more terrified when she meets Ulrich," said the first.

"Come on, Conrad, you liked the man," said the second.

"Thomas, I loved the man; he was like a father to me, but also a friend. I must say, however, that that man was the cruellest, most putrid killer I've ever seen. It was amazing. I remember once when we were out patrolling for bandits, we came across a hidden trap. Of course, it's the lord's forest, and therefore no peasant is allowed to hunt here, so Ulrich had me come along with him the entire day, without food or water, tracking the man who placed the trap. Only at sundown, we found his cabin. It was some old ruffian, but the man knew how to swing a sword. From the moment we spotted the place, Ulrich knew exactly what to do. He told me to wait in the bushes and observe, so I did, and Ulrich silently approached the door. He knocked and immediately ran to the back of the house. At first, I was puzzled, I didn't know why he would do that, but then it had turned out that Ulrich had spotted a hidden door in the back, and after about thirty seconds, the old fool came rushing out of the door, straight into Ulrich's blade. His guts were spilled into the snow right then and there. That man's the most ruthless knight in the empire, no doubt about it."

"What a charming story," Thomas replied. "Herwig, tell me, how was Manfred as a mentor?"

"He was an honourable man, truly. He would never shy away from a fight, but he would also make sure that he was always on the right side. It appears that he took that to the grave with him," Herwig, the third man, replied.

"Amen," Thomas said.

"Amen," said Conrad.

"Tell me," said Enne, emerging from the foliage like a hidden hunter, "Who did you squire for, Thomas?" The three men jumped to their feet.

"Well, well; it appears the assassin has arrived. Stealthily as always?" said Conrad with a grin.

"Did Franz tell you it was me?" asked Enne.

"Yes, why?" replied Conrad.

"That means that Maria wouldn't have let you know why I was to be escorted to Kassel."

"Maria? Kassel? Ennelein, you must be mistaken. We're taking you north to the one man who can keep you safe, Sir. Ulrich on Göttingen."

"Why? Why not take me to Kassel? I want to speak to Maria."

"Well, I'm not one to question orders, but I think it's got to do with the fact that you are the number one suspect on everyone's list," replied Conrad. "Come with us, and you'll be safe."

"Did Maria even set this up, or was it all a rouse?"

"I don't know what you're talking about, but we received orders from Lord Franz, and nobody else," Conrad replied. The three men mounted their steeds, clad in red and blue heraldic horse coats. The fourth horse, unbarded, stood in wait for Enne.

"Mein Gott!" Enne exclaimed. "You're not sent to kill me, are you?"

"From what you heard; do you think so?" asked Conrad sarcastically.

"We don't have time for this; saddle up and let's go. We were told to leave immediately; we have to slip by the patrols around Hardegsen if we want to reach Hanover alive. Hardegsen was ruled over by Reuben, and thus it was a vassal of Friedland."

"Why aren't we going on the main road through Bovenden?"

"Because both Bovenden and Göttingen Town are surveyed by Plesse Castle, which was recently taken by Otto and his men. East of here lies an impenetrable wall of scouts. Otto's son, Benedict, is only nine years old, but he and his mother have already begun securing his father's holds. Reuben's wife, Lara, has run back to her home in Nuremberg with her daughter, fleeing Benedict's juvenile wrath. Like a plague, he has dispatched large garrisons to fortify the holds; I wouldn't be surprised if he sent them to us soon," replied Conrad.

"The boy doesn't wish to appeal to the Imperial Court?"

"I'm sure he has, but you know how the Elector of Saxony is, he'd rather pay off his troubles with coin than with sword," said Conrad. "It's only a matter of time before envoys of the court come. It could be days, it could be months, but before then, we have to ensure that you are nowhere to be seen. Now, mount up, we have a long journey ahead of us."

Reluctantly, Enne mounted the steed. It was a large, chestnut coloured workhorse.

"I don't know how to ride," Enne said.

"Don't worry," replied Herwig, "His name's Rudolph. He'll do all the work for you, just hold on tight." The four riders began to journey northwards, near the border with Hesse, on the way to Hanover.

CHAPTER 60. CASTLE LÖWENBURG

After three long days of travel, Maria and her four horsemen finally arrived at Castle Löwenburg. It was a wide, white structure, far more grizzled and fortified than Plesse. Its thick walls protruded onto the fields in front, and the farthest towers hid among the foliage of the Wilhelmshöhe Forest. Behind the castle was a great labyrinth made of hedges and stone statues, inspired by the sculptures from the Merovingian Dynasty. Small paths meandered through it like the halls of a dungeon, but this dungeon was lined with seasonal flowers and gilded fountains. In front of the castle lay a tournament fence, bisecting a dirt path scathed by hoofprints. In the centre of the fence was a quintain, mounted upon an axel that rotated with the slightest breeze. As the party emerged from the wooded road, they saw a lean knight charging at the quintain upon horseback with a lance in hand. Upon the warrior's surcoat was the coat of arms of the House of Hessen, a red and white striped lion rampant upon a field of blue. The knight's houndskull bascinet was lowered as if the knight was charging into battle; however, one could still hear their voice from across the field.

At the door stood Maria's father, Goetz, stood to greet them. Beside him, instead of his children, was a young couple, husband and wife.

"Greetings, Maria!" Goetz called, elated to see his daughter safe and sound. His porters immediately emerged from behind him to tend to the travellers' horses and belongings. The five riders dismounted.

"Father, it's a... pleasure, to return to these hallowed halls," Maria said, fighting the urge to evade the familiar turmoil that she expected to ensue.

"I'm glad to see that you are all safe," Goetz replied. "Please, come in, I will have our cooks prepare a hot meal right away." He seemed more cheery than his usual self.

"Father, who are these young nobles who stand with you?" asked Maria. Goetz looked to his side. Embarrassed, he quickly spoke.

"My apologies. Maria, you must remember your cousin Wilfred of the House of Brabant? You two used to play together. Anyways, he has returned for a short period while the merchant guild up in the lowlands gets their act together. He stands beside his honourable wife, Lady Fidelma of Friesland. You will have plenty of time to acquaint yourselves over a meal."

"It is a pleasure to meet you, Fidelma. And Wilfred, I am honoured that my family will be hosting you; I am delighted to see you once more," Maria said.

"The pleasure is all mine, my lady," Wilfred said, bowing to her. He spoke in a dutch accent which slightly skewed his words, but his High German was certainly passable.

"You have become quite a man of chivalry, I see," Maria said. "I remember when you would much rather have spent your day hunting with that bow of yours."

"While I aspire to be as honourable as the other noble lords of the North, I must say that I also have a strung longbow in my room which has been put to quite extensive use," replied Wilfred.

"Wonderful; now, let's eat," said Goetz, growing impatient.

"It is a pleasure to meet you, Maria. I have heard many stories about you as a child," Fidelma said in a gracious tone.

"Thank you, my lady," Maria replied.

"Maria, perhaps you and Fidelma can catch up over a lovely roasted pheasant? Or, perhaps a wonderful steak?" Goetz said, beginning to make his way inside. The rest began to follow him, until Roland decided to ask a question of his own.

"Tell me, my Lord Goetz, that knight out there, is he any good?" Roland asked, eager for some competition.

"Yes, my Lord," added Helmuth. "After having practiced against branches and each other for quite some time now, I believe it would be refreshing to exchange passes with another skilled horseman, for a change." Goetz replied to their query with the slightest smirk.

"Yes, yes, he is very good. I don't suppose you would wish to challenge him, would you?" Goetz asked, keeping an eye on the practicing knight in his valiant battle with the quintain.

"I believe I would," said Roland.

"As would I," added Helmuth.

"Well, you two are said to be the best lances in Saxony. But, you're no longer in Saxony, you're in Kassel now. That knight right there has remained undefeated for years. I'll tell you what. After a nice meal, we can all gather out here and watch you three fight for champion. We can invite the castle attendants and make an event out of it. How does that sound?"

"Alright, I look forward to it," said Helmuth.

"Oh, come now. There's no need to wait," said Roland, eager to break a lance on something other than Helmuth. "We have our squires here, a few lances with hollow shafts, and all of our armour is already on. We may have travelled for days, but we're never going to be too tired to pass the lance. Come now, let's mount up and work up an appetite." Goetz rolled his eyes. Maria, Fidelma, and Wilfred all looked as if they agreed with the prospect of enjoying some entertainment before their meal.

"Fine then. Each of you can have three passes at each other, and then, we eat," Goetz replied. "I just want some damn food," he sighed under his breath. The squires quickly gave Helmuth and Roland their helmets, shields, and lances, and the two of them approached the practising knight. They rode up to him on horseback, ready for the joust. As if he could read their minds, upon seeing them ready in armour, the knight ordered his squire to remove the quintain. Then, he made his way with a new lance to one of the ends of the list.

"Go ahead," said Helmuth, allowing Roland to face the knight first. Fidelma, Wilfred, Maria, and Goetz all took their seats on an array of escalating benches which stood beside the list.

"Wilfred, you won't ride with them?" asked Maria. Wilfred pondered for a moment.

"You know what, I will. It will be a nice surprise," he said, sneaking off back to the castle to get armoured up. Roland rode to the other side of the list. He bowed his head to show that he was ready, and his opponent did the same.

"Alright. No funny business; clean and simple. First to break a lance gets a point. How does up to three sound?" Goetz asked. The mystery knight gave a thumbs up, as did Roland. "Alright then, three it is. Take your marks, get set, charge!" Goetz cried. The two riders spurred their horses onwards, urging them to go faster. The two riders met in the centre and clashed against each other with great force. Roland's lance splintered upon his opponent's cuirass, but his opponent missed him entirely. The two continued past each other, reforming on the opposing ends of the list.

"That's one point for Roland. Ready? Charge!" Goetz cried again, waiting to get it over with so that he could sink his teeth into the fatted calf. The two riders charged against each other once more. Angered by their performance in the last pass, the knight aimed their lance a little higher. When the two clashed, the knight's lance struck Roland's helmet, breaking on impact. When Roland had approached, seeing the lance make its way towards him, he tried to evade, moving his lance, and only grazing their arm armour.

"That's one for the champion of Kassel," Goetz said cheerfully. The two knights eyed each other. Roland was angered now. He wasn't content with being made a fool of. On the next pass, he aimed deliberately at his opponent's helmet, knocking them straight from their horse. The knight flew, unhorsed by the lance. The knight's houndskull visor opened as it flew onto the dirt. Revealed, beneath the bascinet visor, was Maria's sister, Lena.

"Lena!" Maria called out, rushing down to greet her sister. Lena rose to her feet, wiping some of the grime from her cuisses.

"It's good to see you, sister," Lena said.

"What are you doing in that suit of armour? I mistook you for one of my father's knights!" Maria said with a laugh.

"Well, I am now."

"Really?"

"Yeah."

"Congratulations! You've wanted to be a knight since you were a child, didn't you?"

"I did."

"Good job! I'm proud of you! So, what do you do for father? Last time I checked, there weren't any wars to be fought."

"Well, even if there were, father wouldn't let me fight. He has me patrol the streets of Kassel like some guardsman."

"So? At least you get to wear that armour all day. I thought that's what you wanted."

"It is. It's good to see you," Lena said, lowering her visor and mounting her horse again.

"What are you doing? You can't keep on jousting."

"I sure can."

"You're hurt. You were just thrown from a horse."

"So?" Lena asked with a smile, galloping to the lance rack to pick up another lance. Roland, impressed, was not willing to give in. Thus, he decided to answer the request and keep jousting. He ended up defeating her, three to two, but she did put up a good fight. As Helmuth approached the list, Wilfred emerged from the castle as well, sporting a black surcoat with the golden lion of Brabant. Upon seeing him, Goetz decided to go and enjoy some food. The four knights jousted late into the evening, working up an appetite and enjoying themselves with the sport. Once all was over with, and Roland had asserted his dominance over the other riders, they all returned to the castle for a feast. Over dinner, Maria and Fidelma got to know each other, discussing life in Göttingen vs Brabant. As well, Roland and Helmuth got along well with Lena, as they all enjoyed jousting for sport. As it turned out, Roland and Lena had met each other a few years prior, at a tournament in Dortmund, where neither of them made it past the second round. After the feast, Maria made her way to her father's study. As she approached the office, she knocked on the door.

"Come in," Goetz said with a terse tone. He was busy with trade deals and land disputes between farmers, so he hadn't much time to speak. Furthermore, he and his head-hunter, Adolf Ratzinger, were leading the investigation into the murder of Otto and Reuben von Göttingen. Maria entered the study quietly and timidly, fearful of her next actions. With care, she began to speak.

"Father, I have something to tell you," she said. Goetz stopped writing and looked up at her, placing his spectacles on his desk.

"Yes, Maria?"

"Father, I... I did it."

"You did what?"

"The murders; I did them."

"No, that's impossible. The guards said that you never

entered the crypt that night."

"How did you know that already?"

"Pigeons travel faster than horses, my dear."

"Well, anyway, I did do it. I told my maid to poison them."

"You asked her to poison them?"

"Well, no, but I implied that she should do it."

"I received a pigeon from Adolf this morning, and apparently, according to Franz, your maid ran off."

"Really? Do they know where she went?"

"They don't have a clue," Goetz replied. A guard came into the office.

"M'Lord," he said. "There's a matter that needs your attention."

"For God's sake. Your brother's probably gotten too drunk to leave the tavern again," Goetz said, hurrying out of the room. Maria was left alone. She returned to her room to contemplate things. As she thought, her eyes grew heavy. She set them upon a painting that had been in her room since she was young. It was of a unicorn, a dragon, and King Arthur's hunting party. She was raised in the literature of King Arthur and his knights of the round table. Her favourite was Sir. Percival, the Grail Knight. She loved how he was always on the move, always questing for something, and never giving up on his goal. He was popular in Germany, but so were the others. But he was special for Maria. Upon her shelf was a variety of literature, from the Homeric epics to Sophocles' plays, to the histories of Charlemagne and Julius Caesar. Maria loved literature, she always had. She looked at the painting with joy as she dozed off into a deep sleep.

CHAPTER 61. THE STAG

Ulrich and two embattled knights rode southwards. As they made their way down the third earthen roads, the occasional pine branch grazed their helmet. They rode in armour. It was uncommon for knights to do so, especially not knights of high status. But Ulrich and his men were of the lowest status possible. They had to remain vigilant. Highwaymen lurked in the woods, threatening their way through the foliage like hungry wolves. The Knights of the Maunch would not be prey, however. They were the shepherds, the watchful guardians of the weak and downtrodden... for a commission of course; all things come at a price.

As the men rode, they heard the peeping essence of a babbling brook, streaming across the wilderness like a wayward wyvern. The knights' flasks were empty of both ale and water. Food was scarce as well. They relied on the occasional nuts they found in the woods. Berries were abundant too, but these were city men who weren't accustomed to the nuances of the poisonous fruits of Eden. Ulrich dismounted, leading his horse to the stream. His men followed, keeping a watchful eye around them.

"By God, it's been over a day, hasn't it?" said Ulrich, stooping upon his hands and knees like a worshipper in a basilica. He gazed upwards, fixing his eyes upon the tall oak trees, towering like altarpieces.

"I think so," Pieter replied, filling his flask with a thin current which descended from the most minute of rocky caverns.

"Stay vigilant, men," Ulrich said, wary of the surrounding woods. After the great journey to the North, Ulrich was tired of travelling. He knew exactly what dangers lurked in the shadows. As Ulrich thought to himself, he heard the crack of a twig slicing through the still air.

"Ready your blades, men," Ulrich cried, pouncing to his feet. He and his men drew their swords, ready for a fight. Instead, however, they found no battle. Emerging from the bushes came the most majestic white stag with a bright red collar. Like a horse, it casually approached the three men at arms. It strode to Pieter, baying its head. Pieter extended his palm, connecting with the beast. Something was off. It was strangely tranquil, as was the rest of the scenery. Birds seemed to stand still upon the trees, pointing their beaks in every which direction, but locking their eyes on the mysterious creature.

"What is this beast?" asked Pieter.

"I couldn't say," replied Ulrich in awe.

"It must be from the heavens," said Ludwig, eying it with skepticism. "Or from the abyss. I say we let it be. We have no need for witchcraft, not the two of us anyways."

"It could be a sign, from Isolde," said Ulrich.

"If it was from your witch, she can feel free to make herself known. I have no business with witches," said Ludwig.

"And yet you are here," said Ulrich. Ludwig felt a tinge of fear inject itself into his stomach like a swarm of bees.

"I'm leaving this cursed forest," Ludwig said, approaching his horses. Then, he stopped. "Scheiser!" he cried, mounting his steed and riding away.

"What's happening?" asked Pieter in a panic. Ulrich

turned his head. His horse galloped off into the distance with his war hammer, helmet, shield, tent, and all. The only belongings he had left were his flask, sword, dagger, and Sir. Ernst's fight manual, which he curiously kept in his satchel. Pieter hastily clamoured over to his horse to pursue the beast as well, leaving Ulrich alone with the stag. It approached him with a calmness only known to the most pampered of men and the most innocent of children. It knelt before the knight like a servant to a lord, offering itself as a mount. Ulrich, bewildered by the paranormal spectacle, reluctantly seated himself upon the back of the beast. Ulrich mounted, trusting in the magic that he had witnessed before. He had seen the work of the divine, whether it was the hand of the Lord or the Devil. The stag bolted into action, hopping over logs and stones in pursuit of Ulrich's comrades. Faster than any steed, the deer made its way through the woods, traversing its way across the earthen scape of foliage and bark. Ulrich rode without control. He had never ridden a stag before. Instead, the animal led the way, plotting the course for the two of them. Eventually, they caught up to their comrades, and together the three watched as Ulrich's horse escaped into the wilderness. It was gone, long gone, and there was naught that they could do.

"This is a sign; I know it," said Ulrich.

"Ulrich, if you are the next messiah, I must know," said Ludwig. "I fear I may play the role of Judas all too well," he added with a laugh.

"Laugh as well as you wish, but you cannot put aside the fact that this creature not only brought me to you but found us in the forest. Just imagine, of all the places it could have gone, it found us," said Ulrich.

"I believe you, Ulrich," said Pieter. "You are no superstitious commoner; I know this well. Speak freely. You are safe from judgement among us, brüder."

"Pieter, I value your loyalty, but I can't tell you what I read in that book. All I can say, is that it's imperative that I return to Adelebsen and meet with Franz," said Ulrich, eager to continue on in his journey.

"Well, how can you do this with no horse?" Ludwig asked.

"This stag has more than proven himself," replied Ulrich. "I need not joust for our mission; this beast will serve me well."

"I certainly hope so," said Pieter. "You pay our wages."

"We are all paid by the robbers, are we not? There is no money to come if we do not return to the road. Brigands infest the roadside bushed, not the trees deep within the wood," said Ulrich. The men returned to their journey, high in spirits, and lusting for adventure. With hungry stomachs, they craved food, but food would not be found without a skirmish first. They treaded woefully, cautious of brigands concealing themselves along the side of the route. Ulrich sported a hood which he found in Ludwig's saddlebag to conceal his identity. The company was soon to reach Adelebsen.

CHAPTER 62. THE INSPECTOR

Franz heard a knock on his office door.

"Come in," he beckoned, placing his quill aside and waiting in anticipation. A guard strode forth, winded and alone.

"Sir, you must tend to the West Gate at once," he said, catching his breath.

"Why? Who goes there that seeks my word?"

"It's the inspector. He calls himself Adolf Ratzinger. He comes from Kassel with a retinue of sergeants."

"Let him in and bring him to me," said Franz.

"You wouldn't wish to greet him yourself?"

"I must take care of a few things beforehand. Off with you," Franz said, ordering his guard away. The guard returned to the gate to inform the guardsmen. In the manor, Franz marched around Maria's room, ensuring that there was no sign of the poison. As well, he, accompanied by a few of his guards, ravaged through Ennelein's belongings in the servant quarters. Of the little she had, there was no poison. It must have been disposed of. Finally, Franz returned to the courtyard to welcome their guest.

Up the hill rode a man and his retinue of sergeants. The man wore no armour but, instead, a simple doublet. At his side was an arming sword and a buckler shielded his loins. All was covered by a long black cloak which draped over both the man and the horse, cascading down to his spurs. The man's beard was large and bushy, waving into a rectangle of brown hair. He rode through the gate and dismounted, sending his horse off with one of the porters of the manor.

"Lord Regent Franz von Plesse, I presume?" the man asked with a stoic grin.

"That is I. You must be Sir. Adolf."

"Just Adolf. Right, may I use an office?"

"Well, I see no reason why you can't use mine."

"You are a gracious host, Franz. Most men scamper like wounded dogs at the sight of a lawman, but not you. You can be our first witness. Once I am set up, you must bring to me a list of players involved in the crime. I wish to speak with them each one at a time," said Adolf, making his way into the building.

"That's not possible."

"Why?"

"After the incident, most people were evacuated from the town."

"So, all the guests are gone?"

"They are."

"No matter. Men, search every home for poison. I wish to see the doctor who treated Maria. After we are done here, we will move on to Rosdorf and Friedland. Let's move," Adolf said. His soldiers sullied out of the building to interrogate the villagers as Adolf made his way into the castle to question Franz. In the town, chaos ensued. Stores were ravaged, homes were disassembled, and peasants were cast out onto the street, restrained from seeing the commotion afoot in their own abodes.

Through the commotion rode three steel-clad men at arms, one atop a pale white stag. Ulrich turned to a villager.

"What's this commotion about? Who has brought this trouble to Adelebsen?" he asked.

"You would be wise to leave at once," she replied in a

frantic voice. "The armies of Kassel have descended upon us. They hunt for a murderer among us, one who undoubtedly abodes in Friedland or Rosdorf. They accuse our people of murder in our own homes. What is this nonsense? They have cast fair Maria away, replacing her with the soldier Franz. He knows nothing of government and hasn't left his keep since he was first inaugurated a few days ago."

"Whoes blood runs our streets?"

"The brothers of Lord Manfred. They were slain in the dead of night. Not a whisper was heard until morning."

"I see. Thank you for your troubles," Ulrich said.

"Answer me now, knight. Why do you ride a stag as if it was a horse?"

"It's a long story," said Ulrich, spurring his stag onwards into the fray to determine the commotion for himself. He saw children separated from parents, belongings ripped from the grasp of the people. He determined that the act was naught but injustice. He turned to his brothers in arms.

"Brüderen, we ride to the manor. Follow me," he said, spurring his stag onwards. They rode through the cobbled streets, avoiding the sergeants and peasants bickering upon the street like hagglers. They made their way up the hill.

Franz sat on the powerless side of his desk. Across from him sat Adolf, quill in hand, wearing spectacles fit or the most learned of stone masons.

"Tell me, Franz, what do you remember from that night?" Adolf asked. Franz's mind was blank. In honesty, he slept the entire night without an instance of discomfort. But he had to make something up. He had to find the perfect red herring to differ Adolf and his hounds from Maria's scent. Franz peered outside his window. Through the stained glass, he could only make one thing out clearly. Some madman rode about mounted on some sort of deer.

"I do remember one thing, sir. There was a man, a suspicious man, who rode atop a deer."

"A deer?"

"Yes, a deer. I didn't think it was possible at first, but as he galloped away from the crypt, I knew he was up to no good."

"Do you really expect me to believe that a man was riding a deer? Can a deer even support the weight of a man?"

"You can either accept my testimony or not. But I do believe I saw him recently in the village. We tried to catch him, but that deer was too agile."

"Interesting. What made him suspicious?"

"Other than the deer?"

"He may be a fool, but not necessarily a murderer. Tell me, what made him a suspect?"

"I had never seen him before, not in the manor at least."

"He was in the manor?"

"In the courtyard, yes."

"And you guards didn't stop him?"

"No, with his beast, he leapt over them like... well... a deer."

"Interesting. I will have my men hunt this brigand down at once. Do you remember anything else?"

"No, nothing abnormal," said Franz.

"Alright then. You are dismissed, for now. On your way out, summon in one of my guards."

"Yes sir," Franz replied. As he left the room, he followed the instructions. But immediately afterwards, he raced to his own brigade, training in the fields behind the manor. He summoned one over to himself and instructed him to find the man on the deer and tell him to leave at once. He needed the hunt to take time. Without Enne or Maria, this man was the only suspect. "Oh, and one more thing," Franz added. "When you find him, and with haste, you must order him to travel to Hanover in search of a knight named Ulrich von Göttingen. That man is the only one who can help us."

CHAPTER 63. UNFAMILIAR FRIENDS

Enne, Conrad, Herwig, and Thomas rode through the woods, northwards. Every so often they stopped along the side of the road to eat, drink, and rest. Herwig played merry tunes on his lute, but nobody sang. They had been riding for a day, and the sun was lowering itself in the sky, returning to its abode of darkness.

"Should we rest here?" Thomas asked.

"No, we have to press on. We must arrive on time," Conrad said, urging his comrades to continue. As they rode, they began to hear the clopping of another set of hooves. Through a dense fog came galloping a sable steed, loaded with saddle, horse coat, and barding, but without a rider. It came thundering towards the travellers.

"Woah, boy," said Herwig, extending his arm to receive the horse by the reins. Conrad and his riders examined the animal.

"Wait... this is Ulrich's horse," he said, unsheathing Menschentöter. The four travellers looked at each other.

"How can you be certain?" asked Enne.

"This is his war hammer. He loved it and would never leave it," replied Conrad.

"Could Ulrich be now stranded in the woods?" asked Thomas.

"If he is, we have to help him," said Herwig.

"Who knows how far this horse has come," said Conrad. "What if... something happened to him?"

"To Ulrich? Impossible," said Thomas.

"We have to help him," said Herwig, galloping off into the fog.

"Wait!" called Conrad. Thomas chased after him, and soon Conrad and Enne did the same, grabbing the war horse by the reins and leading it towards their target. They rode on for hours, scouring the woods until they came across a tall obelisk. Upon it were ancient runes from the old Germanic tribes. Herwig halted to see the object. It was tall and mighty and loomed over the forest with an ominous presence.

"We shouldn't be here," said Thomas, trying to make out his surroundings through the thick mist.

"There's no way that Ulrich is here," Conrad added. Herwig persisted, however, shouting Ulrich's name. The four riders circled around the obelisk, trying to peer off into the woods. Then, they head sloshing in a river nearby. They rode towards it together, in the hopes of finding a bathing Ulrich, but instead, they found nobody. The current roared intensely, launching fish into the air like water dancers. "We must turn back," Conrad said.

"Your master is in danger," said Herwig.

"I have a new master: Franz, and he ordered us to find Ulrich. He's not here in some babbling brook, but he's off somewhere doing something, which obviously doesn't require a horse. Something tells me to head back."

"Something? Like what? You're too afraid. If you're so scared, stay back and guard the murderer as we men do the searching."

"Fine then. No searching, no retreating. We ride to Hanover," Conrad affirmed. He led the horse onwards, and his comrades followed. They rode until sunset, at which point they had cleared the fog and retired for the night.

"We should rest here for the night," Thomas said. Conrad agreed. The three squares laid out their blankets to form beds and set up a campfire around which they told stories and jokes and sang songs. They watched as the pale embers fluttered into the night sky. The dark purple veil was discoloured by the grey smoke. One by one, they fell asleep, watching the stars.

The next morning, Enne rose to the clamour of conflict.

"Up, on your feet!" Ordered a broad and burly man at arms covered head to toe in brigandine and splint armour. His comrades, all in suits of plate and chainmail, held the squires hostage with broad arming swords. "Alright, now tell me, lass, what did you do to Ulrich?"

"What? Nothing! We don't even know where he is!" she squealed. The man lifted Menschentöter.

"You thought we wouldn't recognize this? Now tell me, where is Ulrich, and what in God's name did you do to him?"

"We didn't do anything. We are looking for him, just like you," Enne said, fearing for her life.

"Who even are you?" shouted Conrad. The man turned to him.

"Who are we? Well, we're your worst nightmare. We, my friend, are the Knights of the Maunch, and we eat lying little thieves like you for breakfast."

"We didn't steal anything," exclaimed Herwig.

"Really? So, this war hammer is yours? And this horse, the fifth in your collection, is also yours?"

"I can explain," said Conrad. "I was his squire." The man looked at him questioningly, turning his head slowly. Each scale in his aventail clinked against the buckle of his brigandine like clockwork.

"You say you squired for him, huh? And what happens to be your name?"

"Conrad, Sir. Conrad von Liechtenstein. I come from the West."

"I can see that. I know geography; I'm a knight. Just

because my armour may not look the part, I probably received a better education than any of you louts did."

"I doubt that," said Thomas with a chuckle.

"What was that, boy?"

"I doubt that. I have been sent all the way from Holstein, in Denmark, to squire here," said Thomas. "My father was the brother of the Duke of Holstein, Sir. Herman Rosencrantz. We were taught by Roman scholars in London."

"Ha! Well, how did you end up in a damned place like this? Why aren't you squiring for some Breton prince?"

"I was sent here because my father wished to make amends for his skirmishes with Saxony."

"Interesting, so your father lost, and the Elector asked for you as his prize? So what? He didn't like you enough and gave you to the Prince of Göttingen?"

"Enough about me. You claim to be a scholar, who the hell are you?"

"I am a scholar of sorts, yes. I grew up lowborn, on the streets like the peasant rabble."

"But you weren't a peasant," said Herwig.

"No, I wasn't. My father was the sheriff of Bemerode, but we didn't live like nobility. I was taught in a school, however, in Hanover, with the sons of the local lords and the Prince himself," the man said.

"Now, tell me. Where is Ulrich?"

"We were looking for him. We were told to find him, but instead, we only found his horse," said Conrad.

"Well, he was off to Göttingen himself. We ought to follow him, to see if he's okay."

"We just came from there."

"Ah, but we Knights of the Maunch don't follow the traditional roads. We use the back routes, footpaths, anything that'll get us one step ahead of our enemy."

"Who is that, exactly?"

"Brigands and raubritters, or course."

"Well then, take us via your back routes," Conrad said. The man and his three men at arms travelled with the young riders towards Göttingen. They rode along earthen paths in the woods, hidden to the main road. Along the way, they found remnants of campsites, affirming their idea that he returned. They continued to follow Ulrich's path until they returned to the town.

CHAPTER 64. THE RECKONING

Ulrich trotted about the streets, attempting to secure what little peace he could among the bustling commotion. Continuously, he tried to speak with the marauding men of Kassel, but this was to no avail. He was tempted to take brash measures. At one point, he even clenched the hilt of his blade, ready to strike an invasive sergeant, but instead, his self-control overcame him, and he decided to ride away. Ulrich scampered about on his stag, hoping to distract the investigative force with his presence, but he didn't spark a reaction. Soon, from the Manor on the hill, a unit of sergeants emerged, ready to head into the commotion. Ulrich decided to go and speak with them to figure out what was going on. As he made his way over, he was quickly stopped by a soldier in the retinue of Franz.

"Sir, may I have a word?" the man asked frantically.

"I have no time; I must put an end to this. What in God's green earth is going on here?"

"I must tell you. These men track the killer of Reuben and Otto von Göttingen. You, unfortunate wayfarer, are now their prime suspect."

"Tell me, how did you come about such a foolish notion?"

"My master, Franz, has chosen you to be the suspect, as he knows you can ride away easily on that... steed of yours."

"Alright then. Why wouldn't he reveal the true murderer?"

"It is beyond my place, sir. Look, we haven't much time. Those men dispatched from the manor are coming for your head. You are to ride to Hanover."

"What lies in Hanover?"

"You are to seek a knight named Ulrich. He was a good friend of Franz. He will keep you safe."

"Good man, I believe you have been fooled. The man of whom you speak stands before you."

"What do you mean?"

"You say that I'm to seek out Ulrich, and yet I am the Ulrich of which you speak. It appears that Franz has mistaken me for somebody else."

"By God, then you must hurry. Ride out of this town, ride away. Never let these men catch up to you, or else they will uncover the truth."

"What is the truth?" asked Ulrich impatiently.

"I have no certainty, but the word among the men is that Lady Maria, like a sorceress, poisoned their food."

"Only housewives and bored children fall for such rumours. But, if there is a chance that fair Maria will be charged for this, I should take the blame instead. I abandoned her husband. Perhaps, if I had stayed, Manfred wouldn't have been slain. Nor Freidrich, nor Wilhelm," Ulrich exclaimed. Brushing past the astonished soldier, he galloped towards the forthcoming investigators. Without a word, Ulrich unsheathed his sword and dropped it onto the ground. Then, he dismounted and sent the stag off, raising his hands in capitulation. His hands were soon tied by the sergeants of Kassel, and Ulrich was escorted to the crypt, where the assassin was interrogated. Tied to the praying hands of Manfred's tomb, he was stripped of his belongings. The guards left him with nothing more than a shirt, trousers, and the right to remain silent. Ulrich gazed at the flickering candles - the only source of light in the entire dungeon. "By God, Manfred.

If I had known that my disobedience would have brought about this, I would have stayed by your side into a thousand more battles. I was a fool Manfred, a fool. Now, you have left this world, causing even more chaos than the order you sought. And it's all my fault," Ulrich said solemnly. Tears of pain and sadness emerged from his eye sockets. The grizzled warrior began to weep. "Forgive me Manfred!" he cried. "Forgive me, for I have sinned!" Ulrich looked down at Manfred's effigy's praying hands and could think of no more than the good that Manfred brought about. The brashness Ulrich once accused him of now appeared as courage. The bloodlust now became an intense desire for justice. Ulrich fell to his knees and began to pray. Not for his own life, but for forgiveness for his treachery. A gust of chilled air wafted into the room. The candles blew out. Night fell upon Adelebsen.

CHAPTER 65. THE TRIAL

Ennelein, Herwig, Conrad, Thomas, and their new party of vigilantes entered Adelebsen. It appeared as if a hurricane had passed through, cluttering the streets with belongings and scattering peasants all around the town. Chests and baskets lay dispersed upon the cobblestone, while citizens went about reorganizing their homes, ensuring that nothing was stolen by the brutish men-at-arms. Conrad stopped to ask a wayfaring peasant about the destruction, and the party learned all about the investigation which ransacked the town. Hastily, the party rode up the hill to speak with Franz. As they entered the great hall, they quickly realized that the inquisitor, Adolf, had already found a suspect. In the wooden cage across from him stood Ulrich, battered and bruised, skinny as a twig. Conrad looked in horror as his mentor was entrapped in that coffin-like cage. The party decided to wait in the hall as the case proceeded, but it was in its finishing stages. What the "witnesses" were saying to the judge was inaudible, as they discretely conversed on the far end of the hall. A sea of audience blocked the party's path. Ulrich, encaged, stood like a pillar in the middle of the room. The party watched as Adolf convened with his colleagues. Finally, he rose to a podium to speak.

"Sir Ulrich von Göttingen, knight errant of the late Sir.

Manfred von Göttingen, are hereby charged with murder of the highest degree. You have been found guilty by this very imperial diet. But, as the evidence, although present, is scarce, we will provide you with two options of execution. You may choose to drink the very poison with which you murdered the brother Ruben and Otto von Göttingen. This execution shall afford you a proper Christian burial, for in the eyes of the lord you shall be given forgiveness as a confessor. Your second option is to face a trial by combat. You shall fight me, Inquisitor Adolf Ratzinger, to first blood. The lord shall dictate your worthiness of forgiveness. Should you lose, you will be hung in the main square for all to see, and soon after burned like a heretic. The choice is yours, Ulrich," Adolf said sternly. Ulrich opened his mouth to speak.

"I choose death by poison," he muttered.

Conrad couldn't help himself."No!" he cried. "Choose the trial by combat! I will fight in your place! Choose me as your champion!" Ulrich swiveled his head, catching a glimpse of the young squire.

"You are but a boy; I couldn't do that to you. I must receive a proper burial. I must be forgiven," Ulrich replied.

"Ulrich, you didn't do it. I know you didn't do it. You couldn't have," Conrad shouted across the hall. Ulrich, suddenly realising that he needn't pay for Maria's crime, quickly changed his mind.

"Adolf, the boy is right. I wish to receive a trial by combat, to dictate my worthiness of forgiveness for my heinous crime. But, this boy will not fight in my stead. I will fight," Ulrich said firmly, looking Adolf in the eye.

"So be it," the inquisitor replied. "We shall have you fight tomorrow at midday. Two longswords will await us in this very hall. This trial is officially over. Citizens, you must now exit the hall," Adolf said, descending from his podium. As the room began to clear, Franz approached the party.

"By God, if I had known that I would cast Ulrich into this

terrible chaos, I wouldn't have sent the inquisitor after him. I swear it."

"You made the inquisitor think it was him?" asked Enne. "It can't be. He's innocent. What if they find out the truth?"

"I didn't know it was him, I swear," said Franz frantically. "They won't find out. Ulrich just needs to win this fight, as he always has."

"The poor man's in no shape to fight. He's half starved for crying out loud!" exclaimed Conrad. "Please, convince him to let me fight in his stead."

"No, I won't. I'm going to fight for him. This is all my fault, so I had ought to pay for what I've done," Franz asserted.

"You can't be serious. We have to choose our best fighter. No matter what, we just need to win this duel," said Enne. Pieter, Ulrich's right hand man stepped forward.

"I'll fight. I'm far more skilled than Conrad, well, at least I'm not a beardless youngen. And you, Franz, are older than my father ever lived to be. I'll fight. I can wield a sword like a knight. I can beat that man in a duel, I swear it by the good God," he said. The party agreed that Ludwig held the best chance of defeating Adolf in a duel with longswords.

Franz made his way to the crypt. When the guards tried to stop him from speaking with Ulrich, he ordered them to step aside.

"What do you want, Franz?" Ulrich asked restlessly. He was bruised and battered. It was clear that, since he was last seen, the guards gave him the harshest of imaginable treatments.

"What in God's name did they do to you, Ulrich?" Franz asked with sympathy. Ulrich just grunted. He was starved, broken, and unable to even look the commander in the eye.

"Ludwig will fight in your stead, Ulrich."

"No, he won't."

"You say that now, but the second you step into that hall, you will be carved like a pheasant. Understand me, knight.

313

This is not your fight. I made the mistake of blaming you wrongfully for a crime you didn't commit."

"I must pay for abandoning Manfred."

"What sort of blasphemy is that? You did what any sane man would."

"You didn't leave."

"You don't understand."

"Really? Because all I know by the looks of it, is that I left, and nobody else did. And after I left, one by one, Wilhelm, Freidrich, and Manfred all died. I wasn't there to protect them."

"Throwing your life away now will achieve nothing. If they kill you, do you really think anything will end? Otto's son will still come after this place like a hungry wolf, and we will need every knight and man at arms we can muster."

"Don't be a fool, one man can't stop an army."

"And yet you blame yourself for failing to stop the armies of Poland? Don't be a fool. You're a knight, not a jester. Tomorrow you will let Ludwig fight, or I'll see to it myself that you are given medicine and saved as a captive of Adelebsen, living out the rest of your days with the shame in defeat."

"Where's the honour in that?"

"Where's the honour in suicide? Ulrich, you are a knight, act like one. Ludwig will fight in your stead," Franz exclaimed. Ulrich gave no reply, but the look in his eye said enough. His breath slowed. He accepted the sting of shame, for he knew that he was of more use alive than dead.

"Franz," he said, as the commander began to leave.

"Yes, Ulrich?" Franz asked.

"Wherever my belongings are, fish out my book and give it to Ludwig," Ulrich asked. Franz complied.

Late into the night, as Adolf trained with his longsword against imaginary foes in Franz' office, Franz accessed Ulrich's belongings which lay in a chest near the crypt. From them, he pulled out Sir. Ernst Meyer's fight manuscript. It included pages upon pages of dueling tactics. It would certainly come in handy for Ludwig. When he brought it to him, Ludwig accepted it with content. To him, the best way to evade fear was to practice. Like Adolf, Ludwig sliced the dead of night with his longsword practice. Both were ready to settle the score in the arena.

CHAPTER 66. THE DUELISTS

The next morning was shrouded in mist. Rain descended from the heavens like tears. Streams seeped between the cobblestones, clearing them of dust and replacing the dust with mud. Mud pooled by Ludwig's feet as he practiced.

"Step right, swing from defence one to attack three, and thrust between the shoulders," he muttered to himself, pacing forwards and backwards like a ballerina. But he was no dancer. His sword shone in the faint sunlight, and the rain flowed down its fullers as he swung. The droplets flew from his blade-like projectiles.

"How long has he been up?" asked Enne to Herwig, as they observed Ludwig from the manor.

"He was up before I. I rose at sunrise," Herwig said, gazing at the clouded sky. " I can barely tell, but it ought to be noon soon."

"We should tell Ludwig," said Ennelein. "He mustn't be late." The three assembled in the great hall where the carpenters had erected a crude enclosure. In it stood Adolf, gripping a longsword which rested in a scabbard at his side.

"Well then. Franz has informed me that there's been a change in plans," he said, pacing about the octagon. "Apparently, Urlich has felt a change in heart. Ulrich, can you confirm that this Ludwig will fight in your stead?"

"He will," said Ulrich, shrivelled upon a stool from which

he would watch the fight. Only a sparing amount of viewers were allowed into the hall, so that the adjudicators could have a clear view of the duelists.

"Well then," Adolf said with a grin. He held up two swords in his hand, one of which was his own. "Make a choice." Ludwig handled both, and eventually decided to take the other sword.

"Your blade is fine, Adolf, but not as fine as this one."

"Fair enough," Adolf replied. "I'd rather you have the better one; it makes for better sport." He had a keen grin upon his visage which extended across the entirety of his face. Adolf planted the tip of his blade on the ground, and began to say the opening remarks. "On this day, we men of God appeal to the heavens for divine direction. This man, Sir. Ulrich von Göttingen, pleads for forgiveness from his charges of murder. Murder of nobles no less. To represent him shall fight Ludwig von Hanover. I, Adolf Ratzinger, shall ensure that this man receives no mercy from the Imperial Diet. Let us begin," he said, raising his blade.

The two lightly tapped their swords in the centre to mark their readiness. Then, they got into position. For nearly thirty seconds the two simply stared at each other, waiting to entrap the enemy at the perfect moment. As the perfect moment seemed miles away, Ludwig lunged forth with a slash. Adolf parried it, and made his own strike, which was quickly dodged by Ludwig. The two settled once more into a stalemate. After another moment of dead silence, Adolf plunged his sword forward. Ludwig countered with half sword technique, riposting the blade and striking his opponent on the shoulder. Bruised and enraged, Adolf slashed once more at his opponent, drawing a thick stream of blood from his abdomen.

"First blood has been drawn!" the judges called, ending the fight. Ludwig fell to the ground and cried out in pain, as the stone tiles became stained with hot, pooling blood. Adolf wiped his blade with a handkerchief and made eye contact with Ulrich, who had rushed to his friend's aid.

"Ulrich will be hung," Adolf said, sheathing his blade and leaving the hall. As soon as he opened the door, ten of his men rushed into the hall and grabbed the prisoner.

"I'm sorry," Ulrich said to his friend.

"I failed you, Ulrich," Ludwig replied. Ulrich was ripped from his friend and dragged through the hall. The party followed him after bandaging Ludwig.

The noose already hung in the main square. As they saw the entourage descending from the manor with the reprobate, a horde of peasants gathered in the town square. They knew Ulrich. They had seen him enforcing the law, but they never knew him as a person. They trusted the diet. As Ulrich was brought upon the wooden platform, peasants began to cry out for his execution.

"Kill the murderer!" they chanted. Conrad approached Adolf before he ascended to the platform.

"You can't hang that man; he's innocent," Conrad said frantically.

"That man is a murderer, in the eyes of both Lord and law. He will pay for his crimes against the Electorate." Adolf approached the stand where his guards stayed to keep watch and maintain order. "Men, women, and children of Adelebsen, I bring before you a ruthless murderer of nobles. This man is guilty of murder of the highest degree, for he plotted to kill two innocent men of lordly blood. He will be punished for his crimes. He is hereby stripped of his knighthood. He will hereby be sentenced to death by hanging. He will receive no Christian burial for he has been deemed unworthy by God, as proven in our trial by combat. Have you any last words, Ulrich von Göttingen?"

"Forgive me," Ulrich muttered under his breath. He looked at Franz, then at Conrad, and finally at Ludwig. The crowd booed him, throwing rotten vegetables and stones at him, and shouted at him with slanderous titles. A block was placed beneath the noose. Ulrich stepped on it. Then, Adolf tied the noose around the man's neck. Ulrich prayed as hard as he could. Although the stones hurt more than he ever had in armour, he stayed silent, patiently waiting for his death. Just as the guard positioned himself to kick away the block from beneath Ulrich's feet, an arrow plunged into his eye. The oaf stumbled backwards and off the platform. From the surrounding forest came an army of nearly eighty brigands, galloping on steeds as loud as thunder. The peasant masses scattered at the sight. Adolf, now completely distracted from the execution, called his men to arms. He drew his sword but was quickly turned into a human pin cushion. Franz called upon his men as well, ordering one of his men to return to the manor and muster the entire garrison. A battle ensued in the square. Conrad, Herwig, and Thomas all guarded Ennelein atop the podium, blocking incoming arrows with their shields as they flew in from the forest. Ulrich untied himself and picked up Adolf's sword, helping the three squires as well as he could. The soldiers of both Kassel and Adelebsen fought alongside each other against the intruders, hoping to force them back to the woods. Chaos ensued. Villagers threw tables, chairs, and pottery onto the attackers, dealing heavy casualties. The brigands fought home to home, trying to pacify the residents.

"We have to get out of here," cried Enne.

"I agree," said Herwig, leading the charge to clear a path from the podium. The five of them made their way out of the main square and behind allied lines, running to their horses.

"We should go to Kassel. That's where Maria is," Ennelein said.

"That's stupid. I'm a wanted man now," replied Ulrich.

"Maria won't let you be convicted," Conrad argued, wishing only the best for his mentor. Ulrich capitulated, and the five mounted their steeds and rode towards the forest. They rode deep into the woods, down the road heading south as it was the quickest way to Kassel. In the distance, they saw flames erupt in the small town. After them, they heard hooves. Ludwig and Pieter emerged from the foliage, following the group.

"You made it out!" exclaimed Ulrich.

"It was a lost cause. The village is overrun," replied Pieter, slowing his horse to a canter.

"Well, it's good to see you safe," said Ulrich. "The others? Where are our brothers?"

"Most of them fell," said Ludwig, gripping his side in pain. What was thought to have just been a flesh wound seemed to be an even more serious injury. All of a sudden, a crossbow bolt flew into Thomas' horse. It fell to its side, crushing his leg. From the bushes emerged a group of brigands on foot. Initially, Conrad and Herwig were eager to engage, but they realised that they would be alone in that fight.

"Drop your weapons," their leader shouted. All of their swords hit the ground, except for one. Herwig stood tall on his horse, ready for battle. Although encircled, he bravely charged into one of the captors, striking his polearm aside with his shield, and smiting him with his blade. Swiftly, he rode off. Although the brigands wished to make chase, not a single one of them had with them a horse. Herwig rode back towards the town, into the dense thicket. The rest of the party was forced to dismount, and they were all tied behind their backs. Although Thomas couldn't walk, they made him limp with them. "You idiots just messed up," the leader grunted. In a line, the six were forced to march all the way to Rosdorf.

CHAPTER 67. AN IRON GAUNTLET
AND A LONGSWORD

In the aftermath of the battle, the people of Adelebsen were subjugated under the iron will of Osanna, Lord of Göttingen. The remnants of the Göttingen garrison were forced to make a choice; to either join her or face the wrath of her son's blade. Although many capitulated in fear, many more fell beneath his heavy sword stroke. The nine-year-old boy was ruthless, to say the least. He was completely desensitized as a child. He was raised to be a knight, a warrior without any emotion. Killing like this was not a game to him, but it was no chore either. He was perfectly fine with lobbing off heads all day if need be. But it was not him who really ordered the act. He didn't sit on the throne in the great hall. Instead, he sat on a stool beside his mother, Lady Osanna of Rosdorf. She occupied the central position on the platform. Before her knelt Franz, captain of the guard, and Lord Regent of Adelebsen.

"So, Franz von Plesse. I have heard so much about you," Osanna said. "It was you who helped Manfred and his cronies to Prussia, correct?"

"Under the instruction of your late father in law, Prince Otto the Elder," Franz replied.

"Well then, let's skip the formalities. Either you serve me

or die. Simple."

"I would rather die than serve the vile witch who killed my men," Franz replied.

"So be it," Osanna replied. "Guards, take his head quickly," she ordered with a smile. The sinister woman grieved the loss of her husband, Otto. But, more importantly, she grieved the loss of his inheritance. As he had written no will during his lifetime, half of his wealth was seized by the Imperial Court. The rest was left for her to fight over among dozens of relatives scattered across central Europe. This was her chance to secure a life of luxury for her child, Benedict. As Franz was beaten and subsequently dragged out of the hall, Benedict sat playing with his sword. It was a small arming sword, but it was still sharp and dangerous.

"Benny, put that down," Osanna ordered. "You'll have plenty of time to play with swords when you're older."

After being dragged from the hall, Franz was tied to a wooden block. A guard holding a broad bardiche eyed him carefully.

"Last words?" he grumbled.

"I don't regret a single thing. Will you do something for me?" Franz replied

"What do you want?"

"There's a woman named Katerina. She's a Russian Boyar. If you see her, tell her that I love... loved her."

"Sure," the man said with a smile. "Anything else?" the guard asked sarcastically. He spat on the ground before lifting his axe.

"Wait! There's more," Franz said, desperately trying to salvage what few moment's he could.

"Spit it out then – I ain't got all day."

"I regret nothing. When I was on the quest with Manfred and his knights, it was tough, real tough. We fought countless enemies, brigands, and even wolves. But you know what? I regret none of it. I would go through it all again, maybe with a few tweaks here and there. But I certainly would not give up that adventure, not for any amount of gold, not in a thousand years. You are a soldier. But do you truly believe in what you fight for? I was a soldier, and I can tell you that the only thing that kept me going through the hellish storms and incessant blood was the belief that I was fighting for the side of good. So, I ask you now; what do you fight for? Do you fight for gold? Do you lob off heads for the thrill of it? Because I assure you that you have never, and will never feel the true exhilaration of fighting for a good cause. A just cause. A cause that you would willingly die for. Would you die for your gold?" Franz asked, looking up at the beastly man. The man said nothing. "May God bless this forsaken town." Franz spat on the ground. With one foul swoop, the poor man was turned into a lifeless sack of flesh and bone. His head rolled on the freshly trimmed green, spilling a trail of fresh, hot, blood.

Osanna rode through the town. Benedict followed her like a duckling following its mother across a street. All around the town, the burned houses weren't rebuilt. Instead of focussing on rebuilding the town, Osanna decided to use all of the town's manpower to begin training a militia. She wished to have every man of fighting age able to wield a spear to serve her bidding. As well, the women and children were disbanded from their trades and forced to plough the fields, the job typically carried out by their husbands and fathers. Every day, Osanna would tour the town with her son, ensuring that everyone was fulfilling their quotas and abiding by the law. She let the peasants keep none of the grain and, instead, forced the millers to send it all to Rosdorf. To feed the people here, she relied on whatever small game the peasants could forage after dark. The soldiers were free to loot and pillage whatever and whoever they pleased. Nobody was safe from them, not the church, nor each other. Her army was composed of mercenaries - brigands turned into soldiers. Without any sense of discipline or justice, their rule over the populace was draconian by all means.

In the dark of night, a hooded figure approached the gates of Castle Löwenberg. Blankets of rain cascaded through the castle courtyard as the messenger hurriedly ordered her entry.

"Who is it?" Goetz asked from his study.

"It's a messenger," replied the porter, half asleep. "She says it's urgent."

"Let her in," Goetz demanded. As the great series of castle doors opened, the cloaked informant rushed through the halls to meet with Goetz.

"Lord Goetz, I bring word of Adelebsen."

"Excellent. Has Adolf found the traitor?"

"No, far worse. They're dead; all of them. Adolf, Franz, everybody loyal to Lady Maria," the messenger replied. Goetz shuddered. Enraged, he poured himself a glass of wine. He offered one to the messenger as well, but she declined his offer.

"God damn it! Damn it all to hell! I swear, with all that is left in me and my realm, we will reclaim the town and hunt down the marauders like wolves. I swear it! Tell me, how exactly did you come about this information?"

"My name is Katerina, my Lord. Boyar Katerina Nevskiy of the Principality of Novgorod. I was in the service of Sir. Manfred. My druzhina and I fought alongside him at Grunwald and Marienburg. After escorting the lords' retinues to their respective towns, we became aware of Benedict's plot to invade Adelebsen. In fact, he even tried to buy us, but my Lord, we are not for sale. We serve Lady Maria. Upon hearing of this, we decided to follow their army to the town, but by the time we arrived all the way from Friedland, it was too late. My retinue is now tracking a band of survivors who were taken prisoner. Sir. Ulrich appears to be one of them."

"By God, I would never have thought you to be a fighter. Very well. Although our army is in shambles, we do have one. Thank you for this information. You are dismissed."

"My Lord, I would not wish to seem disloyal, but..."

"But what? What is it you want, coin?"

"I would not decline such an offer."

"Damn Russian. Fine, we'll pay you your just due, but first, you must save Ulrich and bring him here," Goetz said, irritably. "You can sleep here in the castle for the time being." Katerina was shown to a guest room, where she was allowed to stay. She was there given a pouch of florins.

"Bring us Ulrich, and you'll get another," the porter said. Through the night, the six captives stumbled through the dark. Thorns pierced Ulrich's feet as he marched without shoes. No ruth was shown to them. By morning, they reached Rosdorf.

CHAPTER 68. THE LION RAMPANT MARCHES

On the third morning of November, the garrison of Adelebsen heard the horns of war echo through the forest. The blaring cacophony rampaged through the air like the sweet sounds of salvation. As Benedict's scouts rode through the woods, they spied upon a vast army of eight thousand men. The armies of Hessen, Kassel, Brabant, and the Rhinelands were assembled for war. At the head was Prince Goetz von Kassel, garbed in full armour.

"They're here!" cried a messenger, barging through the door of the great hall.

"Who's here?" asked Osanna.

"The armies of Kassel. They have come to take the town. Maria has returned!"

"For the love of God," Osanna muttered. "Garrison the town. We will not give it up without a fight."

"But my lady, we have only a few hundred men," replied the messenger.

"Did I stutter?" the woman shrieked. The garrison of Adelebsen, composed of brigands, mercenaries, and Adelebsen's defects, mustered their forces and prepared for a siege of the town. Benedict and his mother rode out from the manor, ready to discuss terms with Prince Goetz. Wilfred, leading the Brabantian vanguard, approached the gates to discuss with the emissary party. The gates of Adelebsen opened slowly, creaking ever so slightly. The guards stood atop the ramparts with crossbows in hand, ready to fire at any sudden movement. Wilfred's men replied with a similar formation. Upon seeing each other, Osanna and Wilfred began to discuss the impending siege.

"I see you have emerged from your cave, you vile dragon of a woman," Wilfred remarked.

"I don't believe I've had the pleasure of meeting you, young lord. I am Osanna, Lady of Göttingen."

"I am Wilfred of the House of Brabant, Cousin of Lady Maria, rightful Lady of Adelebsen," Wilfred replied. "I have heard all about you. Why don't you let your Lord do the speaking?"

"He is only a boy."

"He is supposed to be in charge, is he not?"

"I am," interjected Benedict. "And I would have your head on a spike if you speak about me like I'm not the rightful ruler of all of Göttingen. It's mine, all mine. The court decided!"

"You killed the judge," replied Wilfred with a smirk.

"What is it you want, Wilfred. Money? We have plenty in our coffers," offered Osanna.

"It's not gold I'm after. I have brought the armies of the Lowlands to ensure that you return my cousin's rightful inheritance to her. Adelebsen is not yours."

"We will not go down without a fight," Osanna replied. Without further discussion, she pulled her horse aside and rode away with speed. Her son followed suit. Wilfred returned to Goetz.

"Goetz, the witch won't surrender. We'll have to take them by storm," Wilfred declared.

"Caution, Wilfred. We shouldn't risk the lives of our men. Send word to the commanders that we set up camp. Nobody is to enter or exit the town until further instruction, understand?"

"Goetz, we need to act quickly. The people of Adelebsen will starve."

"They have enough rations in there for a few more days. We just have to wait for Maria's return, to ensure that they completed their mission."

"Fine then, I'll spread the word," Wilfred replied, leaving Goetz' side. The army prepared for a lengthy siege. They set up tents, dug an earthwork, and selected patrols to ensure that no reinforcements would arrive. But the truth was that this was all a distraction. As all this preparation and commotion was going on, Boyar Katerina, Maria, Roland, Helmuth, and the druzhina made their way to Rosdorf to free Ulrich's company.

In the woods, the troops rode with haste. After a few days of travel, they finally set their eyes upon the glowing hearths of Rosdorf. The flames of candles lit the town under cover of night, sprinkling thin sprouts of luminescence all around the town.

"Halt!" Katerina whispered loudly, bringing the party to a standstill. "We should approach the town with caution. They won't let us in as we are – we'll need to hide our armour." The party members wrapped their cloaks around themselves to hide their identities.

"Let's go over the plan once again," suggested Roland.

"Fine," replied Katerina. "Goetz and his armies marched on Adelebsen two days ago. Hopefully, that means that Benedict has called some troops from Rosdorf's garrison to bolster their numbers, enabling us to slip past their thinly dispersed guard and free Ulrich's company. Understand?"

"Got it," replied Roland. "How do you suggest we enter?"

"I know exactly what to do," Katerine replied. Maria, Katerina, Roland, and Helmuth approached the gates in darkness with only a candle to light their surroundings.

"Who goes there?" bellowed a guard from the ramparts.

"We're four travellers from Tyrol. We would like to enter your town for a place to stay," replied Katerina.

"Come back in the morning," the guard replied.

"Please, we have nowhere else to go."

"I said, come back in the morning. There's not much room here anyways."

"May I speak with your lord?" Katerina asked. "Perhaps he would have something to say about it. Hospitality is one of the pillars of chivalry, you know," Katerina said, urging the guard to open the gates. The guard was now in a dilemma. If they truly where spies or criminals, he wouldn't want them to know that his lord was trapped in Adelebsen.

"There's only four of you?"

"Yes."

"Fine then, come in and be quiet," the guard said. Two more guards opened the gates to the town. The town was walled and well-fortified. The white washed buildings seemed to glow in the dark of night.

As the guards opened the door, the four travellers trotted through. But just when they were about to close the door, Roland and Katerina quickly drew their swords and slew the guards. A storm of arrows was launched by the druzhina from the bushes, pelting down the guards on the wall. Before anyone could alert the garrison, the fight was over. The group made their way into the town, cloaked atop their horses. They rode straight towards the keep, where Ennelein and Ulrich must have been kept. They rode past patrols with ease, cloaked inconspicuously. As they arrived at the gates of the keep, they swiftly launched their arrows into the guard at the door. After opening the door, the druzhina cleared the halls with their axes and sabres, hunting down the guards defending the darkened complex. In the meantime, Helmuth, Roland, and Maria made their way to the dungeon. In the basement, they found a long dark corridor, at the end of which sat a sleeping guard. The poor man awoke to the tip of

Roland's blade held firmly against his neck. Maria grabbed the keys from the man's belt and opened the party cell.

"Maria, is that you?" a frail voice muttered from the darkness. It was the voice of Ulrich. She would recognize it anywhere.

"Be quiet; we can't alert any of the guards," Maria replied. The guard, perplexed, started calling out for help. Roland quickly plunged his blade into the man's throat.

"Quick, we have to run!" he instructed. The group made their way out of the cell. Ulrich's feet were bloody, and Thomas had a broken leg.

"We can't," replied Ulrich. "We need to take some horses from the stables." The party quickly moved through the halls, reuniting with the band of druzhina, making the band nearly fifty men. They quickly mounted up and began patrolling the streets near the stables, while Ulrich's men, the squires, and Ennelein hastily freed some horses. Once all were mounted, they quickly set off for the gate. At that moment, the town bell was rung.

"To arms!" guards cried off in the distance. "They're escaping!" The horde of warriors rushed towards the exit, firing arrows and swinging swords at guards along the way. As they were about to reach the gates, a group of guards quickly assembled before them. Their long polearms kept the riders at bay.

"We have to ride around them!" shouted Katerina. The group split up, making their way through alleys and corridors, all trying to reach the exit. The squires, Ulrich, Helmuth, and Roland all made it out safely, but the druzhina were still trapped inside. Ennelein, riding out of the town, was struck down by a crossbow bolt which had pierced her thigh. She tumbled to the side of the road. Conrad rushed towards her to stop the bleeding. He hastily tore off a part of his shirt to turn into a bandage. Enne looked down at the wound and nearly fainted, but the pain kept her conscious. Panicked, Conrad lifted the stout body onto his horse and, soon after, mounted it as well. They escaped the fray just in time, as crossbow bolts whizzed past them.

"We have to go back in and help them!" Roland shouted. The riders returned to the fray to salvage the remnants of their party, but the rain of crossbow bolts made the escape nearly impossible. Although Katerina made it out alive, many of the druzhina fell. As did Thomas who, dismounted, couldn't walk, and was quickly slain by oncoming guards.

"We have to leave," said Maria, holding Ulrich back. The riders quickly escaped the town, salvaging the lives that they could. They spurred their horses onwards into the dark of night, halting only once absolutely clear of danger. They rode all throughout the night at full speed, galloping quickly to reach their destination, Adelebsen. At sunrise, they saw the small town encircled by trees. Among those trees lay the siege of tents of Goetz' armies. The small town sat trapped among them, encircled by the sea of white military canvas. The survivors rode towards the town to reunite with the rest of the army. Pleased to see their return, Goetz embraced his daughter as she rode in.

"You're safe!" he exclaimed. "Thank heaven almighty!"

"There's no time to waste," Maria replied. "Ennelein took a crossbow bolt to her leg. Goetz quickly called for his surgeons.

"Have you stopped the bleeding?" Goetz asked.

"We applied bandages, yes," replied Conrad. "But the blood hasn't stopped coming." Ennelein was carried off by the military doctors in a stretcher. As she was carried away, they gave her theriac, a sort of pain killer produced from an amalgam of herbs. Once she reached a tent, they doused the wound in a bottle of wine. Conrad and Herwig watched from the entrance of the tent. They both observed with disparity. Although they knew the woman to be a murderer, they also found her to be a good travel companion. They had become attached to her.

Roland approached the tent. Upon seeing the blood and operation, he shuddered. The thick, red liquid acted as a reminder of all the lives lost; a reminder of the hell Roland and the others had faced. It reminded him of the blood that splattered on his bascinet helmet, the droplets of which just made their way through the eye slit every time. It reminded him of Wilhelm, lying in the grass, burned to a crisp and unable to breathe. Roland couldn't watch. He looked away with haste, nearly reaching for his sword. His gut told him there was danger nearby, and yet, there was none.

"Do you know where Ulrich is? Or Thomas?" he asked. Conrad didn't move. His eyes were locked on the operation. At that point, the doctors had begun to rip the bolt from her muscle tissue. She cried out in pain, so they instructed her to bite down on a belt. Herwig gave Roland a grave look.

"Ulrich is alive. You'll find him over with Maria."

"And Thomas?"

"Thomas fought valiantly. Like a lion. He stood his ground to the end."

"Scheiss!" Roland exclaimed.

"Why do all the best men have to die?" Herwig asked. "The Lord steals their souls from us before we can even say goodbye. First Wilhelm and Friedrich and Manfred, now Thomas? What did he do to deserve such a death? He was barely a man – a beardless youngen."

"At least they all died with honour. They all went down fighting. We should be proud of all of them, and all we can do is hope to die with that same glory."

"Tell me. Does it ever get easier?"

"I would be lying if I said it did. This last year has killed more good men than any other. Sometimes, you just have to have faith that they're looking down on us now. Because, if they aren't, we're all destined to either perish forever or live out eternity in the depths of the inferno."

"Thomas is in heaven. So are the others. I know that for certain," said Herwig, with tears in his eyes. The three men stood in silence as they watched the operation. They watched as Enne fought for her life, despite the tremendous blood loss. Enne, on the other hand, could only think that she was now paying for her sin. With every ounce of blood that streamed from the two-inch-wide hole, she felt no guilt and no remorse. She exacted justice on the right people; she knew it. If this was the price for following orders and helping her community, so be it. But she fought. Although she understood the reason for her predicament, she still had no intention of dying that day. Even when a belt was tightened over her thigh to stop the blood flow, even when bandage after bandage was applied with little avail, and even when she saw her skin turn pale, she didn't give up hope. Once the painkiller kicked in, Enne fell unconscious instantly.

CHAPTER 69. MIGHTIER THAN THE SWORD

Maria and Goetz sat alone in a military tent. Goetz poured himself and his daughter a glass of wine each. As Maria watched the deep red liquid trickle into the glasses, she could think of nothing but the murder that had set it all in motion.

"Tell me, Maria, now that we're alone, why did you do it?" Goetz asked solemnly as he took a sip.

"Manfred was gone. I was tired. It was late. I hadn't meant it, truly. I simply conceived of the idea, but to my recollection, I left Enne with a choice. Perhaps it was foolish. But I don't know now whether or not I regret any of it."

"Maria, how much blood has been spilled in your name?"

"Was this not the fate of the town regardless of the murder? Would Benedict not have gotten his grubby little hands on this place following his father's death?"

"Killing is a sin."

"Killing can be a sin. If Manfred ever taught me anything, it's that we sometimes need to take justice into our own hands."

"Maria, what happened to you? Before I left for Sicily you were such a sweet, God fearing young girl? Now you are a murderer?"

"I am the Lord of Adelebsen. When a crime is committed

on my land, I am the one who must deal with it. That's what Manfred would have done."

"But you are not Manfred."

"So? Can I not learn from the man who has run this town so well for so long?"

"Well evidently his tactics don't always work. Look around. Eight thousand men are camped here ready to die for your claim to the throne."

"That's not fair. It wasn't my fault."

"Wasn't it? You're the one who lost the town."

"Because they took it. They killed your man, Adolf. They killed Franz. They killed so many of my citizens. I am not the one to blame here!" Maria began to weep. She felt the shame of her deeds. She felt her father's disapproval radiating throughout the tent.

"Maria, don't cry. You're not little anymore."

"I'm mourning the loss of my husband. My righthand man. All the people who I swore to protect are now imprisoned in their own homes."

"You'll have plenty of time to weep once the town is ours. Until then, grow some gall and stay tough. If not for yourself, for your companions. Do you see them out there? They're barely holding together. You've all been through a lot. So, toughen up, and act like the rightful Lord of Adelebsen. Our armies will attack the town soon..."

"No."

"What do you mean 'no'?"

"No more blood."

"Maria, these men are soldiers; it's what they do. If we aren't paying them to fight, what are we paying them for?"

"You have enough florins, let them have their pay. I'll talk to Osanna. If she doesn't value the lives of her men or even her own, she ought to value that of her son."

"Maria, we'll send a delegate. If you walk into that town, you'll die."

"I don't care. This town is my responsibility. Manfred left it to me. He would have wanted me to give everything for it."

"To hell with what Manfred thinks. Manfred is dead. You are blinded by grief. Let Wilfred deal with her. Or perhaps one of your knights. Roland? Ulrich?"

"Father, I must do this. It's just something that I have to do. For my own conscience. It'll set things right. The Lord will see my repentance."

"You make a strong case, Maria. You're a good debater, just like your mother. If she could see you know she would be proud. But I just can't lose you too."

"Father, I'm making this decision, with or without your consent."

"Maria, I won't have it."

"You will! Or, I will ride off to some distant land away from here, never to be seen by you or your men again! How could I face the shame of returning to a town I haven't even earned?! Would you make me a tyrant? Like Benedict? I wish to go."

"Fine," Goetz grumbled.

"Pardon me?"

"I said fine," Goetz restated. "But you will take with you a retinue of at least ten men at arms. That's not debatable."

"Thank you, father! Ten it is," Maria said with the feintest of smiles. Although she was soon to risk her life, she was glad that her father at least understood her plight.

"If anything goes wrong, you gallop out of there as fast as you can, and we'll ram that gate down with all our strength. Understand?"

"Yes, father," Maria replied.

"Now go. We mustn't spend any more time waiting. We have a town to rescue," Goetz said, finishing the last droplets of wine in his glass. Maria, content with her father's choice, stood up from her chair. The two made their way outside to the encampment, where they split up. Goetz went to inform his commanders of the plan, while Maria was off to collect ten skilled men at arms to accompany her on her mission. First, Maria approached Ulrich, Helmuth, and Roland, who had been catching up together in a make-shift alehouse. Although the men were battered, they were absolutely ecstatic to see each other. She found them playing dice together, while Ulrich entertained them with his adventures in Hanover.

When Maria approached them, the look on her faced foreboded the gravity of their next quest.

"How goes it Maria? I'm so sorry for your loss," Ulrich said kindly.

"Manfred's passing is hard on all of us, but there's no time to mourn, not yet."

"Maria, we will fight with you until the end. We want to be in the vanguard when storming the town," Ulrich replied.

"There will be no need for that," Maria said. "We will instead talk to Osanna, convince her to give up the town."

"Will it work? I mean, that is one vile wench," Roland replied.

"I can't be certain, but we have to try. Will you three accompany me? I have to form a retinue of ten men at arms, and there is nobody who I trust more to defend me than you three."

"Of course, my lady," Ulrich replied. He was sore all over, skinny, and pained with each step he took. But he was ready to accompany Maria, if not for her, in Manfred's name.

"We will ride in the name of all who have fallen," said Helmuth.

"I would be honoured, Maria," said Roland, fastening his sword scabbard once more to his belt.

"Who else will accompany us?" asked Ulrich.

"Well, first of all, I believe that Lena, my sister, would have made sure that she is in this army, with or without my father's knowledge," Maria said.

"A woman?" asked Ulrich with surprise.

"Oh, Ulrich, you haven't seen her prowess on the

tournament ground. She can joust in a league with Helmuth and I," said Roland with excitement.

"Well then, she sounds like quite the fighter," Ulrich replied with a chuckle.

"Believe me, Ulrich, she is quite skilled in the art of combat," Maria added. "As well, I think I'll choose the company of my cousin, Wilfred. He has brought good knights from Brabant."

"Ah yes, the men of the lowlands are good fighters," said Roland. "Just look at Maurits. That man could swing a sword quite well."

"His passing was quite a shame," said Ulrich. "Let's drink in his name," he added, guzzling down the rest of his pint.

"Perhaps we may leave the drinking until after we have the town?" asked Maria.

"Don't worry," Ulrich replied. "I'm far scarier when I'm angry. Now, somebody get me a harness, and let's ride," he said gruffly.

"Before you put on any armour, I should probably give you this," Roland said with a smile. From his saddle bag he drew Menschentöter, Ulrich's trusty war hammer.

"Where on earth did you find that? I thought they took it from us in Rosdorf!" Ulrich exclaimed with glee.

"I picked it up while we escaped. I saw it lying around in the keep armoury," Roland replied. Ulrich was very content with this gift and gave the weapon a few practice swings before the group split up.

The three knights prepared for the mission while Maria travelled off to search for her sister and cousin. Ulrich, with some financial aid from Roland and Helmuth, was outfitted with the best armour the camp blacksmith had on hand. It was nothing compared to his old suit of armour with the flamboyant colours of Göttingen, but it was enough to protect the man's chest, head, and hands. The three knights decided to practice their combat some more with wooden swords – a warmup for if the mission went awry.

Roland was surprised to find that Ulrich had improved immensely due to the fight manuscript gifted to him by Ernst Meyer, the Lion of Magdeburg. The men trained until sundown; they duelled, jousted, and tested each other. They honed their skills, practicing the one art they all bonded over – war. For a moment, it felt as though nothing had happened. It felt as though Roland and Ulrich were practicing again in the fields behind the manor. For a moment, it felt as if they were all still there; Freidrich, Wilhelm, and even Manfred. Ulrich and Roland fought hard. They fought like they were preparing for a war. They fought like they were about to go on a quest to a far-off land with their retinue. But they were the last ones left. There was no more Manfred, or Freidrich, or Wilhelm. There was no more Prince Otto to guide and oversee them. There was no more Franz to coach them on their skills while they travelled through the winter storms. Roland felt a pain in his chest, like his heart was going to break out of his rib cage. Ulrich felt the same way, only to a lesser, more muted extent. It felt like time had stopped, and all the world had turned to a deep shade of grey. The lives of the lost registered in their minds, stinging like a battle wound. They didn't talk with each other. They just fought and remembered.

CHAPTER 70. THE BROKEN WHEEL

At dusk, a messenger came to the three knights.

"We spoke with Osanna. She has agreed to parlay," he said in between tired breaths. Helmuth said a quick prayer and then kissed a cross necklace he had acquired in Marienburg. Ulrich sheathed his sword and mounted up. The other two followed suit. The three men made their way towards the gates of the town. On the horizon, a hot red sun faded below the pine trees. At the gates, the party assembled. Maria was there, as was Lena, Wilfred, and five of his knights. Lena stood in a suit of armour from head to toe. If nobody had already known she was a woman, nobody could have noticed.

Maria, on the other hand, carried no armour. No weapon, no sword nor lance. All she had was a scroll. On it was a pardon from the House of Kassel. They were the results of Adolf's investigation, but with a twist. Instead of blaming Ulrich, they blamed Osanna. As nobody could contest these rulings, and as Osanna had the highest probable cause considering that she was so quick to act, and a whole host of nobles from across the west agreed that her tyranny was unjust, she would be threatened with imprisonment in an imperial diet. It offered Osanna with a choice. She could either submit herself to the Imperial Court alone, or she and her followers, including her son, could be executed in a siege of the town. Maria, Goetz, and Wilfred wrote it together. They decided that Benedict had little say in the matter, and that, hopefully, a gesture of mercy could break the vicious cycle of violence that had already brought so much destruction to the land. To Maria, it was like a wheel. Spoke after spoke rises to the top while the rest role in the dirt. She thought it was time to break the wheel. End the cycle.

Bring peace.

Maria tucked the scroll into a leather-bound case and led the party into the town. She was invited by defector guards, now wearing the coat of arms of Osanna's house: The House of Conradin. They bore three black lions on a field of yellow. Those same banners were now hung up all around the town. As the party passed through the streets, they hung from the walls of many homes and businesses. They stood as a constant reminder of who truly controlled the town. Osanna rode down with a party of her own knights as well. Benedict, young and unaware, rode behind her. His lack in height was compensated with an absurdly tall crown.

"What is that monstrosity that rests atop the boy's head?" whispered Roland. Helmuth gave a chuckle, but the rest of the party remained serious and focussed on the mission.

"I see your son Benedict sees himself fit to be a king," said Maria playfully.

"What is it you want, you witch? First, you kill my husband. Then, you wish to take what I rightfully inherited from him? Are you some kind of usurper?" Osanna replied.

"We come with terms," Maria said, pulling the scrolls from her bag. "I suggest you read them before you make any hasty decisions."

"This new line of Göttingen-Conradin will rule over all of the Göttingen territory, from Brunswick down to Friedland. Understand, murderer?"

"Look, we don't want a battle."

"Really? Because you have brought nearly ten thousand

men to my doorstep."

"This is not your doorstep!" interrupted Roland.

"Ah, I see. You need your knights to fight your political battles for you," Osanna replied with a sneer. "You can take this piece of paper and shove it down your throat. We will fight till the very last, like honourable nobility. Not the kind of nobility who stab their overlords in the back, like you."

"Osanna, it's clear you love your son dearly," said Maria.

"I do. I suppose that it's something you'll never comprehend. A childless widow? Who could be less fit to run an estate?"

"Please Osanna, you don't want him to be killed in battle."

"He would die like a chivalrous knight."

"He would die! That's the important part. Listen to yourself. You took this town for him, but if you don't give it back, your son may pay the price," said Maria, pleading to the woman.

"You would kill a boy?"

"Arrows find many targets," said Ulrich. "When an archer's volley is shot, they don't know who they'll hit."

"Read our terms. Think about it. Surely, we can come to a compromise," said Maria, offering the scroll. Osanna ripped it from her hand and opened it, realising she didn't have many options. "All we ask is that you pay for your crimes. Your son is innocent. So are your men and your citizens."

"You would have me repent for taking revenge on my husband's killer? And my brother-in-law's killer?" Osanna replied.

"We would have you tried by an objective source. The Imperial Court will investigate the matter, should you choose to submit yourself to them. Or, you could run off, and start a new life in France or Hungary. Just stay away from Göttingen," said Maria firmly. At first, Osanna was ready to order their arrest right then and there. But then she realized that these people had chosen to spare her men. They chose to spare her son. And, realizing that to save her son she had no other option, she agreed.

"I agree," she replied after careful contemplation. She had one of her men hand her a reed pen, and she signed it against the neck of her horse. She handed it back to Maria shortly after. "Benedict, I'm doing this for you," she said, turning to her boy who was completely oblivious to the situation.

"Thank you," Maria said. "You will not regret this."

"If you touch a hair on my boy's head, you will suffer a fate worse than your husband's. Understand?" Osanna remarked.

"You can trust us," Maria replied. Osanna smirked.

"I suppose I must come with you now."

"We'll give you time to say goodbye to your boy," Maria replied. Tears formed in Osanna's eyes. The woman who she once made out to be a ruthless murderer had actually turned out to be merciful. Osanna knew the gravity of what she had done. She intended on submitting herself to the court. All she wanted now was the best life possible for her son. She dismounted from her horse and helped Benedict off of his. She bent down to his height to speak with him.

"Benny, don't cry. I'm going to leave you now," she said with a pink face and tears streaming down her cheeks. Benedict now knew what was going to happen. He thought she was going to trick them. He thought his mother was always in control of the situation. But not this time.

"Where are you going, mamma?" he asked in a sad and timid voice.

"I'm going away for a long time. I don't know where," she replied, fighting the pain that swelled in the back of her throat. "Our maid, Susanna will take care of you. I'll send for my brother, Karl to come to Rosdorf and raise you, I swear it."

"Why do you have to go?"

"We… no… I did a bad thing. A very bad thing. And now, because I did a bad thing, I have to pay for what I've done," Osanna replied. "Stay strong Benny. Stay strong like a knight.

Stay strong like your father." Osanna hugged her child for a long moment. She wept over his shoulder. Benedict felt extremely somber as well, but he was raised to be a knight, so he tried not to show it. Tears streamed down his face though, and everybody empathized with his pain. Then, Osanna rose to her feet. Her knights held Benedict back as she left.

"Mamma!" he cried out, wanting to go after her, but her men held him back. She mounted her horse and began to ride away from the town with Maria and her knights, but she peered back once more over her shoulder to see her boy one last time. As she trotted away from him through the dark, candle lit streets, his visage disappeared into the night. The party returned to the camp victorious.

CHAPTER 71. THE SAGA

The following morning was cold and dark. The first snowfall descended on the town, painting rooftops white with fluffy white crystals. Osanna was gone. In the dead of night, she was taken away by Wilfred once and for all. Where they went, even Maria didn't know. But what everyone could be sure of was that she had no hope of escaping. Wilfred's army, comprised of thousands of men, was ready to teach the wench a lesson if she ever tried to escape.

Maria rose to a cold breeze bighting at her fingertips. She lay in a tent, beneath the dark grey sky. Her horse outside neighed. It was spooked. Maria rose to her feet, dusting off some of the straw on which she slept from her dress. The three knights that inhabited the tent with her were still fast asleep. Maria felt an urge to stroll outside. One foot after another, she made her way through the camp.

"Perhaps I'll use the latrines," she thought to herself, out loud, with a whisper. She made her way through the rows upon rows of tents. By the next day, all of those tents would be gone. Every soldier lying there would return to their homes unscathed. Maria felt proud of herself. She walked and walked until she reached the tent with the toilet in it, but just as she was to enter, she felt there was no longer any need to go. She walked towards her horse and mounted him. She felt like going for a ride instead. She just didn't want to sleep.

Maria rode into the forest. The snow on the ground melted and turned to slush beneath the hooves of her horse. She rode quickly, as if she was chasing someone or being chased. The pine trees swayed in the wind, as if they were urging her to sally forth into the unknown. Maria rode and rode until she finally reached a clearing. In it, she saw naught but a small wooden cross sitting atop a mound of dirt. "That ought to be where Manfred and his men put those brigands," she said to herself. She approached the flimsy structure with caution. She didn't know why it was intriguing, but she did find it alluring. She felt as though it represented the lifestyle led by Manfred and his men. She also felt like she had a share in it, at least that she experienced it. Maria knelt and said a quick prayer.

As she knelt, eyes closed, a figure emerged from the foliage. Maria immediately scrambled to her feet, ready to fend off an assassin. But there was none. Instead, there was an old lady. In her hand, she carried a thick, leather-bound book.

"Who are you?" Maria asked. Her heart still thumped like a drum after the startle.

"They call me Isolde," the woman replied.

"You, Manfred told me about you. He saw you, in Prussia."

"Indeed, he did."

"What are you? A witch? Did you bring this upon us?"

"What specifically are you referring to? The plague? Or the murder?"

"I don't know. Both? Either?"

"Well, I can assure you that I am responsible for neither. These things are out of my control."

"What do you mean?" asked Maria, slightly calmer now.

"Here, read this," Isolde replied, handing Maria the book. Maria grabbed it and held it out in front of her. The cover had little decoration. It was titled: 'The Red Castle'.

"What is this?"

"It's a collection of Manfred's adventures. I thought you

might benefit from it."

"How did you get this? Who gave it to you?"

"A man named Renault d'Anjou gave it to me. He told me to deliver it to the Lord of Adelebsen."

"I presume he meant to give it to Manfred. Well, Manfred's dead now. I'm the Lord of Adelebsen in his stead."

"I know, Maria," Isolde replied. "Take the book. Read it. It will be something to remember him by."

"Thank you, Isolde," Maria replied. Isolde nodded, and slowly retreated into the wood. Maria was curious to chase after her, but she realised that the matter was probably best left here. She stashed the saga in her saddle-bag and returned to Adelebsen, riding at a calm pace. When she reached the town, the army of Kassel had already begun a procession towards the manor. She observed as crowds gathered to welcome the liberators. They cheered, tearing down the banners with the Conradin coat of arms, and burning them in the streets. But there was confusion as well. Goetz led the procession, followed by the three knights of Adelebsen. Nobody saw Maria. So, she rode forth to the front of the procession, reuniting with her comrades. Ulrich pulled out his flask.

"To Manfred!" he toasted atop his steed, pouring the clear liquid straight into his throat. Roland pulled out his flask as well.

"To everyone who died for this God-forsaken place!" he cheered with a smile and took a large gulp as well. Finally, Helmuth pulled out his flask.

"To Maria," he toasted, sipping the schnapps in his flask lightly. Cheers echoed throughout the town until the procession finally reached the manor. Inside, the guards had burned their tunics bearing the Conradin coat of arms and wore their Göttingen tunics again. Maria reunited with many of the courtiers. She was greeted by a host of her employees, happy to see her once more. It was picturesque, yet, something was missing. It reminded Maria of how well things ran during Manfred's absence. It was smooth and jolly, and yet Manfred wasn't there to accompany her.

The day was spent settling disputes left by the shift in power. Every hen, loaf, and egg that changed possession during the reign of the Rosdorfers had to be dealt with. Plenty of people came to Maria, looking for an unwavering source of justice and anchor to guide them and solidify this new era for Adelebsen.

In the afternoon, Maria bid farewell to her father.

"I'll see you soon," she said. She promised him that she'd visit more often, engaging further in her family politics. Lena, now outed as a warrior for all to see, was incorporated into Maria's retinue. Sir Lena von Kassel pledged her unrelenting allegiance to the Princedom of Göttingen, renouncing her affiliation of Kassel, and eventually becoming knighted by the Elector of Saxony himself. Although that day was far from this one, both Maria and Lena anticipated it since the day Lena took up arms.

At the end of the day, once the armies of Kassel, Hessen, and the Rhineland had all marched off into the forest of Adelebsen, Maria threw a feast. It wasn't to mourn the deaths of the fallen, but instead to celebrate their lives; to celebrate the new era of peace and friendly politics that would fall upon Adelebsen and the rest of the Princedom of Göttingen. It was grand, and full of lively singing, dancing, and delicious foods. Unfortnately, they weren't prepared by Ennelein, however, as she had to recover from her battle wound. She instead lay in a cloister bed, waiting to recover. She would live out the rest of her days as the unsung hero of Adelebsen. All of the knights and lords of Göttingen would know her secret, and to them, the deaths of Otto the younger and Reuben were well welcomed.

"Good riddance," most of them had secretly maintained upon hearing of their deaths. This support for the rejuvenated township was shared by the new rulers of Göttingen. Benedict especially grew up to be a friend to Maria and her knights, finally taking good care of her in her later years. She guided him and raised him like a son; only, they were separated by a day's ride.

Following the feast, in the night time, Maria, Helmuth, Roland, Ulrich, and the squires all secretly met down in the crypt. They left their weapons at the doors, obliged to do so by the guards. It was a new mandate installed following Manfred's assassination. The party met by Manfred's tomb. Together, they conversed somewhat gloomily. Maria, escorted by a couple of handmaidens, brought wine for all to enjoy. She passed the tray around, allowing all to indulge in the sweet, crimson liquid. Ulrich, however, declined.

"You wouldn't have a glass?" Maria inquired.

"Freidrich was right. I shouldn't be drinking every God-damn second of the day," he replied, pulling out his flask. As it had turned out, the clear liquid was not schnapps nor moonshine, but instead water, cultivated straight from a fresh spring. "Good health," he toasted.

"Good health," the others replied in unison, clinking their goblets together with cheer. But the cheer was limited, for all had suffered great sacrifices and hardships throughout the past year. The meeting was merely a reminder for some. For others, it was a comfort.

"To new beginnings," Maria said, lifting her chalice and taking a sip. The group talked well into the night. They told tales of the mighty adventures they had on the road to Prussia and the great battles in which they fought. All the while, a snowy tempest echoed against the stone walls of the crypt. It appeared that winter had once again graced the rooftops and cobblestone streets of Adelebsen. At the door, and hooded man approached the guards. He was somewhat short in stature, wearing common clothes. His shirt and pants were both as white as the snow surrounding him.

"Who are you?" asked one of the guards, drawing his weapon.

"Please, I mean no harm. I seek refuge from the storm. I've been robbed. Highwaymen have taken everything. I think they were pagans by the looks of it," the man replied, pleading to the guards like a sinner at mass. The two armoured men let him in.

"Who are you?" asked Ulrich.

"Please, there are brigands afoot. They have everything I own," the man said in a panicked voice. Ulrich cast aside his flask and chugged a full glass of wine.

"We have some work to do," he replied. Lena, Helmuth, Roland, Ulrich, and the squires all donned their armour, drew their weapons, and mounted their steeds, riding off into the cold winter night.

POSTLUDE

"And so, ends our tale, not with a whimper, but with a battle cry," announced Walter. "And now, half a century later, we recount the tale of this heroic knight and his merry men. His honourable wife, and his devastated town. Did this Sir. Manfred and his men really exist? Well, you might find the odd mention of his father and brother in the historical record, but one must comprehend that many more tales rest untouched by pen and paper. Thank you, God, for the strength and memory to..."

"Wait, wait, wait... it's over? Just like that?" asked the king in confusion. "We've been listening to this story every night for a fortnight. That can't be the ending! What happens next?"

"My King, some tales are best left unfinished."

"What does that mean?"

"Well, how would you like it to end?"

"The knights should capture those criminals and have them executed. But just because I want that to happen, it doesn't mean that it did happen."

"My Lord, the story is over. The town is saved! Why would one care about such a minute mission?"

"But there is still action and adventure to come in the story."

"There always is, my King. History always unfolds at its own will. It doesn't stop to let a story tie itself up with a nice big bow. No, no, history unfolds as it pleases, incessantly flowing forth like a river. The truth is that the story never ends. It simply continues on and on, as more characters are added and the characters we knew pass away."

"But this isn't a history, it's a story. An entertainment. Wouldn't you entertain us for a little while longer?"

"My Lord, there is no more story to tell. My memory fails me."

"Please?"

"Alright then, fine. The knights chased after those brigands, rung them by their necks, and everybody lived happily ever after. The end."

"That's not a good ending."

"Well then, how would you have it end?"

"I don't know. I wish Manfred could come back from the dead."

"But my King, that's not possible."

"So? It's a story."

"My King, I think we had ought to call it a night," Walter insisted. By now, most of the lords and ladies of the court had left. Despite the king's discontent with the ending, they were tired and were fine with letting the long and grueling tale end with a bit of excitement. Walter looked around, realising that most of them were gone.

"Fine then. You'll get your pence in the morning," replied the king, also noticing the lack of popularity that the discussion held. He made his way off to bed.

"Good night, Henry," Walter replied, packing up his things. The curtains were drawn closed, and the band of troubadours who had entertained the courtiers for all those nights, descended from the stage.

ABOUT ATMOSPHERE PRESS

Atmosphere Press is an independent, full-service publisher for excellent books in all genres and for all audiences. Learn more about what we do at atmospherepress.com.

We encourage you to check out some of Atmosphere's latest releases, which are available at Amazon.com and via order from your local bookstore:

Tales of Little Egypt, a historical novel by James Gilbert
For a Better Life, a novel by Julia Reid Galosy
The Hidden Life, a novel by Robert Castle
Big Beasts, a novel by Patrick Scott
Alvarado, a novel by John W. Horton III
Nothing to Get Nostalgic About, a novel by Eddie Brophy
GROW: A Jack and Lake Creek Book, a novel by Chris S McGee
Home is Not This Body, a novel by Karahn Washington
Whose Mary Kate, a novel by Jane Leclere Doyle
Stuck and Drunk in Shadyside, young adult fiction by M. Byerly
These Things Happen, a novel by Chris Caldwell
Vanity: Murder in the Name of Sin, a novel by Rhiannon Garrard
Blood of the True Believer, a novel by Brandann R. Hill-Mann
The Dark Secrets of Barth and Williams College: A Comedy in Two Semesters, a novel by Glen Weissenberger

ABOUT THE AUTHOR

With a passion for storytelling, Noah Verhoeff has taught a course on Creative Writing at the Horizons Summerschool program and is the founder of the Young Writers Society at Upper Canada College. Beyond *The Red Castle,* Noah has published a selection of short stories in *The Forgotten Sagas Anthology,* including "The Janissary," "The Joust," and "Red Army Men." An avid history buff with archaeological experience from the Sebastien Site, Noah likes to focus his writing on adventures of epic proportions that maintain historical authenticity. *The Red Castle* in particular takes place in one of Noah's favourite historical settings - 15th century Europe. Noah's primary aim is to keep his readers on the edge of their seats, keeping them guessing at what the future holds.

Lightning Source UK Ltd.
Milton Keynes UK
UKHW010729040521
383104UK00006B/854